*She waited for him
to say something.*

He didn't, he just stood looking at her. He'd turned his back to the house, so she couldn't see his expression, only his outline against the stain of light that showed through the draperies in the windows behind him.

But he could see her clearly. She wore an elaborate satin gown the color of copper pennies. It had many flourishes, draping over her form, concealing everything and yet hinting at all he remembered seeing the day she'd worn that simple milkmaid's frock.

"Shall we go in now?" she asked.

"Shall we?" he asked slowly, in return. But he made no move to go. Instead, he brushed a curl back from her cheek.

It was an odd sort of caress, hardly a caress at all, tender and affectionate rather than passionate. But it made her breath stop. "I thought you were going to be mindful of my reputation," she said.

"I am. Oh, Kate, you have no idea of how much I am."

Now he stroked a curl at the side of her head. She knew that if she turned, her lips could touch that hand.

"I thought you said this was to be a mock flirtation," she said.

"So I did," he said, and moved closer.

EDITH LAYTON

THE DEVIL'S BARGAIN

HarperTorch
An Imprint of HarperCollinsPublishers

This is a work of fiction. Names, characters, places, and incidents are products of the author's imagination or are used fictitiously and are not to be construed as real. Any resemblance to actual events, locales, organizations, or persons, living or dead, is entirely coincidental.

❦

HARPERTORCH
An Imprint of HarperCollins*Publishers*
10 East 53rd Street
New York, New York 10022-5299

Copyright © 2002 by Edith Felber
ISBN: 0-380-81864-7

First HarperTorch paperback printing: May 2002

HarperCollins ®, HarperTorch™, and ❦™ are trademarks of Harper-Collins Publishers Inc.

Printed in the United States of America

Visit HarperTorch on the World Wide Web at www.harpercollins.com

10 9 8 7 6 5 4 3 2 1

To the newlyweds,
Susie and Ed,
and all their happily ever afters

Prologue

He put down his bags, looked around, and smiled. It wasn't a pleasant smile. He'd followed a trail that ended where it had started, at home, in England. Not at home, he corrected himself. Home wasn't anywhere near this crowded coaching stop, home wasn't London, filled with strangers. Home was in the north, a great house, long, green, sloping lawns. Home was where generations of his family lay, where his youth and hopes and friends had been. All gone now. Only the house and lawns remained, abandoned, empty as his heart. But not for long. Soon he'd know triumph, he'd have his revenge.

He'd worked so long for it.

He'd sacrificed, devoted his life, risked his neck and his name, given up chances for love, rid himself of self-respect, comfort, and peace, all to this end. Now it was almost done. He had all the evidence, all the documents, witnesses, testimony, papers signed, sealed, only yet to be delivered. He could have done that months ago, he could have ended it then. But he'd held back. His revenge had been his life's work, and it was, even for what it was, a work of art. There wasn't a seam in it, not a loophole, not a place for his prey to get out. Even if they killed him now, they wouldn't escape his vengeance, because his death would release the truth.

He'd spent his years creating a masterwork of vengeance, and so the finishing stroke to it had to be as brilliant as its creation. His triumph had to be respected, relished, appropriate to the enormity of the work and the crime that had begun it. He'd bring them down. He'd exult in it. But for it to be perfect, he had to see their faces when it was done.

They knew he had the evidence. He'd made sure of it, step by step along the way. They'd tried, but couldn't stop him. Nothing could, then or now. They knew that, and he was sure they also didn't know why he was waiting. They had come to London, at last, their last home and now their lair. They hid themselves behind closed curtains, afraid to go out into the light. They knew what was coming.

But that was the best part. The waiting. He had time to enjoy it. He had only to find the right moment, the exact weapon, the perfect tool to help him right the wrong that had changed his life forever. As he would change theirs, paying them back for their treachery with public humiliation, disgrace, and exile—if they were lucky.

Something struck his side. He crouched, swerved, spun, a pistol appearing in his hand between one breath and the next. His narrowing vision focused on a white-faced man in front of him, eyes widened in terror. A fattish middle-aged man, pale hands up, wavering fingers trembling in the air.

"Sorry, sorry, excuse me," the fellow gasped, his

protruding eyes fixed on the pistol. "I was hurrying to meet the family, pardon me, excuse me, didn't mean to jostle you, sir, sorry . . ."

The pistol vanished again up the tall, dark, powerfully built gentleman's sleeve. "No, your pardon, sir," he said smoothly. "I've just returned from traveling in dangerous lands, my reaction was purely reflex." He bowed. "It will take me time to get used to London again. Please forgive any distress I caused you."

The fellow looked like he'd excuse him anything if he could only get far enough away from him to do it. He backed off, babbling, "No matter, I quite understand, no offense taken, makes sense, I assure you . . ." His voice trailed off as he backed away, then turned and hurried from the coach yard.

The tall gentleman smiled again. He was sorry to have startled the poor fellow, but a man who relaxed vigilance often ended up more than relaxed, and forever. Soon, though, if he could find the right moment and method, he could relax again. That would be . . . strange, he supposed.

His smile faded. There'd be plenty of time for smiling later when he was finally done and could put down a greater burden than these bags he'd carried over the face of Europe and back again. He picked up and strode out of the coaching house.

It was time to begin.

1

The gentleman was up to his neck in hot water. It seemed to please him very much. He stretched out his long powerful naked body and relaxed. Arms outflung to either side against the rim of the pool, head back, he let the rest of his body float. This seemed to interest the young woman in the gauzy gown who came wading toward him through the long shallow pool. She balanced an urn on one shoulder like a woman on an ancient Greek frieze. Her rounded hips moved to an even more ancient rhythm. The water in the pool came to her upper thighs, making it abundantly clear she was wearing nothing but that gown, the urn, and a smile.

The pool had a mosaic-tiled floor, the theme of which was more Roman than Greek, in that it had more to do with an orgy than a philosophical discussion. The room was white, a domed ceiling soaring overhead. Skylights poked in it showed only the night sky, but flaming torches everywhere made it bright enough for the bather to see that the young nymph with the urn was as pretty as she was scantily clad. The sheerness of the gown and the dampness in the room made her look bare as any of the many life-size replicas of Greek statues that stood by the pool.

The room made a halfhearted attempt to show Classical Greece in the heart of London Town. No one was there to study history. White marble benches were obviously for the use of bathers to sit before removing their clothing. Removal of it was necessary for more than just bathing. Settees and cots at the side of the room were for fellows who preferred to do their thrashing without splashing. There were private rooms upstairs, but this converted orangerie was a new attraction of one of the most popular brothels in town.

Such baths weren't new in London. Apart from the ancient Romans, Hummum's in old Covent Garden had lent its name to them in its day. But everything old is new again, and London doted on anything new.

The gentleman opened his eyes as the young woman with the urn neared him. He smiled at her. But there was nothing but lazy good humor in that slow smile. She looked down at his body and sighed. There was a wondrous lot to see, but all of it as banked and tempered as his smile. None of it offered her any encouragement.

"More hot water, sir?" she asked.

He shook his head. "Thank you, but I'm fine."

"Should you like anything else, sir?" she asked hopefully. "I mean, anything?"

"Oh, I know very well what you mean, love," he said in his rich deep voice, "but I'm fine, thank you. Perhaps some other time?"

She nodded, and waded away toward a man who was watching her from the other end of the pool.

"Can't be feeling fine," a voice steeped in irony commented. "Not if you turn down the likes of that. You must be ill, Alasdair."

The reclining gentleman's eyes opened again, humor sparkling in their midnight depths. He looked up at the man who'd paused at the side of the pool. A slender young gentleman, fully dressed in the height of fashion, gazed down at him.

"If boredom is illness, then behold me dead," the man in the water said. "Care to resurrect me?"

"My word!" the other man said. "If she can't do that, then you are dead. Or changed beyond recognition."

"Or here for other reasons than play. If I wanted steam and hygiene, I'd go to a Turkish bath. This place is full of wenches—and gossip. How have you been, Leigh?" the man in the pool asked. He gathered himself, then stood in one easy motion, looking like Prometheus rising from the waves.

Water sheeted off him. As unconcerned about that as his nakedness, he offered his friend his hand. In truth, he was no more naked than any of the stone fellows standing nearby. His body was a similar masterpiece, only of smooth burnished skin and well-knit muscle. He was a young Hercules rather than an Apollo. His heavily muscled frame was made of massive bones, but altogether well formed, down to the high arches in his narrow, classically molded feet. If it weren't for the masculine pattern of dark hair on that rock-hard chest and the shield of it below, he might have been the model for one of those statues. Except for that—and his face. It would never have graced any Greek statue. The ancients believed only balance and harmony made for masculine beauty.

Sir Alasdair St. Erth was not remotely beautiful.

Only his mouth was well shaped, deceptively tender. His face was a collection of plateaus and planes, his forehead too broad, jaw too pronounced, chin too large. His nose arched at the bridge and turned down at the end like a bird of prey's, ruining any chance it had for beauty. Much that mattered. What he had was too irresistibly human to translate to marble.

Surprisingly luxuriant lashes softened that angular face. The eyes gleamed like starlight on shards of coal at midnight, his teeth were even and white. His dripping hair was stygian black, and would be even when it dried. The occasional melting look that came into the fathomless eyes was beguiling, as dangerous as an undertow. The man was dark as a thundercloud and slick as oil on water, and devilishly attractive in all his imperfections. And the devil knew it, they said. A great deal was said about him. His close friends knew there was more that wise men only hinted at.

"I was going to come round to see you tomorrow," Alasdair said, running a hand back over his sopping hair. "Yes, I'm back. As for tonight, this is just a way of letting the world know it. As for the other? I never was much of a one for public spectacle," he said with the merest expression of distaste as he twitched one shoulder toward the woman he'd rejected. She'd put down her urn, bent her head, and was vigorously attending to the chap floating belly up in bliss at the other end of the pool.

"But you, Leigh," he asked his friend, "are you coming? Or planning to? By which I mean, are you coming or going now?"

It could only have been the play of torchlight on the other man's cheeks that looked like a faint blush. Few things made Lawrence Fane, Lord Leigh, show any emotion he didn't want to. "I'm leaving," he said with a faint smile. "And you?"

"Oh, I've made my appearance. That's the only reason I came here. And for the hot bath, so soothing. Now I'm off to the Swansons' ball. Care to join me?"

"Swansons'! Lord. You *have* changed. Talk about public spectacles! Throwing yourself to the lions would be more pleasant, I'd think, and the Coliseum less crowded—and more exclusive. The Swansons hold balls as often as other Londoners have hot dinners. No." He paused in thought, then went on: "Too many Londoners don't have hot dinners that often. But then I suppose the Romans wouldn't have given house room to daughters like that. They'd have thrown *them* to the lions. Now that would have drawn a crowd."

"Unkind," Alasdair said, as he scooped up a towel from a bench and began drying himself. "A family with many marriageable daughters, one less attractive than the other, must do what it can. Their daughters may look like draft horses and have conversation almost as lively, but you only have to dance with each once. And mind, so far as I know, at last count there were only three left unwed. A small price to pay for good food, tolerable music, and all the fresh, hot gossip you can ladle up. Most of London, at least anyone at loose ends tonight, will be there. So will I. Not for long, but long enough to let everyone behold the magnificence of me again."

"And let anyone who cares to make certain things known to you know that you're there to pay for them again," Leigh mused. "Alasdair, I wonder if you'd heard. The War with France is over."

"Oh, *that* one. Yes," his friend said blandly.

"Oh. I see," Leigh said thoughtfully. "I'd forgotten yours. Fine, to the Swansons' then. Why not?"

"So you're at loose ends?"

"My dear Alasdair. I always am."

Swanson House was a grand one in a good part of town. It was packed to confusion with people, which meant tonight's ball was a success. The host and hostess were beaming, because they'd snared some fascinating guests.

They even beamed at Sir Alasdair. If they'd heard the rumors about their unexpected guest, nothing in their glad welcome showed it. St. Erth had a pedigree as noble as any man's, after all. Wealth, too. Of course there were those rumors about him, and tales of his misspent youth. Still, he wasn't a youth anymore. Yet he had only thirty-some years in his cup. A man could change. At least, they fervently believed a rich, titled bachelor could. So whatever his past, he was welcome here in the present, with hope for the future. And he'd brought an elusive gentleman with him, Viscount Leigh. They always welcomed marriageable gentlemen.

There might be a cloud over St. Erth's name, but Viscount Leigh was eminently eligible, from a fine old family with a fine fat fortune. The fellow also had excellent manners and quiet good looks. He was known to be a scholar and amateur scientist. Known to those few fast friends he had, that was. Because he wasn't a social animal, not shy at all, but seldom seen at society's events. He occupied himself in libraries and political clubs, as well as the more raffish places single gentlemen visited, and was said to have a keen sense of humor and a questing intellect. He might be here tonight for curiosity's sake, he might actually be looking for a wife at last. The Swansons eyed him with rising hope. If they eyed St. Erth with less hope, they were no less interested in him.

They weren't the only ones. A clutch of fashionable young men who'd been idly noting arrivals, straightened when they saw who had just come in.

One gasped. "*St. Erth!* After all this time? That devil's back in London?"

"He's back, can't mistake him for anyone else," another commented. "What's the matter? You look terrible. Oh, good God! You haven't offended him, have you?"

"Don't be an idiot," his friend snapped. "If I had, I'd be out of here and halfway to the docks by now. The man has a bad reputation—or rather, a good one—with sword, pistol, and fivers. No, it just means my plans for success this Season are in jeopardy. If he just glances at a female, she's his."

"Not likely. I mean, that's true, but it won't mean a thing to you. Said you was looking for a wife, right? Well, he ain't in the market for one, unless she's someone else's. And come to think of it, he'd probably look for two. The man"—he paused, lowered his voice, and said enviously—"is *insatiable*, they say."

"*I* heard two isn't enough, and that he goes to orgies for even more," another young gentleman whispered in scandalized delight.

"How'd you know?" the second man sneered, "You never even been to the Continent. That's where he's been all this time. Fighting duels, too, and winning every one."

"I heard a fellow could die of a wound from one of his cutting remarks."

"Well, but I never heard of him slicing up anyone what didn't deserve it. Though what he thinks is deserving is what worries me."

"He left England poor," one man mused. "Now he's rich as a nabob, they say."

"They say, they say," another man mocked. "What's the fellow actually done?"

"People he don't like have disappeared. Women he does like run to him. The man gets what he wants, and you'd better take care he wants nothing to do with you."

"I wonder what he's doing here," the first gentleman mused after an awkward silence. "Surprised he was invited."

"Why not? He was asked everywhere on the Continent. With royals, even. Even though he was seen hanging about in low places, gambling hells, dens of thieves, and with all sorts of rogues, doing who knows what. . . . Aye—less said the better. But he was seen doing we know what at every kind of house of assignation, too. And as for orgies! He openly attended infamous ones, I heard."

"Some one saw him *at* it?" a very young gentleman asked in thrilled horror. "I mean, doing *it*? Right in front of everyone?"

"Him? No. But he was often seen at them."

"What's that to say to anything? I'd go to one if someone asked me."

"Point is," the second young gentleman said patiently, "he knows where to go. And what to do when he gets there."

They thought about that, and every other dark rumor they'd heard about the notorious St. Erth.

"Well," one of them finally said sadly, "see how much any of that matters. Just look at them."

They turned to where their friend was looking. And saw all the ladies staring at St. Erth.

Sir Alasdair didn't seem to notice. He made his way

to the punch bowl and soon stood talking and laughing with other gentlemen. He might not be acceptable to the highest sticklers in the *ton*, his past had too many shadows for that. But many men liked him even so. Many females loved him especially so.

It was hard to ignore him. Even if one were mad enough to want to. For one thing, he was too tall to overlook. For another, he was too pleasing to watch and listen to.

This afternoon, he'd looked like a gladiator in his own skin. Tonight he wore correct evening dress and looked every inch the fashionable gent, although every stitch he had on was corbeau black except for his white linen. But with that regal bearing, whatever he wore would seem correct. Sir Alasdair commanded the eye and delighted the ear. The most delicious part was that he obviously didn't give a tinker's damn if he did.

Some women whispered about him, others dreamed. One did more. A regal lady in a silver gown stood by a back wall, gazing at Sir Alasdair. She stopped talking with the man at her side. She smiled. "Yes," she said with satisfaction, "I'll have him."

The gentleman nodded, turned on his heel, and strode away. The lady continued watching the baronet.

So did everyone else, to see whom he'd dance with. Would it be one of his host's ill-favored daughters? Maybe some well-bred tart? A dewy young thing? Or the wife of a friend, to prevent gossip? As if he could. They waited. They'd have to wait longer.

A footman wound through the crowd and delivered a note to him. He opened it, scanned it. A brief flicker of disquiet crossed his face before he wore his usual blandly serene expression again.

"Bad news?" Leigh asked.

Alasdair folded the note. "No. I've no idea what it is, actually."

"Aha!" another gentleman chuckled. "A 'billy due,' unless I miss my guess. Sweet nothings and an invitation to more. Leave it to him, man's got the luck of the devil. Never got one of them at a ball myself."

"You never got one of them anywhere, sir," another gentleman drawled. "If you had, your lovely wife would have slain you."

"Likely," the other admitted good-naturedly. "That's what comes of having married in my infancy. Miss out on all the merry moments you bachelors have. Secret perfumed summonses are the stuff of my dreams, I fear."

Alasdair drew the note under his nose. "This one was scented with cigar smoke."

"And in handwriting bold and black as your heart, my friend," Leigh observed, peering over his shoulder. "Since Napoleon's left St. Helena for hell, I doubt it's a summons from the War Office *or* a note from a French spy. I don't think the nation has anything to worry about. But maybe you do. I wouldn't care to meet the lady who wrote that!"

"I would," Alasdair said with a smile. "Though I doubt it's from a lady. My curiosity knows no bounds. If you'll excuse me?"

He bowed his sleek dark head, turned, and strode away. His friends watched him go. Then they began chatting again, with no further comment about him. It wasn't so much that he was a man of mystery. A man had his reasons, and Sir Alasdair likely had more than most.

Alasdair left the ballroom at full stride. When he got to the hall, a footman approached. "The gentlemen are gaming in the little salon," he told Alasdair, indicating the long hall on the right. "The gentleman's withdrawing room is to the left."

"And the library?"

"Past the gent's room, down the hall, sir," the footman said.

Alasdair turned left. Gentlemen at lavish balls were often given more means of diversion than dancing, eating, and gossiping. The gambling was small stakes, set up to ease the boredom of papas, husbands, and confirmed bachelors. The library was the best place for a nice nap until a fellow's wife or daughter was done with all the tomfoolery and a chap could go home again. But Alasdair was looking for the blue salon the note said would be beyond the library. And he was looking for something more interesting there.

He didn't know who the anonymous fellow who'd sent the note was. Nor what the "... *meeting that I've cause to know would be most especially suited to your keenest interest and most pressing desire* ..." was. But he had a pressing desire, and it was known in certain places that he was always in the market for a special sort of information, arranged confidentially and paid for secretly.

There was no sound as he padded down the hall swiftly and silently as a wraith. This part of the house lay still around him. The quiet was a relief to his ears, but his heartbeat picked up. He had high hopes. Sending a note to him in the midst of a ball might mean someone had something new and valuable to sell him. Not that he hadn't enough information now. But a man would be a fool to pass up any cream to go on top. Whatever he was, and he admitted that was a great many none too palatable things, he was no fool. Woe to the man or woman who took him for one. He was done with being a fool, forever.

The door to the library was open. He glanced in as

he passed. The place was as crowded as the ballroom, but private as a mausoleum, and just as lively. One stout gent sat back in a deep chair with a newspaper folded over his face, another dozed in front of the fire. There were other old parties littered on the furniture everywhere. Alasdair moved silently on.

There was a closed door a few feet farther down the hall. He eased it open.

The room was blue all right. At least the walls were covered with watered blue silk. It was difficult to see the rest of the room, much less the colors in it. The few lit lamps and blazing hearth only showed glimpses of fashionably spindly chairs and settees in the latest Egyptian style. The long curtains were pulled closed. The place looked deserted.

Alasdair knew better than to trust first appearances. He stepped in and closed the door behind him.

"Good," a throaty voice said with deep pleasure. "You came."

"As you see," Alasdair said, peering into the shadows, "though I can't. Am I to talk to shadows? It wouldn't be the first time. Deuced uncomfortable though."

"Not at all," the voice said with husky laughter. "Good evening, Sir Alasdair."

A tall woman stepped out of the shadows. Alasdair's eyes narrowed. She was elegantly dressed in a silver gown with a black overskirt. Her shadow-colored hair was bound up high, exposing her long aristocratic neck and the sparkling diamonds on it. She was whippet thin, her face handsome rather than pretty. He estimated she wasn't yet thirty years old, but not much less. The back of his neck prickled. She could be an informant, she could be about his omnipresent business. But he had the uncomfortable feeling that though her business was his, it wasn't what he wanted. He always trusted his feelings. He didn't trust her.

"Good evening, ma'am," he said, inclining his head in the merest bow. "I don't believe I've had the pleasure . . . or have I? But so long ago I don't recall? Many of my pleasures from the old days are ones I confess I have the damnedest time remembering now."

It wasn't what he would have said to a lady. But he was beginning to believe she wasn't one, at least not in manners. She laughed again, reassuring him that she wasn't.

"Lud! No, my dear Sir Alasdair, we haven't met, in any construction of the words. It would be best if we get that over with now, and quickly, for we're going to know each other a deal better in future, you see. I'm Lady Eleanora Wretton, of Wretton Hall. My father is Duke Wretton. We're twenty-seventh—or -eighth—in line for the throne, not that it means much, but it will give you some idea of our standing."

"Indeed," Alasdair said lightly, though his face was still and he stood motionless. "And I should have that idea . . . because . . . ?"

"Because it will show you the futility of trying to rush out the door now. My brother's already stationed on the other side, you see. And his word will be taken far more seriously than yours."

"I see. And it was his handwriting on the note?"

She nodded. "I'm sorry. But we felt a note from a smitten female would have been ignored."

"Clever," Alasdair said. "So it would have been. And so, unless I'm very much mistaken, this is not an invitation to dalliance, is it?"

"No," she said, "That must come later."

"Ah! Then it's a proposal of marriage?"

She smiled. "Yes, I'm sorry, but there it is. Although

it's much more than a proposal at this point, sir. After luring me here, alone, for your sole enjoyment? With the door closed so I can't escape, and I, the unmarried daughter of a peer? It is, I fear, a certain engagement."

"Is it?" Alasdair mused. "I wouldn't bet on it, my lady. I have some options. I can challenge your dear brother to a duel, you know. Or your dear father, if it comes to that."

"So you can," she said mildly, "and maybe even kill them, you're very good at that, I hear. But then," she added sweetly, "you'd hang, surely. Or be forced to go abroad for the rest of your days. And you so lately returned to England from the Continent," she said with sympathy. "I'm sure that would inconvenience you."

"Aye, it would be the very devil," he agreed.

"So then, there it is. Now, you've only to decide whether to walk out of here and announce the thing graciously, or let my brother do it, in much less amiable fashion."

He said nothing. She sighed. She rubbed a hand over her lips to make them blush ruddily, and stepped toward him, shrugging her gown off one shoulder as she did. "I'd hate to expose myself entirely," she said, looking down to see the silky material had stopped sliding, caught on the puckered nipple of one little breast. "I'd thought to keep that a treat for your eyes only. But this—and this," she added, shaking her head back, letting her hair loose from its pins so it lay on her shoulders, "should suffice, I think." She raised her arms and ran both hands through her hair to muss it even more. "Such ardor you showed, my dear sir!" She laughed when she saw her motion had bared both breasts. "Naughty fellow."

"Yes, but not this time," Alasdair said, standing aloof. "A pretty sight, but wasted. There are gaps in your trap m'lady. I can exile myself, and will, I think, rather than be forced into wedlock."

"Indeed? But everyone is saying how happy you are to be home at last."

"So I was," he said. He cocked his dark head. "Why me? Some baroque form of revenge?"

She laughed again. "Lud, no! But needs must when the devil drives . . . a singularly apt phrase in your case, you'll agree. Look, my dear sir," she said, suddenly serious, "you're a fellow with a desperate reputation. I, unhappily, have one now, too. You may have committed all sorts of indecencies with all sorts of creatures. I merely forgot myself with one man who forgot his wedding vows. Yet I'll suffer more for it than you with all your immorality. His wife is the vengeful sort."

She shrugged again. "So my name will be ruined, and I'll have to leave the social scene for years, if not forever. Is that fair? Hardly. So since I had to choose someone to cleanse my name in a sudden but acceptable marriage, we felt you'd be the most apt and the last to cry foul. You ought to understand. And you are, after all, getting a wealthy, titled wife, with the best social standing. I have a great deal to bring to the bargain, after all."

"Including that forgetful fellow's get to raise as my own?" Alasdair asked thoughtfully.

She had the grace to look away. "No," she said after a moment. "I've some sense of fairness, you know."

He seemed genuinely amused, though his hands were knotted to fists at his side. "No, my lady. I think not. I'll do many things, and, as you say, have done. Not that you're not charming," he added, gazing with slow care at her breasts. "Indeed, I think if you'd met me in the normal way of things, you might well have achieved something like your aims. I do like a woman of courage, not to mention guile. And who knows what time might have wrought?"

He raised his head. His expression was mild and his voice remained urbane, but his stance resembled a stag at bay. "But we've had neither time nor opportunity to know each other, nor will we. I'm no man or woman's slave, or toy, or prey. Do your worst. I won't marry you. Sorry."

"You will be sorrier," she warned him. "Your reputation can't recover from this. I've had a good name—until now. If I marry, the other matter will be forgotten. The gentleman's wife only wants to know that I'm safely away from her husband. She won't pursue it once we wed. You are, among other things, greatly feared. One of the other reasons we chose you."

He didn't answer.

"And so?" she finally asked after a bit of wood snapped in the fire and broke the silence. "One last chance, sir. I look well kissed, I am half-dressed. Make me a pretty offer, or I'll take the decision out of your hands. One more moment, then I'll cry out. My brother's waiting for that summons. He'll rush in, accuse you of all things. How tedious. How bourgeois. But everything he says will be believed, you know. Come, Sir Alasdair. Though you hesitate, I *am* considered attractive. They say you did every vile thing in your wild youth. No one will be shocked to see you returning to such behavior now. But they *will* be shocked, and appalled, that you violated a gentleman's code by attacking another gentleman's daughter. Last chance, sir. We'll be wed anyhow. Wouldn't it be better to do it in dignified fashion?"

He shook his head. "No," he said, "I shudder at the thought of the outcry, of course. But I've no intention of marrying you, certainly not like this. So shout, have your damned brother in, have the world in, if you wish. Screech away, my dear, but even if you cater-waul like Catalani herself, I won't have you."

She looked shocked. Then her expression grew cold. Her body stiffened, and her widened eyes glittered.

He braced himself.

"Oh, my," a light, breathless voice said from the corner of the room. "Oh, my dear lady, please don't! My family would hate my name involved in a scandal. It's what I get for always being in the wrong place at the right time . . . or is it the other way around? Whatever it is, I beg you, please don't shout! Or at least, could you wait until I leave?"

2

Alasdair and the lady spun around to stare at the young woman standing in front of the curtains, twisting her hands together. A very pretty and very worried young woman, simply dressed in white. She was white-faced, too.

"I was here, resting, when you came in," she told Lady Eleanora quickly. "I thought you'd only be a moment, that you were here to fix your gown or some such. When the gentleman arrived, I hoped to slip away because then I thought you and he . . ." She hesitated, clearly embarrassed. "But it was nothing like that. I mean to say, you wanted him to, but he didn't. Oh, Lord!" she said miserably. "What a strange situation! I'm making it worse, aren't I? But please, don't shout. I couldn't bear it!"

"A servant," the lady spat, spinning around to stare at Alasdair. "Never mind. She's nothing. She won't be believed."

"I beg your pardon!" the young woman said,

sounding even more upset. "I'm not a servant. I'm not dressed for a grand ball, to be sure, but I only recently arrived in town, you see. I'm a cousin to the Swansons and very respectable, I assure you. I may not be dressed in the first stare of fashion," she said, drawing herself up to her not very considerable height, "but at least I *am* dressed."

Alasdair began laughing.

Lady Eleanora drew herself up, too, in every way. She pulled up her gown and swiftly retied her hair. "Good evening," she said through clenched teeth. She walked past Alasdair, drew open the door, and swept out of the room. Only the door slamming behind her gave hint of her wrath.

Alasdair stopped laughing. "My thanks, and from the bottom of my heart," he told the young woman. "But now we have to get you out of here, unseen, and fast. She'll be bent on vengeance. She'll cry rape on us, and then you'll be in the soup."

"And you, too," she said wisely. "But don't worry. I'll leave the way I came in." She gestured to the curtained wall. She saw his dumbfounded expression and smiled at last. "No, I'm not a ghost."

"No, you're an angel," he said. "But you walk through walls?"

"Yes, as a matter of fact, I did. This is an old house, and there are hidden corridors for the staff to use throughout. They didn't want servants lugging chamber pots and such through the halls for everyone to see in the old days, it seems. So I came in that way."

"But why?" he asked, "Why did you come in here tonight?"

She hesitated. "Because it wasn't fair," she said. "We heard what she and her brother were planning. Overheard, that is. Sibyl and I. Sibyl's the youngest Swanson daughter. She's not been presented to Society yet. We were standing at the back of the ballroom and heard them whispering together."

She looked even more uneasy. "Not precisely the back of the ballroom," she added. "Sibyl knows all the hidden places in the house, and was showing them to me. It's really fascinating, architecturally."

He raised one eyebrow.

She looked embarrassed, ducked her head, then raised it as she hurriedly went on. "But that's not the point. The lady and her brother didn't think anyone was there, of course. We couldn't believe our ears! So gothic. And mean-spirited! Sibyl was on fire to rescue you. I couldn't let her risk her name. She's very young. And to possibly be ruined by a gallant gesture? I'm not very brave. Nor was I sure it was the right course. But she was so upset that she was going to rush in to mend matters if I didn't. I couldn't have that."

They heard a commotion in the hall, the sound of several voices. She glanced at the door, and then back at him.

The first time he'd seen her he'd been too busy thinking about his predicament for a good look. He'd the fleeting impression of a charming face, a mass of curls, a slender but bountiful figure, loveliness that needed closer inspection. Now he gazed at her, and in that moment felt something shift in his perceptions, something alter his pulse, something he couldn't name. It was gone in another moment. He never forgot himself for longer. There wasn't time to think about it, not now. One thing was clear though, she was dressed plainly, but plain she was not.

She looked at the door and then back at him, and froze as her eyes searched his. He'd seen that reaction before, but never from a female. *Fear?* Of him? But why should she fear him?

The sound of voices came closer. She only kept staring at him. She didn't move a step.

His nostrils flared. "Oh," he said softly, his face going still, "I see. I was rescued so as to be given a more deserving bride?"

She gasped as though he'd hit her in the stomach. Her head reared back. "That's vile! I'd have done the same for any animal caught in a trap." Even in the inconstant light he could see her cheeks flame at what she'd said. "I didn't mean it that way," she said at once, "I don't mean to be rude," she added, backing a step, "But I certainly don't want *that.* I can think of few things more repugnant than marriage to you. Except for being caught in here right now. Good-bye." She turned, hurried to the other end of the room, and drew back the curtain.

"Wait! I'm sorry," he said, "I didn't mean that. Or if I did, put it down to my disordered thinking, under the circumstances. I'm entirely in your debt and I know it. Please forgive me."

She nodded curtly and ducked behind the curtains.

"Your name—at least that!" he called after her.

Her tousled head popped back out. "But you don't have to thank me again, or worry about anything. I'm no one, really. Good-bye!" she said, and disappeared behind the curtain again.

The door to the blue salon flew open. A group of men burst in, led by an agitated gentleman. They glanced around the room, and saw nothing but Alasdair. He wore a pained expression.

"Where is she?" the agitated gentleman demanded.

"Who? And lower your voice please," Alasdair said, wincing.

"These fellows think you've got a woman in here, Alasdair," Viscount Leigh said with a wry smile as he stepped into the room, looking around curiously. "They claimed you were bent on rape. I tried to tell them it was always the other way round, and came to see if I had to rescue you from some besotted female."

"Thank you, Leigh," Alasdair said. "No such luck. I was summoned here with that damned cigar-perfumed note, but when I got here the place was empty. I was just waiting to see if anyone would appear. I didn't expect a mob."

The agitated gentleman stalked into the room, frowning ferociously. He looked in every corner, even peering behind furniture. Then, on an obviously sudden inspiration, he turned toward the curtains. With a triumphant flourish, he tore them back.

There was nothing there but a wall, a picture of an overfed ancestor, and the blank, black panes of a window staring into the night.

"Many things I have done, Wretton," Alasdair said sweetly, "but I've not yet mastered the trick of pulling females out of thin air. God knows, I've tried. Now, if you don't mind, I'm leaving. Speaking of air, I need some fresh. The atmosphere's too stifling for me here. Good evening," he said as he strode out the door.

The agitated gentleman looked confused. The others in his raiding party glowered at him. Some of them had unmarried sisters here tonight, too.

Kate reeled into her room, one hand on her midsection.

Her cousin Sibyl popped up from the chair she'd been curled in. "Kate! What is it?" she cried.

"Lord!" Kate said dazedly, sinking to her bed. "He's

so *big*! He took all the air out of the room. He just siphoned it out, somehow."

"Did you save him?"

"Consider him saved—if that's at all possible," Kate said on a shaken laugh. "At least I routed *her*. You should have seen it. Shocking! She pulled down her gown, and her breas . . . bosom was hanging out. He stared. Well, who wouldn't? They were very nice," she added generously. "Another man might have been left speechless. *I* was. I suppose he's seen too many to care. She told him to marry her or else, just as she said she'd do. She had him cornered, but he didn't give up. 'No,' he said. 'Do your worst,' or something like that. I was all admiration. She was about to shout, and her evil brother was outside the door, too. Then I stepped out and pretended to be stupid. Which I was.

"Who could have expected it?" she murmured almost to herself. "I thought I was so much older and more responsible than you. How could I have known? I never saw the like of him before. Sibyl," she breathed, her eyes widening as the implications of what she'd done sank in, "my name could have been ruined, too."

Some of the exhilaration began to wear off. "What a fool I was!" she marveled. "I'd heard so much about him. If half of it were true, it was too much. But I was ready to sacrifice myself to save him. I said it was to save you, too, but the truth was I felt sorry for him. I never blamed him because, I suppose, we tend to romanticize wild gentlemen, allowing them things we'd condemn women for."

"But men are different. They have different needs."

"Do they?" Kate murmured. "Well, at least they pay different consequences for them, don't they?"

"Lady Eleanora was going to trap him, blackmail him. That was never right."

"So it wasn't," Kate shook her head. "Lord! I did it!" She held up her hands and saw the fine trembling in her fingers. "How could I dare? I'm amazed at myself—and by him. Sib," she said, "you can't know how monumental the man is! I'm amazed I could speak straight at all."

"He's that handsome up close, too?" Sibyl asked breathlessly.

"Lord, no! Not with that face of his. It's a mass of contradictions, nothing matches, that jaw is *impossible*. I've hung lanterns that were of subtler design. There's no balance. But the sum is so much better than the parts. No, he's not handsome. It's better and worse than that."

"You sound smitten," her cousin said.

"Smitten?" Kate echoed, considering it, her head to the side, "No. 'Smote,' though. Yes, absolutely. But what's that got to do with anything? He's too much for me, but I wasn't angling for him, and I'm not going to have to deal with him again. But, as for *she* who was trying to," she said with a sudden triumphant grin that made her look like a girl, "I did it. I banished the she devil, and set him free!"

Her cousin looked at her with admiration.

"Don't think he was grateful," Kate said with a laugh. "He couldn't have been ruder. He accused *me* of trying to snare him! Yes. Because when she left, instead of nipping right out of the room the way I was supposed to do, I suddenly felt I couldn't move. It's the truth. I couldn't. My legs turned to water. I'm glad he accused me of what she tried to do; it was like a bucket of cold water in my face. I fled—as much from him as those who were coming. Oh, but my dear cousin! He terrified me almost as much as the people who were coming to the door."

"People came to the door?" Sibyl asked, her eyes widened.

Kate nodded. "She probably sent them after she left, trying to get him into trouble, no doubt."

"And you." Sibyl looked worried. "She might harbor a grudge and try to do you an injury."

"Much chance of that," Kate scoffed. "What? Send me home again? I'll go soon anyway. I'm a country mouse in from the haystacks for a few improving weeks. No one knows me, or knows I'm here, and no one will know where I go, or when I do."

Sibyl looked down at her lap, "I'm sorry. It's just that Papa and Mama are having a hard enough time springing off Frances, Henrietta, and Chloe. If they gowned and presented you, you'd be too much competition."

"Don't feel sorry for me, there's no need for it," Kate said quickly. "I couldn't be any kind of competition either."

"What?" her cousin squeaked, gazing at Kate. "With your looks?" The excitement had put high color into Kate's cheeks, making her piquant face glow. "Why, you've the most beautiful eyes, such a pretty shade, they match your hair. As for hair, you don't have to spend hours in curl papers, you simply tie yours up with a ribbon, and *voilà*! It's instantly in perfect style, *à la Meduse*."

"Yes," Kate said with a grimace, shaking her head until some of her curls tumbled from their moorings to dance around her face, covering her eyes. "Very appropriate. Because if I didn't tie it, it would look just *like* a nest of snakes. My hair is brown, my eyes are ditto, I'm not impressed with my looks at all. Now, if I were slimmer and . . . Never mind that." She swiped her curls back with one hand and looked keenly at her cousin. "I'm not talking about my appearance. It wouldn't matter if I looked like Venus. I can't be competition for the gentlemen your sisters are on the hunt for."

Sibyl began to protest, but Kate held up her hand. "I've no money, at least not the kind you need to be a social success in London."

Sibyl fell still and looked at her own hands as though they suddenly fascinated her.

"Yes, exactly," Kate said. "And though I'm 'connected' to just about everyone, I've no social standing either." She saw her cousin's expression. "It doesn't matter. I'm glad I'm here. *Glad?* Ecstatic. If I hadn't visited you, I'd never get to see the sights of London."

"But your parents sent you in the hopes . . ."

"That once I was seen one of the royal princes would come waddling over, fall to one knee, and ask me to be his wife?" Kate smiled ruefully. "I love my parents, but I'm three-and-twenty and firmly on the shelf. Sending me to family I hadn't seen since I was christened was a wild hope. Not mine. I don't fit in here at all.

"What a face! You look like you're about to cry for me." Kate laughed. "There's no need. We're not poor, mind. We've a neat, comfortable farm and a steady income. But the thing is we have to think about income, and it's clear no one here does. When I first saw the gowns on the London ladies, I was staggered. I'd only seen such in fashion plates. And the way the gentlemen dress? Why, the pin in Sir Alasdair's cravat could have bought a horse! We don't have funds like that. What am I supposed to do, snare a footman? Not that Ffelkes isn't pretty," she added, to make her cousin giggle, because poor Ffelkes had spots and no chin, "but I don't think he reads any more often than he bathes. I vow, the fellow must have himself dusted every day, along with the furniture. And oiled, too, just look at his hair."

Sibyl laughed, but then grew serious again. "No, I mean it, Kate. You've got *such* looks. And the loveliest figure. Why, you don't need expensive gowns."

"Of course I do!" Kate said in annoyance. "That's the point. It's not that I want them, it's just they're required in your set. It's a uniform." She sat straight up and lectured like a schoolmistress. "I reasoned it out after I'd been here a day. London's a crowded city. I imagine you could live here all your life and still not know everyone walking on the street with you. So expensive clothes are how the rich can recognize each other, even from far away. It's necessary. Like in the army or navy, where you can tell whose rank equals yours at a glance. Or more appropriately, and since I'm a country girl, it's exactly like the way birds put on their spring plumage for mating. To attract their own kind.

"Don't giggle," she chided, "I'm quite serious. Just look right outside this window. Every person dresses for his station in life. It takes the guessing out of things. It's true that these days, with all the new money being made after the war, there's bound to be some confusion. Commoners are getting as rich as noblemen. But money speaks to money, even so. I've little, and everything about me shows it. Education," she went on, holding up one slim finger to silence whatever Sibyl was about to say, "can be got cheap, in a book, or from someone wise, so it doesn't matter. And breeding only serves the well-bred person.

"But don't pity me," Kate warned. "If your parents bought me expensive gowns, it would be dishonest, like a false front, because there'd be nothing behind it. We're only third cousins. It's a wonder we get on so well, and I'm glad of it. Your parents owe me nothing, nor do I expect it. The crime is what they're doing with you. Or rather, not doing. You're pretty as you can stare, nineteen, and *never* presented at a ball? They keep you like a mad wife in an attic. And you're their own daughter and the best-looking of the lot!"

Sibyl shook her head. "No. But I'm the youngest, and so shouldn't be upset at being the last to be 'popped off,' Papa says."

"Well, you'll be the easiest to pop off," Kate insisted, gazing at her cousin fondly. Sibyl had the sweetest temperament of all seven Swanson sisters, with not an ounce of the competitiveness that ruined the others' personalities. She was the changeling child in all ways, looks and manners. She lacked her sisters' sturdy bodies and heavy features as well as their jealous natures. But she couldn't even show her face at a ball until the last of her elders was wed. It was the only way to keep peace in the family. So Sibyl was left to wait, alone. Kate knew she'd been invited to keep her company and didn't mind, except for Sibyl's sake.

"But you saved Sir Alasdair," Sibyl said eagerly, glad to get off the subject of her future. "I'll bet he'll be *intensely* grateful, when he thinks about it. Like the lion in that Aesop fable."

"Absolutely," Kate agreed, "I saved him like the slave did the lion with a thorn in his paw. And nearly got my head bitten off for it, too!" She winced. "And didn't I just about tell him that in so many words? I said I'd do as much for any animal caught in a trap."

Her cousin gasped.

"Well, but that was after he insulted me by guessing I was trying to snare him. But he *is* like some mighty animal at that," Kate mused. "The man's larger than life, full of pride and vigor." She shivered and wrapped her arms around herself. "He terrorizes as much as fascinates. *Exactly* as they say. One thing's

sure, for all I think Lady Eleanora's a monster, she's a
very brave monster, indeed! I saved him, but I'm glad
I'll never have to see him again."

"But you seem so taken with him."

"What's that to do with anything?"

"Is it his reputation?"

"Lord, Sib! No. Haven't you been listening? Please
do. It's this world, his life, your life . . . all this." She
threw her hands in the air. "I've been impressed by so
much since I arrived here. Not just the sights, but the
people seeing them. The elegant men—dandies, poets,
Corinthians, more types than I've seen in one place in
my life. Goodness! More *people* than I've ever seen in
my life! I'm just as overwhelmed by the ladies of fashion. And by the women you pointed out, the expensive
Cyprians we saw riding in the Park. Yes, even those
poor creatures I saw from the carriage, selling themselves in the streets. Sib, as far as I'm concerned they're
all from another world. As is Sir Alasdair. I've traveled
in books but nowhere else. I'm dazzled. Of course. But
I know the difference between fiction and fact. What
has such a fellow to do with me? Or any of them for
that matter? I'm here to visit and learn, and I am.
There's an end to it."

Sibyl gazed at her cousin sadly. "It's a shame." She
sighed. "You're *so* very pretty."

Kate smiled gently. "How pathetic! We sound like
old spinsters trying to cheer each other up on a lonely
night. *'But you've still got four lovely teeth, dearie,'* she
said in a quavering falsetto. *'Aye, sister, but you can still
see out of one of your pretty eyes, my sweet.'* "

"But, you—*you've got most of your hair, too,*" Sibyl
said in a trembling voice, getting into the spirit of
things.

"More hair than wit," Kate muttered, suddenly serious. "Lord," she said in wonder, "I actually went and saved the most dangerous man in the *ton*!"

"Well, I don't know about that," Sibyl said thoughtfully. "Markham's rumored to have killed his wife, remember. Dearborne is an utter cad. FitzHugh has a wicked temper and is fast with his fists. Lord Dance and Mr. Jellicoe are always ready with pistol and sword, but so many gentlemen are that it's hard to say which one is worse. Wycoff was even naughtier in his day. As for lethal, everyone knows Drummond and his friends Dalton and Sinclair, and a whole slew of others were involved in dangerous doings for His Majesty during the war. So, as for *dangerous* . . ."

"Sib," Kate said with authority, "you weren't there."

"No," Sibyl admitted with deep envy.

"It's another good tale to bring home," Kate said. "That's all."

"With all your protests," Sibyl said with a grin, "I begin to believe you wish it were more."

"Of course," Kate said with a touch of acid, "I wish he'd clasped me to his chest, thrown me on his steed, and carried me off to his flaming circle of hell."

Her cousin laughed.

Kate sobered. "The more I think about it, the more frightened I get," she said with total honesty. "It was a very stupid thing for me to have done—for us to even think of doing. If I'd been caught there with him, it would have been dreadful. He'd have despised me. With reason. But I'd have never allowed him to offer for me to save my reputation. That would be absurd.

"And you know?" Kate mused, remembering that dark face and the chilling look that had come into those obsidian eyes when he thought she was about to do the same thing Lady Eleanora had tried. "Even after only a few minutes in his company, I begin to realize I actually may have done him a great disservice. Eleanora Wretton might have been the perfect mate for him."

"But she's crafty," Sibyl gasped, "and cold. And she has no principles, or morals—at least where her own comfort and desires are concerned."

"Exactly," Kate said.

3

It was a rare spring afternoon that came as a surprise after a damp, misty morning, the kind of tender day that sent poets scrambling to their inkwells and more realistic Londoners rushing to get their hats to go outdoors.

Two gentlemen of fashion came out of the Swanson town house that afternoon, the day after the Swanson ball. Only years of breeding prevented them from being jammed together in the doorway as each tried to be the first one out. Only decades of careful tuition kept them from hurtling down the stair to the pavement once they'd actually sorted things out and stepped outside. It had nothing to do with the weather.

"Hours wasted in that cramped parlor!" Alasdair said in disgust, straightening his shoulders and shaking out his sleeves as though he'd been bound in a box.

"Only a half hour, and it was a large room," his friend Leigh commented.

"It felt like eternity in a coffin," Alasdair said. "And

not for a minute did they let on they'd yet another daughter, much less a visiting country cousin. I couldn't bring up the subject. It's obvious she wasn't supposed to present herself to company. And I didn't want anyone to know I'd been alone with Eleanora Wretton, much less saved from her clutches. I sat and smiled until my face ached, but didn't get a chance to see my savior, to thank her. I hinted my head off. Much good it did me."

He walked on, muttering. "All they kept doing was praising those three lumpkins of theirs. Who sat staring at me as though they were going to toss a coin to see who got to gnaw at my bones or grind them to make bread. God. Poor old Swanson. I even pity the wife, though she didn't stop talking, beaming at her ill-begotten lot as if they were fairy princesses. Those girls look like ogresses, damned if they don't. I almost expected to hear one of them mutter 'fi-fi-fo-fum.' And I'm not even considered prime husband material, not really. You must have felt like a lamb patty."

"I'm used to it," Leigh said blithely. His friend didn't react to this outrageous remark by so much as a smile, or laugh at his conceit. It was simply true. Fair-haired, slight of build, and of medium height, the viscount's face was pleasant, but his remarkably intelligent gray eyes lifted it from the ordinary. He might be overlooked in a crowd, but he never overlooked anything, which was why he'd been a vital link in His Majesty's service during the war. Brilliant as he was reclusive, and unfailingly polite, he was a man who made up his own mind, which was why he never faltered in his friendship with the baronet St. Erth.

"They've given up on me," Leigh explained. "It was you they were sighting today. You're new, rich, unattached, and untried. What did you expect?"

"A chance to thank the young woman. She did me a service, and I repaid her with an accusation."

"That's all?" the viscount asked, idly swinging his walking stick. "Their footmen say she's pretty as she can stare."

Alasdair's dark head turned, and he gave his friend a darker look. Leigh shrugged. "My footman made the acquaintance of theirs and asked a few questions for me. It turns out that the Swansons keep her as company for their youngest daughter, but never take her into society. Their older girls don't like competition, for some reason."

"You might have mentioned it sooner. We could have avoided this interminable morning."

"But there was always the chance they'd let her appear, with the youngest."

"No," Alasdair said in annoyance. "Their butler says they don't dare show their youngest because they know she'll be snapped up. This would shame her unmarried elders, and their wailing would be heard cross the channel. So they're keeping the young one back until they can bounce off the others."

Now Leigh shot his friend a keen look.

Alasdair shrugged. "My butler happened to meet theirs."

"But you came here this morning anyway?"

"Like you. In hopes I'd find out more myself."

"The country cousin is a nobody," Leigh said thoughtfully.

"So I heard, too."

They turned east in unison without a word of consultation. As the park gates came into sight, the viscount turned his head to look at his friend, his eyes bright with laughter.

Alasdair's own eyes sparkled. "I heard she was in

the habit of going to the park in the morning. As you did, of course."

"The footmen, especially the one with spots, waxed rhapsodic over her looks," Leigh said. "I confess my interest's whetted. I can't wait to see her for myself. I knew there had to be a reason you were so intent on thanking the chit personally. She's that attractive?"

Alasdair shrugged. "Hard to remember, I was so distracted last night, one surprise after another."

His friend remained silent. He knew Alasdair better than that.

"Curling hair, a charming smile," Alasdair went on casually, as though he hadn't seen her face in his thoughts all night. "But I was so grateful for her being there I'd probably say that about a Gorgon. It's not her looks that interest me, it's a debt I owe."

"Of course," Leigh agreed too amiably. "But the park will be crammed with females. If you don't remember her, how will you find her?"

"I'll look for a young woman in a pink gown, wearing a yellow straw bonnet with a paper rose on it. If that doesn't do it, I'll look for her companions, a thin pale girl with no eyebrows, accompanied by a maid-servant in blue. A half guinea more and I'd have the exact number of their teeth. Swanson's housemaids feel underpaid, too."

Leigh chuckled. "Why in the world did you roust me up this morning, saying you needed me today? You could find a needle in a haystack at midnight with your eyes closed. I wish you'd been about my business rather than your own when I was working on the Continent. The War Office would have been thrilled with you."

"They were, sometimes," Alasdair said. "But spare me the bouquets. I'm not so patriotic. It's just that now and then in the course of my own peculiar investigations, while straining through the slime, I chanced upon a particularly nasty tidbit that could be of use to His Majesty. Whenever that happened I passed it on— or went a bit further, if they asked me nicely enough."

Leigh stared at him, all laughter gone from his eyes. "So I thought,—later. Lord, you're good."

"The point is that I'm bad," Alasdair said seriously. "That's why I need you today. Wait. Ah. Good." He stopped walking as he spied a well-dressed elderly couple approaching.

Alasdair swept off his high beaver hat as they neared. Leigh did the same.

The old gentleman paused. He looked irresolute, then stricken. He finally removed his hat, his frail hand trembling. His wife stood stiff as a poker, looking anywhere but at the two gentlemen who had greeted him. The old man put his hat back on and, looking miserable, resumed walking. His wife looked triumphant as she marched away at his side.

"There you are," Alasdair said with grim satisfaction, clapping his hat back on. "What's a proper browbeaten gent to do when confronted by a rakeshame? Worse, when the rascal's accompanied by a good man? I made poor Bryce come to a moral decision. He can tell his lady he could hardly ignore you. Ordinarily, I wouldn't have greeted them. But you had to be shown. Proper ladies and gentlemen don't acknowledge me."

"But at the ball last night . . ." Leigh began.

Alasdair cut him off with a laugh. "I live, I breathe, my income comes in with the regularity of my wicked heartbeat, so I'm acceptable at the Swansons'. In certain circles, I'll never be. I can find the girl, but in doing so I risk ruining her reputation. So make yourself most in sight and stand by me, please."

"The Bryces are ancient, their opinions antique,"

Leigh said angrily. "Your reputation's no worse than many men's."

Alasdair looked at his friend and arced one black brow.

"The Wretton woman wanted you," Leigh argued.

Alasdair smiled, bitterly. "My name's bad. But hers will be worse if she doesn't change it promptly, and legally. No matter what she said, I doubt she was strictly alone last night in that desperate endeavor. And I'm not just talking about her brother."

"But you're not carrying someone else's babe," Leigh protested, "A man can change . . ."

"Don't sound like a matchmaking mama, please," Alasdair said brusquely. His broad shoulders went up as though he felt a chill wind at his back as he stalked on through the warm bright afternoon. "The Bible-pounders are right. A man can't change any more than a leopard can. I can paint over the spots but, believe me, they're there. I've done things. Whether I regret them, deny them, or do them in future or not, doesn't change what has been done. The past *is*. Some things stain the soul. Some things are irremediable. I've a bad name. I deserve it. Have done. I just want to find a young woman who did me a favor and thank her without harming her. Will you help me?"

"Of course," Leigh said. "But I believe your past haunts you more than it could ever hurt anyone else."

"Then be glad your heart's innocent enough to think that. Let's look, shall we?"

His friend held his tongue. There was a lot to look at. The park paths were filled, every bench occupied, even the grass was strewn with people enjoying the day. Saunterers, idlers, ladies, gentlemen, and resting workers, the park was crowded with blissful-looking adults, tumbling children, and frolicking dogs.

"Whatever else our Regent does wrong, this is very right," Alasdair commented. "I may regret his onion domes and gilded kitchens, but at least he keeps creating new green spaces for recreation. I've always thought it was our parks and not our politics that saved us from the ax. If the French aristocracy had built more than Versailles or let the peasants in to gambol as much as Louis did, they might have kept their king and their heads, too. Is there anything more democratic than a park on such a day?"

It certainly appeared democratic, but a more careful look showed the classes behaving differently. It was a warm day for spring. Workingmen had their sleeves rolled up, their shirts open at the neck. Gentlemen wore their jackets unbuttoned, but their necks were still covered and would remain so in public even if it were steaming, or they were. Ladies, luckier because fashion called for almost transparent gowns, idly flapped their fans as they strolled. Ordinary women tugged at their necklines and kilted their skirts. Alasdair smiled at a saucy milkmaid when he saw her lay down her yoke and milk pails. She winked at him, plumped her considerable self down on the grass, hiked her skirts to her knees, and tilted her chin up to the sky.

Leigh also eyed that white flesh as it came into view. "We'll be a nation of cooked lobsters by evening," he said dryly.

"But sometimes the pain is worth the pleasure, however momentary," Alasdair said. He grimaced. "Yes, I know. A singularly poor example, coming from me."

"There's a pink gown," Leigh said quickly.

"On a female shaped like the tree she's standing under," Alasdair sighed. "Use your quizzing glass."

"You didn't say she was shapely."

"I'm saying it now. There's a straw bonnet! No, look what's under it. Blast, is the chit here at all?"

"Patience," Leigh said. "This path goes all the way round the Serpentine. Shall we? What shade of pink?"

"What do you mean?" Alasdair asked, frowning.

"There are different hues of pink—rose, apricot, coral, and salmon pink, petunia . . ." Leigh said patiently, "Petal, dawn, blush, and tulip . . ."

"*Tulip*, is it? Very apt. I never knew you were such a tulip of the *ton*," Alasdair said in amazement. "How do you know all those ridiculous names for colors?"

"It happens a flirt of mine modeled gowns for Madame Celeste. She often talked about fashion."

"And, obviously you didn't see her for her conversation," Alasdair said sardonically. "*Flirt*, is it now? What a nice euphemism. I'll bet you spent a pretty penny for the right to a *'flirt'* of an evening."

His friend looked away, his lean cheeks taking on one of the shades they were discussing.

"But what else can a fellow do?" Alasdair went on. "Doesn't it get to be a bore, though? The only women worth both looking at *and* talking to are either married to others or want to marry you. At least, that's how I've found it. And I won't indulge in liaisons with married women."

"So moral, then?" Leigh asked with a smile.

"Not in the least. Sinning is not the same as cheating. I abhor a cheat."

"And you don't want to marry?"

"If a female considers me eligible, she's not looking at more than my title and bank account. I'd rather do it the honest way and pay for a quick"—he grinned—"'flirt.'"

"And love?"

"Curious question coming from you," Alasdair countered. "We're of an age. I've been gone from England for months, and I don't see any rings on your finger or through your nose."

Leigh's face grew a gentle smile. "Haven't succumbed, I'm afraid. Oh, I thought I had a time or two. But that's the point. I *thought*. I've been told that when one loves, thinking is not possible."

"Probably," Alasdair commented, "that must be why there are so many stupid people in the world."

They laughed aloud. They'd been noticed by every woman in their path, but their full-bodied laughter made those who hadn't seen them turn to look.

"There," Alasdair said with satisfaction. "If we'd kept on, we'd have walked right into her."

She and her companions had turned at the sound of his laughter. She stopped in her tracks when she saw him. He stilled, too, looking at her as she gazed at him. Shadows had made her elusively charming. Daylight showed her to be vividly so. The simple rose-colored gown she wore showed her neat figure to perfection, but was too obviously homemade to be fashionable. But she transcended fashion. She wasn't beautiful, not in the current style of imposing women with long necks and aquiline noses. Better than fashionable, she was unique, and very appealing.

She had delicate, even features, clear white skin, and a pretty, curving mouth. But he'd have known her by her eyes even though he hadn't seen their color before. They were clear, fully opened, tilted, the color of coffee shot with gold. Flyaway brows arched over those dazzling eyes. Shining coffee-colored curls escaped from under her bonnet and coiled around her forehead and neck. The sunlight sparked gold in those twining tendrils.

"Extravagantly pretty," Leigh murmured, quite impressed. Alasdair was already striding toward her.

Her companions were a servant and a slender, pale young woman dressed in white, a color she blended into. "The invisible one must be the Swanson girl." Leigh sighed as he followed Alasdair. "It only makes sense the charmer would be the one who saved you."

Alasdair approached the pair, then stopped and stood silent, looking at Kate.

Leigh came up to the pale girl. "Good afternoon, Miss Swanson," he said, and bowed.

"How do you know my name?" she asked, startled.

"You could be no other," he said. "I've just come from your house, and the resemblance to your sisters is remarkable."

There was a stunned silence at the outrageous lie.

Alasdair winced. "Forgive him," he told Kate, his eyes on hers. "I asked for a proper introduction, and he's obviously still working at it. Let's dispense with that. I had to thank you again and apologize for what I said. I owe you much and wanted you to know it. Oh, give you my friend, Viscount Leigh," he added belatedly, as he stared down at her.

She looked at him, shocked, appalled, delighted. The emotions chased across her face. Alasdair had to sternly throttle the desire to take her hand and walk down the path with her so he could watch more responses come and go on that lovely, expressive face. She stared at him as though mesmerized, and he felt an unmistakable mutual tug of attraction. Daylight couldn't disguise the flicker of response in her widening eyes. He recognized that reaction too well to mistake it.

"You don't have to thank me," she said, never taking her eyes from his.

"Of course I do. I wish I could do more," he said, and meant it.

She searched for words. That surprised her. She could talk the knob off a door, her family said. But standing in the shadow of this big dark man stole her breath and froze her wits.

He'd been formidable in a darkened room, he was overwhelming in daylight. She'd thought men of his reputation needed moonlight to be seductive. She was wrong. Fit and athletic, he looked like he'd be as comfortable on a horse as in a boudoir. His black hair shone like a crow's wing, the sunlight showed his skin smooth and clear. His mouth was firm, and she found herself fascinated by his lips. They were shapely, almost tender, at least so they looked in that angular masculine face. The sable eyes were still fathomless, only now, as she tore her gaze from his mouth, she could see those eyes had long dark lashes, and now, too, they sparkled with humor and interest, making her think he was aware of every stirring reaction to him she was trying to suppress.

She wet her lips. He watched. Her companion made little coughing sounds that turned to squeaks. Alasdair turned his head to look at her. She was nervous and frightened. It reminded him of where he was, and what he was.

Their maid bustled up, looking anxious. These two gentlemen were well-known to the servants of the socially prominent. Both wealthy, titled bachelors, she considered them dangerous to her young charges, each in their separate ways. One, because few mamas knew him well enough to know if he had a heart. The other, because they said he didn't, and that was why he stole so many.

She needn't have worried. Alasdair was himself again, shocked at his own lapse. He tipped his hat. "And so I merely wanted to give you good day, Miss— Good Lord! I don't even know your name."

"Corbet," Sibyl Swanson said in a tiny voice. "Kate, we must be going," she said, and then looked agonized, realizing her rudeness to the two men.

Alasdair relieved them all, except for Kate, who stood staring at him, her eyes searching his face as she still sought something to say. "Good day," he said, bowed, turned, and left.

He walked away so fast he didn't hear what the littlest Swanson said to her cousin in disbelief. "You said you didn't care if you ever saw him again. But when you did see him you looked like a sleepwalker!"

"I felt like one," Kate said as she watched his broad back retreating. "Oh, my! Oh, drat! He's gone! He must think I'm a fool. The man's so imposing he just stole my wits away! No wonder he left so fast. I couldn't think of a thing to say to keep him here."

"Then you weren't a fool at all," Sibyl said. She saw her cousin's flushed face. "And what does it matter what he thinks?"

"Oh. Yes. Right," Kate said sadly.

"You didn't want to stay and chat some more?" Leigh asked after he'd walked along with Alasdair for a few minutes in silence.

"No," Alasdair said grimly. "I had to thank her, I did. If there's ever a chance for me to do her any good, I will. But the best thing I could do, I've done. Which is to leave her alone."

"Pity," Leigh said again. "I think you'd suit. She's unique."

"Yes, and so am I," Alasdair said. "Exactly."

"Leigh!" a hearty male voice called.

They paused.

Two young gentlemen hurried up to them. "What? You, out in public, promenading in a park?" one asked Leigh. "Now there's a wonder."

"Unlike some gents I could name, I've been known to leave my house by day, even when it wasn't on fire." Leigh laughed. "If you'd ever been out before nightfall you'd have known it. Oh, allow me to present my friend, Sir Alasdair St. Erth. Alasdair, give you these hopeless fellows, Lords Reese and Covington."

The men bowed to each other. The newcomers looked at Alasdair with naked curiosity. He smiled. "Excuse me, gentlemen. Have your chat, Leigh. I'll just go on ahead, I see an old friend."

"Fine. Go on, I'll catch up," Leigh said.

Alasdair strode on. He hadn't seen anyone he knew. *His* acquaintances were the sort who came out after dark—or a heavy rain, he thought with bitter humor. He rounded the path, walked off to the side, bowed his head in thought, and waited. The sun was warm on his shoulders and neck, but he felt nothing but the chill in his heart.

Yes, he thought, she was extravagantly pretty. He was definitely attracted. But he had other business to attend to, business that required all his attention, wit, and focus. Besides, she was a decent young woman, he couldn't court her if he wanted to. Not now, not yet, maybe not ever. 'Pity,' Leigh had said. No. He didn't want that. Not for himself, certainly. And not for her. She had, after all, done him a favor. So there was an end to it.

He'd long since learned to hide his emotions. He'd learned to deny them even earlier than that. And so when Leigh caught up with him, he had his mood and expression under control again. He looked up, as though he'd only been contemplating the day.

"Old schoolmates," Leigh said with a shrug, "but bores. And, I fear, boors. They can be counted on to have many, many children," he added to make Alasdair laugh, because he saw more in that bland expression than his friend knew. "They saw us chatting with the Swanson chit and your rescuer. I had to laugh it off, making myself the goat, convincing them it was a case of mistaken identity on my part. They knew her, you see," he said, as they started walking again.

Alasdair looked at him.

"Yes. The Swansons may think they're keeping their youngest a secret, but they can't. They're too well connected, and they do manage to pop off the odd daughter now and then. One of Reese's brothers actually married one, last year. So he knows the whole bloodline, even the visiting cousin. He met her when he paid a call with his unfortunate brother the other week, and can't seem to forget her either. She's a gentleman farmer's daughter from Kent. Of little money and no particular account, they said wistfully, because of the little money. Still, she's connected to half the House of Lords, so she could stay with anyone, they say, but seems to like the invisible Swanson girl. She was invited to visit with the Norths as well as the Deals, here in London. She even has a standing invitation to stay with the Scalbys. But she refused. Seems your gentle rescuer has taste as well as remarkable eyes."

Alasdair stopped in his tracks. He wheeled around and stared at Leigh, his black eyes ablaze. "*Scalby?* She's *related* to them?"

Leigh was taken aback. He hadn't been thinking, just prattling, to cheer his friend. Too late, he realized his mistake. He damned himself. "Well, yes," he said slowly. "On her mother's side. But she's no more kin to them than the Swansons. They're blood, but twice or thrice removed, too. You can't think she's tainted because of it."

"But close enough to be invited to stay with them," Alasdair said urgently, his face alight. "So close enough for them to know whatever she does wherever she stays."

Leigh's eyes widened as he stared at his friend's suddenly animated face. "No," he said, as understanding set in. He slowly shook his head. "I'll support you in many things, Alasdair, and have done too. But you can't be thinking of making her part of . . . your plans. No. She's blameless. Let her remain so."

"So she is," Alasdair said with triumph, "but I'm not. I'd make God or the Devil part of it if it would help."

"But to hurt an innocent? That's not like you."

"I wouldn't go that far. But far enough, Leigh, far enough to get enough rope so they can hang themselves."

"And the girl?"

"She looks able to skip rope. That's all she'll have to do."

Leigh said nothing, and kept his expression bland though he was deeply troubled. Alasdair never showed his hand. That he did now meant that his excitement overrode all his training. It was as rare as it was ominous. Leigh knew his friend well, so there was nothing more he could say. No one could argue that Alasdair didn't deserve his revenge. And he wouldn't listen if they did.

But there was more he could do, Leigh thought.

There was every possibility the young woman would be sent home before anything happened. Every possibility, plus another. He'd see to it.

Alasdair walked on, lusting for Katherine Corbet as he never had for any woman. All thought of her lovely face and appealing figure was forgotten. In one blinding flash she'd become infinitely more desirable to him than beauty could ever be. Revenge was more important to him than sex, after all. Or food, wealth, or health, or breathing itself.

She was fascinated with him, obviously. She could be useful.

She was only a little straw, he reasoned with dark glee, but enough to break the camel's back. Or better yet, kindling enough to start the purifying fire he'd been building toward all these long, miserable, and dangerous years. A little straw was all he needed to start a conflagration. She wouldn't perish in it—he'd snatch her out before she did. But it would be a fatal fire. He'd see to that.

4

"Again!" Lady Swanson asked anxiously. "What was said, how was it said, and who else was there to see or hear?"

"Ma'am," the maid said miserably, wringing her hands, "I told you all, every bit, every scrap. I can't remember every word nor one other, I swear. As to who saw? Anyone in the Park, I'd think."

"It's clear you didn't think!" the tall blond woman sitting next to Lady Swanson boomed. "You should have taken Sibyl away the minute they appeared! Oh, get out, do!" she told the trembling maid with a wave of her hand. The maid scurried from the room.

"This is too much," the blond woman said angrily, turning to face Lady Swanson. "Leigh *and* St. Erth? Trying to scrape up an acquaintance with *Sibyl* on their own? In the Park?" She stamped her foot, making a porcelain shepherdess on the mantel do a little jig, "I will *not* have her marrying before me, Mama. Life is hard enough as it is!"

"Before you?" another fair-haired young woman cried from her seat by the window. "What about me? You can't allow it, Mama."

"Ho!" another thickset blond young lady said angrily from the chair where she sat, staring at her feet. "*Allow?* Are you mad, Chloe? Much Mama has to say about it. She allowed Mercy to marry before me, didn't she? And Mercy's a year younger."

"But McIntyre offered for her and wanted no one else, so Mama's hands were tied," Chloe said with a touch of malice. "But, Mama, you *can* do something to nip this in the bud!"

All three pairs of eyes swiveled to stare at their mother. Lady Swanson repressed a sigh. She was such a delicate-looking little woman, it was hard for people to believe she'd given birth to these three strapping young females. For herself, too, sometimes. Still, she loved all her daughters, even though there was, she admitted, perhaps a surplus of them. But though she loved, she didn't dote. It was hard to play favorites when one had seven daughters. Impossible, when they'd been so blessedly brought up by maids and governesses, she'd never experienced intimacy with them. Until now. No hired servant could see to marrying them off.

Lady Swanson gazed at her daughters and sighed more deeply. It would cost a fortune. She had that, and had spent a great deal of it already. Which is how she and her husband had popped off the older girls. But so far these three hadn't agreed to marry any of the gentlemen her parents offered to buy for them. And she couldn't find it in her heart to insist on any of those who had proposed because they'd been from the bottom of the barrel. It seemed even fortune hunters had some standards these days. Or maybe it was because the peace was finally offering some prosperity, so times weren't as bad as they'd been when her elder girls had been wed.

She felt as bad for her daughters as for herself and her husband. She knew what marital bliss was. She and her husband loved each other and always had done. He didn't blame her, as some men might have done, for producing no sons. And how could he object to the fact that the girls she'd borne had inherited almost everything from him? That was the problem.

Lord Swanson was a man's man, with a face and form that suited a man. He looked hale and hearty with his big broad bones, round red face, and prominent nose. It gave him weight and character. His eyes were a nondescript color, but well opened. And he'd thick brown hair, when he'd had it. His wife had lovely blue eyes, but they were small. No one noticed because her features were so charming and delicate, as was her body. The girls had inherited her blond hair and eye shape. Everything else was a feminized version of their father. Only not *that* feminine, Lady Swanson thought, and sighed again.

Most of her girls had got their looks from their father, that was to say. Her youngest, Sibyl, was Lady Swanson's own image, but faded, as though the imprint had got fainter being so many times removed from her. Still, a dash of soot on Sibyl's eyelashes, a rabbit's foot's worth of color on her cheeks, a wash of henna to give some depth of color for the hair, and her mama was sure she could marry her off in a second. But that second would have to wait until an hour after the last of her elder sisters' weddings. And that might take centuries, Lady Swanson thought unhappily as she looked at her daughters' wrath. It wasn't a flattering expression for them. They wore it often. For some reason, they hadn't inherited Lord Swanson's easy-going personality either.

But, their mother thought sadly, it must be difficult growing up to realize that though you thought you had everything all your life, when push came to shove, it turned out you had nothing a man might want in a wife—except for the money in your father's pockets. It would sour a saint, which they were not. But they weren't wicked children. It was just that they felt things too deeply. Things like envy, rivalry, and malice.

"Now, you know very well that Sibyl didn't approach *them*," she said now, to calm her daughters. "And you know even better that a mere hello in the street does *not* a courtship make."

There was some grumbling, then Henrietta spoke up. "But why should they even bother to seek her out? After spending the morning with us, going off and trying to start a conversation with Sibyl, of all people? I mean, two of London's most eligible men accosting *her*? What other reason could they have?"

"Goodness! I'm not sure they're *that* eligible," Lady Swanson said quickly. "I mean, Leigh is not a social creature and is new to us, so we don't know much about him, really. And as for St. Erth! We know too much! His reputation and all . . ."

"'And all' won't matter at all once he *is* married," Chloe said, aggravation in her deep voice. "You know that."

"Sibyl's not of marriageable age," Lady Swanson declared. "Or only just," she added quickly, remembering that she'd been married even younger. "And she hasn't been presented. Therefore," she said on a sudden happy inspiration, "it can only be that they are trying to scrape up a closer acquaintance with you girls!"

Three pairs of eyes stared stonily at her.

"Leigh *and* St. Erth interested in us?" Chloe's lip curled. "Odd that we didn't see any evidence of it when they were here."

Her mother ducked her head. She raised it and saw her daughters' expressions. She felt a tug at her heart but steeled herself to speak with forced cheer. "They're the best of friends. You know how men are! Maybe one was lending the other support. Perhaps he wanted to know more before he went further."

There was a stonier silence.

Lady Swanson shrugged, and gave up trying to sugarcoat the thing. "You have excellent birth and generous dowries," she said firmly. "Your standing in Society is irreproachable. That still matters. Leigh's a recluse, an only child of elderly parents. Who knows what pressure may have been brought to pry him from his house and hurry him to the altar? I haven't seen his parents in years, but they could have asked to see him settled before they die. He won't find a better lineage to suit them than here. As for St. Erth?" She pursed her lips. This was a more difficult courtship to imagine or explain.

"He's been abroad," she said on a sudden inspiration. "Who knows what became of his fortune there? Maybe he needs to repair it in a hurry."

It was a hard thing to tell hopeful young women, essentially saying it was only the blood in the veins and the gold in their dowries that could interest their suitors. But it was evidently the right thing. Her daughters mulled this over. Lady Swanson eyed them sadly as they did. Chloe's neck was not as thick as Henrietta's, but her nose was larger. Frances's nose was smaller, though her shoulders were broader. They would have been *such* imposing men, their mother thought wistfully.

Still, the bright side was that each was more attractive than their older married sisters. In fact, it seemed her daughters improved in looks in age order, the younger improving over her elder every time, as though Nature had kept trying to get it right. Sibyl would be so easy to be rid of—marry off, Lady Swanson thought.

After a moment of considering their mother's harsh explanation, her daughters looked happier and gazed at Lady Swanson with renewed interest.

"So!" their mother said gaily, seeing that. "We'll try to make it easier for St. Erth and Leigh. We shall have another ball!"

There was a chorus of groans.

Lady Swanson looked puzzled.

"Our father's balls are the joke of the *ton*," Chloe said.

One of her sisters snickered.

Lady Swanson's eyes sharpened, and there was a sudden silence. Fond she might be, but she wouldn't have her dear husband ridiculed.

"They're too frequent," Henrietta explained.

Lady Swanson nibbled the tip of a finger. "Then, a musicale?"

The groans were louder this time.

"No one enjoys them," Frances said. "Except the old ladies, and that's only because they can catch up on their sleep."

"Then," her mother said patiently, "we'll all simply have to go to every fashionable affair St. Erth and Leigh attend, to give them an opportunity to further your acquaintance."

"You plan on taking us to gentlemen's clubs?" Chloe sneered.

"Or to brothels, boxing matches, horse races, gambling hells and that nasty Hummum's in the Strand?" Henrietta asked bitterly.

There was a silence.

"We might have a rout," Chloe said. "A supper and dancing, nothing formal."

There was a hum of agreement.

"*And* we might want to ask Sibyl some questions," Frances said darkly.

Sibyl's three older sisters left her room after a fifteen-minute interrogation. They felt much better. Their sister sat staring after them, looking a little pale after all their questions and accusations.

But "no," she'd kept saying, "I don't know why they introduced themselves. The viscount said I looked like a Swanson, and then they both made polite conversation. That's all."

That was finally accepted, and obviously pleased her sisters. They left soon after, discussing plans for their rout.

"No. I do *not* feel like 'Ella, Sit by the Cinders,'" Sibyl protested to her cousin a second after the door closed.

Kate sat in the window seat of Sibyl's bedchamber. The Swanson girls had questioned her, too. But it was their sister they'd asked about. They hadn't for a moment thought either man she'd met in the park had been interested in her. They didn't consider their cousin much more than a jumped-up servant.

"I have a soft bed," Sibyl went on, bouncing on it for emphasis. "I eat good food, and have any number of gowns. No one beats me, my sisters usually ignore me, in fact. I just have to wait until they marry before I am courted. And," she added, before Kate could speak again, "even if I could receive gentlemen callers, I wouldn't want either Leigh or St. Erth. Leigh is quiet as a clam, and he never stops watching people, so who knows what he's thinking? It makes me anxious. As for St. Erth! He's so big, so dark . . . so overwhelming! I don't even know how you managed to speak with him!"

"I didn't," Kate said glumly.

"Because he's everything you said and worse. Terrifying! And Viscount Leigh? I wonder why he doesn't just take out a scale along with his quizzing glass when he studies a person. Who'd want either of them? Apart from my sisters, of course. I'd want a comfortable husband, a man I don't feel nervous with."

Kate almost agreed, until she remembered that though Sir Alasdair had terrified her, it was a delicious sort of terror, like when she was a child and went swinging too high, feeling her stomach drop as she did. Then she remembered how she always begged someone to push her so she could swing that high again. And it wasn't precisely her stomach that had reacted to him, although the region wasn't that far from it.

She changed the subject quickly. "Thank heavens your mama told your sisters the gentlemen must have been asking about them!"

"Well, I couldn't lie that much," Sibyl said, "but I didn't have to. They believed it. I can almost pity those two men. Now my sisters are going to be watching them like hawks whenever they see either one of them."

"So they'll arrange not to see them," Kate said. "Those two are resourceful. And who knows? Maybe they might be interested in your sisters. I know, Sir Alasdair said he had to thank me. But who can tell what really goes on in a mind like that? At least it's over for me. He thanked me, and that's that." There was wistfulness in her voice when she said it.

Sibyl heard it. "You're the one who's sitting by the cinders," she said sadly.

"I'm sitting by the fireside in London now," Kate said, forcing a smile, "and that's something to remember!"

She told her cousin only half the truth. Because she also knew that the notorious baronet was something never to forget.

Viscount Leigh stood in his friend Alasdair's dressing room, watching him as he raised his chin and wound a clean white neckcloth around his neck.

"I hope you purchased an extra length," Leigh commented. "The only longer neck I've seen is at the Tower menagerie. But that fellow also had hooves, horns, and spots all over his back."

"I'm spared that," Alasdair commented as he slowly lowered his chin and settled it into his precisely tied neckcloth. "At least the spots. I manage to conceal the hooves and horns. And tail."

"I wasn't commenting on your resemblance to the devil. I was remembering a giraffe. But speak of the devil, why did you ask me here today?"

"I didn't," Alasdair said, putting his arms out as his valet held up his jacket for him. "I merely asked to see you at your leisure."

"All I have is leisure. I'm at your service."

"Are you?" Alasdair mused, shifting his shoulders as he got the tightly fitted jacket on. "Yes, that will do. Very good, thank you, Pierce," he told his valet.

The man nodded, picked up the clothing his master had decided not to wear, and quietly left the room. When the door had closed behind him, Alasdair fixed his guest with a long look. "I paid an interesting call on an old friend yesterday. Now, what I'd like to know is why Viscount North felt impelled to make inquiries into my relationship with his distant relative, Miss Corbet? Kate Corbet, the little lady we met in the Park the other day, in case you've forgotten."

His voice became cooler as he stared at Leigh. "But I doubt you've forgotten. You see, Jason North's an old friend of mine. And he tells me it was you who urged him and his good wife to take Miss Corbet into their home and under his protection, because of the dangers facing an untried girl here in wicked old London Town. Naturally, Jason asked me why my name was brought into this equation. Though I understand the wicked part, of course, I confess, it made me wonder, too."

Leigh's expression grew shuttered. He looked away from his friend and studied his walking stick instead. "Dear me," he said with an attempt at flippancy, "I'd no idea you two were old friends. A misstep, that." He raised his gaze. His eyes were steady. "The truth then. I worried about the girl."

"Woman," Alasdair corrected him, turning to view himself in the looking glass. He seemed totally preoccupied with his appearance, but kept careful watch on his friend's face, reflected behind him. "She's three-and-twenty, North says. And clever as she can hold together, as I thought. Well able to handle herself. Was it my handling her that worried you?"

Leigh grimaced. "It wasn't her morals so much as her heart I was worried about, Alasdair. Even if her morals failed, I trust you know the precise line you can walk in a flirtation with a lady of quality. You always have in the past. But you had plans for her, you said as much. You also blithely said you felt she could fend for herself. I just didn't think it was fair to involve her in your machinations. The Swansons certainly aren't interested in her welfare. Someone had to be. She may be three-and-twenty but anyone can see she's not a woman of experience."

"I see," Alasdair said gently. "*You're* interested in her, then? If that's the case, I'll gladly step aside, and congratulate you on your unexpected good taste in women. She's charming."

"No," his friend said quickly. "She's charming, but I've no plans for her. You do. That's what bothers me. Be damned to it, Alasdair! I'd have the same reaction seeing a snake eyeing a mouse."

"Snake? Giraffe? Lord, you think well of me," Alasdair said as he buttoned his jacket.

Leigh sighed. "Alasdair, you want the girl to help you revenge yourself on the Scalbys. From what North told me, and believe me I know how to ask in a roundabout way so he didn't guess my intent, they aren't close to her. There's a thought! Why bother with an untried chick? Why not use one of the Swanson women instead? They'd love your company, if only because it would call other men's attention to them."

"It's not merely a question of aesthetics," Alasdair said, adjusting a sleeve. "They aren't related to the objects of my interest. The Corbet woman is, on her mama's side. The Swansons are connections to her father. And if my attentions would delight the ogresses, why shouldn't they please Kate Corbet as well?"

"She doesn't have any town bronze. She's obviously more sensitive and sheltered," Leigh persisted. "North said her father's relationship with all his London relatives is distant, in every way. So you won't find out anything about the Scalbys from her. Why not just give up the idea?"

"Oh, but I don't need any more information about them," Alsadair said, running a hand back over his raven hair. "I have enough to hang them three times over now. Speaking metaphorically, of course. They have enough money and titles to keep their necks from the noose. Their crimes are many and heavy but not punishable by anything but eternal flames. But certainly enough to make them lepers in polite society forevermore."

"That's not enough for you?" Leigh asked.

"*No.*" Alsadair said, his mouth suddenly twisting as though he'd bit down on something bitter. "I want to see their faces when *I* reveal all. But how am I to do that?" he asked, recovering his bland expression again. "They've become hermits since they returned to London, or at least, since I have. I can hardly set fire to their town house to smoke them out, can I? Now Fate's thrown me a chance to do that in another way. Come, my friend," he said, turning to face Leigh. "That's all I want. Not much is it? Not after what's owed me. If I keep company with their relative, I'm bound to see them, sometime, someplace, in public. That's all I'm after. A chance for a public denunciation. How can that hurt the young woman you want to protect?"

"You told North this?"

"No, of course not. But North knows me and trusts me. Do you?"

Leigh ignored the question. "And when you've done it?" he persisted. "What's to become of the girl?"

"The *woman,*" Leigh said patiently. "I won't take anything from her, if that's what's bothering you. Not her maidenhead, not her reputation. Good God, man, I have discretion and control, you know. Nor will I leave her wanting, either. The Swansons are keeping her a secret. My squiring her around London will bring her to the attention of many more eligible gentlemen."

Leigh still looked troubled. "And if she loses her heart to you?"

Alasdair laughed. "She won't. You spoke about my knowing which lines to walk. Trust me to know the ones I can't cross."

"She seemed infatuated with you."

"Infatuation is no bad thing," Alasdair said with a smile. "It can be amusing and, if handled properly, can be a learning experience so that when she meets a man who suits her, she won't be tongue-tied or awkward. Infatuation can only grow to love if there's fuel to feed it. Trust me, I won't do a thing to nourish any grand passion. I'll entertain the woman. But I won't let her entertain any misconceptions." He threw back his head and laughed loudly. "There'll be no conceptions of *any* kind, I promise you!

"So then," he added, sobering, "if I promise to be good and bring nothing but good to her? You'll stop trying to have her far-flung relatives rescue her from my clutches?" His expression grew gravely serious. "Leigh, I'm asking if you trust me. No. I'm asking for your trust. Do I have it?"

There was a moment of silence, then Leigh looked at him gravely. "You're my friend, and I have no friends I can't trust. But what if the Scalbys don't rise to your bait?"

Alasdair smiled, and shrugged. "Then I'll settle for merely ruining them without the joy of seeing their expressions when they realize I've done it. Half a loaf is better than none." But his smile showed he wasn't a man who settled for half of anything. "You can see for yourself."

"Yes, I'm afraid I will," his friend said with regret.

5

Sir Alasdair and Viscount Leigh presented their cards and then were left to cool their polished bootheels in the Swansons' drawing room. It wasn't a thing they were used to doing. Or a thing they wanted to do, either.

"If it were for anyone but you," Leigh finally said softly as he paced the room, "I'd be down the street by now."

"If *I* were anyone but me, I'd be three steps ahead of you," Alasdair answered. "But I can scarcely come calling by myself."

His friend looked at him with bemused inquiry.

"I've faced assassins in dark alleys and violent men at knife point," Alasdair explained, "but even I draw the line. I will not take on the Swanson women alone. Apart from the fact that coming here by myself would give rise to even more speculation." He shot Leigh a keen look. "You didn't have to come along. Are you obliging me? Or playing watchdog?"

"Don't worry about it. A watched dog never bites," Leigh said lightly. "I'm just interested. You're throwing yourself to the lionesses. Such entertainment doesn't often come my way."

Alasdair gave a cough of a laugh. He looked up as the door to the drawing room opened. Leigh stopped pacing. Both men stared.

They were stared at, too. The three older unwed Swanson daughters entered the room with their mama. The popular quip around London these days was that one Swanson girl was worse-looking than the other, and the other wasn't good to look at either. This morning they bore that out. It wasn't their gowns, which were made by the best dressmakers in town. One wore white, one yellow, and one was draped in flowered muslin, but none of the gowns was flattering. It was difficult to flatter forms or faces like theirs. It wasn't just because the women were large and ungainly, a smile could go a long way to soften anyone's appearance and bring charm to the plainest face. But they wore identical expressions, and the only word for them was smug.

Two of London's most eligible bachelors had come calling. Whatever the Swanson daughters didn't have, they believed they had what these gentlemen callers were after. One of these attractive men probably needed money, and the other had to have a highborn wife. The Swanson women didn't flutter or simper or try to make themselves attractive to gentlemen once they knew they were suitors. Instead, they frankly eyed their callers, as though they were on display in a window, for sale. But there were three of them and only two suitors, so each finally smiled as she curtsied, while her mama gushed greetings.

"My lords! How charming to see you again," Lady Swanson exulted.

"My ladies," Alasdair said, bowing. "The delight is ours, I assure you. I come this morning on an errand of some delicacy."

Lady Swanson beamed. Her daughters preened.

"My friend Leigh came to bear me company," Alasdair said. "You see, I've a message for someone you harbor under your roof, and an invitation for her, too."

Lady Swanson smiled more widely. She knew how to dissect flowery speech. The "under your roof" part filled her with glee. The invitation also sounded promising.

"My friend North told me his cousin, Miss Corbet, is staying on here in London with you," Alasdair went on. "I encountered her by accident the other day in the Park. As it happened, I told him I'd done so. Well, the moment he heard he begged me to present her with his greetings and an invitation to take tea with him and his lady today. Another invitation. It seems he'd asked her to come visit when she came to London, but she has not yet done so. Miss Corbet seemed to me to be somewhat reclusive. I told him that, and added the fact that I didn't know if she could or would visit him on such short notice. But I promised him I'd try to convince her to. Sometimes sudden invitations can result in instant decisions. Thinking about social engagements can make them seem more terrifying to the timid.

"At any rate," he went on smoothly, "I've come to relay the message and offer to escort her if she wants to visit her cousin."

There was a stunned silence. But Lady Swanson hadn't already married off three of her difficult daughters for no reason. "Why, certainly," she said as soon as she recovered her wits. "She ought to have visited her relatives here in town, and so I've told her. But she was so occupied with seeing the sights. How kind of you to offer to take her. Of course she should go. And so I'll tell her, I promise you. But, though you two gentlemen are certainly good company, she'll need the escort of a respectable female, won't she? Might I suggest one of my daughters and her maid accompany you, too?"

Frances smirked at her sisters as their expressions grew sulky. She was the eldest, and would be the one who got to go.

"What a good idea!" Alasdair said. "Yes, I should have thought of that. Your daughter Sibyl, of course. It was clear to see the two were best of friends. That should certainly put poor Miss Corbet's fears at ease. How clever of you, ma'am."

Lady Swanson excused herself and left the room to tell her daughter and Kate about the invitation. Her other daughters sat and stared, thunderous as an August afternoon, unblinking as lizards, as the two gentlemen struggled to make polite conversation with them.

Both men looked ready to bolt by the time Lady Swanson came back. She breathlessly reported that her cousin accepted the invitation, but that Kate and Sibyl had to dress for the outing. "So if you don't mind waiting a few more minutes?" she asked the gentlemen, and shot a significant look at her mute and angry-looking daughters.

They got the hint. Frances began asking Leigh about his ancestors. Henrietta asked Alasdair about his estate and what sort of repair it was in. Chloe wasn't as subtle. She asked both of them about their families, finances, and plans for the Season.

When Sibyl and Kate appeared, they were greeted by the two men as though they were seeing dawn after a long, dark night.

"Well, time to depart," Alasdair said quickly as he

stood. "I'll take every care of them," he told his host-ess, "and have them back directly after tea. Good day, ladies, it's been a great pleasure," he lied, bowed, and hurried to shepherd the two young women from the house.

Once outside, Alasdair looked down at Kate, seeing her clearly for the first time that day. She was wearing her pink gown, and her unruly curls escaped from un-der the pretty straw bonnet with the pink paper rose on it. But she was obviously upset. Her eyes were downcast, her face pale, her lips held in a tight line. *Poor little thing*, Alasdair thought with a surprised pang of sympathy, *she really is timid. My work's cut out for me.*

Leigh saw a blushing Sibyl into the coach, her maid-servant following, then Alasdair handed Kate up into it. He was the last to enter the carriage, and the first thing he saw was Kate's blazing eyes as she leaned to-ward him.

"How could you!" she hissed at him.

"I beg your pardon?" he said, taken aback.

"Well, you should! I mean, really!" she said, her voice shaking with suppressed fury. "I *told* you I didn't need to see you again. I *said* I didn't want you thanking me or singling me out. To accost me in the park was bad enough. But to ask me out? Do you know what problems you're making for me? And *poor* Sibyl!"

Alasdair sat back. "No," he said thoughtfully. "You're mistaken. I have an excellent memory, and what you actually said was, 'I can think of few things more repugnant than marriage to you.' You did not say that you never wanted to see me again."

"Well, I thought you'd guess it," she said in aggra-vated tones. "And what a humbug! To say that North was yearning to see me. That I was too timid to see him? I didn't see the need! I've met the man precisely twice since I've grown up, I doubt he'd recognize me if I showed up dead on his doorstep. What is the meaning of this, sir?"

"I think he'd recognize you if you showed up dead," Alasdair mused, holding his smile back. "Unless you were terribly mutilated, of course."

She looked as though she'd gladly mutilate him. "Yes, go on, make sport of me," she said through clenched teeth, color returning to her face, blooming in her cheeks. "When you're done, pray tell me why you asked me out, set the Swansons in an uproar, and made poor Sibyl's life miserable! Or didn't you realize that her sisters will make mincemeat of her now?"

" '*Poor Sibyl*'?" Leigh asked Sibyl with a small smile. "Said twice? So, it can't be an accident. But how unusual. I'd no idea your first name was 'Poor,' my dear. Does it run in the family?"

Sibyl ignored him because she was as impressed as dismayed by her cousin's fury. Even her maidservant sat shocked, staring at Kate.

Kate noticed. "I'm normally the mildest of creatures," she went on, trying to keep the anger out of her voice, "but unless I get some answers, I'll tell the coachman to stop, and I'll walk all the way home if I have to."

"It's only been two streets," Alasdair remarked, glancing out the window. "But, wait, no, no," he laughed as Kate reached for the pull to signal the coachman. He captured her hand. "I'll tell all. Lord, what a firebrand," he mused as he held her hand in his.

It was a very small hand, and he could feel how cold it was, even through her glove. It trembled, but not with fear. He saw her militant expression, and realized she was fighting with herself to keep from pulling her hand away—in order to clout him, no doubt. He chuckled, and saw her color rise higher.

"It's true North wasn't on fire to meet you at first," he said quickly. "As you say, why should he have been? But I did mention you to him. Then he did say he wanted to see you. I can't pretend that I was instantly smitten with you, either, Miss Corbet, but I was fascinated, and wanted to pursue our acquaintance . . ."

"Gammon!" Kate said, in a rage now. "Don't try that one with me, sir. I've two eyes and three brothers. I know how men think, and I think I smell a rat. You are a clever man of wealth, title, and experience. I'm not that rivetingly beautiful, and I don't have a penny to fly with." She glowered at him. "Plain truth. You're up to some rig or other, and that's a fact. And I tell you I'll leave if you can't tell me the plain truth!"

She sat back, her breath hitching, her pulse racing, and her hand still in his. She still heard a buzzing in her ears, too. She'd gone up in a flame. Whenever she did she literally saw red and exploded with rage. Even so, as her vision cleared, she could hardly believe what she'd done. She'd been speechless in his presence, because she'd been seeing him in secret, rosy, sensual, and improbable romantic daydreams since she'd clapped eyes on him. But as always with her, once she got angry, she forgot everything.

Well, it was outrageous of her, but it was just as well! she thought on a shaking breath. She scarcely noted the viscount. Sir Alasdair had all her attention. He was one dangerous fellow. There could be no room for daydreams around someone like him.

Alasdair exchanged a glance with Leigh, saw his raised eyebrow, then turned to Kate again. He sighed. "Truth, then," he said. "Your cousin North wanted to see you. I owed him a favor, so I said I'd escort you to his home. My friend came along for the ride, to give me some respectability. Which I sadly lack."

"Your friend also came along in order to have the fair Sibyl's delightful company," Leigh added meticulously.

Sibyl's expression showed how much she believed that.

But all of Kate's attention was on Alasdair. "That's all?" she asked, incredulous.

"That's all. For now."

"Oh," Kate said, and thought about it. It seemed reasonable. Why should such a man lower himself enough to make a fool of her? When she'd done it so well for herself, she thought in chagrin. That last bit, *'for now,'* was troubling, but he was probably just incurably flirtatious. She wished she'd held her tongue. But what did it matter? She'd be gone from London soon anyway. And at least she wasn't tongue-tied in his presence anymore.

"Please accept my apologies," she said, keeping her eyes downcast. "I thought you were making fun of me. Now I see you were only doing a friend a favor."

"I was grateful to you, too," Alasdair said. "I thought reuniting you with your family might be some small way of repaying you for . . . being so kind the other day." he added with a glance at the fascinated maid, "when we met in the Park." He absently ran a thumb over the back of Kate's hand, stroking it as he thought of what else to say. "Some ladies would have shunned me. My reputation's not the best."

It sounded right, and felt much too good. His hand was very large, and cradled hers in dry warmth.

"You'd have a great deal more respectability if you didn't steal people's hands," Kate said. "May I have mine back, please?"

He released her hand and gave her a tilted smile. "Not so timid as your cousin believes, are you?"

"I don't think so," she said, putting her tingling hand in her lap. She cocked her head to the side. "Well, I don't know. When you live in a place where everyone knows you and you see the same people day after day, it's hard to know if you're timid or not. Since I've come to London, though, I suppose I may have been timid."

She didn't add that she had no way to test herself either, since she hadn't met anyone new since she came to London. But there were things she could say because they were true. "It's such a huge bustling place," she said, sitting forward in her eagerness to explain. "I've never seen anything like it. It's like market day in my village, only on every street! Every day! So many people, so many new faces. You have to get used to that, and I'm not yet. But, oh, it's exciting!"

The sunlight made her eyes glow. Her face took on life from her animation. She looked lovely, refreshing. Alasdair smiled. His work was indeed cut out for him, he thought ruefully, he'd have to watch himself as carefully as he did her.

Both Sibyl and Leigh shifted uncomfortably when they saw his expression. Leigh, because he'd seen it before, and was wary. Sibyl, because she'd never seen anything like it, and was terrified even if that long languorous look wasn't directed at her.

Kate could only stare, trapped in the reflection of his slow, sensuous smile as surely as if he still held her hand fast. Because she couldn't look away. Even if she'd tried. Even if she'd wanted to.

Kate's cousin, North, was as spectacularly handsome as she remembered. Quite the most good-looking male in the family, as her mother always said, to tease her father. But as her father always answered, though North had used his looks to earn the worst reputation in his day, marriage to a charming beauty had settled him into the ultimate boring husband.

Kate didn't find him boring. The viscount might be settled, but he was still dashing. Fair, with flawless features and the most interesting eyes, one blue and one gray. When she'd been a girl she'd thought him the best-looking man she'd ever seen. He was still handsome. But Kate suddenly realized growing up had changed her preferences. It seemed she preferred dark to light.

Viscountess North was as attractive as her husband, in her own way. She had a piquant face and a mop of curly hair, done up with a simple ribbon. She looked so charming and effortlessly fashionable, Kate was determined to try the same style herself.

They were the nicest hosts she could imagine, too, asking her how she liked London, telling her stories about it, urging her to visit them again before they headed back to the Lake District. At least, they said that when they could. Because they also had three lively young sons with curly heads, fascinating eyes, and never-ending prattle.

"Forgive us, we're unfashionable," her cousin North laughed as one of his sons, ensconced on Alasdair's lap, refused to give back the watch he'd been given to play with. "Children are supposed to be in the nursery with their nanny. But we enjoy ours too much to let her have all the fun."

"Now you see why we asked you to come back again," his wife told Kate. "No one else will!" She grinned as Alasdair made a terrible face at one of the little boys in his lap, making him giggle.

Kate watched, enchanted. She was as taken with the

children as with St. Erth's reaction to them. There wasn't a trace of the raffish noblemen in his attitude. He was so tall, so big in every proportion, he had room on his long knees for two of the boys, and yet was gentle and knew exactly how to play with them. Kate had three younger brothers and could tell when an adult was shamming. Sir Alasdair wasn't. Viscount Leigh's smile was bemused, but he was obviously wary of children. Sir Alasdair seemed genuinely amused by them, and made them laugh until they got hiccups.

"Oh, but I'll be happy to come back and visit," Kate assured her cousins eagerly. She hesitated. "For as long as I'm here, of course. I'd planned to go home in a few weeks, but my aunt has just told me my parents wrote to her asking that I return sooner."

"Indeed?" Alasdair said smoothly, taking his eyes from the gold watch the two children were now vying for and fixing her with his dark gaze. "She told you that just this morning, did she?"

Kate nodded. "Yes, but they wrote to tell me the same thing only the other week. They miss me, you see."

"Well, I can certainly understand that!" the viscountess said. "I'll miss my children when they grow up. Which is why I'm so pleased we'll soon have another. This time, a girl, I think, for me."

Everyone exclaimed and offered good wishes, and the subject of Kate's leaving was dropped. But Alasdair didn't forget it.

He mentioned it to her when he said good-bye later, in front of the Swansons' town house. He helped her down from the coach, but didn't release her hand. "Yes, it was a good afternoon, and I'm glad you enjoyed it," he said. "Now, what's this nonsense about you running home?"

"Not 'running home.' If I'm needed there, there I'll be." Kate looked away as she said it because she knew it wasn't so much as she was needed, as she was missed. But she realized she'd miss London, too. She'd have the rest of her life at home, and hated to leave just when things were getting so much more interesting.

He seemed to know that, he studied her so closely she had the eerie feeling he knew every thought she was trying to hide from him. And surely it wasn't proper for him to keep holding her hand? Sibyl was talking to the viscount, her maid was flirting with a footman, so no one saw it. But Kate couldn't ignore it. It was only her hand held in his light, warm clasp, but his presence was such she felt as though he was holding her by his side with far more than that. It made her stomach feel strange, and robbed her of breath. She forced herself to look at him. And took her hand back.

He smiled. "I'm sure when your aunt realizes there are benefits for her daughters in my continuing to call, she'll stop reminding you of your duty at home. You're only here for a little while, so surely it can't hurt if you stay on a little longer?"

She hesitated.

"Because," he went on in that deep, rich voice, his eyes intent on hers, "I begin to believe it would do me a great deal of harm if you left now."

Too much! Kate thought. The thought straightened her spine and brought any nervous airy fancies down with a thump. She knew her worth as well as this man's experience. The two didn't tally. She snapped back to attention. "Cut line, sir," she said, looking him straight in the eye. "I'd be best pleased with truth."

He laughed again, but nodded. "You're right. It was only a half-truth. I'd like to see you again. I enjoy your company. I can't say more now, because as you so rightly think, it's too soon. But if you leave, it can never be later."

He stood before her, his broad shoulders blotting out the sun. Fortunately for her composure, his fascinating dark face was also cast in shadow. Kate gazed at that shadowy face with mistrust. What she'd told him when they'd set out was unfortunately still true. She might have dreams, but she was a realist and knew what she was and was not. She wasn't a famous beauty. She wasn't rich. It was flattering to think he'd been smitten with her, but she doubted it. She hadn't gotten so much flattery in her life that she could be comfortable with it, and didn't believe she deserved it. Especially not from this man. Why should he single her out?

Everything she thought was there to see in her eyes.

"Your expression, Miss Corbet!" Alasdair said. "All right then. What I said was true. But it's also true that since I returned to London I've had some difficulty reestablishing myself in certain circles. I had a wild youth. I went off to the Continent and rumor grew. Now I've returned to find my reputation preceded me here. I'd like to repair it, and the company of a respectable female would go a long way to doing that."

Kate felt a twinge of disappointment and a wash of relief. She was suddenly freed from something too deep and dangerous to contemplate. It seemed that anger wasn't the only thing that could break the spell this man could cast over her. Nonsense did it, too.

She shook her head. "Fiddle! London's stuffed with respectable young women, old ones, too, who'd be thrilled to keep you company."

The front door to the Swanson house swung open. Alasdair glanced over to see a footman in the doorway, and the curtains to the front salon windows pulled back. Swanson faces looked out, Leigh was slowly strolling toward the front steps with Sibyl.

"No, please listen," Alasdair said quickly, turning his body so Kate couldn't see the window or door. "My thanks for the compliment, and it is true that eligibility often does outweigh reputation in some circles. But I'd rather be liked for myself. Please hear me out. I have the uneasy feeling that if I don't tell you now, I won't have a chance later. You're poised to leave, in more ways than one. I'd rather you didn't. And not only because it's hard for me to keep company with a wellborn, respectable female."

She raised an eyebrow.

"But that's true," he said earnestly. "Not just because of my reputation. I *am* a gentleman and can behave like one. But think about it. If I do call on a lady, it will give rise to certain expectations on her part—and her family's. You saved me once, and I have the uncanny feeling you could do it again. And you're the most sensible woman I've met in a long while. There may be more for us, too, though it's clear you doubt it. You seem sadly impervious to my charms."

Kate blinked. He thought she was impervious to him? Lord! What did the other women who fancied him do? Salivate on his boot tops? Fling rose petals at him?

"Think of the advantages," he persisted. "Not just the delight to be found in my presence," he added with a self-mocking smile. "It will bring your cousin out of seclusion, too, and give the Swansons some much needed cachet. Not from my presence in their parlor. Fortunately, though I have a bad reputation, I rejoice in having good friends. My friend Leigh, for example, is a very respectable fellow and much admired. Where he leads, others will follow."

Seeing the arrested look in her eyes, he quickly went on: "Think about it. It could be amusing for you. Going to parties, balls. We can see the sights during daylight, too. We can go riding or touring. Did I mention picnics? And fairs, if you like, as well as art exhibitions, poetry readings, whatever you want. Company grows thin in London as summer goes on, but it's never extinct. There'll be things to do and see. It will give you a chance to see London and have some pleasure in it."

That last part was exactly what worried Kate, though it also tempted her.

"So, may I continue to call on you?' he asked.

She looked at him closely and saw entreaty in his eyes and earnest hope in his expression, and experienced the slight dizziness she felt whenever she looked him straight in the eye. She could only nod, as charmed as she was flattered. His plan made sense. For the time being, that was all she needed it to do. And she reveled in it.

6

Kate waited for her cousin to speak again. She sat in Lord Swanson's study and watched his broad forehead furrow in thought. He was a fair man and a good fellow, or so her father said. She couldn't say. She hadn't seen much of him when she'd been a girl. That hadn't changed. She'd been a guest in his house for weeks now and hadn't exchanged more than a few sentences with him there either. He wasn't rude, just occupied with his own affairs, which obviously didn't usually include his guest or his daughters. But now they obviously did.

"Sir Alasdair didn't come to ask my permission," he finally said.

"He isn't asking for my hand," Kate answered carefully. "At least not for more than the time it takes to help me up into his carriage. He isn't proposing walking down any aisle with me but one in a theater, you see."

An unexpected smile lightened his expression. He

had a wide red face, not a very attractive one. But when he smiled Kate could understand why wispy little Lady Swanson spoke so fondly of her husband. If his daughters only smiled more, she thought. If only they tattled less, she thought with a slight frown. Their father wouldn't have called her in for this embarrassing talk if they hadn't run to tell him wicked Sir Alasdair was about to compromise their poor innocent country cousin. Or, at least, they'd done it after they'd picked their chins up off the floor, restrained themselves from throttling her, and gone in outrage to their mama. That poor lady, not knowing how to stop their squalls, had sent them to their papa. Who looked at her hopefully now, as though she could solve his problem.

"One doesn't want to offend Sir Alasdair," he said slowly. "Because though he has a certain notoriety, he's certainly an eligible suitor." He hesitated. They both knew how true that was. If the baronet really were a monster of depravity and had asked Kate to the theater, the Swanson sisters would have simply smirked. They did that very well.

"You couldn't go alone, of course," he went on thoughtfully. Before Kate could argue that of course she wouldn't do that, he added, "And my wife and I are otherwise engaged that night."

"I doubt he means to get up to any sort of debauchery in a theater," she blurted. She hadn't realized that an invitation to a young woman included that woman's relatives. She'd thought he'd meant a chaperone.

He looked unhappy. "It isn't that, though the theater does have a shocking reputation. My dear cousin, it's because a young woman of breeding cannot just attend a theater with a gentleman on her own. Especially one like Alasdair St. Erth."

Kate sat back and held her tongue. She didn't know London. And she did know Sir Alasdair's reputation.

"Still, I suppose we could have Mrs. August accompany you. She's entirely respectable and always willing to do a favor. She might even find it a treat."

Kate couldn't think of a word to say. Old Mrs. August lived with the Swansons, the way a ghost could be said to live in a house. She was an ancient, faded lady, a distant connection to the family, who drifted on the margins of life in the Swanson household, taking her meals in her rooms and showing up at some of their innumerable parties, though always disappearing early in the evening.

"It could be done. If you wish. But, my dear," he added, "do you think he has serious intentions toward you?"

Kate hesitated. If she said no, and told him Sir Alasdair's reason for asking her out, he would definitely disapprove. It sounded too smoky by half. Well, it probably was. But if she could keep her head, she'd have such fun. She knew she could. Her wits could guard her heart because she didn't trust the gentleman by half. No matter how attractive he was, she doubted she'd fall heedlessly in love with a man she couldn't trust. And she was certain she'd be able to deal with whatever he really wanted of her when she discovered what it was. The mystery was half the fun, she assured herself.

She decided to skip over the direct question and instead tell Lord Swanson half the truth. With a little flattery to soften it. That usually worked when she played intermediary for her parents in their disputes.

"Please excuse my plain speaking," she said, "but my parents brought me up to be forthright. I was joking about the debauchery, but whatever his plans, I doubt Lord Alasdair means seduction. Whatever cloud there is over his head, he is, after all, by no means insensible to the conventions."

Her cousin nodded, slowly. "And with all the beautiful women here in London," Kate went on, "it's hardly possible that he's consumed with a sudden passion for me. Even if he's suffered a head injury and has fallen under my spell," she added, grinning, "the fact is that I *am* under your protection. The Swanson name is not one to be trifled with."

"Indeed," he said, obviously much struck by that thought.

"And so whatever his intention, it can't help but be amusing for me. He wants to take me to the theater. We'll be seen at all times, I'll be back home soon enough, and it seems like such fun . . ." She paused, determined to keep that note of pleading out of her voice. She had to convince him she wasn't a lovestruck chit, but a sensible woman. "It will be good for my cousins, too," she said more firmly. "Sibyl will be coming along, Sir Alasdair said his friend Lord Leigh will be accompanying us, and surely the viscount is a model of good behavior."

"As to that," Lord Swanson said, looking a little hunted, "perhaps you might consider leaving Sibyl home, and taking one of her sisters instead? Sibyl is not yet out."

Kate had thought this over carefully. "Yes, exactly," she agreed. "But she's my friend, and of an age to go out of an evening," she added, to hint about that oversight. "Sir Alasdair already knows her, as does Lord Leigh. And exactly because she isn't out yet they'll know she isn't expecting any offers. Their friends will know that, too, so it will put them more at ease with her. They'll feel freer about visiting here in the future, attending your parties and such, don't you think? That will be better for everyone, won't it?" She fell silent, hoping he'd accept that.

He glanced at her from under his bushy eyebrows. There were no fools in her father's family. Her heart sank.

"Yes, I think it will," he finally said. "So you may go. Sibyl, too. But, Katherine? If there's any hint of impropriety or difficulty, or any pressures brought to bear on you because of this, don't hesitate to come to me. And I don't just mean those that may come from St. Erth."

Kate stilled, thinking of his daughters' spite. No, there were no fools in her father's family. Her smile was gentle and heartfelt. "Thank you."

"And Katherine?" he added as she stood. "It's not without the realm of possibility that a gentleman might fall under your spell. Especially when you smile. Just remember that."

"Thank you again, cousin," she said, her eyes growing misty. "I'll try to remember." She laughed. "I'll try to *believe* it, actually!"

"I can't believe I'm actually doing this," Leigh told Alasdair as he settled himself opposite his friend in his carriage. "I've risked my neck any number of ways for King and country, for friends, too. But this! This surpasses all. I'm taking a child to the theater," he marveled. "And she's one of the *Swansons*! Lord, the things I do in the name of friendship!"

Alasdair sat back as his coachman pulled away from the curb. "She's hardly a child. Just a pale little mouse, as overwhelmed by her sisters as you are. Can you even remember what she looked like? I think half the reason Kate Corbet's agreeing to this is to get that girl out of the house and into the company of a single male before she's ninety. Because if she has to wait to be presented until all her sisters are married off, that's how old she'll be then."

"Fine. You escort her," Leigh said. "I'll have the Corbet woman on my arm . . . lap . . . or wherever she cares to perch. She's a fine-looking woman and seems to have a brain in her head."

"Certainly you may have her anywhere you wish," Alasdair said, "*after* I've achieved my goals with her."

"Alasdair," Leigh said seriously, "that sounds terrible, even coming from you."

"But of course you know better," Alasdair said smoothly. "My motives may not be good, but they're not evil. There's a paradox for you. I don't mean her harm, at any rate. I have my faults, too many to list, but I know a gentleman can't give a respectable female pleasure without giving her his name, too. At least the kind of pleasure you mean. So her sweet body is safe from me. I can't have it, and I know it. What I can have is her name—bruited about town in the same breath as mine. At least until it's noted in certain quarters. Only that. Then you may do what you will with her. But not until then."

"But what if she thinks you want more?"

"I don't think she will," Alasdair said thoughtfully. "The other reason she's going with me is that she's wondering why I asked her. She's suspicious, and curious as a cat. That's refreshing. And she's open about it, which is even more so. Some of it must be that country upbringing. The rest is because she knows she's leaving here soon. London has a certain unreality for her, I think, because I suspect she's a very realistic woman on her own ground. We do things when we're away that we'd never do at home, you and I certainly know that. Travel gives us the freedom to be foolish. But I don't for a minute think she's ever that foolish. You're right, she's got more than a pretty face, she's got a sensible head on those pretty white shoulders of hers."

"But you noticed they're pretty, and white," Leigh said quietly.

"I'm well intentioned." Alsadair laughed. "Not dead. Since when have you become your friends' conscience?" he asked more soberly.

"I beg your pardon. A fault of mine. You've no idea of how much it limits me."

"No," Alasdair said. "It's one of the reasons I value your friendship. You're unique, my friend, a complete gentleman, but one who has a heart."

"No," Leigh said. "If I had one, I wouldn't still be a single man."

"You're reclusive, and it's difficult to find the love of your life under your chair. So I'm glad I've given you a reason to venture out, too. It's time. You've a cautious heart, but you have one, never doubt it. I wonder if I possess a heart anymore. It got in the way, so I put it aside a long time ago, along with my morals."

Alasdair laughed at his friend. "Don't look so worried, I tell you all I want from Kate Corbet is her company, in public. But she is attractive . . . and I am what I am. So if I seem to be asking for more of her, let me know." He stared out the window into the dark. "I don't want to cause troubles while I end my own, because when I'm done with this business, Leigh, I'm done with it all. I'll want to start life on a fresh page and finally forget the past.

"It's been a long time and a lot of work. I think I'm becoming as eager to lay the burden down as I was to assume it. You know?" he asked reflectively. "I worry that in time I may even miss this vile mission of mine. It's consumed me. I can't imagine life without it. I don't know how to lead a normal life anymore and don't know if I ever can again. But I'd like a chance to find out."

"It's almost done then?"

"It *is* done." Alasdair nodded. "All but the final touches. I have enough information about them to make sure they can never be so much as seen in polite company again. I only want to be sure their names can never be spoken in it either."

Leigh hesitated. "But—it's possible you may sully your name, too, if you do that, isn't it?"

Alasdair laughed. It wasn't a pleasant sound. "*Sully?* You think the son of a suicide, with a cloud of dark rumors over his own head, can shame his name further?"

"Knowing what you're capable of? If your plans bear fruit? Oh, yes. Alasdair," Leigh said, leaning forward, his hands clasped between his knees as he stared at his friend, "I've never asked you for specifics about the matter, and I never would. But I hope you know that if you ever choose to confide in me, I'd never let it go further either."

There was a silence. When it became uncomfortable, Leigh sat back, and went on, "Well, just so you know. The rumors about you are many. And unspecified. If what you do makes them clear, and they're as bad as you seem to believe, then certainly, yes, it will ruin your name further. Completely. Why risk it? You've done so many good things for your friends and your country, why rake up old coals?"

Alasdair stiffened. "Because they're coals from a fire that destroyed my life as surely as it did my father's!"

His voice was too loud in the confines of the coach. He thumped his fisted hand on his knee for emphasis. "I *will* have my revenge. The rest doesn't matter, it just does *not*."

He took a deep breath, uncurled his hand, and looked at it. When he spoke again his voice was calm, too calm. "They caused my father to kill himself. They almost drove me to it, too. Yes, that's true," he said to Leigh's appalled silence. "I chose to live only in order to revenge myself on them. I will. If it harms me in Society's eyes, so be it. If it loses me my friends, then they weren't really friends, were they?

"But I will destroy the Scalbys once and for all and forever." Alasdair spoke the words like an oath he'd pledged many times. "I could kill them. Don't think I didn't consider it often in the early days. I could have done it then and anytime since. Slowly and fairly painfully, too. I learned to do that. But that's not enough and would be too easy. It was then, it is now. Their pride must be crushed. Their name must become a definition of 'monster.' Because it is. Not just in my case. They've destroyed others by means so unsavory even I don't want to discuss it. But I can prove it. I will. That's a worse fate for them. Because they'll have to live with that. Or not."

He shrugged. There was nothing casual in the gesture. It was a tic of one shoulder. His voice was dark and deep. "If *they* die, let it be by their own hands. Let them do as my father did. But I must be the one who causes it, and they have to know that. They have to see and hear it from me. In public. Then and only then, I'll consider what else—if there is anything else—I want or need in this life."

This time, the silence in the coach was profound. Alasdair eyed his friend's rigid form. "I've never showed you this side of me, have I? But it exists. It's *why* I exist. I don't usually get so carried away; I suppose I'm getting overanxious. As I said, the time is near. I could end it all for them right now if I chose. But the long wait has made me greedy. I want to draw them to their fate rather than bringing it to them. The Corbet woman is the bait. I'll see that she doesn't get swallowed up, I promise. Now," he said in a lighter voice, "let's forget it, shall we?"

Leigh sat silent, still looking troubled.

"Of course," Alasdair said with another shrug, "if you're having second thoughts, I'll have the carriage turn around right now and take you home. But I will go on. I honestly don't know what will happen when the truth is finally out, Leigh. It may all blow up in my face. You may not want to be associated with me then. A man must be careful of his place in Society, at least I'm not insensitive to the fact that other men must be. So if you want to be out of my plans now, I'll let you off and make excuses to the Swansons for your absence."

He gazed at Leigh as though trying to see more than the outline of his face in the flickering coach lamplight. "Leigh, I've known you a long time and kept up our friendship because even as a boy you were of unimpeachable honor. Our paths diverged after my father's tragedy, but I made sure to maintain our association even so. Why *you* agreed still puzzles me. In fact, I never knew why you chose to be my friend in the first place; I suppose it's a case of opposites attracting."

Leigh didn't join in with Alasdair's forced laughter.

"And so, my friend?" Alasdair asked softly, "final chance. If you want to end our association now, I won't pretend to be happy about it, but I will understand."

Leigh made an exasperated sound. "Give me more credit than that. A conscience doesn't make a man a cad, I hope. What you want is reasonable, I suppose, even if the way you're going about it disturbs me. But if this means an end to the business, then I certainly want to help you complete the job. Just be careful of Kate Corbet's feelings. She's clever, yes. And curious. But even the most clever woman can forget her wits when a fellow like you campaigns for her attention."

"It's her cousins' attention I'm campaigning for," Alasdair said. "She is clever and suspects something of the sort. But she's only a lure, and won't lose by being one. I'll show her a good time in London. She won't regret it."

"And who knows?" Leigh mused. "In turn, she may help you find where you put your misplaced heart."

Alasdair was still laughing when the coach pulled up to the Swansons' house.

$\mathcal{L}$ady Swanson insisted Kate couldn't go out wearing the same old things now that she'd attracted a gentleman's notice, even though Kate's gowns had been specifically made for her trip to London. So if Kate was going to appear in public with a famous man, especially with an infamous one, her hostess insisted she had to be properly dressed in the latest fashion so no one could say her cousins weren't taking good care of her. Since even the best dressmaker in London couldn't cobble together a new wardrobe in a matter of days, a seamstress was called in hurriedly to make over some of the Swanson daughters' gowns for Kate until her new ones were ready. Kate protested almost as hard as Lady Swanson's three elder daughters did.

In the end, though, Kate had to admit that what she'd imagined was the highest kick of fashion in London must have changed while she was on the coach driving there. After much arguing, Henrietta, Frances, and Chloe finally agreed to donate a gown apiece to

Kate. They watched jealously as their mother picked over their wardrobes to see what might suit their cousin. Though they constantly jockeyed for position with each other, none of them wanted to win the competition for most suitable gown to give away.

Kate hadn't wanted to enter that contest but had to admit she was the one who won it. She had on the most expensive, elegant, and beautiful thing she'd ever worn. Clad in heavy *café au lait*–colored figured silk that gleamed and shone as she turned to see herself in the mirror, she felt like a different person. A privileged, sophisticated one. The silk felt heavenly against her skin and made her look and feel regal. The gown was extravagant, both demure and seductive. Kate didn't know how it accomplished all that, but it did. High at the neck and waist, it nonetheless showed both to their best advantage. Long cream-colored sleeves emerged from little puffs at the shoulders to hug her arms, but not as much as the silk hugged her form. And what a form! The material seemed to know just where to cling, molding itself to her shape and flattering it. The silk sighed when she moved, but not so much as Kate did as she looked at herself.

"Whatever he's up to, I think he's getting more than he bargained for," her cousin Sibyl commented, eyeing her. "Kate, you look absolutely beautiful."

"Yes," Kate agreed, gazing at herself, enthralled. "How I wish I could call in an artist and have him sketch me now! I'd love my family and friends at home to see how I look."

Sibyl frowned. "They will. The gown's yours, Kate. Chloe gave it up. Besides, she'd never fit into it now."

"I don't mean that. The thing is, I won't fit into it again either, not in the same way. It won't look like this at home. This is a *London* gown. It fits me, *here*."

"And there and there," Sibyl commented wryly. She looked down at her own dress and sighed more deeply than Kate had. Sibyl wore the correct color for a young girl and was all in white. The color seemed to have erased her—she fit into her gown the way a white rabbit fit into a snowdrift in January. She knew it and that made her fade even further away.

Kate had campaigned for a new wardrobe for Sibyl, too, but the three elder Swanson sisters had been adamant about that. Bad enough their infant sister got to accompany Kate and the most deliciously eligible men they'd clapped eyes on in years, the chit would not be able to outdo them in anything else while they had any say about it. Their voices were loud and angry enough to make that say the final word. So Sibyl wore her best gown, which looked exactly like her worst one.

"What a pity it will be so dark in the theater we won't be seen!" Kate said, to make Sibyl feel better.

"It's never that dark," Sibyl said mournfully.

Kate's eyes arrowed to Sir Alasdair St. Erth when she saw him waiting for her in the salon. She told herself any woman's would.

He wore a black jacket, impeccable white linen, and slate gray pantaloons. Dressed to a shade, and such a somber one, he nevertheless commanded the eye. Though his friend Leigh, at his side, was dressed correctly, the bold strokes of St. Erth's dark palette, as well as his stature, reduced the slender Leigh to a mere watercolor.

Few women could have missed the erotic speculation and slow admiration that sprang into Sir Alasdair's dark and lingering gaze as he bowed to Kate. Few could have withstood the heat in that pensive yet passionate regard. But it looked as if Kate could.

She rose from her curtsy with calm, sedate grace. No one guessed she was so stricken by Sir Alasdair's appearance and terrified of showing it that she had to focus all her energy on breathing and standing upright.

Kate's three older cousins glowered. They'd accepted an invitation to a ball just so they could be in their finery when the gentlemen came to call. But no one noticed them any more than they did the elderly Mrs. August, who'd been called on to be chaperone for Kate and Sibyl. That ancient lady was all in gray—gown, hair, and wrinkled face were all the same faded hue. That changed when Alasdair turned his attention to her.

"Though I'd like to stay and talk," Alasdair said smoothly, "I fear the curtain may rise without us, and that would be a pity. Mrs. August?" He offered her his arm.

Faint color appearing in her wrinkled cheeks, she straightened as much as she could and placed her hand on his arm. Mrs. August glided from the room with the baronet like an empress off to give an audience to her subjects.

But she fell asleep minutes after she'd gotten settled in her chair at the theater. Kate didn't know how she could, because it was noisy and as bright as noon in Piccadilly Square. She'd thought Sibyl had been exaggerating about how noticeable they'd be, but she'd never been to the theater in London before. Even before the play began the audience was busily and happily watching itself, and babbling about it until her ears rang.

The lobby had been confusing and crowded, such a mass of faces and pushing people that Kate got only a sense of pandemonium as theatergoers rushed in to their seats. The long staircases to the loge were jammed, the corridors to the boxes packed. She'd been relieved when they finally filed into the box Alasdair had engaged for the night.

Snugged high into a tier of boxes on the right side of the theater, the private box was filled with gilt chairs. Kate looked down before she sat down, and felt as though she was in the crow's nest of a mighty ship, looking out over a surging sea of glittering playgoers. It was a dizzying experience. She was less happy when she saw faces turned up to her and realized she'd be as much a part of the play as an observer of it. Then she sat quickly and huddled down, looking hunted.

"If you crouch any more, you'll look like Mrs. August's twin," Alasdair whispered in her ear as he pulled a chair close and sat beside her.

"Well, I feel a bit—on display," she murmured, darting another glance out at the audience.

"You are," he said simply. "But if you shrink from the limelight, you'll call even more attention to yourself. The audience is here for gossip as much as theater."

"Gossip *is* theater," Lord Leigh commented as he seated Sibyl and himself nearby.

"Exactly," Alasdair agreed. "And often more entertaining than what's onstage. Everyone here wants to know who's with whom tonight so they can speculate about it. It's part of the pleasure of theatergoing, but instead of a lively art, they make it a blood sport." He smiled at Kate and explained. "Like any hunting pack, they bay when they get an interesting scent. If you run, they *will* pursue. If you stand your ground and meet their gaze, they'll look for better sport."

"Ohmygoodness," Sibyl said in a small voice.

That made everyone laugh, except for Mrs. August, who was dozing. The moment lightened. Kate sat up straight and dared to look down at the glittering assembly, so she didn't see the tension in Alasdair's face as he turned to look, too.

Nor did she see how his gaze swept over the crowd as he sought the two faces he'd come to find, or how his lips tightened when he failed to see them. His eyes sharpened when he recognized others in the throng. He gestured to a woman seated below, looking up at them.

"There's an old friend of yours," he told Kate, looking across to another box where a thin woman sat, her opera glasses raised in their direction, obviously focused on them. "Lady Eleanora. And her new fiancé, Mr. Jellicoe. He looks boggled, as he should be."

"A sudden engagement, that," Leigh commented dryly.

"So sudden poor Jellicoe is only now becoming aware of it, I imagine," Alasdair agreed, gazing at the dazed-looking gentleman at Lady Eleanora's side. "It just happened . . . precipitously, at a musicale at the lady's home I hear. It was announced at the end of the evening, a great surprise to everyone, including Jellicoe, one surmises."

"Oh my," Sibyl gasped. "Did she snare him the same way . . . I mean," she said, biting her lip at her slip, "did she . . ." Her voice dwindled as she realized she shouldn't have mentioned Lady Eleanora's foiled plot to snare Sir Alasdair.

"Oh, likely," Alasdair answered, noting how nervous she looked. "And don't worry, Leigh's aware of the matter. If I forgot to offer you my thanks, Miss Sibyl, allow me to remedy that. I understand you got wind of the plan and took pity on me."

"You've nothing to thank me for," she said quickly. "It was all Kate's doing!"

"And all forgotten now, right?" Leigh told Sibyl

with gentle censure. "Because though it was kind, and daring, it isn't at all the thing to talk about."

Alasdair smiled to himself at the way Leigh spoke to her, like a patient father might speak to a child.

"Oh," Sibyl said in a small voice. Then she asked, "I forget. What *is* what's not at all the thing to talk about?"

"Good girl," Leigh said, making her blush rosily.

"Poor man," Kate said, looking across at Lady Eleanora's fiancé.

"Yes," Alasdair said. "And poor Lady Eleanora, believe it or not. She's well served. Jellicoe's hers now, however she got him, but I wish her joy of him, he'll lead her a merry dance. Best take care to avoid the lady in future, my dear, she isn't the forgiving sort."

Kate laughed. "I'll avoid her here in London but I won't have to worry after that. I'm bound for the countryside soon, remember?"

"A great pity," he murmured, making her look away, pretending interest somewhere else.

Alasdair enjoyed flustering the practical Miss Corbet, but reminded himself not to flirt with her, since she wasn't used to it. Conversation diverted her, laughter made her forget to be self-conscious, and that was better. There were too many people gaping at her for even his comfort now, and it was rumored he was so impervious to insult he could make Medusa blink. Besides, he found himself feeling strangely protective of her.

It was her air of fragility, he decided, studying her pretty profile as she looked out at the audience with interest again. Not her great beauty, because by no stretch of the imagination was she that. But he thought she was very attractive with her unusual almond-shaped eyes, straight nose, and the slight overbite that emphasized her precisely etched upper lip, accentuating it, making it more tempting. Her halo of curls intensified an illusion of tender femininity, though she wasn't at all frail. Her frame was slender, but her body was lush. Still, her features lent her a certain charming delicacy. Odd that he was so attracted, she wasn't his type of female at all, he thought—and was brought up short.

His type? That almost made him laugh aloud. His type was the sort of female who was important or expedient to make love to, or simply necessary to have sex with when the need was on him. His type was any woman who could amuse him, ease his boredom or his loneliness. Because there were times when it wasn't diversion or lust he was seeking, times when he simply needed to feel close to the living skin of another human being, perhaps to reassure himself that he was still of their number.

Cleanliness and comeliness in any of his partners were extras his fastidious soul applauded but his vengeful spirit never found strictly necessary. Charm and wit had never been part of those requirements either, he realized, so no wonder he was reacting so strongly to this candid and friendly young woman.

He found himself wanting her for his purposes as well as others he hadn't anticipated, yet wanting to save her from him at the same time. *Fine*, he thought with bitter humor. *Leigh's got himself a charming young daughter to entertain tonight, and I seem to have gotten one that I desire.* But he didn't feel fatherly toward Kate in any other way, and desire was the driving force of his life, so it was a situation he could deal with.

He looked over the crowd with satisfaction. The Scalbys weren't in attendance, but they'd hear of his being there that night, as well as who had accompa-

nied him. They kept up on his activities as carefully as
he did on theirs, he never doubted it. They didn't have
friends but they had victims and toadies, those who
feared them and those who tried to placate them. And
many more they paid for information.

He'd be noticed. He had other enemies, too, and
even more people simply found him good fodder for
gossip. He'd give them that tonight. His guests were
young ladies who hadn't been seen on the town. Anyone interested would soon discover that he and Leigh
were out with a Swanson chit, as well as an unknown,
with a respectable old female playing chaperone. But
they'd be intrigued by the fact that he was dancing attention on the unknown. She wouldn't be that for long.

He could almost hear the gabble from where he sat.
St. Erth here with a new female? Who is she? They'd find
out. *Why, she's a nobody from nowhere, but related to
everyone,* they'd say. Cousin to the Swansons. Penni-
less, or so the gossip would run, since the only money
gossips found interesting to talk about was either a
fortune or none at all.

A country mouse. Charming, they'd say, *but, my dear,
no station and no money. What could Sir Alasdair be up to
this time?*

The Scalbys would hear it. And they'd know her
name and what he was up to, or imagine they did,
which was better. Imagination was the best weapon in
a war of nerves. They'd certainly think about this news
and wonder if it meant anything to them, if it was the
beginning of the end. Their end.

That was all he wanted, for the time being.

"There's the earl of Drummond and his new bride,"
he said, saluting an old acquaintance with a languid
wave. "There with him, his cousin, the Viscount Sinclair and his beautiful wife." He smiled at the way his

friends enthusiastically returned his greeting from across the theater.

"They could lead Society if they raised one finger, but they don't care to," he told Kate. "Which is why they're still pleased to see me. That pleases me, so I'll return the favor by not getting too close to them until my reputation is closer to being mended. I met the viscount through my work abroad in the past. The spectacularly handsome couple sitting next to him is Damon Ryder and his wife. They have more money than the Bank of England and less concern about society than your grocer's cat. Again, they're friends who don't care about gossip, and I stay away because I care for them.

"Now, to their right—the fellow looking like a stuffed goose with an egg halfway out? He's more like the rest of Society. His name is legion, but he answers to Lord Bight. He's narrow-minded and guilty of most things he condemns me for, but he commits his sins with stealth. He's exactly the kind of person I'm going to have to win over. *We're* going to have to win over," he corrected himself.

He entertained Kate by pointing out others, showing her a host of people in the galaxy of stars of the London firmament that glittered around them. But never for a moment did he show her how he was also making sure they themselves were seen, so word of their appearance together tonight would be certain to get out.

Alasdair was sorry when the houselights dimmed and the other show the audience was there to see began.

And curiously, because she'd been so fearful of Society and so eager to see a real London play, Kate was disappointed then, too.

She got to see that play, and heard its lines being

shrieked, because to her amazement, the audience kept right on chattering. They threatened to drown out the actors, which made every comment from the stage become a scream. By the time intermission came, her ears ached.

But that was only the beginning. The moment the curtains fell the audience was released, and set into even more frantic motion.

"Care to promenade?" Alasdair asked, rising from his seat.

"We'd better," Lord Leigh said, as he also stood. "Or else this box will become so stuffed with the curious that we won't be able to breathe. At least we can get some air while on our feet."

Kate looked to Mrs. August, who had woken and was as confused as a little bat squinting at a sudden light. Kate was sure the old woman had forgotten where she was.

But she soon remembered. "Run along," Mrs. August said, seeing them all standing. "It's quite all right for you girls and the gentlemen to be seen promenading at intermission. I fear the crowds would be too much for me."

"A wise decision," Alasdair said. "Would you like us to bring you something to drink?"

"That would be very nice," she said gratefully.

"I don't know that it isn't too much for me!" Kate told him. But she put her hand on his arm, raised her head, and followed his lead.

The corridor was so filled with people, it was hard to edge out into the hall. But Alasdair was large and determined and clove through the crowd like a ship under full sail. Kate soon found herself out of the long corridor and in the great hall. And separated from Sibyl.

She looked back in momentary panic.

"We'll find them later," Alasdair said. "Stop now, and we won't be able to move again."

She went on blindly, until Alasdair paused in a niche by a staircase. Out of the surging flow, Kate breathed more easily. But her breath stopped when she looked at Alasdair. She only meant to talk to him. The words dried on her tongue. He was looking down at her, she was suddenly the focus of all that considerable power of personality.

He wasn't smiling. His dark eyes were rapt, a look of such melting ardor in them that she could only catch her breath, and blink the way old Mrs. August had when she'd found herself waking up in a strange place. He was so big, so dominant, so very attractive and intent—on her. Flattered, a little frightened, and fascinated, she could only gaze back at him.

That would never do. She fought for control and found it in conversation. "Lord!" she said, fanning herself. "Everyone's watching and listening so closely I feel as though I ought to have lines to say."

"They couldn't hear them and wouldn't listen any more than they did to the actors," he said with a smile that made her toes curl in her slippers.

She swallowed hard and looked just over his shoulder. That helped.

"You look bemused," he said. "Or is it aghast?"

"Both," she admitted, too disconcerted to find an easy lie. But she found a way to change the subject. "I was just wondering," she said, "am I making you respectable? Or are you making me a scandal?"

"A little of both, I suspect. But it will tilt toward respectable when they realize my heart is pure."

A genuine laugh escaped her.

"Does what they think of us worry you?" he asked.

"It might," she answered honestly. "If I were plan-

ning on staying here. No," she said, after a second's
consideration. "Not even then. My real friends and my
family would know the truth, and that's all I'd care
about."

His expression grew shuttered. "How fortunate you
are," he said blandly.

This sudden coolness after all the heat he'd projected left her feeling confused and chilly. When he
glanced away to acknowledge someone who called his
name in passing, Kate drew a shuddery breath. She'd
have to control her emotions or give up seeing him.
She must have looked like a fish in the millpond gaping at the full moon. Speaking of theater! She'd reacted
to him like a stock character in a bad farce, a country
gawk being overwhelmed by a polished seducer. *The
poor man,* she thought in chagrin. He couldn't help the
fact that his purring voice made the hair on her neck
tingle, or that when he looked at a woman she found
herself wishing his hands would follow that look. He
was only playing the game they'd agreed on. She was
the one who had to rein herself in. He needed her to repair his reputation, not add more fuel to the fuss about
his wicked one.

When he turned to her again he seemed as pleased
as she'd ever seen him.

She whispered nervously, "So, do you think this is
working? Or perhaps not?"

"I'm vastly content," he said, his expression showing it so clearly she had to look away again.

He was delighted with her. Everyone had seen him
gazing at this sweet young woman with fixed lust—
and whatever else the gossips would certainly invent.
They'd also have to see how she looked back at him,
with enchanting distraction, and a little fear. Perfect.
She could be pretending for his sake or she might be

genuinely overwhelmed. It didn't matter. It would be all over town in hours and on the Scalbys' plate with their morning paper, if not before.

Things were going just as he planned. He only had to be vigilant and make sure they didn't go even further than that.

8

The word about Sir Alasdair and his latest flirt went out fast because it was delicious gossip. In fact, the rumor about the infamous St. Erth and his unexpected infatuation with a nobody from the countryside flew so quickly it was old news to many in London by the time the moon set on it.

There were others who were intensely interested in anything to do with Sir Alasdair but who spent their nights in different ways, and so only heard the rumor with the rising sun. But they listened very closely when they did.

It was hard to tell it was morning in the darkened breakfast room. The shutters were closed and the drapes drawn, locking out the bright new day. Breakfast was being served in such dimmed light it might have been dusk except that, as a bow to reality, no candles were burning. The messenger who brought the news to the lady and gentleman couldn't see their faces as he told them about Sir Alasdair's latest escapade. He counted himself fortunate.

"I see," the lady seated in shadow finally said when he'd finished. He stood, turning his cap in his hands. "My man will give you your money, as usual," she said. "You may leave."

He bowed, backed away, then turned and scurried out the door into the hall.

"So, what do you think of that?" she asked the man at the head of the table when they were alone again.

He shrugged.

"So," she said, picking up a fragile teacup in her long thin fingers, "our relatives the Corbets have a lovely daughter. Who would have thought it? Had we thought of it, we'd have acted first, I'm sure. She is, after all, our cousin. *Ours*. Exactly. Why else would he dance attention on her, pretty though she may be? 'Pretty' is nothing to him. 'Exquisite' is nothing to him, for that matter. He has always been hard to predict."

She took a sip and grimaced, though it had nothing to do with the taste of her morning chocolate. "As now. He could have his pick from the highest, we know he has his choice of the lowest, and yet here he courts our obscure cousin. What do you suppose he wants us to do about it? More to the point, what does he expect us to do about it?"

The man merely picked up a piece of toast, closed his teeth over it with a snap, and began chewing.

"Quite right," she said, nodding. "Nothing. What can we do, after all, except sit here and wait for him to come to us? We will. And he will, you know. He'll have to. I doubt he wants to marry our cousin. I doubt he wants to enjoy her in peace and obscurity either. He may, however, ruin her in an attempt to lure us to him.

I wish him joy of it. I envy her the joy of it, though."
She laughed. It wasn't a pleasant sound.

But it started her companion laughing. That made
her wince.

Outside, in the broad light of the new morning, the
man who had visited the lady and her husband scuttled through the streets, head down. He held the coins
their butler had given him fast in his fist. When he'd
gotten far from the elegant district he slowed at last,
dropped the coins into a pocket, and began to saunter
as though he owned the mean streets he now traveled
through. He didn't, but he was on his way to a man he
thought did.

His shoulders went down, and his back grew less
straight when he entered the tavern. He was a man
who knew how to trim his sails when the wind
changed, since his life often depended on it, and his
livelihood always did. His always being what people
expected to see was the secret of his trade. He snatched
off his cap and held it in his hands as he approached
the man who'd sent him on his errand.

He gave his news.

"Well, well," the man he reported to murmured.
"So I thought, din't I? Good, good. Her Ladyship don't
like the news. His nibs and her young cousin making
eyes at each other? Ha. But now, the thing is, does St.
Erth do it for the joy of the cousin, or the vexation of
Her Ladyship?"

The other man shrugged. He was good at his work,
he had eyes and ears and knew how to scurry and
lurk. But the question he was asked was as yet unan-
swerable, and they both knew it.

"Aye, there's the crux, of it, ain't it?" his employer
asked. "If it's for his pleasure, I want to know about it,

'course I do. But what sort of pleasure is it? If it's for the pleasure of tormenting the Scalbys, that's old news." He raised one stubby finger in the air. "Ah, but if it's for a different sort of enjoyment, that's another question."

He paused in thought. "If he just wanted body work, there's enough females panting for him, so that ain't it. Why bother courting a decent woman for that? Ah, but if the gent think he's grown himself a heart at last . . . and if he thinks it's set on this little country mort? *That* would be something to get my teeth into. Then we'd have something to work with. Well, we'll have to keep our eyes peeled, won't we?"

The other man nodded. It was as he expected. And it was good, because it was work for him. And how else was a man to live? No matter if his doing that work in order to live sometimes meant another man might not live for very much longer.

The word went out so fast that when the hour to pay a polite call came, the Swansons' town house was as crowded as the theater had been the night before. The Swansons were dumbfounded. They'd had more daughters than most families could boast, and since those girls hadn't been anything to boast about they'd had to pay a small fortune in their time to lure eligible gentlemen to their door. Now they hadn't done a thing and found they'd never netted so many.

The staff rushed around, stowing capes and cloaks, greatcoats and walking sticks. The butler sent footmen to the cellar to bring up more wine, the housekeeper badgered the cook, who dispatched servants to the shops for more cakes to serve. The Swansons entertained lavishly, out of habit. They'd always had to in the past. Today their callers only seemed to want or need a look at their country cousin.

But Lady Swanson hadn't already married off three of her difficult daughters because she was slow on the uptake. The company would be served lavishly anyway, and maybe her own purposes would also be served.

"Now, look," she told her three older unmarried daughters after she'd assembled them in her bedchamber so she could lecture them. "Our drawing room is filled with the most eligible men in town. I know they aren't here to see you, but they aren't here to see Sibyl either, so stop complaining about her. She's down there with her cousin, which is how it should be. They're here to see Kate.

"Stop blaming Kate, too. It's not a situation that has anything to do with her looks *or* wiles. It's a matter of common curiosity. Or, uncommon, I should say. The men are here to look Kate over because of Sir Alasdair. He showed a preference for her, and they're all dying to see why. So what if that's the reason? They're here. That's the point. There's only one of her and three of you. Get dressed, get downstairs, and be charming."

"Much good that will do," Chloe muttered. "They've seen us before."

Her mother nodded. "So they have, so it will be easy for you to strike up a conversation then, won't it? It wouldn't be the first time a fellow who came to see one young woman walked off with another. But it would be a miracle if you look like that—and I tell you if you continue to, I'll be very angry.

"Worse," she said, as they kept glowering at her. "You'll be very lonely, too, that I promise you. Because I won't spend another groat on you if you don't cooperate in this. So. If you want to stay here with your sisters forever, fine. Remain in your rooms, continue wearing those bilious expressions and mumbling together about how cruel fate is. And prepare to spend a lifetime together, too."

"You always say that," Henrietta complained. "About how we should befriend other girls, because who knows if we won't net a fellow who can't get them, or meet his best friend, or his cousin or some acquaintance?"

"Well, *I* know," Frances spat. "We meet them, and the gentlemen marry them or their friends, and we're always left to meet other girls, and the same thing happens, and that's that."

"Try befriending them for themselves, for once," their mother blurted, because she was at the end of her patience, and that patience had held for too many years. "Try a smile, or a kind remark about someone, anyone, sometime. Try being *nice* once in a while! Or don't," she said, turning to leave the room. "I wash my hands of you, and if I do, how can you expect any gentleman to take you off my hands!"

Her daughters stared at her, then at each other. It was more than Lady Swanson had meant to say, and less than she wanted to. She stormed from the room. It had been cruel, it was harsh, it was necessary, she decided as she went downstairs to oversee the formidable amount of company at her house that morning.

Her youngest, Sibyl, wore another white gown, and seemed ever paler in her nervousness at all the attention she was getting from those gentlemen callers who hadn't managed to wedge themselves into the tightly packed circle grouped around Kate.

Kate was dressed in a pretty concoction, a breath of a gown of striped shell pink. It made her glow as much as all the flattery she was receiving did. The gown hadn't looked remotely charming when Henrietta had worn it only the month before. Henrietta grimaced when she saw it, though, when she and her sisters arrived in the drawing room within a half hour of their mother's lecture.

Lady Swanson was gratified to see them there, and pleased to see them dressed well, too. With a sigh of relief and a short prayer for success, she turned her attention to the company again, smiling and chatting with as many men as she could. She tried to charm the cream of the *ton* who graced her salon so they might come back again, even when they didn't need to find out more about her husband's cousin.

But she frowned when she noticed the men her eldest daughters were spending their time with.

Henrietta and Chloe had cornered Lord Markham, or had he cornered them? Their spite would have drawn him like a magnet. The room was full of acceptable gentlemen, he was barely that. Dark of eye and mood, attractive in a sullen way, the fellow had a title and some money, but he spent that money on himself and let his estate go to wrack and ruin. He also had a vile disposition and few friends, and those he had were no better than he was. A widower whose wife had died young, it was a measure of his popularity that some said she did it to escape him and others whispered that he did it to be rid of her, but that she was better off either way.

Even so, Markham was seen everywhere because of his name, and the fact that there were still some mamas who thought a good woman might be the making of him. Lady Swanson wanted her daughters married, but even she wasn't that desperate. She frowned to see her daughters so interested in him, not because she thought they were in any danger, but because she knew them well.

The lady's brow furrowed further when she saw

her daughter Frances in close conversation with Eugene Polk. They were more than likely tearing apart someone's reputation, a thing they both did constantly. He was a weedy, spotty youth whose braying laugh made him an unpopular guest, though he was tolerated because he always knew the latest gossip. Well, *that* might be a match, Lady Swanson thought, and shuddered.

It was much more pleasant to entertain her other guests, because every man there was trying equally hard to please her. It was a novelty and a pleasure, and she made the most of it, because single daughters or not, a person had a right to a little amusement now and then. But she worried about why her elder daughters looked so pleased as they conferred in whispers with Lord Markham and Mr. Polk. And so when a sudden hush fell over her company her heart sank, and she wondered if it was anything they had said.

She looked up and smiled in relief. The room had grown still because the star of the morning had just given his cloak and hat to a footman and was entering the room.

"Sir Alasdair," she said, as she hurried across the room to greet him, "and Lord Leigh! Good morning, gentlemen, do come in."

The company in the room all looked to the newcomers, ignoring Lord Leigh, who was fashionable but never newsworthy. Instead, they greedily noted St. Erth's clothes and bearing. They saw his slow smile growing at the attention he was getting—and his dark eyes narrowing as he spied the woman he'd obviously come to see. He gazed at her intently, taking in her appearance from the curls on the top of her head to her toes, as he advanced toward her.

Kate was being entertained by a cluster of town

clowns, the sort of fashionable men who were always willing to even the numbers at a dinner party or take a wallflower off a mama's hands in exchange for the latest jokes or gossip. One moment she was paying attention to them and the next . . .

It was as if she felt the force of Sir Alasdair's gaze, or so the impressionable among the company later said—though some argued it was the draft from the opened door that had warned her of his arrival. But she looked up and saw St. Erth, and smiled with sudden joy of recognition, looking as though she'd been treading frigid water in the company of sharks and he'd just thrown her a lifeline.

He advanced, took her hand, and smiled at her like one of those sharks.

"Good morning, Miss Corbet," he said, everyone hanging on his every word. "Have you recovered from the crush at the theater—not to mention the performances there—yet?"

She laughed. "I have much to talk about when I get home."

"But now you've dimmed my day," he protested. "Let's not think about such unhappy events, especially since the future is so uncertain. Instead, let's celebrate the present. It's such a lovely day Leigh and I thought that if you were free after this morning's calls, we could take you and your cousin for a whirl around the Park."

Her face lit—before she quenched the sudden excitement that had leapt to her eyes. She cast her gaze down. When she looked up again she was obviously under control. "A whirl?" she asked with a quirked grin. "On horseback? I don't think I'm a good enough rider for that! In a carriage? Dangerous, I'd think. On foot? That would be delightful, if dancing through the

Park is permitted. And if my cousin agrees. And of course, if Lady Swanson gives her permission."

Alasdair smiled. The other gentlemen exchanged glances. No wonder Sir Alasdair was interested in the chit, she had a sense of humor. And courage, to banter with the devil like this. They turned to hear St. Erth's answer, glad, to a man, that they'd come there this morning. This was better than a night at the theater.

Alasdair inclined his head. "I'd be happy to waltz through the Park with you, Miss Corbet, but I imagine Lady Swanson wouldn't be as pleased. Actually, it was a carriage ride to the Park I had in mind, with a walk once we got there."

"I'd like that," she said simply.

The other men looked cheated. They had been. It was so early into the morning call they hadn't had the time to get to know the girl well enough to ask her out. That devil, Sir Alasdair, did know her, and knew their habits, too, and so in one bold move had stolen a march on them. But they couldn't compete with him for her, and not just because they never had been able to.

She was respectable, and so their interest in her had to be as well. And it couldn't be. They could call on her once or twice, of course, and ask for a dance the same number of times, but asking her out was drifting into dangerous territory. In their world marriage was a business undertaking for men who couldn't go into business, a venture embarked on for profit and betterment. Most men only got the one opportunity at it and so had to take their best chance at improving or consolidating their holdings and positions. This woman had little to offer on the marriage market. She had scant money and no rank, everyone knew that. St. Erth didn't care. But perhaps he wasn't seeking her hand? The morning became even more fascinating.

"Now, shoo! Go away, Sir Alasdair," one of the callers said with a wave of his hand to show Alasdair he was only joking. "You've got her for the afternoon, so let us poor creatures have at least this hour."

Alasdair bowed and left to find Lady Swanson to get her permission. He was sure he'd have it. He kept his hands at his sides to keep from rubbing them together. The morning's encounter would be through the polite world by the time luncheon was served. That, along with his appearance at Kate's side last night, would double the talk. He'd see what he could do in the afternoon to triple it. He wouldn't have to do much. Which meant he could just enjoy himself.

He looked back at Kate as she stood listening to various fools and fops trying to amuse her. She sensed he was watching, and cast a roguish conspiratorial grin toward him before she turned it into a laugh at something someone said. He corrected himself. No, that meant he could *really* enjoy himself. The thought bothered him for a moment before he dismissed it. Nothing wrong with finding pleasure in one's work, after all.

9

"**S**o cruel! But so true!" Kate laughed.

Alasdair looked down at her where she walked by his side. Her head came up to his shoulder, and when she turned her gleeful grin up at him he almost missed his step. She made him forget what he'd said to make her laugh, but he was very glad that he had.

"I'm having such fun!" she went on. "You've turned a walk in the Park into a party. It's not so much what you say as how you say it—no, it is what you say. Outrageous! But so funny. Whatever your other plans are, whatever happens with them, know this, Sir Alasdair. You're giving me the time of my life. I'm so glad I fell in with your mad scheme."

He smiled, then had to hide a frown. His reaction to her genuine pleasure in his company surprised him, and he wasn't comfortable with surprises. But she was right. It was such a simple diversion and yet so diverting. They were only walking through the Park. It was more pleasant than most things he did, more amusing than most conversations he had, and the most exciting time he'd spent with a woman in a long time, and that included interludes in dim, perfumed boudoirs.

Kate and he just talked. Or rather, today she listened to his running commentary on things they saw, laughing in all the right places, and for a miracle, actually made him laugh, too. *Really* laugh, not just assume a knowing smile as he so often had to do. His pleasure in the day, and hers, was seen by everyone they passed. They looked as though they were having a wonderful time, and they were. She was a perfect accomplice.

Alasdair's admittedly lax conscience was clear. Kate Corbet had no pretenses, but that didn't mean she was naive. A well-informed mind saw the humor in life, just as a strong streak of practicality made her see nonsense for it was. She had a lively sense of fairness that sometimes made her chide him for being unkind, even as she struggled to restrain her laughter at whatever unkind thing he'd said. He congratulated himself on a well-conceived plan. Whatever the outcome of this adventure, she might profit even if he didn't. Now that Society had noticed her, some real suitors might take an interest in her, too.

He ought to be content. It was a good day's work. The fashionable in the Park noted his interest in Kate. That was the only difficult part of it for him. Not his interest—but letting others see it. That wasn't his style.

It was a masterstroke that Sibyl Swanson was there, too, partnered by Leigh. The pair strolled along behind Alasdair and Kate, a maidservant pacing decorously after them. Few had even known of Sibyl's existence, but now anyone could see she was the best-looking of that ill-favored lot, so she and Leigh attracted their share of stares and comment. There was a lot for idle and active observers of society to notice, and more to feed the gossips. It was going very well.

But they only had the afternoon to show the world their courtship. He couldn't take Kate out by day and night, at least not in the same day. They were playing an intricate game, and he had to leave her some reputation when they were done with it. That didn't mean he couldn't make the most of it. Laughter was all very well. They needed more to really make tongues wag.

He bent his head. "We have to go back soon," he told her softly. "Our revels must soon be ended, or your uncle will be waiting for us with a preacher."

"Go back? Already?" she asked in surprise.

"Too soon, I agree," he said, lowering his voice, "But tomorrow we have the night. We'll meet in public then, too, but the advantage is that not even the keenest eyes can see everything we do in the night." The smile he bent on her was gentle, intimate, knowing.

Her eyes widened, her color rose. She lowered her eyelashes, and he knew she was searching for a comment to lighten the moment.

". . . Which will help our charade enormously," he went on smoothly, his smile becoming wider when he saw her reaction. It was relief, and chagrin, and possibly, regret.

"Good," he whispered to her. "Laughter is good, but blushes are better. The world will certainly note that."

Her chin rose, she looked him in the eye. "Aren't you afraid you'll look like a jilt when we're done?" she asked with asperity.

He laughed. "But no, my dear Kate. You'll be the jilt. It will enhance your reputation enormously."

She bit her lip.

"And I'll be pitied, which will help me, too," he

added. He patted her hand where it lay on his arm.
"Don't worry, no one can lose by this, and I'll be
helped so much. Have I said thank you lately?"

"You're welcome," she murmured, still looking
troubled.

So he made her laugh again, and then again.

But then it was night, and Alasdair found himself pacing his study, curiously edgy, anxious to do something,
with no idea of what that was. He trusted his instincts,
they'd always served him well. The damnable thing
was that though he racked his brain, he couldn't find a
reason for his unease. Everything had gone as it ought,
he should be relaxing now.

He threw himself into a chair and stared gloomily at
the unlit hearth. What was troubling him? His plan
was afoot, victory was near. He was too keyed up, that
was it, he needed diversion. He wished he could see
Kate, that would be amusing . . . but impossible. It was
late, no gentleman went running to a woman's house
at this hour without a previous appointment, if she
was respectable. But he wanted to be with her, see her,
discuss things with her, see those amber eyes crinkle
as that pretty pink mouth curled up in laughter, smell
her perfume, touch her. . . .

He threw his head back on the chair and let out a
gusty sigh. What a dunce he was! Such a simple thing.
It wasn't Kate he wanted now, he just needed a
woman. Since his attention was being focused on Kate,
he thought she was what he wanted. *There* was a piece
of nonsense he could never share with her!

No denying she attracted him, and vigorously. But
half that attraction was because he wasn't used to
women like her. The other half was just as clear to him
now that he thought about it. He didn't belittle her

charms, he couldn't. But they were obsessing him too much. For good reason. It had been a while since he'd enjoyed the favors of any woman. He'd come to London with a plan that had occupied his mind so much he'd forgotten about his body. Now his body was reminding him. He sprang from the chair.

Simple problems had simple remedies. And such simple remedies were easy to find in London. What a good idea! Relief from tension, if only for a few moments, would be welcome. He felt a surge of expectation as he strode to the door.

He paused halfway there.

Matters of the body had always been simple ones for him. Light affairs with adventurous women, temporary trysts with playful widows, money exchanged for services rendered by experienced courtesans, those sorts of liaison were easy outlets.

He suddenly realized none of them was possible now.

A call on any of his former playmates would be noticed—if indeed, those women were still free. He'd been abroad a long time. They might be married, or dead, by now. He never bothered keeping in touch with his casual paramours, and he had no other kind. He wasn't about to roam London by night, knocking on doors, asking their whereabouts. And this certainly wasn't the time to set up a new flirt.

He could go to a brothel. It wasn't the best thing, but a jolly woman who could make it seem that she liked her work was acceptable on nights like this. But he stayed where he was, irresolute.

Sometimes anonymous sex was necessary. *If* it was safe. He wouldn't go to an inferior brothel for the same reason he'd never take a woman who walked the streets. He'd no desire to end up raddled with the clap, the disease of incautious pleasure. There was no cure for it, and it disregarded rank and fortune, leveling the rich and famous as well as the poor and unknown. The afflicted poor could be seen begging in the streets, gone crippled and disfigured with it, but Alasdair had seen too many of the mighty fallen with it, too. Ladies of a sportive nature who suddenly gave up dalliance, going veiled to hide the ruin of their skin. Gentlemen of interesting reputations who began to forget important things, like their names.

The wages of sin were too often slow wasting of the body and secret erosion of the brain. Alasdair wanted to have his body and his wits in his old age—if he was lucky enough to reach it.

Anyway, if he went to any of the better brothels, he'd be seen. That would put paid to any hope he had of convincing the world he was serious about Kate! A gentleman could dally and it might be winked at—but not if he was supposed to be in the throes of ardent longing for a particular woman. He felt desire ebb away.

So what to do? Impossible to sit still with a book. Ridiculous to drink until he fell asleep. He had to *do* something.

He reviewed his options. A gentleman's club wasn't the answer. Nothing they had to offer would do tonight. He wouldn't wager—when he was restive like this he'd leap at any dare. Even political discussions might come to mayhem while this wild mood was on him. So he'd also have to avoid those friends he had. It would be too easy to alienate them with some misplaced word.

No play of any sort was available to him.

Alasdair felt caged and thwarted. It was too dark to ride, too late to stroll the streets looking for diversion, too late to reorder his life. But he could do business. His spirits rose. Yes, the business of his life, his revenge. Yes. He'd see how his plan was doing, first-hand. Or, actually, secondhand, which was better, because that was the way his enemy saw it. He needed to know what the Scalbys were thinking.

Alasdair knew he'd made the right decision if only because of the way his heartbeat picked up when he bounded from his house and walked out into the night.

The Old Cat was an historic tavern on an old street near the river. Somehow it had escaped the Great Fire and weathered the centuries since, though the building was tilted with age and the front was still blackened by smoke and soot from the fire, as well as the accumulation of years. Travelers visited so they could mention the name in their journals, men of fashion dropped by, workers in the district met there, too. It was a place where the high and the low could meet without notice or comment. That was why the Honorable Frederick Loach was usually found there, because he did business with all kinds of men.

Alasdair's restlessness had been somewhat cooled during the long walk to The Old Cat, so he was his usual self when he ducked his head under the low door and strolled into the taproom.

The place smelled of smoke and ale, but it wasn't unpleasant. The light was dim and yellow, but not so much so that Alasdair couldn't see the Honorable Frederick seated at his usual table.

Alasdair strolled to the table.

"Give you good evening, Sir Alasdair," Frederick said easily, indicating a chair. "I hadn't thought to see you so soon again."

"I was out on the town and thought I'd drop by," Alasdair answered lazily as he seated himself. "How are things going with you, Fred?"

The Honorable Frederick Loach was a slender gentleman with fair hair as thin as his smile, and a smile faint as his voice. Fred came from a good family and ran with bad sorts, his vices were many and his money soon parted from him. Fortunately for him, his morals were just as meager. He had entree to all the best places and insinuated himself everywhere else. He heard everything and sold what he heard to those who had a use for gossip: caricaturists and writers of scandal sheets who spun the dross of other people's folly into their own gold, reselling it to an eager public. Frederick earned even more by selling specific gossip to anyone, for a price.

Alasdair reached into his pocket, extracted some coins and put them on the table. "I recall now that I lost that wager the other week. Never let it be said that I forget my debts."

Frederick's hand moved fast as a lizard's tongue. He had the money in his pocket before the echo of Alasdair's words faded. "Thank you. You are indeed a man of your word."

Alasdair sat back, his eyes half-lidded to conceal the gleam in them. Pretense had been kept, proprieties observed. Now he'd get what he paid for.

"I hear you've been courting Miss Corbet, cousin to the Swansons," Frederick said in his die-away voice, so softly that Alasdair had to listen closely to hear him above the general babble. "Everyone's buzzing about it. *How* charming for you. I understand her cousins are in *alt* about it because it's brought so many suitors to their doorstep. How pleasant for their youngest, the heretofore unknown Sibyl. The latest rhyme goes:

> "'As I was going to take the waters,
> I met a man with seven daughters.

> *Six could turn Medusa to stone,*
> *but I have eyes for one alone.*
> *Who is Sibyl, what is she?*
> *Not like her sisters—there's a mercy.*
> *No wonder they kept her under wraps,*
> *away from the eyes of us eager chaps.'*

"Not inspired verse, but *ever* so amusing, don't you think?"

"I'd hoped you'd heard something more to my taste," Alasdair said with barely concealed impatience.

Frederick's gaze sharpened. Alasdair wasn't a man he wanted to trifle with. "Oh, *that*," he said quickly. "*They've* heard, of course. Almost at once. I wasn't the first to tell them either. They pay well to hear about you. But you'd want to know how they took it and what they thought. How can I tell you that? I had no intimation from their expressions, of course. Don't be vexed with me, I am a veritable *fount* of information, sir. But I cannot crawl beneath their bed to know their true reaction, can I?"

Alasdair frowned. "They go nowhere? They see no one?"

"They do not *stir* from their house. But they have visitors. Not friends of mine although all of them are known to me and all serve the Scalbys in rather the same capacity that I do. So there they sit, and yet they're in the thick of things, as it were. One bit of news, though."

Frederick paused to take a sip at his tankard. Alasdair restrained himself from throttling the news out of him.

Frederick saw Alasdair's face and set the tankard down. "Some of their informants also work for those of lesser rank," he reported. "A ranker rank, if you'll forgive the jest. For example, that wispy fellow by the tap, the one between those two carters? You have to squint to see him, then focus hard to keep him in sight. He has a gift for disappearance," Frederick added enviously. "He's employed by an old friend of yours."

"Yes, so I guessed. He's good, but not quite invisible. I've seen him before."

Frederick fell still and looked at his drink.

"I seldom pay merely for poetry," Alasdair added evenly, though there was a note of warning under his words.

"Oh, well. The fellow is in the employ of a lout known as Lolly Lou. He's a larcenous boor. A low creature, though he's done well enough for himself. He has his podgy digits in many a disreputable enterprise in the lower parts of London. If a thing can make money for him, he'll do it. He has no discretion at all," Frederick added fastidiously.

"I know him," Alasdair said, nodding. "He'd sell out his country as soon as any one of his wives."

"So you heard about that, too?" Frederick asked in disappointment. "Well, I suppose you would, having met up with him in your adventures during the late wars, I suppose . . ."

He turned pale. Alasdair's face had grown cold. His eyes seemed to glow with an infernal glare as he leaned forward so that his soft cold voice could be heard. "You will promptly forget that line of reasoning and anything to do with my work during the late wars. *If* you wish to remain in your fastidious line of work—in one fastidious piece, that is. All things are for sale with you, I accept that. *We* accept that, I should say, because there are others concerned, and believe me, they would be if they heard how free you are with our histories. Inane gossip about fashion or love affairs is one thing. A man's work for his country is another. The wars are past, our parts in it often are not, so it's not a matter for discussion even now. Is that clear, and understood?"

"Certainly," Frederick breathed, his hand to his throat. "By all means."

Alasdair rose and towered over the table. "Good," he said. "If you hear anything else, you know where to find me. As I know where to find you—anywhere in London. Good evening, Fred."

He stalked from the tavern, only letting his shoulders relax when he'd left it. He walked to the corner, turned it, stepped into a shadow, and waited. It wasn't long before the slight man who had been at the tap scurried out, looked around, and hurried down the street. Alasdair eased out of the shadows and followed, even though he was certain that he was being followed, too.

He lost the furtive man in the mists, but Alasdair thought he knew the way anyway. He walked to a dark street by the river, then went down a few old stone steps and opened a weathered door. There was no sign over the door. Those who came there didn't need one. He knew he'd come to the right place by how utterly still it got when he did. The gin shop was small and dirty, packed with bodies that hadn't seen much water since it had last rained. There was so much smoke the candle flames had to leap to be seen, but they might have been hopped higher because everyone's breath was so soaked in spirits. The smell was indescribable. Which was fortunate, Alasdair thought. Because those who could describe it by comparing it to anything else they'd experienced were truly damned. The patrons of this place looked it.

The men and women in the gin house were danger-

ous. Their faces showed they'd nothing to lose but
their lives, and that those lives were the least of what
they had. These were people who scraped together liv-
ings from the leftovers of others' lives, or stole them
outright, or sold themselves so they could buy what
the others stole.

There were mudlarks, black with muck, still reeking
from hours of plodding along the banks of the Thames
searching for lost treasure, and that was anything that
could yet be sold. They, and the many prostitutes in
the place, at least worked for their living. The others
were thieves of every rank. The better dressed were
those who met the public, running confidence games,
passing counterfeit money, or keeping clerks busy
while their mates lifted merchandise. The other
thieves who frequented the place didn't worry about
appearance because they hoped no one would ever see
them. After all, it was hard to see someone who crept
up behind you and stole your purse, or waited until
you were asleep and crept down your chimney and
looted your house, or did that after they smashed your
windows, or your head.

Everyone stopped talking to stare at the big gentleman who loomed in the doorway. He was obviously
rich, and just as obviously looking for someone. He
was either out of his mind, in which case he'd be out of
his money as well as his boots before another hour
passed—or he was out for them. Most of the denizens
of the gin shop believed the latter, and tried to look innocent, or started to edge toward the back exit. Lolly
Lou looked up, saw the dark, dangerous gentleman on
the doorstep, and smiled.

Alasdair saw him immediately. Short and grimy, as
round as he was tall, with a bald head and barrel chest,
Lolly was holding court at a side table. He was dressed

in mimicry of a gentleman's garb, but his clothing was as soiled as it was out of fashion. The elusive man Alasdair had followed was at his side, but he winked out of sight as soon as Alasdair's sharp gaze lit on him.

Others at the table moved away, too, but the hulking man standing behind Lolly stayed where he was. He looked like he could crush anything or anyone without thinking, because for him crushing was easier than thinking.

"Look who's here!" Lolly said. "Come in, Sir Alasdair. If you've come in peace. If not . . ." He waggled one finger in the air, "You'll leave in pieces, I think. The advantage is mine this time, ain't it?"

"No," Alasdair said as he came up to the table. The hulking man followed, coming to stand behind him. Alasdair ignored him, fixing his dark gaze on Lolly. "It never was, and never shall be," Alasdair said. "I need a word with you, and I want it in private."

"Ah, well, *I* want a bag full of king's faces all clinking together," Lolly said. "Gold makes such a nice sound when it's jostled, don't it? But I take what I can get, because I know the way of things. Now, to my way of thinking, you've got power because of your name and your money. But I have all my friends here, which weighs more right now, do you think?"

"You tell me," Alasdair said, reaching down, taking Lolly's grimy neckcloth in one clenched fist, and hauling him to his feet. "You're having me watched, Lolly. I will know why."

Lolly didn't answer. He stayed rigid in Alasdair's clasp. But Alasdair saw the glint in Lolly's eye as he looked over Alaisdair's shoulder.

One of Alasdair's elbows went back and crashed into something that felt like living lead. With his other hand he swung Lolly around so he bounced off the

huge man's chest as he approached. It bothered Lolly
more than the giant, who didn't seem to notice.

Alasdair let go of Lolly. The mammoth was a head
taller than he, and built along the lines of a barn. He
was thick-necked and dull-eyed, but there was im-
placable intent in those bovine eyes as he reached for
Alasdair. His intended victim knew that if the giant
reached him, he'd be picked up and would be lucky if
he were only thrown out the door. Alasdair took a step
back. He heard Lolly laugh. A few in the crowd of
spectators jeered.

"Hutch will teach you to mend your manners," Lolly
said, catching his breath. "Don't kill him, Hutch," he directed the giant. "Only make him wish you had, eh?"

The giant nodded and moved forward.

Alasdair swung his fist and connected with a jaw
that felt like an oak door. Hutch blinked. Alasdair
flexed his aching hand, gritted his teeth, and drove his
other fist in the giant's belly. It was like hitting the side
of a cow. But the cow might have reacted. Hutch
didn't even grunt. Someone in the crowd laughed,
others were too busy calling odds and making bets.
The odds, Alasdair was grimly amused to hear, were
on his chances of living through the beating Hutch
would deliver.

Hutch threw a punch. Alasdair absorbed the blow
on the side of the head. It made his ears ring. But the
man's fists weren't as strong as his body or Alasdair
would have been on the floor. It was often so with gi-
gantic men, their size did the work their uncoordi-
nated bodies could not. That was what Alasdair
needed to know. He straightened and waited.

The crowd was delighted. Their catcalls showed
what they thought of a nob who was too stupid to run
and too much of a milksop to strike back. Keener eyes

also took note of the fact that the gent was also togged out in the latest store of fashion, meaning his tightly fitted jacket didn't give him much room to move his wide shoulders. He'd flicked open the buttons on that jacket as well as his waistcoat, but he was also limited by a high neckcloth. Hutch was dressed in old, loose clothing. The odds on the gent surviving went down further.

Hutch moved in and swung a meaty fist. His eyes opened in surprise as he felt that fist captured in his supposed victim's hand. His reaction was slow, Alasdair's was not.

The crowd saw the gentleman spin around, drag his huge attacker's arm behind his back, and bend it upward. Alasdair was behind Hutch now, and he pushed him. Hutch stumbled and fell, because the gent's boot had been interposed between his own feet.

Hutch rose from the floor with a roar and lunged back again. The gentleman's reactions were so fast no one in the crowd could tell if it was a boot or a fist that got Hutch in the nose this time.

The next blow made Hutch grunt. Those who blinked missed the way the gent then turned, making Hutch's enraged drive forward send him flying into the wall headfirst. Everyone saw Hutch climb to his feet and, growling, pick up one of the stout wood tables and hold it at arm's length above his head as he glowered at the gent. They winced as they saw the gentleman duck down and charge—forward. Then, somehow, the table went crashing across the room, with Hutch following, his nose streaming blood.

Lolly stopped it. "Have done!" he shouted. "Hutch. *Down!*" he commanded. Hutch, obedient, sat where he was.

"Now," Alasdair told Lolly, his words loud in the ut-

ter stillness of the room, "that . . . private conference . . .
I wanted. Here, or in the street. Your choice. In a minute,
it will be mine. I don't think you'll care for that."

"I have more friends," Lolly said, his eyes darting
around the room.

Alasdair nodded. "Yes. But I do have that name and
rank you mentioned. Fighting man to man is fair. Murder, however, is not. Don't even think it. I remind you
that it will out. In my case, especially. You have too
many witnesses, I have too much of that name and
rank you mentioned before."

Lolly's smile grew flat. "Aye. Never let it be said I
don't fight fair neither. Well, then. Have a seat, and
we'll have a chat. What are you all staring at?" he
asked the crowd.

They went back to their tables, their voices rising as
they made noise to show Lolly they weren't staring or
listening.

Alasdair didn't move. "You want me to discuss my
business, and *yours*, here?" he asked with a mocking
smile.

Lolly froze. "Ah, well. Come on in the back then,"
he said with a forced smile. "There's an alley there."

"Only a madman would go into an alley with you,
Lolly," Alasdair said. "Or a suicide too lazy to do the
deed himself. We can step outside, though."

Lolly followed Alasdair out the front door.

They stood in front of the gin shop, only the lantern
on the ledge above the door giving Lolly light enough
to see Alasdair's expression. He wished he couldn't.
"Now, then, what's your question?" he asked with
false composure.

Alasdair raised one dark eyebrow.

Lolly fidgeted. "You know why I'm watching you,"
he finally said. "Same reason I heard you were paying

good coin to keep an eye on them. Aye, the Scalbys. They have enough brass to have His Majesty watched in his bath. They want reports on what you're doing. I tell them, that's all."

"It has nothing to do with your personal feelings?"

"Oh, that. Water under the bridge. A man in my line of work don't bear grudges."

"Who do you think you're talking to? Grudges are your stock in trade," Alasdair said with weary patience. "Mine, too, so I understand you very well. Now listen," he said grimly, "I queered your game once. You passed some time at the pleasure of His Majesty in Newgate because of it. That's true. But I could have had you hanged."

Alasdair's expression stopped Lolly from interrupting. "I never believed your excuse that you thought the Frenchman was merely a smuggler bringing in wine for you to sell. But I could never prove what I thought you'd given him to smuggle out of the country either. Treason's a hanging offense, and so in spite of my misgivings I didn't let them drag you to Tyburn Hill. Neither did I let your friends here know my suspicions, or they'd have scragged you in far less elegant style, and you know it. They're not gentlemen, but don't be deceived. They *are* Englishmen. They lost limbs, friends, fathers, and sons in the war, too. It wasn't charity on my part. I couldn't be sure, and I have morals, in my fashion. But anything you do now makes me wonder about my compassion then, Lolly, it really does."

"My watching you's got nothing to do with that!" Lolly protested.

"Be sure of that," Alasdair said, biting off each word. "I don't care what you report to the Scalbys. But I am not His Majesty. You can't station your ferrets in my water closet. Watch if you want, but from afar. Make me forget that you're watching, as well as existing. *And don't get in my way.* Or this time I won't care if I can't prove anything."

Alasdair straightened his cuffs, dipped his head in a mock bow, and paced off into the night.

Lolly stood watching him. As did others, from the shadows.

10

"**I** must talk with you," Kate said as she took Alasdair's hand.

"Anytime," he answered as he turned away from her.

"I meant alone," Kate answered before the figure of the dance parted them again.

When Alasdair came back to her, he said, "How delightful. Of course. I'm flattered and more eager than you. Name the place and we'll slip way. To a dark corner, or the garden?"

She controlled her temper. "I mean just talk. And you know it."

"Behold me crushed," he said, and grinned so suddenly she forgave him his jest. "Why not now?"

"It's private," she said before she stepped down the line of dancers again. "About a problem. It can wait, but I'd rather talk about it tonight."

"At dinner then," he told her when the dance brought them together again.

She nodded, wishing again that there was a simple way a single woman could speak privately to a man. It was absurd how people in London seemed to think men were so heated by their passions that they'd attempt to violate a female the minute they were alone with one. Kate grew even more indignant thinking about it, until she thought about the passions of the man she wanted to speak to, and almost missed her step.

Even so, however murky his past, the man hardly had to attack a woman. From what she'd seen, the assault would probably go the other way round, at least to judge from the way the other ladies were eyeing him that night. Which was the same way they always did. Still, he'd never been anything but a gentleman to her. Those heated looks he bent on her for others' eyes to see, and she never forgot it. It was maddening that she had so few opportunities to talk to him in private. There was always a relative or a servant within earshot when he was near.

Now she'd told him she had a problem. Whatever his sins, she believed Sir Alasdair was a man who knew how to solve problems. Especially the sort that involved getting a woman alone.

Kate watched Alasdair as he stepped through the dance with consummate grace. Not precisely grace, she corrected herself. He was much too large for leaping or pirouetting, he didn't caper or posture the way other men who styled themselves fine dancers did. He simply moved in time with the music, that big frame of his keeping to the rhythm but not flaunting it. He made it seem as masculine as riding a horse, as effortless as the way he strolled down the street. She couldn't help being flattered that she was his partner at this ball, and was dismayed about how flattered she was.

After all, this was all a pose, a favor she was doing him. It was just unfortunate that the more she did the more she found herself regretting that when her task was done he'd be fair game for other women, the ones he needed that veneer of respectability for. That was nonsense, and she knew it. That was exactly the problem.

They'd been together often in the past days. Not all the time, of course. They didn't want the rumors of his interest in her turning to talk of imminent marriage, because then no matter what he said when they parted she'd look like a jilt. A flirtation was different. Anyone could cut off a flirtation and come out of it unscathed. That they were having, and they'd managed to see each other often enough to make the point. Daytime saw them sharing rides and walks. Evenings they were together, as tonight, at this ball.

Kate didn't have to pretend her interest in him, the man could interest a rock. She could only hope beneath the careful fabrication there'd also been some real pleasure on his part. She thought she'd done her part well. They'd always found something to talk about, whether it was gossip or a discussion of the state of their world. They never spoke about anything significant, yet they were always talking. She felt triumphant whenever it seemed she might really be amusing him.

But the more she saw him and other women's reaction to him, the more she wondered why the devil the man insisted he needed her to make him respectable. Worse, the more she saw him the guiltier she felt. He'd said she was the perfect person to pretend to court because she knew his attentions for what they were and wasn't susceptible to him. She wasn't sure of that anymore.

Because she truly looked forward to seeing him. He was the best thing she'd found in London, more interesting than any man she'd ever met at home, and certainly the most attractive. His face and voice and form projected a magnetism that was nearly overwhelming. She firmly suppressed those reactions to him. Or tried to. Beyond all that, and that was more than she'd ever experienced, she discovered she liked him enormously.

Of course she knew he wasn't really courting her. But she hadn't realized how good an actor he was. While he was convincing others, it was too bad that he sometimes convinced her, too. She, of all people, should know how ludicrous it was to think the worldly Sir Alasdair St. Erth wanted to make love to her, even if he could! His torrid gazes had a purpose, they both knew it. It was all for show, that was the point of their association. So it was unreasonable that she found herself beginning to hate the day the deception would be over. Unreasonable, irrational, neither sensible nor good for her.

The music ended. Alasdair bowed and let her new partner claim her. That was another thing, Kate thought as she took another man's hand. Her dance card was filled. Sir Alasdair had given her popularity. Some men wanted to see what had captivated St. Erth, others sought instant fame, hoping to capture some of his shine by dancing attention on his latest flirt. She'd little to offer but her hand in the dance and knew very well that was all they sought it for. Their interest in her was limited to their interest in gossip.

So Alasdair had accomplished his aims. But he was making hers harder, which was why she had to talk with him, and soon.

She danced with a vapid young lord, which let her concentrate on watching Alasdair dance with a ravishing brunette. He wore black, as usual, but his waist-coat was celestial blue laced with gold. It seemed to Kate that he was in his perfect setting. And what a setting it was!

They danced across a magnificent ballroom. The floor, when Kate could see it through the crowd of swirling dancers, was intricately inlaid mosaic marble. The lofty domed ceiling was covered with frescoes of mythological heroes and heroines, the background awash in tones of pink, peach, sky blue, and gold. The walls were saffron, outlined in gilt and leaf green. Fluted ivory columns held up the divine ceiling, myriad candles in crystal chandeliers suffused everything with gold.

The scene looked magical and mythical, reminding Kate that it was exactly that for her. It might be Alasdair's natural element, but it certainly wasn't hers. She couldn't wait for dinner, and not because she was hungry. The sooner she spoke with him, the better for her state of mind. And heart.

Alasdair reclaimed her when the music stopped. The ballroom doors were flung open so the throng could enter the room next door for dinner. It was a lucky thing Kate wasn't hungry. It seemed to take forever to get to a table. First, she had to wait as Alasdair was stopped by curious partygoers asking questions. Then he hung back, waiting at the entrance to the dining room as others took their seats or milled around the buffet tables.

"Why are we waiting?" she asked curiously.

"You wanted to speak to me in private," he answered as he surveyed the room. "So we need a table away from the crowd, close enough to the horde for propriety, and far enough from your cousins, most of whom are here tonight, I see."

She nodded glumly. Sibyl was with Leigh. But tonight Sibyl's other siblings had come as well, including two of her married sisters and their unfortunate husbands. Except for Sibyl and her mother, the other Swanson females were unpleasant company. They were still fierce rivals, to each other and any other female who came within their orbit. Being raised in such a competitive atmosphere had left its mark. They weren't any happier about their country cousin's sudden social success than Kate was with them.

Alasdair took Kate to a table set far from the long buffet, the punch bowl, and any Swansons. He pulled out a chair for her, signaled a footman, ordered some wine, and then looked at Kate. "I'll get you something to eat. What do you prefer?"

"Don't bother," she said. "I prefer getting my dinner myself."

He shook his head. "That will never do. An attentive gentleman waits on his lady."

"That's exactly what I want to talk about," she said eagerly. "I can skip the food, but I must speak with you."

"It will look odd if you're not eating. Still, if you prefer to sit staring into my eyes, transfixed by me, that would do, I suppose. At least for our little plot. But not for me. You see, I'm hungry. Dancing isn't hard work, but all that incessant smiling is."

"Oh, go get some food then," she said crossly.

"I'll wait. On second thought, it's a better idea not to join the first wave of invaders. There's some trampling over by the aspics and the scene at the shellfish display is getting feral. I hope no one gets bitten. I imagine they've held some food in reserve for those who don't choose to fight for it." He sat and turned his attention to her. "So. Tell me what's bothering you."

He stripped off his gloves, folded his hands on the tabletop, and smiled at her. She looked down quickly because he was still playing the game, and that smile was dangerous even though she knew it was only a game. Her attention was caught by the state of his hands. He had wonderful hands, she'd noticed that right away, large and powerful, with long fingers, broad palms, and strong wrists. Unlike the pale white hands most London gentlemen took pride in, his looked like they were actually capable of work. But now she saw they looked like they'd been ill-used. His knuckles were bruised, striped with dark red scrapes.

Kate couldn't help the little lurch in her stomach at the thought of his being hurt. Liking him was more dangerous than being infatuated with him, because it was even more foolish and futile. They'd never be lovers. And given the state of their world, they could never really be friends either.

He saw the direction of her stare. "I see you've noticed my wounds," he said, flexing his hand and looking at it. "Don't worry. I richly deserve them. They're from a bout at Gentleman Jackson's boxing saloon."

"Who won?"

"Need you ask?" he said with mock surprise.

"Never mind," she said. "The thing is . . ." She had to pause while the footman delivered the wine, sitting quietly through the ritual as Alasdair sipped it before nodding acceptance. "I think our scheme has worked," she said as soon as the footman left. "I think you're respectable as houses now and can court a royal princess if you choose."

"One doesn't have to be respectable to do that," he said with a smile. "At any rate, I don't think you're right—at least, not entirely. Our courtship has obviously startled people, and some are impressed by it, true. But it's much too soon to have changed their minds about me. If we part now, even on the best of terms, it will only convince them they were right to doubt me. Because just see how wicked St. Erth couldn't stay with a respectable young woman above a fortnight? No, though I'm delighted with our progress, there's a long road ahead." He leaned closer and lowered his voice. "For example, do you think your own relatives entirely believe our mutual state of infatuation so soon in the game?"

She thought a moment. "Well, Sibyl knows all, of course. Lady Swanson is a dear and believes the best of everyone. The fact that I've attracted so much company to her house pleases her very much. My cousin, Lord Swanson, likes me, so I think he doesn't find it strange that you might, too. But as for his other daughters? They believe the worst of everyone and nothing anyone says would convince them otherwise."

"I meant your other relatives here in London."

She frowned. "Oh, you mean Lord and Lady North, Baron Chadwick, and the Deals? The Norths are your friends, too, so you can tell them what to think. The others hardly know me well enough to care at all."

His expression was bland, but he persisted. "I thought you had more relatives here in London."

"I do. There are the Brentwoods, Sir Fane and his lady, Lord Ross, and the Hopes. But they don't know me, so why should they even care? I suppose they would if we really were going to marry, but even then only enough to wonder what to give as a wedding present. Of course, there's our cousin, His Grace, the Duke of Tarlyton. But he's so old one hardly ever sees him, and his son, who seems to be a very nice man, is still in Vienna."

"I heard you were also related to the Scalbys," Alasdair said carefully.

"Oh. Them. Yes, I am. But to tell the truth, I try to forget that." She saw his expression and stammered. "I—I'm sorry, are they particular friends of yours? Forgive me."

"I knew them once upon a time, but no, they're not particular friends."

She breathed a sigh of relief. "That's good, because I didn't want to say anything rude. It's nothing they ever did to me, you see. But I've always been uncomfortable with them. One hears stories . . . It's not just that. The few times I saw them when I was young, at family affairs, funerals, and weddings and such, they frightened me. Well, they were so lofty, elegant, world-weary and—how can I say this?—they seemed threatening. That's me, not them, because they've never done anything menacing. But even when I saw them again later, before they went abroad, they made me uneasy."

She smiled at him. "Idiotic of me, isn't it? But the more they tried to be nice, instead of putting me at my ease, they made me more uncomfortable! She's very beautiful, isn't she?" Kate asked wistfully. "She seems polished to a high sheen, face, form and voice. And even though he dresses in old-fashioned styles, or maybe because he does, he was the most elegant gentleman I had ever seen. But they look at a person as though from a height, and always seem to be secretly amused. Maybe everyone *is* a provincial compared to them, I certainly am. But I don't like feeling like one.

"I expect they're very well known, and so I suppose I should have mentioned them when I spoke about my relatives," she went on with a small shrug. "But there you are. I avoid even thinking about them. I suppose I should visit them while I'm in London, if only for the look of it. Truthfully, I've been putting it off."

"They are off-putting, to be sure," Alasdair said. "Don't worry, it's no problem to me. Or to them. They are very worldly, after all. . . . They haven't asked you to visit, have they?"

She shook her head. "No. There's a standing invitation to everyone in the family, but we've never accepted it. My parents didn't ask me to call on them either. So I'm only too happy to end my visit here without that honor . . ." She sat up straight. "That's exactly what I wanted to talk about. I think it's time for me to start planning on going home."

He suppressed a startled movement. "Is there trouble at home?"

"Not really. It's hard to explain. You'd have to know my family," she said ruefully.

"I'd like that."

She laughed. "You don't have to play the game with me, you know. What would you have in common with my family?"

"Tell me about them, and I'll see."

She looked at him skeptically.

"It's hardly fair," he said. "You know so much about me, but here I am keeping company with a woman of mystery."

That made her laugh outright. "All I know about you is rumor, and you've asked me to discount that."

"But at least you know that much. I don't even know gossip about you. We talk about everything but your past. If not for my sake, think of our masquerade. People will think it odd if I know nothing about you but your taste in clothes and politics. Tell me about your family."

She gave him a quizzical smile.

"No, I mean it, please," he said.

She couldn't resist his earnest look, and so began to tell him about her parents and brothers. He sat watching her intently as he listened. Half the undivided attention he focused on her was for the effect, they both understood that. The half she didn't know was that he liked watching her.

Tonight she wore a tawny gown, a simple silken column that became less simple as it clung to her body, pointing up her sweet little breasts. He had to keep reminding himself not to stare. Gazing into a lady's eyes was a sign of love, looking down her bodice was very pleasant, but not the message he wanted to send to anyone watching them. He knew what he liked, though, so it was difficult to keep his eyes and his thoughts elevated.

He didn't have to pretend to be enchanted by her. She was enticing, and became more so as he got to know her, since hers was the kind of appeal that grew on a man. Her neck wasn't swanlike, as fashion admired, and though her eyes were large, her mouth was, too. It was made for kissing, just as she was made for lovemaking, and it fascinated him that she didn't seem to know it.

He found her ignorance of her charms intensely erotic. Maybe because she thought herself completely safe with him, she didn't try to entice him, and so enticed him even more. He genuinely liked her and was bemused to find himself wanting her so much. He'd promised he'd leave her as he found her. But tonight the errant thought occurred to him that he'd never really know how he'd found her until he tried her, would he?

"I beg your pardon?" he said, when she paused for the answer to a question he hadn't heard. Contemplat-

ing his inconvenient desire for her made him lose track
of what she was saying.

"Sorry," she said, grinning. "I do go on about them,
don't I? How fascinating can my stories about my
brothers be if you don't know them? Anyway, they
aren't the problem. Not that my parents are," she said
hastily. "But they *are* why I think it would be better if I
went home sooner than I'd planned."

She lowered her voice. "My parents sent me to London, but now they're finding it hard to do without me.
They have misunderstandings from time to time, you
see. Nothing dire. But they can make them seem that
way. They have these little arguments that escalate to
hurt feelings and long silences. Mother walks off in a
huff, Father locks himself in his study and is a bear
when he has to come to meals. It's easy to fix; they just
have to be diverted. I usually find some problem they
have to work on together. That gives them an excuse to
talk again, and soon their disagreement's forgotten.
They love each other deeply, but they're very dramatic. I think they actually enjoy their tiffs, so long as
someone's there to mend them. The problem is that I
usually do, and they're starting to miss that."

"But if you marry, they'll have to learn to live with
that."

She grinned. "Yes, and that's what's got them feeling so unsettled! They sent me away because they felt
guilty that I was so content at home. I am. But they
thought maybe they'd leaned on me too much, making
me forget I should be planning my future. Now they
miss me terribly. Anyway, when I wrote to say I was
bored here and ready to come home, they leapt at the
chance to agree."

His eyebrow went up. "Bored? Why, thank you."

"Oh, I wrote that before I met you. It takes days for

letters to get back and forth. And"—she looked away—"I didn't tell them about you. Why should I?" she asked defensively. "Why should I get their expectations up? Well," she added to his smile, "whatever you say about your reputation, you are intensely eligible, you know."

She went on before he could speak. "It's true. That's just it, too." She leaned forward on her elbows, and whispered, "I don't know why you need me to lend you respectability anymore, because although I admit I heard whispers about you before, I haven't heard a word since we started seeing each other. You have many worthy friends too—just look at Leigh, or the Norths. They don't exclude you. In short, sir, you seem entirely respectable to me." She sat back, having made her point.

"Believe me, I am not."

She shook her head. "I can't see that."

"You don't know all."

"Well, there you are," she said triumphantly. "You said you didn't know about me, but there's little enough to tell. You're supposed to have this dreadful reputation, but I've never heard a word of it. In fact, I don't know much about you at all."

"There isn't much to tell," he said, and with a tilted smile added, "not in the edited version, at any rate, and that's the only one I'd tell a respectable young woman. Let me see. I have no close family. I'd some siblings who died in infancy. My mother died when I was thirteen. My father when I was sixteen. A suicide. I'm surprised you hadn't heard that, at least."

"I'm sorry," she said quickly.

"Thank you," he said gravely.

"That's dreadful, but not what I meant," she said. "Why do you say you still have a bad name, and what did you do to get it? Surely you can couch it in polite language, you're good with words. If you couldn't do that, you wouldn't even be allowed in here!" He didn't smile at her joke. "I really should know," she added, "because if we keep this up, and anyone said something terrible about you, I'd have to defend you, wouldn't I?"

He didn't answer right away.

"There you are," she said a little too briskly. "If *you* can't even tell me, then I suppose it *is* high time I cut line and went home."

He looked up from his glass. There was heat in his dark eyes, despair, and much bitter mockery. It was a look she'd never seen on his face before. It made her want to comfort him and run from him, at the same time.

"I tarried in many dark places," he said softly, lowering his gaze again, turning the stem of the glass in his fingers. "I had experiences many men have not experienced, and no decent women shared. But I didn't tarry with decent women. I never cheated at cards or failed to pay my debts. I cheated nonetheless, and my debts were many. I'm not a good man, Kate. But I'm not evil. It's just that I have scores to settle and am never nice about how I settle them. A great wrong was done to me once and I've never forgotten it."

He held her gaze with his own. "I told you no lies, although I didn't, and won't, tell you all. I hope, one day, when the last wrong is righted—and that will be soon—to be acceptable again. That much is true, and is what I'm working toward. I hope you continue to help me in this because my need is greater than your parents'. After all, they have each other. I only have you."

The way he said "have you" made Kate's ears grow hot, while the earnestness in his voice made her feel guilty. He spoke about need and revenge and looked like he was burning for it. Though he was doubtless a good actor, she heard honesty in what he said.

"And that great wrong," he added, "is one that has never been righted. I must make sure it is. Then I'll be done. I need you to help me gain my ends. Nothing's changed about that. No harm will come to you, that I promise. I can't say more now. Please trust me. Just a few more weeks, Kate, and then whether I've achieved my aims or not, I'll release you from our bargain. I thought we had one. Didn't we?"

She knew what she had to say, and was a little dismayed at how happy that made her. "Yes," she said. "All right. I gave my word. In for a penny, in for a pound. I promised. But I can't stay here forever. That was never part of the contract."

He'd been holding his breath. She heard him let it out. He rose from the table. "Thank you for honoring our bargain," he said. "Now I'll get something for us to eat. And fetch a long spoon for you while I'm at it." He touched a finger to her cheek and chuckled at her puzzlement. "A long spoon, my brave darling, for dining with the Devil, of course."

11

The private dining parlor at the restaurant was decorated in red and gold, lit by candles and enhanced by the glow of the fire that leapt in the hearth. The two well-dressed gentlemen who had engaged the room sat and discussed politics until they were left alone with their desserts. When the door closed behind the last waiter, the slighter gentleman leaned back and fixed his companion with a steady look.

"How much longer will you continue this mock courtship of yours, Alasdair?" Leigh asked.

His friend didn't raise his eyes from the walnut he'd just selected, but he did raise a dark brow. "A rather abrupt shift from affairs of state to affairs of the heart, I think, isn't it?"

"If it were an affair of the heart, I wouldn't ask."

Alasdair smiled. "Yes. Because you doubt I have one. But I do still have a conscience. Don't worry. The lady in question won't suffer at my hands, and is not suffering now."

Leigh frowned. "I know that. Kate's having the time of her life. That's exactly my point. You've brought her into fashion. Every fribble in London is after her. I saw her riding with Skyler the other day. He wouldn't bother to pass a minute with anyone who isn't top of the trees. She danced with both Babcock and Farnsworth the other night, and those fashionable idiots were shooting evil looks at Atwood when he asked her for a dance, too. And that twit, Clyde Jeremy, hangs around the Swanson parlor like lint, in spite of the terrible Swanson sisters eyeing him like a spring lamb with mint sauce on the side."

"A monstrous thing I've done, isn't it?" Alasdair laughed.

"Yes," Leigh said seriously, "because when you're done with her, they will be, too."

"I doubt Kate will lament that," Alasdair said as he put the nut in the nutcracker's jaws. "She's constantly amazed at their nonsense, she's told me so."

"Nevertheless, it's bound to be embarrassing for her when this charade is over. They won't have the time of day for her when you stop seeing her."

"It won't be embarrassing in the least," Alasdair said, closing the nutcracker and fracturing the nutshell with a loud crack. "She won't see them. She'll be back in the countryside with lovely memories of her triumphant visit to London."

"And perhaps a broken heart as well?" Leigh asked. He saw Alasdair's hand still, and went on: "Yes, she humors them. You're right, you can see it in her eyes, she's as amused as you are by their attentions. But she glows when she's with you. There's no mistaking it, or disguising it either. She comes to life when you enter a room. Did you know that? She won't glow when you're through with her, that's what I'm worried about."

Alasadir put down the nutcracker. He tapped a perfect globe of walnut meat from the shell and turned it in his fingers, paying close attention to it as he answered. "Then don't worry. I don't. Kate and I have a good time together, that's true. But there's no deception involved, she knows what I'm up to."

"No one knows what you're up to," Leigh said quietly.

Alasdair met his eyes at last. His own dark gaze held anger, but his voice remained cool. "And what do you think that is?"

"A good question, Alasdair. I guess you want your courtship to reach the Scalbys' ears. You despise them, I don't doubt you have good reason. You've never told me all of it and I never pressed you for it. A man's secrets are his own, even a boy's are—and that's what you were when you met them. I know that, but little else. Except it has to do with your father. I suppose you're seeing Kate because she's their cousin and you think that will dismay them. It's a rococo scheme, even for you. What's the point?"

Alasdair leaned back in his chair and stretched out his legs, affecting calm. But his eyes denied it. "The point? Revenge. Revenge is a strange thing. If a man's angry at someone, he wants satisfaction, of course. In the first pure flare of rage, killing the object of his fury is the only thing that will do it for him. Fortunately, with most men, Reason takes over. He remembers that murder's a mortal sin. Moreover, if he succeeds, there's the nasty fact that Society will then usually do the same to him. A duel? But they are illegal and unsatisfactory. Apart from the fact that if you win you might have to go into exile, it might satisfy your anger against one person, but what if you're offended by two?

"Mayhem is good, too," Alasdair said. "But it's so

temporary. A burned-out house can be rebuilt, can't it?" He spoke as though he were amused. But he wasn't and neither was his friend. He held up a finger, "But say anger has been thwarted for decades. Suppose the sin is too great to be settled by a lawsuit or even the spread of scurrilous gossip. What then? I'll tell you what. As years go by, a man discovers he needs more than simple reprisal. Years *have* gone by," he said harshly, "and I'm not just any man. I need their complete destruction. Now even a rope around their necks wouldn't do. Death's too sudden, too complete. I want them to live with defeat, I need to see their eyes when they know I've beaten them."

He looked down at his hand as though suddenly noticing the tight fist it had closed to, and opened it. He dropped bits of pulverized walnut into his plate.

"They've hidden themselves," he said softly, brushing his hands together. "They're more cloistered than nuns, nested like eggs, secret as a nut in the shell. No one's seen them since they returned to England. I will. I must. Yes, I could end it without doing that, but I *will* see them as I ruin them. They've hidden themselves well and can continue to, because they can turn away friends—if they had any. But they can scarcely turn away family. Kate's my key."

He looked at his friend soberly. "They caused my father's death, Leigh. They ruined him by enticing him into a fatal financial scheme. He might have recovered from that. He was a gentle man, never a coward. But they made it worse, visiting him and mocking him, dancing on the grave he hadn't yet dug, promising him shame for years to come, ruining every last thing he held dear. He felt he had no choice. As I have none now.

"I'm no prince of Denmark," he added, a slow, sad

smile spreading across his mouth, easing the tight
lines of it. "I didn't choose to procrastinate. I tried to
make them pay right away. But I couldn't. They were
powerful, and I wasn't. How could I be? They were
grown, I was still a lad. And I was unmanned by grief,
deep in shock and sudden crushing debt, only sixteen,
suddenly poor, with a name to try to salvage and an
estate to save from total ruin. I've worked and grown
and hardened since then. Now I'm no longer poor, or
young, or powerless. Now, too, I will take my time.

"It's a little thing I'm after," he added in cajoling
tones as he stared at the fire seething in the hearth.
"Just a few minutes in their company, to face them and
tell them what I know, what the world will know, and
how little credit or reputation they'll have in the world
once I've done it. That's all. Not much, is it? No harm
will come to anyone else. Least of all to Kate."

"It's a madness with you, Alasdair."

"Yes. True," Alasdair said with a quirked smile.
"But I'm a lucky lunatic, because when it's done I'll be
sane."

"And Kate?" Leigh persisted. "Is there a possibility
of a future for her in your plans?"

Alasdair's smile grew cold. "So, after all the denial,
the truth. You've a care for her, after all?"

Leigh shook his head. "I do, but I don't know her
well enough to have more than that. I doubt it would
matter if I did. I told you before, have you looked at
her when she looks at you? Or are you too full of your
own plans even to see her?"

"I see her," Alasdair said. "I like her. But I've no intention of allowing myself to have serious intentions
toward any woman until I'm free. Don't you understand? I'm married to this scheme of mine, Leigh. I'm
faithful to it. I have been for almost two decades, and I

can't commit myself to anything or anyone else until I've fulfilled my oath. I restored my fortune, I *will* restore my father's good name, to let his soul finally rest in peace. And," he added more quietly, "I will regain my own peace of mind."

When Leigh spoke his voice was sorrowful. "My God, Alasdair. What did they do to you? It goes beyond revenge for your father, doesn't it?"

The dancing flames in the hearth reflected on the surface of Alasdair's dark eyes, and his expression held darker fires. "Yes," he murmured. "It goes beyond that. I can only hope when I'm done, it will be done too."

"Memory can't be killed by killing of any sort."

"No. But it can be appeased. Have done," Alasdair said in lighter tones. "It will be over soon, and then we'll see. You may yet drink a toast to my bride. But I'm damned if I know who that unlucky lady will be. Yes, I know, I'm damned anyway," he added with a true smile. "I do intend to marry, to continue my line, that's always been part of my plan. But as I said, I like Kate, and want the best for her, and I don't know if that would be me. For that matter, I don't know if there'll be enough left of my heart to share with anyone. And she deserves no less. So if you've a fondness for her, don't let me stand in your way."

"You stand in my way by simply standing there."

Alasdair shrugged. "I won't repeat my father's actions, even for you, dear friend."

Leigh winced. "I never meant that."

"I know you didn't, I just wanted to see you squirm. And since you're pleased to dissect my life and intentions, what about you and the little Swanson chit? Have you seen *her* when you enter the room? Speak of incandescence, she lights from within at the sight of you. She's charming, you know."

"Yes, I know. But she's a child. As for her lighting up when I enter a room, well, why not? Of course the poor girl rejoices when she sees me. I'm kind to her. I make her laugh. I take her out of that house and treat her like a lady. And she has no one to compare me with, no man has ever paid attention to her. She has that clutch of hideous sisters to contend with, and they've helped keep her a secret, like a mad relative in the tower."

Alasdair grinned. "So she's your charity work, is she?"

Leigh paused. "I suppose she is."

"And Kate? If I cry off, I should think you'd at least try your hand at entertaining her. Even though you'll have to travel to the countryside to do it."

"I've a carriage and horses, so, as you said, we'll see," Leigh said with a challenging look in his eye.

"Very good," was all Alasdair said, as he selected another walnut. But this time he quickly and neatly cracked it in his hands.

The two men parted in front of the restaurant.

"I'm to my club," Lord Leigh said. "Care to come along?"

"No, thank you, I'm going home. I'm not quite respectable enough for your club yet. No, don't offer to accompany me to another. I don't feel like gambling and can't go wenching. It's a book by the fireside for me. This respectable life will be my ruin. I'll see you tomorrow at two. We have an appointment with the ladies, remember? The art exhibition? Then tea?"

Leigh nodded. "I remember. But your debt to me is rising. Any more enlightening exhibitions, and I think I'll ask you for some disreputable addresses."

"Oh, I don't doubt you can hunt up some of your

own," Alasdair said, "I go to the baths merely to be clean, I remind you." He chuckled at his friend's rising color, clear even in the lamplight. Waving a negligent hand, he ambled off down the street.

It was a busy section of town. Streetlamps glowed, private coaches and hackneys clattered down the street, lanterns fore and aft adding their own wavering lights. Passersby chatted as they strolled, boys carrying torches lit their way along the cobbles. Many sections of London were dangerous by night, but all the light in this district kept crime down, and the safety that provided lured ever more people out for a night on the town.

Deep in thought, Alasdair stepped around slower pedestrians as he made his way toward his town house. Leigh's comments had started him remembering, and he hated that. He wasn't thinking of Kate, or revenge. He was too busy trying not to think about why he needed both.

He'd long since ringed the thing round with so many plots and plans, snares and schemes, that it was hard to see clearly. He seldom had to think about the actual reason he needed revenge. But time had passed, and he'd enacted most of his schemes, so now the ugly thing could sometimes be glimpsed, pulsating like a worm surprised in the center of a rotting peach.

The worst nightmares had stopped long before, the moment he paid his first informer for information about the Scalbys. That was literally blood money. He'd earned it by working with his hands and back beside his tenants in the fields, trying to raise enough crops to keep the estate in good heart. His tenants had worked harder for him because of it. He was lucky in that, at least. The war effort required food for the troops, and his farms produced. He was lucky in his friends, too. He learned how to invest his money, growing it as carefully as he'd worked his fields.

By the time the Scalbys left England, Alasdair was a man, and a fairly rich one. His finances were in order, his life free to follow his dream. That dream was of revenge. When the Scalbys left, so did he. They established a home away from home on the Continent entertaining as lavishly as they ever did. Never political, they changed allegiances with the times and so were useful to every side. Alasdair crossed the Channel too.

As the war with France dragged on, Alasdair joined a select group of gentlemen abroad. He spied for His Majesty, and himself. As his pile of incriminating documents about the Scalbys grew, the incidence of his night panics—those dreams that dragged him screaming from his sleep—shrank in proportion to information received. It was like raking a midden, but the higher the mountain of filth he amassed, the more peace he found.

Sometimes, though, even now, he'd wake in a sweat, mocking voices still echoing in his ears, the stink of opium and patchouli in his nose, the imprint of those cold hands still on his hot, shrinking flesh. But now, at least, he didn't remember the exact words or feelings magnified so intensely in his dreams. He didn't allow it.

He'd learned to rise from bed, throw open a window, and breathe in clean air. Then he'd turn on all the lamps to banish the night. Then he'd pace and plot and plan to keep his mind from its sleeping horrors. The echoes of his shame would fade into dawn.

He accumulated information. The Scalbys had played at every evil game. They'd debauched the innocent. They'd gorged on forbidden pleasures. That wouldn't matter, Society forgave that if it was done discreetly. But by following their adventures, by interviewing the fallen and promising vengeance to the grieving, Alasdair finally had enough proof to hang them—if he cared to. More than enough to ruin them, and that was his aim.

A man could take another man's innocence and get away with it. He might trick another man out of his life, sully his infants and shame his name, and yet still be permitted in polite society. But one rule couldn't be broken. Society did not forgive noblemen who swindled other noblemen out of their fortunes. They'd done that to many more men than Alasdair's father.

That was good, and it was enough. But by digging in lives the Scalbys had touched, Alasdair discovered that they'd also committed treason. It was his crowning achievement, capping all his years of work. Because that was absolutely unforgivable. That, all their money and influence couldn't wash away.

It was a bit of carelessness in a lifetime of callous betrayals. The Scalbys had always deftly danced around politics, but once, they'd stumbled. They'd found out some things from a drunken officer who had stayed at their home for their pleasure, and his. They'd told those things to another friend of theirs—in a letter. Not for money, but for favors. It didn't matter. The secrets were military ones. Luckily for Alasdair, the old friend was, like so many of their friends, also an enemy of theirs.

Alasdair had the papers. He had them at last. Utterly. He had them, but never forgot they were still dangerous. Serpents could slither out of the tightest corners. But if they were helpless it wouldn't be half as satisying a game. So he kept watch on them as surely as they did on him. They obviously were waiting for his next move. When should he make it?

He turned it over and over in his mind as he walked, as he'd been doing for weeks, because it was such a delicious problem, too rare a treat to gobble down. He'd waited too long to waste such a wonderful opportunity for ultimate revenge; he had to have the precise moment for it. He deserved it as much as they did. He might have been working for his country as he tracked them, but that wasn't known outside of the War Office. What everyone did see was how he filthied his name by following their star. He'd had to go down into the gutters with them, and had come up with his own reputation ruined. They'd pay for that as well.

The streets grew darker as Alasdair neared his house. He lived in the best part of town, where bright lights weren't tolerated any more than loud noises. A single lantern glowed above each door. It was quieter here, too. The Watch, an old pensioner hired to carry a rattle to sound the alarm if he saw trouble, dozed safe in his little booth at the corner, as comfortably nestled in his high chair as the wealthy he was supposed to be guarding were in their beds.

Alasdair strolled home, deep in thought, trying to guess how long it would be before the Scalbys asked Kate to visit them. Or would they? They knew he was courting her, did they guess why? Did they know just how much he knew? He slowed as a disagreeable thought occurred to him. If so, would they resist the impulse to interfere? Would he have to do something bolder?

He picked up his pace again, his bootsteps ringing on the pavement. Even if the Scalbys didn't guess the ultimate weapon he'd gotten hold of, they wouldn't be happy at the idea of him marrying into their family. Maybe they'd have her visit so they could find out? . . .

but then when they saw her, would they try to see if they could make some profit from her?

His mouth tightened at the thought. He wouldn't permit it.

He just wanted her to be invited. He'd invite himself along with her, send her from the room, and have his triumph. But they were lying low. He'd have to force their hand. Maybe cause more gossip they couldn't ignore. Not enough to ruin Kate, just enough to fuel rumor. Keep her out too long one night? Kiss her in public? He smiled. It would be a pleasure to mix work with pleasure.

How *would* it feel to be able to run his hands through that crop of buoyant curls at last? To pull her close against his body, feel those high shapely breasts burning against his chest, to nuzzle her neck and breathe in the wild spring scent of her, feel that smooth downy cheek against his lips, taste, at last, that smiling mouth . . .

He turned at a noise. But not fast enough.

. . . Just enough to get the bludgeon blow on the side of his head, not the back of his neck. So he didn't go down, but only staggered. He managed to dodge the next blow, but he couldn't get his bearings because his head was ringing too loudly. He swung out wildly and hit his attacker flush in the mouth, he felt teeth against his knuckles. But there were two attackers. He was dazed, and it was dark. He shook his head to try to see straight. He couldn't gauge how far his attackers were from him because the blood from the cut on his temple was flowing down over his eye.

The pain in his head was so bad he hardly felt more than a punch in his chest as the knife went in. But he could hear it scrape against a rib as the man pulled it out, and he became infuriated. He lunged and grabbed, wrestling for the knife he saw glinting in the lamplight. He wrung the wrist that held it, and when it fell free, he grabbed the knife in his fist. When the other man came clawing for it, Alasdair swung it hard. It sank into the fellow's chest. Alasdair didn't let go of the hilt, so he and the other man fell like lovers, tangled together, striving together.

He rolled on the ground struggling, until total darkness fell.

12

They were coming for him. It was time, but he wasn't ready yet. Alasdair wished he'd drunk more and had more of what they'd given him to breathe in, because muzzy as he was he could still feel and hear. He was much too aware. He kept his eyes closed. Not tightly, because if they saw his eyes squeezed shut they'd know he was feigning sleep, and he wouldn't have them think he was a coward. But he was, and he hated himself for it There was shame enough to deal with without that. He had to keep remembering that he was mature now, old enough to handle anything, and this was just another thing he had to contend with.

He forced himself to breathe slowly and evenly, letting his lids lie smooth, praying they'd leave him. No, he was beyond prayer, obscene even to think of it now. But he hoped they'd leave him if they thought he was oblivious. He felt a hand on his chest and knew that it wouldn't matter, because even if he wasn't insensible, they were.

He heard voices murmuring, he thought he heard laughter, too, they were having a good time. They always did.

"Is he awake?" someone asked.

"I don't know," another answered. "It doesn't matter at this juncture."

Indeed, it didn't. He'd done this in a thousand dreams, and it never mattered. But this time was different because this time he felt pain, and it wasn't just in his heart and cringing soul. His head was ringing, there was a sharp pain in it as well as a stab of pain in his chest every time he took a breath. The sickly stench of opiates was in his nose once more. He tasted spirits on his lips. He knew he lay vulnerable, naked before strangers again. He despaired. There might be variations, but this *was* the dreaded dream returned.

Yet it was not. Because the more aware Alasdair became, the more he hurt. He actually felt pain. That had never happened before. And this time he felt coverings on his body. So though they were at the stage of gathering round him, watching him closely, excited by their victory, this time perhaps he could wake before it began. He struggled to open his eyes. Now he was determined to see who his tormentors were.

"I think he's stirring," a male voice said, and Alasdair felt a cool hand on his shoulder.

He didn't even have to try, it simply happened. He felt the hand on his body and his own fist clenched, he lurched up with a snarl and swung with all his might. He connected with someone's jaw and felt a wild surge of delight as the man cried out and tumbled away, falling with a crash, somewhere out of his sight.

Then he sank back, exhausted, but exhilarated. Until he heard the man speak.

"Jesus!" Leigh said, picking himself up off the floor. "What the devil did you give him?"

"Laudanum," another man said in a worried voice. "Brandy when he woke the first time. Laudanum, the second. This has never happened before. I hope we won't have to restrain him."

No restraints! Alasdair tried to shout, struggling to wake. He managed to pry open an eye. His eye burned, his vision wavered, but he recognized Leigh standing, looking down at him.

"No restraints," Alasdair croaked. "I won't do it again. Leigh? That is you? I'm not dreaming?"

"Want me to punch you to be sure?" Leigh said sourly. "No, you're not dreaming. I wish I was, though." He touched his jaw, flexed it, and winced. "Gads, that's lucky, it still works. I thought you'd broken it. You can stop fighting. You're safe, old man. In your own bed, with a physician in attendance. You were set upon in the street. The Watch came running and startled them off. Well, startled one of them off. You polished off the other."

"Who were they?" Alasdair asked, clinging to consciousness.

"We'll find out. You rest now."

"What happened to me?" Alasdair demanded, because the light was fading, and he had to know if he would wake again.

Leigh understood. "You'll be all right. You had a blow to the head and a knife between your ribs. But the knife missed your vitals and your head is hard. Rest, sleep, let us do the work."

Vastly relieved, Alasdair nodded, and the pain of doing it sent him spiraling into the dark again.

* * *

"It's absurd!" Kate muttered as she paced around her room.

Sibyl watched, wide-eyed, from a chair in her cousin's bedchamber. Kate was throwing a fit. Not the sort of fit Sibyl was used to seeing, because Kate didn't shout, screech, or threaten, as Sibyl's sisters did when they were thwarted. But she was very angry and talking recklessly, not at all her usual, calm self.

"The man is hurt," Kate said. "He's sick. Lord, for all we know he could be dying! It happened two days ago, after all. He was supposed to go to the opera with me tonight, but of course he can't. I've gotten a note with his regrets—and it's not even written by him! What am I to think?"

She took another agitated turn round her bedchamber. "And I'm not allowed to go visit him? Why, if I was home, and he was a neighbor, I'd have been on his doorstep with a pot of soup two hours ago. *And* asking if I could help with anything else, too."

"But we're not in the country, and he's not a neighbor," Sibyl said. "Mama says it's a pity, but you can't visit yet, because if he's in bed, you certainly can't see him."

Kate glowered at Sibyl. "He can't debauch anyone; he's in bed because he's sick," she said through clenched teeth. "We are speaking of the milk of human kindness here."

"No, we're speaking of one of England's most notorious bachelors. And you're not the only one whose nose is out of joint, Harriet and Frances wanted to go with you. Because they think he might have some bachelor friends visiting him, too," Sibyl added fairly. "But Mama's right, Kate. If you go to his house, it will make things look more intimate between you two. If you were a married lady, it would be one thing. You could go anywhere. If your mother were here, you could visit with her. But my mother doesn't know him well enough to call on him, and you can't. You're a single female, Kate. It's just not done unless you're married or betrothed. So if you did go, at the very least it will seem as though you two have an understanding."

"We do!" Kate said. "It's just not the kind your mama means. You know that, if she doesn't. I've agreed to help him, and I'd think it would make him look even more respectable if I visited him now," she added in a burst of enthusiasm.

Sibyl gave her a long level look. Kate had the grace to look away.

"All right then, maybe not," Kate admitted with a trace of embarrassment. "But I have to know what's happened to him. All I heard is that he was set upon by robbers and left for dead!" She shivered. "I thought it was all country talk, but London must be a very dangerous place if a man like Sir Alasdair is set upon and almost killed. And in one of the finest districts, too! I can't sit back and wait patiently. I want to know." She paced another step, then turned. "And I shall," she said with determination.

"Your reputation will be ruined," Sibyl said. "And it will reflect on us. Mama will kill you, if my sisters don't do it for her."

"She won't. My reputation will be preserved and so will yours. I'll go in disguise."

Sibyl clapped her hands together. "As a boy!" she cried.

Kate gave her a look of disgust. "You really do have to stop reading so many gothic novels. Do I look like a boy? Can I walk like one, talk like one, behave like one? No. I'm not an actress." She was diverted for a moment. "You know? Every time I see a Shakespearean play I wonder that the audience doesn't giggle when they see *Twelfth Night* or any play where a boy acts like a girl pretending to be a boy. I mean, in his time all the female roles were played by men and boys, so a boy pretending to be a girl who was pretending to be a boy was probably convincing, and why not? He was actually just playing himself. But now it just seems foolish ... You know what I mean," she said peevishly, because Sibyl was starting to grin.

Kate marched over to her wardrobe. She flung its doors open. "I'll go as myself, but no one will notice. I still have clothing I wore at home. I think I packed everything I owned, even though I haven't used any of it because your mama wouldn't allow it. Just as well. I'm not interested in fashion now. I have good, decent gowns, for a good decent countrywoman," she said as her head disappeared into the wardrobe. She rummaged through her gowns.

"Aha!" she said triumphantly, drawing out a plain muslin round gown. She held it up for Sibyl to see. "This. And my old walking boots, the ones for rainy days. Still serviceable, and absolutely unfashionable. I think your mama would swoon if she saw them. But she won't. Because who looks at country girls fresh off the farm? I'll wear a kerchief, too, and walk with my head down. There's not a soul in the street who'll look at me. Even the servants won't, because they consider themselves of a higher class. And the upper classes don't look at servants, do they? So, safe all round. And so I *shall* see him, so there!"

"I'll come, too!" Sibyl cried, carried away by the idea.

"That you will not," Kate said as she drew her gown over her head. "Then your mama would kill me and

you. In the remote chance that anyone notices, that is,"
she hastily added. "No, I'll go alone."

"You can't. It isn't done!" Sibyl protested. "At least
take a maid with you!"

"No," Kate said, tossing her fashionable gown aside
and dropping the other one over her head. "I can't take
anyone, and I don't need to. Servants talk. Anyway,
servants don't take maids with them."

"It's dangerous," Sibyl wailed.

"Not at all. I'll go and be home in time for dinner
and no one will be the wiser."

"You yourself said London was dangerous."

"Yes. For someone who looks rich. Come, do I look
rich?"

Sibyl privately admitted Kate didn't look rich, in
fact she looked as though she might be seeking work.
Her gown was indeed an old one, not threadbare, but
its tiny pink floral pattern had turned almost white
from repeated washings. It didn't have a style or a
flounce, and was so thin the only shape it had was
Kate's own. Which was rather spectacular, Sibyl
thought with a trace of wistful envy. With Kate's mop
of curls, appealing face, and charming figure, ill
dressed as she was, she didn't look slovenly; instead
she looked quaint, adorably so.

"You'll be accosted then," Sibyl said. "You can't just
defy Society's rules."

"Oh, can't I?" Kate asked, her hands on her hips.
"Well, I have done, if you'll recall, and you encouraged
me to do it, too. And last time I did, it was actually
more outrageously daring, and I wasn't accosted, was
I? I didn't even know Sir Alasdair then, but I stole into
a room and interrupted a lady when she tried to trap
him, didn't I? I routed her, but I could just as easily

have disgraced myself if he'd a mind to have her. Or me! And after that I was alone in the room with him. It was at night, too, he didn't know me, and he wasn't wounded then."

"You don't know how wounded he is now," Sibyl argued.

"Exactly," Kate retorted. "That's why I have to go see. Last time I saved him. This time I'm saving myself from my conscience."

"Your curiosity," Sibyl corrected her.

"It's more than that."

"Why not just ask someone who *has* seen him? I know! Send a note to Leigh!"

"Alasdair may be at death's door," Kate said, picking up a kerchief and folding it in half. "What sort of friend would I be to sit back and wait for someone to tell me what's going on? If *I* were set upon, maybe left dying, and he didn't know, he'd call on me, wouldn't he? He'd want to know firsthand what happened to me. Fie on Society if it believes women are any less true to their friends than men are! He *is* a friend. I won't sit and wait when my heart tells me to go."

She faced Sibyl. "What's the worst that can happen? My reputation will be hurt? I'll be sent home? Much I care. My parents will understand, and I'm going home soon anyhow. No, the worst thing that can happen will be if he die . . ."

Kate's face blanched at what she'd almost said. She swallowed hard, put the kerchief on her head, drew it in a knot under her chin, raised that chin, and said, "I'm going."

Kate knew the way to Sir Alasdair's house because Sibyl finally told her—after Kate threatened to ask a passerby for directions if she didn't. Kate stole from the Swanson house, crept down the street in the shadows of the other houses, then once she'd turned a corner, marched briskly forward. She didn't slow until she'd gone three streets, when the exhilaration for her own daring wore off and she realized she was alone in London, for the first, and hopefully last, time in her life. Because now she *was* a little worried about being discovered.

It was a calm bright day, a little before breakfast, not yet time to pay morning visits. Even so, the streets were busy. Most of the wealthy people who lived in this district might still be indoors, preparing to step out to dazzle the world with their elegance. But that didn't mean that their needs weren't being served. Servants bustled about their errands. Strolling peddlers cried their wares, shouting about their fresh meats, fish, fruits, and vegetables, offering to grind scissors, mend pots, or offer other services to the housekeepers and butlers who ran their prosperous masters' homes.

Kate walked quickly. She kept her head down, more so when she noticed the looks she was getting. It seemed to her that those who saw her sneered at her. One thing was sure. She didn't see any servants dressed as badly as she was. Even the peddlers had a certain raffish style she lacked. She definitely looked as out of place as she was.

Only four more streets to go, she thought, and plunged on. But her pace slowed again. Now that she was almost there, she was getting nervous, and not just about being found out. Would *he* think she was rash, impetuous—worse, presumptuous? *Would he be in any condition to think at all?* The thought horrified her.

She remembered the queer feeling she'd gotten in her stomach when she'd seen his bruised knuckles. But this! It was almost impossible to think of that strong, commanding man beaten into submission. That smiling mouth, the memory of which kept her stirring restlessly in her bed, broken by a fist? Those intense dark eyes, always brimming with humor and hidden fires—puffed and blackened? The strong bones in his face broken—or worse?

It was almost criminal even to entertain the notion of how Alasdair might have been damaged. Kate had tried not to for the last two days. But he might have been, that was why she was heading toward his house. Still, much as she wanted to see him, just thinking about his injuries made her steps falter.

"Oh, my dear child!" a soft voice said. "Are you lost? In any distress? May I help?"

Kate's head snapped up. She froze. The woman who had spoken was so well dressed in the latest stare of fashion that Kate had to stop and think if they'd met before at any of the elegant affairs she'd been taken to. But she couldn't place that lovely face and was sure she'd have remembered had she even glimpsed it before. The woman was raven-haired, slender, of middle years, but still attractive, dressed in lavender to match her remarkable eyes. Her maid stood a pace behind her, watching Kate suspiciously.

"Oh. No, thank you, ma'am . . . missus," Kate stammered, remembering her role just in time. "Just gettin' my wind, mum. I been walking a ways. But thankee for asking."

"Have you lost your way?" the woman asked. "I shouldn't wonder if you have. London's vast and very confusing, is it not? Lud! I can remember when I first arrived here, indeed I shall never forget. It was nothing like my country home. I suspect it's the same for you. You *are* from the countryside? Perhaps I can help you?"

Kate ducked her head, ashamed of her imposture,

embarrassed because she'd troubled this kind lady, terrified that the kind lady might know her. "No, mum," she blurted, casting her gaze down, "I know where I'm bound."

"But you may have gone astray," the lady persisted. "Where *are* you bound, my dear?"

Kate was sure that if she said she was going to the Swanson house, that's where she'd be led. If the servants saw her, how could she explain her way out of that? Even if she managed to sneak back in the house, if she went there she might jog something in the lady's memory and be discovered for who she was. But she could scarcely pick up her skirts and run for it. She was almost at her destination, the lady would know that, so there was nothing for it but the truth. The truth—a wobbly little bow, a hurried "thank you"— and then she could be off again, with no one the wiser, she hoped.

"Sir Alasdair St. Erth's house, my lady," Kate said quickly. She ducked into a bow—and stopped short before she could move on. Because the lady was laughing merrily.

"I thought I was on to something, but I've come with too little too late. St. Erth, is it? Gawd love the rascal!" The lady laughed. "He could be on his deathbed—as I heard he was—and still be looking for a tasty morsel between the sheets. What a stallion— just as I always heard. I wished I'd believed all the stories, I could have sent him a rare bouquet to help him recover—or plant him under, but at least with a smile on his face. Who sent you?" she asked Kate. "Madame Birch? She deals in the country trade. Some men like them rosy-cheeked—top and bottom."

The lady's maid laughed with her this time.

"But I'd think a fellow who wasn't feeling up to par

wouldn't have the energy to break in a virgin . . ." the woman said thoughtfully. "Or are you not what you seem? Then was it Madame Johnston who sent you to him? Depend on it," she told her maid. "That old horror has all the actresses. A great mistake," she said, shaking her head. "Trust me, *I'd* never have sent him a piece like this one. A fellow on a sickbed don't need games, he needs a game bit of muslin who can get the deed done even if he can't move a muscle—a lass with ways to move at least one. Aye, a piece who can do it neat, slick and quick, by word or mouth, hook or crook, or handily." She grinned at her maid's fit of giggles.

"Now, me," the woman in lavender went on, "I'd have sent Violet—or Tansy, those two know more tricks than an organ grinder's monkey—and can they grind organs!" She laughed along with her maid. "Come, who was it?" she asked Kate, sobering. "I like to know my competition."

Kate could only stand gaping at the lady, who she now realized was no lady, but a bawd. But bawds were all fat, and old . . . at least the caricatures of them she'd seen had shown them like that.

The woman's eyes narrowed as she studied Kate's flaming cheeks.

"She don't know what you're saying," her maid murmured.

"Indeed?" the woman mused, watching Kate. "Then just why are you going to St. Erth's, girl?"

Kate had heard that London bawds accosted girls from the countryside, luring or even kidnapping them to force them into a life of sin. She'd always thought that was a fiction to keep wayward girls at home. Now she felt her bones turning to ice. Too late to bolt and run. Besides, that would cause a commotion.

"I am . . . I was . . ." Kate thought fast, looking up, trying to look dumb as a clod of soil. Which gave her an inspiration. "Begging your pardon, mum," she said, "but I were sent to help with his garden. Aye! See, I come to town with the others when our mistress, Miss Prine," she invented quickly, remembering the starchiest old lady she'd met in London, "needed extra help with her garden here. I've a fair hand with flowers and such, and when my mistress she heard Sir St. Erth was sick, she sent them that works for her to help where they could. Jem, he went to the stables this morning early," she said, praying Alasdair kept a stable, "Lizzie to the kitchens, and I were sent to help with the garden." She hung her head again.

There was a silence. The woman stared at Kate, obviously thinking hard. Then she smiled. Kate's stomach clenched.

"Well, my dear, if you find yourself weary of such backbreaking toil, I'd be willing to find an easier, more amusing, and better-paying job for you. Yes indeed, you could make a great deal of money. Simply call on me, in Clarke Street. Ask anyone for Madame Pansy." She lifted a gloved hand, raised Kate's chin, and looked at her. "I'm famous for the lovely flowers in my garden, and I believe you could be one of them."

Kate nodded, ducked a bow, and, heart beating like a drum, backed away. Then she scurried off.

It was a white-faced, subdued young woman who raised a shaking hand to sound the knocker on Sir Alasdair St. Erth's front door a short time later. Kate stood on the doorstep, catching her breath, and finally found the resolve to let the door knocker drop. Then she held her breath. She'd always thought she was capable, intelligent, and resourceful. But she was very afraid of what she'd learn here. And now she was also too frightened to run away.

13

"The servants' entrance is in back," the butler said, and slammed the door in Kate's face.

She raised the knocker again, her face flaming. When the door opened, and then immediately began to close again, she spoke up sharply. "I am not what I appear to be," she said, mimicking her cousins when they were being insufferable. "Do not close the door again, my good man, or there will be consequences."

The door stayed open. Kate went on speaking, but into thin air. She didn't so much as look at the butler, because she'd noticed that the finest ladies in town never looked directly at servants. "I am Miss Corbet, from Kent, presently staying with my cousins, Lord and Lady Swanson," she declared. "I can perhaps forgive your ignorance, because I realize I am in dishabille at the moment. When I heard of your master's accident, I was gardening, and not wanting to waste a moment, I simply came here at once."

Kate paused, head high, and prayed. She knew

there were more holes in her story than in any garden she'd ever seen, but hoped her name and attitude would carry the day.

"Sir Alasdair sent me a message," she added a little desperately, and then clenched her teeth and suppressed a silent yelp at the folly of the weakness of *that* lie. What if he couldn't have done that because he was insensible? Or worse?

"If you will wait a moment, miss," the butler said after a long moment.

He didn't ask her in. But he didn't order her off the front step. And he left the door open. Kate saw a footman peeping out at her, but stood rooted to the spot, feeling shamed, wishing she weren't so impetuous, while at the same time wishing she were a man so she could be done with this nonsense and stride right in.

The door swung wide. "Kate!" Leigh said in astonishment, looking her up and down, then looking to see who else was there. "What the devil . . . ! Is no one with you?"

"No," she said, holding her head high. "But I had to come and find out how he is, and no one knew, and no one would come with me, and it's not fair that I should have to sit and wait, like a ninny or a child, just because of some ridiculous rules of etiquette." She paused for breath, surprised to feel tears prickling at her eyes.

Leigh took her hand and pulled her into the house. "They aren't ridiculous!" he said, "But the devil is that the situation certainly will be if you stay out there. You came alone? And dressed like that? A disguise, I suppose," he said on a huff of a sigh. "Of all the foolishness . . . I thought better of you. If no one would come for you, why didn't you send for me?"

"Because I'm not a beggar. Nor should I be made to feel like one. Can't you see the folly of it?" she asked in exasperation. "That I should have to go to such rigs simply to see if a friend's alive or dead?"

He hesitated at the word "friend." "Yes," he admitted. "But, oh, blast. What's done is done. He's fine. He'll live. And so long as you're here, you may as well see him before I take you back. Which I will as soon as I can. But I think it might do him good, actually. If he's up to it, you can visit with him and see for yourself. Wait here," he said, taking her elbow and ushering her into a side room.

He went to the door and paused. "Who knows you're here?" he said suddenly.

"Only Sibyl," she assured him.

"Of course," he murmured, nodding. "The bland leading the blind."

"I *beg* your pardon!" Kate said angrily.

He chuckled. "Just wanted to see you look a little livelier. You do look as though you expected lions lurking in the woodwork, you know."

Kate thought she'd been very daring, and his criticism stung. "I just think that's a terrible thing to say about Sibyl," she said haughtily.

"Yes, it was," he admitted. "Unjust as well. The child can't help the fact that they try to keep her invisible, can she? Forgive me, and please don't tell her."

Kate nodded imperiously.

He sketched a bow. "Now, if you'll wait, I'll be right back."

Once he'd left, Kate's bravado faded. She hugged herself and glanced around the room. She supposed Leigh was right, she *had* expected the equivalent of lions in the woodwork, and felt curiously let down, because this was nothing like what she'd imagined Alasdair's home to be. She stood in a study furnished with a desk and a few comfortable chairs. Bookshelves

lined the walls, a few ancient prints of horses adorned
the cream-colored walls. The floors were polished, and
covered by faded patterned carpets. It smelled of
beeswax and lemon polish, and the lingering, faint
scent of past woodfires.

She didn't know why this commonplace room
made her feel both safer and sadder. Maybe it was because she'd envisioned Alasdair living in sumptuous
rooms done in tones of red, crimson, black, and gold,
instead of this simple masculine austerity.

"All right," Leigh said, interrupting her thoughts as
he came back into the room. "We've talked it over, and
he's convinced you're not trying to compromise him.
Come along."

"As if *I* . . . !" Kate sputtered. "I saved him from that
once, remember?" But he'd already turned and started
up the long stair. Kate followed, telling him exactly
what she thought of his estimate of her character, only
stopping when they got to the head of the stair and he
paused outside a door there.

"Alasdair," he called as he gently pushed open the
door and peered in. "Are you ready?"

"Yes," a familiar deep voice answered. "The opium
pipe's hidden, and the dancing girls have climbed out
the window. Bring in the human sacrifice."

Kate entered Alasdair's bedchamber warily. Now
that she heard his voice and knew he lived, she was
aware of how improper it was for her to be in a man's
bedchamber. Worse, to be going into not just any
man's bedroom, but Sir Alasdair St. Erth's! Then she
saw him, and all her apprehensions faded, to be replaced by a flood of shock, horror, and wrenching
sympathy.

She didn't notice the furnishings, but she'd got the
colors right. Her eyes were instantly assailed by red,

black, and gold. Alasdair sat in a chair by the window, dressed in a crimson-and-gold dressing gown. His face was battered, marred by vivid patches of red and black. There was a deep black circle under one puffed, half-shut bloodshot eye. A dark bruise spread over that same cheek. There was a scrape on his forehead, a scratch along the top of his nose, and crisscrossing stripes of red were etched into his long jaw.

He saw her reaction, and his mouth—untouched, she noticed with a surge of wild relief—tilted in a crooked smile.

"*That* bad, eh?" he asked.

"Oh, no—that is to say . . . Yes," she said. "What happened?"

"Do have a seat," he said.

Leigh indicated a chair opposite Alasdair. Kate absently sank into it, leaning forward as Alasdair told the story of the attack on him. The tale was brief and to the point, since he didn't remember much after he'd fallen.

"So I've a few contusions that will mend soon enough," he said. "And yes, the luck of the devil was with me, and so everyone will be sure to say. Because the knife slid in alongside a rib, bruising it but missing everything vital. Now it's just a matter of inconvenience, waiting for things to mend. The fellow with the knife wasn't as lucky. He didn't rise again. The other one got away."

"And it was all for your money?" Kate asked. "But I thought this was a safe district!"

"No part of London is entirely safe," Alasdair said with a shrug that made him wince. Kate saw how stiffly he held himself and realized he must be bandaged tightly.

"Should you be out of bed?" she asked worriedly.

"See?" Alasdair asked Leigh, "They all want me in bed, even respectable ones like Miss Corbet. It's like a curse, isn't it?"

Kate's face flushed.

"Now you see why it's not proper to visit him," Leigh said. "Under *any* circumstances."

"I've nothing to fear from him even when he is healthy," she said absently, her eyes never leaving Alasdair's bruised face. So she didn't see Leigh's eyebrow go up, and couldn't interpret the rueful look that came into Alasdair's one good eye.

"And now I hope you also see what a bad idea it is to travel around this wicked city by yourself," Alasdair told her with sincerity. "What made you do such a foolish thing?"

"Necessity," she said briefly. "And convention. How could I sit waiting for news, when I was so worried about you?"

"I'm flattered," he said, "but appalled at the risks you took. You should have sent word to me. Do you know the risk you ran—and not just to your reputation?"

"Well, now I do," she admitted. "I wouldn't have thought so, but the most awful thing happened on the way here!" She paused and bit her lip at the blunder she'd made. Now that she'd mentioned her meeting with the madam, of course they'd want to know about it, and apart from convincing them that she'd acted wrongly, she wasn't sure it was a conversation she should repeat to gentlemen she wasn't related to.

Of course they insisted. So, taking great care with her words, pausing to search for and insert euphemisms wherever she could, she told them about Madame Pansy and their meeting.

Alasdair had to stop laughing every so often, his

hand on his ribs, to assure Kate that the laughter was worth the pain it caused.

"It was brave of you not to take to your heels and run," Leigh said when she was done.

"Nonsense," Alasdair said with a grin, his good eye on Kate. "Bravery had nothing to do with it. She was too captivated by Madame Pansy's offer to stir a foot from her."

Kate shook her head. "You know? I think I *was*! Not captivated, but fascinated, I think. As well as horrified, of course," she hastily added. "But to be fair, consider: I couldn't run. I didn't want to attract attention."

"You were lucky," Alasdair said more seriously. "Because this *is* a good district. Mrs. P is famous, or rather, infamous. She has plenty of money, but even she hasn't got enough nerve to buy herself apartments here. I wonder what her errand was, but the streets are free. She's proud of her own sordid reputation, which is honest enough, in its fashion, so I doubt she'd have resorted to violence. But some of her competitors might have."

He looked at her gravely. "Tell me you'll never do anything like this again, please, Kate. I'm grateful for your concern, and I do understand how frustrated you must have felt at not being able to find out what had happened to me. I don't think I could stand to bear a woman's burden in society for one minute. But then," he added with a tilt to his mouth that wasn't quite a smile, "I don't bear many of society's burdens, do I?

"Yes, precisely," he answered himself more briskly. "And that leads me directly to our situation, doesn't it? I'm sorry, but obviously, I'll have to skip our appointments for the remainder of this week. Still, I mend fast. I hope to be able to continue to escort you here, there, and everywhere by next week."

Kate looked down at her lap. "Maybe. But your injuries will surely win you sympathy. Do you want to go on with this? Are you sure you still need me?"

She held her breath. She hadn't wanted to ask, but her newfound vulnerability toward him forced her to. It was only prudent. She hated being so prudent and didn't know what she'd do if he said no, any more than if he said yes.

There was a moment's silence. Alasdair gazed at her and tried not to smile. Her clothes were really appalling. She didn't wear a ribbon or a feather, and her hair was a tangled mop under that dreadful kerchief she had on. And yet though she'd been appealing before, now she was the most adorable thing he'd seen in weeks . . . years . . . longer than he could recall.

She looked charming. More than that, she looked available. It wasn't that her gown was indecent. It was so absolutely innocent of adornment it let a fellow focus attention on what was under it. Alasdair, usually the most suave of men, had a hard time not focusing all his attention on that. But he could scarcely ignore the fact that her breasts lifted high from her slender frame and swayed when she bent forward. When she'd taken her chair he couldn't help noticing her charming bottom. Clothes might make the man, he thought, they certainly changed his perception of this woman.

She looked like a simple countrywoman. Someone he could approach with honest lust because at the very least she'd be flattered, and at the most, would consent to a request for lovemaking. Raw as his wounds still were, Alasdair was surprised to find his body yearning—no—actually straining—toward hers. The pain he'd suffered must have weakened his usual self-control, he thought in astonishment, and was glad he was seated, enveloped in a dressing gown. He ached in every part except that one, although that ached, too, of course, if in a different way. She couldn't notice his discomfort. That, at least, was a mercy. Bad enough he surprised himself, he didn't need to embarrass her with it.

Yes, definitely. He still needed her. But not as she'd meant. He needed to take her in his arms, bear her to his bed, and warm himself at her warmth, seek her heat, and match heat for heat.

But of course he couldn't. Not now, wounded as he was. Not ever, damaged as his soul was. It was an inconvenient desire brought about by stress and circumstance. He'd deal with it by not dealing with it at all, relegating it to the recesses of his mind, where all inconvenient yearnings went. It wasn't difficult. After all, he had one desire—all else was always subordinate to it.

"Yes, I still do need you," he said mildly. "My reputation isn't established yet, not by a long shot. People feel sorry for homeless beggars, too, that doesn't make them socially acceptable. So, if you don't mind, can we go on a bit longer?"

"Oh well, then, yes. Of course." She hesitated. "How much longer, do you think?"

"It's hard to say. Is there any particular hurry?"

"Well, I never intended to stay until autumn," she said thoughtfully.

"Nor did I intend to ask you to. But a little while longer?"

She was studying his scrapes and bruises. She couldn't deny him anything now. "Fine," she said. "The Swansons don't mind, and though my parents miss me, as I miss them, they'll understand."

"Will they?" Leigh put in quickly. "They won't

worry because you seem to be keeping Alasdair company? Rumor will certainly reach them."

"It doesn't matter," she said. "I've written to them, telling them he's just a friend."

"They won't worry about his reputation?" Leigh persisted. "Or mind the fact that you won't be going home betrothed to him?"

Alasdair's dark brows went down, he shot Leigh a quelling look.

Kate didn't notice. "No," she said. "My parents aren't like my cousins. They're in no hurry to see me married and gone. We have good times together, I'm very content where I am, and they know it. They trust my good sense, too. And I *have* good sense," she said, paused, and added with a rueful smile, ". . . usually.

"At any rate, they know I'm having fun here, meeting all sorts of people, visiting and . . . Oh! Speaking of visitors," she told Alasdair, "I've gotten an invitation to pay a call on some of my relatives. They asked if I could stop by to see them. I was going to set a date because I thought I'd be leaving London soon. Now that I know I won't be, I think I'll just put it off a while longer. You remember, we were speaking about them just the other day? My cousins, Lord and Lady Scalby," she said to Alasdair's polite look of inquiry.

His body stiffened. Kate thought he'd felt a stab of pain because he'd jarred something, and was trying to hide it.

"Indeed?" he breathed. "And when was this?"

"Just before I heard about you," she said. "Are you all right?"

"I think Alasdair's just a bit tired," Leigh put in smoothly. "Sitting up this long is a strain. He'd never admit it, of course. But once he has no one to show off to, he might take a nap. Which is what he needs," he said, before Alasdair could speak. "So I think it's time we reckoned how to get you home, don't you think?"

Kate shot to her feet. "Of course," she said in embarrassment, "I just needed to know how he was, I don't want to make him worse!"

"*He* is not an object," Alasdair said. "You might ask him."

Leigh ignored him. "The problem is that even if Alasdair's reputation were fine—which it is not yet— seeing you delivered home in his carriage would ruin yours. So I'll call for a coach. No one will associate it with our friend here, or me. I'll take you to within a street of the Swansons, let you off in a quiet place, and watch to be sure you get home safely."

"That would be fine," she agreed. "I'll slip in the back door. Sibyl said she'd be waiting for me there."

"I'll send for a carriage, I'll just be a moment," Leigh said. He went to the door, and paused. "It's not at all the thing to leave you two alone," he said worriedly.

"It's not at all the thing for her to be here, dolt," Alasdair said. "And you were just proclaiming my fragility, weren't you? Go. The only way the girl will be compromised is if she attacks me. You won't, will you?" he asked Kate. "I'm so weak I don't think I could fight you off."

She laughed, Leigh shook his head, and hurried down the stair.

When he left, Kate did feel a little awkward. Since she didn't know what to say she took the moment to look around the bedchamber at last, and wished she hadn't. The room she was in would ruin any woman's reputation.

Alasdair's bed was massive, mahogany, with a carved headboard and fluted bedposts that held a great canopy suspended over it. The bed itself was piled with

crimson silk coverlets and so many pillows, it looked
billowy as the sea. It was a bed a person could sink into
and float away to sleep, or linger in, daydreaming, Kate
thought. She suddenly pictured Alasdair lying in it. It
wouldn't be too big for him. She could imagine his
powerful body eased by all the silken splendor . . .

She hurriedly looked away, her eyes sliding over
fine furniture and ornate draperies that edged the tall
windows. This was the sort of room she'd envisioned
him in. She tried not to picture him waking and sleeping in it. She could hear the clock on his fireplace mantel ticking. She wished she knew what to say.

She looked back at Alasdair, and looked away. He
was watching her. She didn't think a little pain would
matter to him if there was something he really wanted.
She wished he'd say something so she could stop
thinking of seduction. It was because he was always
joking about it, she thought. It was because she was always thinking about it, she realized.

She turned back and looked him in the face, and
was sorry she did. He was still staring at her, looking
at her hungrily.

"Kate?" Alasdair asked softly.

"Mmm?" she said, trying to look as though she
wasn't thinking any of the things she was thinking.

"Tell me," he said. "What else did your cousins, the
Scalbys, want?"

She looked confused.

"I mean," he said quickly, "though I need you, it
pains me to think I'm keeping you from your family
any more than I have to."

"Oh," she said, smiling. "Don't worry about that.
Remember what I told you? Any visit I pay to them
will be purely for appearance's sake. They won't care.
Why should they? I scarcely know them, or they, me."

"Didn't you want to remedy that here in London?"

She laughed. "You can only cure something that's amiss. I don't feel the need of them any more than they do of me. It's all for show. Why, they haven't written to us in years."

"They did invite you to stay with them."

"Because they had to. As the most senior members of my father's family, they're expected to. I knew better than to take them up on it, though."

"So they're patriarch and matriarch of your clan, are they?"

"Yes. Oh my!" she said excitedly. "I never thought! How foolish of me to prattle on about them the other night and never realize . . . How selfish of me! Whatever the strange stories one hears about them, they're world travelers, so sophisticated, they're sure to be important in the *ton*. Did you want their approval? Would it help establish you? I can certainly bear a visit with them for a good cause. If I arranged for us to meet them together, would it help, do you think?"

"Why, yes, so it would," Alasdair said. "I'd like that. When I'm recovered, of course."

"But right now, she must go home," Leigh said from the doorway.

"Fine, there's no hurry," Alasdair told him.

"I'm no longer so sure of that," Leigh said. "Come, Miss Corbet. Time to leave. Past time, I begin to think."

14

$\mathcal{L}$eigh cracked open the door and peered inside.
Alasdair wasn't sleeping, he wasn't even in his
bed. He still sat in the chair he'd been in when Leigh
had left with Kate.

"You can go to sleep now," Leigh reported, "She's
home and safely so. No one saw her. I'll be back
later."

"Come in now," Alasdair said. "I can't sleep yet, I'm
expecting a visitor or two. Don't scowl. I have to know
who attacked me and why, and I won't find the answers in my dreams."

Leigh came in the room, frowning. "What else is
there to know? My friends in His Majesty's service and
the redbreasts at Bow Street agree. The dead man was
a well-known villain with a dozen such crimes to his
name. The other was probably his partner, and they
know who he is. The only reason the pair haven't
swung at Newgate is because they're too efficient.

Their usual victims aren't as fit or well trained as you are, and so they've been able to dispose of them more neatly."

"Exactly," Alasdair said with grim satisfaction. "I wasn't their usual prey. I want to find out why I was favored with their attentions the other night."

"You were there, it was late, no one else was around. It was a crime of opportunity," Leigh said patiently. "The two of them must have been coming home from some enterprise in the neighborhood, or setting out on another, because they were far from their usual haunts. They happened to see you, a well-set-up gent alone at that hour of the night. They saw there was no one else around, thought you might be drunk and careless, and they dared. They lost. At least one did, and when the Watch set up a screech the other was too flustered to go for your money. He cut line and ran. A simple attack and theft gone wrong. What else could it be? Oh Lord," he said, looking at Alasdair's grim face. "Not *that* again."

"And why not?" Alasdair said quietly.

Leigh ran a hand through his hair. "Of course," he muttered, "I should have known. That's why you're pushing poor Kate into taking you to them. You think it was the Scalbys?"

"*Poor* Kate?" Alasdair asked. "I told you she would be unscathed."

"I begin to wonder. She cares more than you think, or I imagined. And even if she doesn't," he went on before Alasdair could disagree, "see how she almost compromised herself today for your sake? The woman doesn't do things by half measures. She's wholehearted and sincere. I wish you'd reconsider involving her."

Alasdair's face was too bland. "Again, I ask, though

it grows tedious. Have you an interest there? If so, I'll of course step back. But consider your answer carefully. I won't ask again."

Leigh was still.

Alasdair nodded. "Then, let it be. I'll see she comes to no harm."

"You actually believe they hired someone to attack you?" Leigh asked. "Why? Oh," he answered himself, "you think they got wind of your schemes and think killing you will save them?"

"It wouldn't. I've made provisions in case of my untimely end. But they don't know that, do they? And of a certainty they have wind of my schemes. I made sure of it. That adds the spice to the dish I plan to serve them."

"But if they're as dangerous as you say, then Kate . . ."

Alasdair cut him off. "They are," he said. "But not to Kate. She's only an obscure young miss from the countryside, a distant relative of theirs, so they've nothing to gain by harming her. Or perhaps they do," he murmured, his dark brows knitting together. "Or would. She *is* lovely. They haven't seen her for years, but they'd take note of that and find a purpose for her if they saw her now."

"Then for God's sake, whatever else you do, at least tell her that," Leigh declared, "and keep her away from them."

Alasdair frowned. "I suppose I must." He paused, thoughtful. "It changes my plans somewhat, but it won't be difficult. She didn't want to see them until she was ready to leave London, then she said she'd go with me. I'll forestall that. Kate's already served my purposes, she's gotten them to break their silence. I can do the rest alone. By the time I'm done with them they'll no longer be a threat to anyone. There's no point in frightening Kate if I don't have to, is there? I'll keep abreast of the situation, don't worry. I may look like I'm at my last prayers, but I can still protect her."

Leigh seated himself opposite his friend and looked at him gravely. "Alasdair, this passion of yours about the Scalbys borders on obsession."

"No, it doesn't!" Alasdair laughed. "It crossed over that border years ago. Don't fret, my friend," he added seriously. "I'm not mad. Or rather, I am, that's the problem. Mad, as in enraged. Not daft, not by a long shot, not yet. I need my wits for what I want to do and I've kept them sharp." He saw Leigh's set expression. "I'll settle this and move back over the border to sanity, all right?"

Leigh was silent.

"You don't believe me?" Alasdair asked. "You don't think I'm capable of rational thought when it comes to them? Then I'll try to convince you. If you'll be kind enough to interview the fellows I'm expecting, and find out if there's any news of the man that got away, or who sent him, I'll go to bed now. You're right. My ribs ache like the devil."

"I'll do it and gladly," Leigh said, rising. "I'm pleased that you're finally making sense."

"Oh, absolutely," Alasdair grunted as he rose with painful care and leaned on his friend's offered arm. "Because how else can I heal soon enough to see Kate again, and maybe this time, find out more?"

"I worry about you." Leigh sighed.

"That makes two of us," Alasdair replied.

Alasdair lay in his great bed waiting for sleep to join him there. He had hopes of it even though it was broad daylight, because he'd drunk an evil draught the doctor had given him to ensure it. There were important things to be done, but he knew this was the first. Sleeping would knit his wounded body and calm his mind so that he could be up and about his business again.

The draperies on the windows were drawn, the ones around his bed never were. He didn't like feeling as though he were sleeping in a closed box, that made him too vulnerable. Nor could he nap, drowsing away the afternoon as so many gentlemen did. A fashionable fellow would have a heavy luncheon, well fortified by ale or wine, then go to his club to settle in a chair for an afternoon doze, or return to his house to sleep until it was time to get up, dress and go out for a night's pleasure that would last until dawn.

Alasdair considered that a waste of daylight. Besides, sleeping by day gave rise to strange dreams. He also hated to wake disoriented, finding dusk where there should have been dawn. Still, the bed was soft, the sheets clean and fragrant. He found a position that if not comfortable for his abused body, was at least bearable. But when he closed his eyes, he still saw too much.

Was he too obsessed with revenge? Of course. Was Kate in any danger? Perhaps. He hadn't anticipated that, so he'd have to move quickly—when he could move again. Which meant he had to sleep.

He shifted to another position. Was he in any danger? That meant nothing to him. He'd been in danger many times before. It didn't matter what happened to him so long as he won in the end. Now he knew he would. He'd made sure the Scalbys knew it, too.

So, in effect, he'd already won.

That made their attack on him something he could appreciate. It hadn't been to stop him, as Leigh had thought. Alasdair knew them too well for that. The attack was to take revenge on him for what he'd done and would soon finish doing. But they'd failed. It was all over except for the celebrating.

So where was the vaunting joy? The exquisite reward for all his hard work? He didn't feel much of anything anymore, but he'd been sure he'd feel a rush of joy at knowing he'd have his ultimate triumph. He didn't.

But when he faced them at last and saw the knowledge of his triumph in their eyes, then surely he'd experience the exultation, the thrill that eluded him, the final taste of victory that was due him.

The doctor's sleeping draught began to work. Alasdair felt his body relax, his thoughts swirling, losing their tight focus. He thought of Kate, smiling as he envisioned her pretty face. A lovely woman, he thought lazily. Game, brave, and just unconventional enough in her thoughts and habits to constantly surprise him. Maybe, one day, when this was done . . .

His thoughts drifted back to that day when this would be over. He pictured the Scalbys' impotent fury, and smiled. But it was hard to envision that, or them, because he saw them both as they'd been when he'd last seen them, from afar, a few years past, and yet just as clearly saw them as they'd been, so long ago.

Lady Scalby was beautiful, he'd never denied that. Then, and now. That last time he'd laid eyes on her she'd kept to the shadows at the edge of the candlelight, as many older women did, to hide the traces of the years that her slender form denied. Hers was always a beauty that masked the rot within. She was tall and dark, sloe-eyed, with the sort of elegance that defied the increasing years. Slender as a stripling lad and strong as a racehorse, almost masculine, with those strong features and spare form, but altogether a woman, and insatiably determined to prove it.

Her husband was dark, too, but small for a man, and stocky, which might have been why he clung to the styles of his youth. That way he could have lace frothing over the back of his stubby fingers to hide them, and wear long jackets to conceal his thick body and lack of length of leg. Everything about him was hidden, except the strange look in his eyes. They were so unusually light they hardly seemed human. Alasdair had seen dogs with such eyes, but theirs held more humanity.

Lady Scalby's eyes were so dark it was hard to read her thoughts. But Alasdair knew them.

Their faces shimmered and shifted in Alasdair's own mind's eye. Yesterday and today blended as his drifting waking dream telescoped to nightmare. He saw eyes intently watching him. He squirmed, trying to escape them and what was fast descending on him. Sleep was coming, with familiar monsters to haunt it. It was unendurable. He wanted to wake, he had to leave the bed; but now, as then, he couldn't. Once again, he was sucked under and swirled down into unconsciousness, silently screaming all the way.

"Now are you convinced?" Leigh asked with a slightly smug smile the next day.

Alasdair looked doubtful—and exhausted. He'd made it down to his study under his own power. The strain showed. He looked at his guests with a jaundiced eye, but could scarcely help that since it was still only partially opened.

"Leigh tells me you think a personal enemy engineered the assault on you," the middle-aged gentleman sitting with them said. "I doubt it. Benny Lick was a bad man, but he and his partner always worked for themselves, never hired out to anyone so far as I know."

"And Lord Talwin does know," Leigh said. "There's nothing going on that our guest doesn't hear, Alasdair. He has his finger on the pulse of London. It's valuable now, but when we have a real police force—as we are working for—it will be invaluable."

"Oh, I agree." Alasdair said. "Not just because of what happened to me. London's grown too big as well as too poor since the war, there are too many hungry people in a city with too many well-fed ones, which is never a safe equation. A man's servants can't protect him all the time. Stationing pensioners and retired soldiers on our street corners won't work either, not just because the poor fellows fall asleep at night. They're too feeble to do more even if they were awake. Bow Street's useful, but only for finding villains after the fact. A municipal police would be good, and will come. But not in time to solve this. So. Are you certain of your facts, sir?" he asked the older man. "No one's caught the other rogue."

"No, he's vanished. Utterly. No one's seen or heard of him since the night you were set upon. They think when he botched his work and lost his partner he left town, if not the country. So when you're able to go out again, you should be safe enough, if you have some caution, like the rest of us. But you won't be able to test that theory for a while."

"But I intend to," Alasdair said. "I have promises to keep and appointments to meet. Since the late unlamented Benny's accomplice is long gone, I'll go about them more easily."

"Surely you won't be venturing out soon?" the older man exclaimed.

Leigh sighed. "Surely, you don't know St. Erth."

* * *

"And if you're wrong," Alasdair mused after Lord Talwin had left, shaking his head at Alasdair's folly, "and someone *is* after me, what better way to draw them out again?"

"You're mad," Leigh said.

"No, only half-mad, as usual," Alasdair said. "Lord Talwin was a gentleman spy, a fine one in his time. He knows the criminal mind, but he knows educated ones. Not those from parts of the city he never ventures in. I do. I have some of them in my employ. They won't speak to anyone but me, and they certainly won't come here to do it. I have to go to them, the sooner the better. If an attack fails, there are always other ways to annihilate a foe. Arson is one of the things that comes to mind. And I rather like this old place. Poison's another, and I've gotten rather fond of this old carcass, too."

Leigh nodded, half-convinced. Until he saw Alasdair's curling smile.

"*And* there's to be a ball on Saturday next," Alasdair said, "and I've promised a waltz to Kate."

One minute they were waltzing among all the company, the next, the music picked up and Kate was whirled around until she was giddy. She was delighted. Alasdair was recovered enough to come to the ball with her, and well enough to enjoy it. She certainly did. Dancing with him was delightful. She danced until her head spun, until the room swirled around her, her only anchor his laughing eyes. But when she finally stopped spinning in his arms, she found he'd waltzed her through a long door and entirely out of the ballroom. The music stopped, she looked around.

They stood on a terrace that ran the length of the house. Golden light leaked from behind the draperies on all the long windows that gave out onto it, and she could see by lamplight and moonlight that they stood overlooking a garden. There was a white marble balustrade around the terrace, twin white marble stairways led off and down into the garden beyond. Kate turned her flushed and smiling face up to Alasdair.

"We have three options," he said dryly. "We could stand here where we oughtn't to be, and block the way of other couples going where they shouldn't. We could go back inside and pretend it was the enthusiasm of the dance that swept us out here. Or, we could stroll to the end of this terrace and find a place where we can't be seen."

She stood absolutely still.

"You *did* say there was something you wanted to talk to me about?" he asked gently.

Well, yes, there had been, Kate remembered, feeling both relieved and disappointed. But now she couldn't recall just what it was. She was too dizzied by how quickly they'd left the ball. And standing alone in the dark with a man changed everything—with *this* man, she corrected herself.

He was formally dressed in black jacket and black satin pantaloons. He even wore a black patch over one eye. Everyone had joked about his resemblance to a pirate. She hadn't, she'd worried about it, because she knew what the patch concealed. It should have been too soon for him to be up and about, but his bruises were almost all healed, and his ribs must have been, too, because he moved with his usual fluid grace.

She looked at him, as worried about his health as her own peace of mind. Dark and dressed in black, yet in no way did he blend into the darkness. His linen was too white, his smile gleamed too brightly. She thought that smile was mocking, and that she deserved it.

"Yes. There was something I wanted to talk about," she said. She glanced down toward the darkened edges of the terrace. "But I thought you worried about my reputation."

"I do," he said, laughter in his voice, "which is why I suggested a darker location."

She nodded, feeling like a fool. But she took his hand and walked down the long terrace with him until they came to a dark place at the end of it. Then she slid her hand from his, because his touch made her senses fizz too much. She could see him clearly once her eyes adjusted to the darkness, but only the bolder expressions on his bold, piratical face.

"Now," he said, "what's the problem now, Kate?"

"My cousins," she said, and frowned, trying to find the right words. Even with rehearsal, it was difficult. The darkness, and being alone with him, made everything different.

"Your relatives? Which ones?" he asked, his voice suddenly less amused.

"The Swansons," she said, and thought he relaxed.

"Shall I have them removed?" he asked.

"I don't know that there's anything you can do," she said, ignoring his joke. "But I did think I'd ask your advice, because it might influence our plans. You see, they're trapping me into all sorts of engagements with men I don't want to see. They tell Sibyl they're doing it to save me from you," she said in frustration, "because you're too much for a simple girl like me to handle. But I wonder about their real reasons."

"You think they're jealous? I'm flattered." His voice was warm with suppressed laughter. "But they might have a point."

"I don't know what their reasons are, but it means I won't be able to see you as often as you'd planned," she explained. "Because, for example, I had to see Lord Markham yesterday, and I don't know which of us was more unhappy about that."

"Markham?" Alasdair asked. His voice let her know she'd shattered his lighthearted mood. "But he's a very bad man, Kate. I know, I'm hardly the fellow to say something like that. He has a deservedly bad name. Those rumors about his late wife are bad. I'm the last man on earth to credit rumors. Still, there are other stories I know are true. I could tell you more, but I won't. His reputation with women is not one I care to share with you. That should tell you enough. Your cousins shouldn't encourage him. Why the devil did you agree?"

"How could I say no?" she asked in frustration. "They said if I didn't, it would ruin Frances's day, because his friend asked her to go walking—if I went along, too, with Markham. So I was caught. It turns out Markham thought I had a fortune! Now, I ask you, where do you think he heard that? I explained the truth to him, but I think he thought I was just being coy. That's not all. I have to go to tea with Lord Fitzhugh tomorrow, because *his* friend is taking Chloe. I escaped before Henrietta came down this morning, or who knows who I'd have to walk out with next!?"

"Did you never consider simply saying no?"

"How can I simply say no to them? I might be able to deal with it, but my poor aunt! And Sibyl? It would be too cruel for them."

"You have a point. But I think you have it wrong. They don't have dark motives, they simply need you to go with them because the gentlemen wouldn't take them out if it weren't for you. Didn't that ever occur to you?"

"Whatever their reasons," she said, refusing to hear

the tender amusement in his voice, "my visit to London has not been . . . quite what I envisioned. I'm only staying on here now because of our agreement."

"There's a neat solution. When we're back inside we'll go over days and make appointments. I'll reserve your time in advance so you can safely turn down other requests, because of me. Let me play the villain, I'm used to it. I'll make a great many requests so you don't have to ever see anyone you don't want to."

"But if we see each other all the time, we really will have to become engaged!"

"All right. Then you have my permission to make any date for any day you want, and let me know later. I don't have that full a social calendar—that's why we're doing this, remember? Will that do?"

"It would. Oh, that is a relief. Thank you," she said, smiling radiantly at him.

She waited for him to say something.

He didn't, he just stood looking at her. He'd turned his back to the house, so she couldn't see his expression, only his outline against the stain of light that showed through the draperies in the windows behind him.

But he could see her clearly. She wore an elaborate satin gown the color of copper pennies. It had many flourishes, draping over her form, concealing everything and yet hinting at all he remembered seeing the day she'd worn that simple milkmaid's frock.

"Shall we go in now?" she asked.

"Shall we?" he asked slowly, in return. But he made no move to go. Instead, he brushed a curl back from her cheek, his long, cool fingers just barely grazing the skin at the top of her cheekbone.

It was an odd sort of caress, hardly a caress at all, tender and affectionate rather than passionate. But it made her breath stop. "I thought you were going to be mindful of my reputation," she said.

"I am. Oh, Kate, you have no idea of how much I am."

Now he stroked a curl at the side of her head. She knew that if she turned her head, her lips could touch that hand.

"I thought you said this was to be a mock flirtation," she said.

"So I did," he said, and moved closer.

He was so tall he had to lean down to let his breath stir her hair as he breathed in her scent. They stood like that for a moment. She felt his warm breath against her eyelashes and caught the scent of his shaving soap. It smelled like pine and berries. She closed her eyes so she couldn't see his face, so she couldn't be held responsible for what she discovered she most wanted him to do. And so she only felt his lips barely, fleetingly, touch her own. Warm, soft, they only brushed against hers, leaving a bright, tingling shock—before they lifted away again.

Her eyes flew open. "You said you'd do nothing to endanger me," she said, surprised how breathless she sounded, how weak her protest. Embarrassed when she realized what she was really protesting about.

"Yes," he said. "Do you feel endangered?"

But this sounded like a game to her now. "Is this a test? Are you trying to frighten me away?"

"Am I? Do I frighten you?"

"I thought you wanted me to help you reestablish yourself. So then, why try to confuse me?"

"Why indeed?" he asked, sounding surprised.

It shattered the moment.

He stepped back. "Forgive me. I meant what I said

in all sincerity. I didn't count on my own rude impulses. See what comes of meeting a man like me alone in a darkened place?" he asked on a forced laugh. "Instinct overpowered reason. But not for long, my reasonable friend. Come now, let's steal back into the house and forget this lapse of mine, will you?"

She nodded, because she didn't like to lie.

"But, Kate," he said suddenly, "believe me, I'd never endanger you. And if you should at any time feel awkward or unhappy about our agreement, tell me, and we'll be done with it."

"I'm not such a poor sport as that."

He looked down at her and said, in a tight voice, "Understand me, Kate, before you so flippantly agree to continue our bargain. It might be dangerous for you in other ways. I have a past, I have enemies. This last incident, I was attacked in the street. It put me in mind of it. It occurs to me there are people who might endanger you, as a way of spiting me. So. You still agree?"

"Of course," she said, troubled by this sudden earnestness. She realized that the attack had unsettled him, he sounded very unlike himself. He might be able to dance, but now she saw he really wasn't yet healed. It accounted for his worry, and maybe even for the strange moment they'd just shared. He'd been rocked, she saw that now. She did what she could to allay his fears; she had none, except for him.

"I think I'll be safe," she assured him. "I wouldn't have agreed otherwise. Unless, of course, you think your enemies will come snatch me out of my bed?"

"No. That's not my point. It's just that my incident, and your cousins' manipulations, made me realize you're vulnerable. I ask you to be careful. Don't go with people you don't like or trust. I'd never let them harm you. Believe that. But I can't be everywhere."

"So you *will* deal with my cousins?" she asked, striving for a lighter note.

"All of them," he said with no trace of humor. "I promise you."

He offered his arm. She placed her hand on it, and they went back to the door they'd left by. They waited for the right moment. Then she went dancing in with him, as though they'd been carried away by the music and then carried back in by it again, should anyone see them, dare anyone ask them.

But they'd been seen, of course. He'd counted on it.

15

Kate was very quiet in the carriage on the way back to the Swansons' house that night. She bid an absentminded good night to her aunt and cousins when they got home and told a disappointed Sibyl that they'd have to postpone their usual after-event discussion about everyone and everything until the next day because she was so weary. She was, but the truth was there were some things she couldn't share with Sibyl. She refused the services of a helpful maidservant, went into her room, and closed the door firmly behind her.

Now she had time to reflect on what Alasdair had done. It hadn't been much. He'd only let her know that he was a man and she was a woman he desired, if only for a moment. But that was more than enough for her. She was surprised, shocked, flattered, titillated, and deeply concerned about it.

It was like having a dear friend turn on you, she thought as she stripped off her gown. . . . It was not, she realized as she lay it down slowly. Because Alasdair St. Erth hadn't turned at all, he'd simply gone straight down the path his life was set upon. She'd always known who and what he was. He'd never denied it. And though he made her laugh, and their ideas often meshed, he wasn't really a friend, and if she'd deluded herself about that when she'd agreed to his odd bargain, there was no way she could anymore.

Kate went to the pitcher and bowl on her dresser and washed herself vigorously. Then she slid her nightdress over her head, turned down the lamp, sank to her bed, and sat quietly, hands in her lap. She remembered how still he'd grown, the air of expectation that had vibrated between them, the feather-light touch on her cheek, the soft kiss that was as much an inquiry as an advance. She hadn't known the answer to his silent question, or if she had, hadn't dared give it. But one thing was clear. In that moment, he'd wanted more. He might have said he'd reverted to type, and maybe it was only that. But when he had, he'd wanted to keep on kissing her. And she'd wanted him to. Oh, how she'd wanted him to.

That simple kiss, that merest touch of his lips on hers, had set her senses fizzing, waking her to lusts she didn't know she had. She'd wanted to drag his head down to taste more. It shocked her that she hadn't as much as it shocked her because she'd wanted to.

There it was. It was really too bad she hadn't been as blithely impervious to him as she'd told him she was. Maybe she really had been then. Not now, not anymore, and she couldn't deny it anymore either. It wasn't just that he positively radiated masculinity. Not masculinity, she corrected herself. She knew many men who did that, from the local blacksmith to her own father. No. What Alasdair St. Erth radiated was something else. Something she'd never known, and only a man like him could do it—but since she hadn't done it, she didn't know quite what to call it and was sure a well-brought-up young woman wouldn't even try.

Her convoluted reasoning made her smile.

She absently ran a hand over her coverlet, smoothing it. The plain truth was that the thought of their making love had occurred to him, and to her, too. Her hand stilled. The blasted man *made* a person think of it. His face, those knowing eyes, his purring voice, the very scent of him. He entered a room, and everyone became his audience. He stood on a terrace in the dark with a woman, and made her wish it were darker so she could blind herself to the truth of the night and bury herself in the unknown splendor she might discover in his dark embrace.

Kate shivered at her own melodramatic thoughts, pulled back the coverlet, crept under it, and lay very still. She was a realistic woman. But Alasdair was a very dangerous fellow. She was sure she had the self-control to prevent anything of the sort ever happening again, of course. After all, apart from considering herself a moral person, she believed in hard facts, and they were all on morality's side.

He'd always been honest with her. Except for his one lapse tonight, his interest in her was solely his interest in their charade. He trusted her not to be attracted to him, not take anything he said or did seriously as he pretended to be courting her. He wanted to be reestablished in society. He would be. Then he'd look for a wealthy titled woman to wed, as men of his kind and class did. Whatever his pleasures were—and she'd thought about them much too often— he wouldn't take them with a respectable young woman from the countryside. That thought was a relief as well as a sorrow to her these days.

She'd be going home soon. However exciting love-making might be—would certainly be—with him, it would be foolish and futile, if not downright disastrous for her, if indeed, he'd even consider it when he was in a more rational mood.

Kate sat up. She actually ticked off more reasons on her fingers, to be sure of them. She'd want to marry someday. Her husband would expect her to be virginal. Even if she could somehow get around that, she couldn't dare jeopardize herself, because however pleasant Alasdair might find it, he could simply walk away when it was done. She might have to walk away bearing his child. Even if not, she'd walk away bearing his imprint, and she was certain she'd never be able to forget that, mind or body. She was running out of fingers when a thought struck her, and it made her want to strike herself on the head. Instead, she flung her head down hard on her pillow, as though that would drive some sense into it.

She moaned into the feathers of her pillow. However pleasant he might find it? *Alasdair St. Erth?* Apart from danger and the immorality of making love to him, the man was an expert at lovemaking. And the truth was that he might not find it pleasant with her.

Kate had a frank mother and chatterbox girlfriends, so she knew more about the mechanics of the act of love than many more sheltered misses did. Lovemaking entailed the removal of clothing, if it was done right. Alasdair would surely do it right. She looked down at herself, and saw nothing but coverlet. But she knew the geography of her own shape. Too well. Her body was not perfect. One of her breasts looked a little higher than the other, and though she hadn't seen any more naked women than she had men, her thighs were probably too plump.

The women he'd known were experts at the art of
seduction, they must certainly have better physical attractions. Her own experience was limited to the few
kisses and embraces she'd experienced here and there
in her career. Resourceful young men and women,
even if respectable, managed to get a *little* wooing
done. There'd been Jeremy Porter, but they'd been
much too young. Peter Price, who'd been much too eager. John McMasters, who'd been too clumsy, and Simon Fletcher, and he'd been impossible. But Alasdair!

Kate sighed. She might dream of his touch but he
was way above hers. It would be like an accomplished
dancer trying to teach someone who had seldom
danced a set of intricate steps. It could be done, but it
wouldn't be much fun for the instructor. Certainly not
half so much as dancing with another expert. Although, if a person had a sense of rhythm, it might
be . . .

Kate sat up straight. What was she *thinking*!

She stifled a moan. She was thinking of him, of being with him. Wondering what that kiss would have
turned to if she'd cooperated, what would have happened next. She needed to know, her body wanted to
know. It was buzzing with excitement just remembering that moment on the terrace, her breasts were tingling, her stomach felt strangely liquid and warm, and
her . . .

Kate itched and burned and grieved for her impossible yearnings. Alasdair was a *very* dangerous man,
she thought with sorrow and trepidation.

And she'd given her word to keep seeing him.

Well, she muttered as she gave her pillow a vigor-
ous thump and turned it over to a cooler side before
she laid her troubled head on it again, her word was
her bond. And that was that. She'd help him, then

clear out of London as soon as she decently could—in every sense of the word. She could only hope she could clear him out of her head someday.

Kate lay absolutely still in the hopes that sleep would eventually find her, because she was fairly sure she wouldn't find it very soon herself.

Alasdair strolled home from the ball alone, head down as though in abstracted thought, body tensed, waiting for another attack. He wasn't looking for trouble, precisely. Only looking to see if there'd be any. He could have taken a coach or walked with Leigh, but he was using himself as a lure to see if anyone was still interested in obliterating him. This time he'd be ready—and eager. The streets were empty, so there was ample opportunity, and he was giving anyone interested even more by seeming to be so lost in thought. He wasn't entirely healed, but mostly so, the thing that hurt most now was his pride. He was a master of revenge. He'd been surprised once, and wanted a chance at reprisal.

There were streetlamps on each corner and a lantern in front of every house he passed, still, as Alasdair knew too well, it wasn't really safe. London was a city of shadows at night no matter how wealthy the district. Streetlights and lanterns didn't dispel the dark. Instead, they actually lent deeper shallows in which to hide. He ambled onward. He had to go more slowly than he usually did, because the damned patch on his eye gave him a one-sided look at the world. It was there for cosmetic reasons, the eye didn't look good, though his sight was normal again. But he wanted to look unconcerned, and whipping the patch off when he left the ball would make him look too mindful of his surroundings.

He left it, and walked on. To anyone who might be

watching him he looked unarmed and unaware. He
was neither. But as he paced down dark streets nothing troubled him but his thoughts.

Those thoughts were of Kate. She was walking out
with the likes of Fitzhugh and Markham? Alasdair
scowled. Markham was rumored to have killed his
wife. No one could be sure of that, but everyone in the
know knew he enjoyed beating the women he bought
for temporary pleasure. And Fitzhugh had a hot temper and a cold heart. Surely Kate's cousins knew they
weren't the sort of men she should associate with.
What was their game? Were they so starved for com-
panionship they were willing to compromise their
cousin for a chance at a few moments in her reflected
popularity? Or was it something else? He'd have to
watch that situation more carefully.

It felt strange to be worrying about someone else.
Strange, but somehow right. In fact, he'd felt impelled
to warn her about another danger. He'd tried to caution her about her other cousins, the Scalbys. Instead,
he'd only hinted at danger and warned her away from
himself. He hadn't meant to do that. Hell, he hadn't
meant even to touch her, but she'd looked so damned
touchable.

He'd seen her upturned face, her lovely body, the
way she waited for him to make the next move after
he'd led her down into the darkness. She'd grown as
still as he had as the possibilities of their situation became clear. He'd heard muted snatches of conversation from strollers in the garden, the music from the
house faint and far away. But he clearly heard Kate
swallow, as she waited for him to make a move.

He'd had to touch her. He simply had to feel the tex-
ture and quality of her skin. He'd never kept such
steady company with a woman he hadn't touched. It

was ridiculous to see her so often and have to keep his hands to himself. She must have thought so, too. She stayed still, her eyes wide and her breathing rapid, obviously waiting, complicit.

Her skin was cool and smooth. And so then he couldn't resist the impulse to feel what her mouth was like. Her lips were pliant and warm, very sweet indeed. She hadn't responded. She'd only stood there quiescent, submissive. Thank God the very artlessness of her reaction had awakened him to danger, or he'd have gone further, though he'd never meant to. If she'd responded with ardor, he'd have been lost.

Alasdair's shoulders tightened at the thought. Passion not only muddled a man's thinking, it destroyed his ability to react to his surroundings. It was dangerous, it distracted a man, distraction disarmed him, and that could kill him. Fortunately his passions never overwhelmed him, because he never gave himself over completely, always reserving a part of his mind, always aware of where and who he was. Desire had always been a simple urge for him to satisfy, like being thirsty and taking a glass of water. He'd see an attractive woman, and react to her. She'd let him know by word or gesture if she was available. That was that.

His reaction to Kate tonight was different. It was swift, unexpected, irresistible. He'd found her attractive when he'd first seen her, but he hadn't felt an overwhelming spike of lust. He'd never have enlisted her help if he had. Alasdair smiled grimly. He would have. He'd have enlisted the Devil himself if it got him closer to his foremost desire in life. If she'd been of easy virtue he'd have used that to his benefit, too. But she wasn't, she was respectable. He'd accepted that, and thought that in enlisting her help he was safe from any entanglements.

Instead, he found her more alluring every time he saw her. He liked her, had come to know her, and liked her even more. And wanted more, though he hadn't thought of acting on it. Until tonight.

That was so untrue that he frowned fiercely. Things had come to a pretty pass if he was beginning to deceive himself. He'd been thinking about doing more for some time. Contemplating how good it would be to make love to a woman he liked. How nice to wake with one he still desired the next morning, and then make slow tender love again by the light of day so he could see as well as hear every breath of pleasure he gave her.

Nice? Good? Tender? Alasdair shook his head. Those words had never stirred his desires before. But Kate had. She'd done it to the point that he'd reacted without thinking. It startled him. And interested her. He was sure of it.

He wanted her, and that wasn't something he'd anticipated. He'd given his word not to harm her, and an affair certainly would do that. He smiled at his folly. An affair would likely be the last thing he'd get from Miss Kate Corbet—in every meaning of the word. Even if he'd given in to his inconvenient desire and had taken her in his arms to discover more, she'd have been upset and remorseful the moment she stepped out of his embrace. One didn't have affairs with women like her, one married them. Only this one man couldn't do that until his mission had been accomplished.

But it almost was, wasn't it?

Well, well, well, Alasdair thought, his steps slowing as he was struck with the notion. Once his lifelong mission was done, what better thing than to start a new life with a wife at his side? His reputation was tarnished, not utterly eroded. It was the plan he'd spelled out to her, he really hadn't lied to her about that. He was redeemable. And she was . . .

Alarm shot through his brain, his shoulders leapt. A streetlight was behind him and he saw a wavering shadow thrown in front of him—a shadow carrying a long stick.

Alasdair spun around, the pistol he'd kept in his pocket now in his hand, pointed straight at . . . an old man in baggy clothing. Who gasped when he saw the pistol, clapped a hand to his heart, and gave off a terrible loud clang that startled them both.

A *clang*? Alasdair froze. Stared. He was trained not to fire without thinking. That was a lucky thing. Now he saw that the poor old fellow carried a huge cowbell in one hand, the hand that he'd struck his chest with. He held a long truncheon in the other, which shook as he stared wide-eyed at Alasdair and his pistol.

"I ain't harming you, sir," he cried, throwing both hands up in the air. Alasdair winced at another loud clash of the bell. The old man dropped it and the truncheon. "I was just about to give you a good evenin', 'tis all," he cried. "I vow 'tis so."

Alasdair recognized him. The Watch. He'd seldom seen him off his high stool in the watchman's box on the corner.

Alasdair straightened, the pistol disappeared under his jacket again. "I wonder which of us frightened the other more," he said ruefully. "I heard your footfalls and thought you were about to attack me." But it was clear the only thing the old man had that could attack anything in any fashion was his heart.

The Watch, seeing that Alasdair wasn't going to shoot him, bent and picked up his bell and stick with unsteady hands. "A fellow was attacked hereabouts t'other week, and I bin keepin' a sharp eye. I was goin' to tell ye to do the same." He squinted. "Why, 'tis you, sir! How are you keepin'? No permanent injury, is there?"

"None," Alasdair said. "I sent a small token of my appreciation round to you for frightening away the villains the other day. Did you get it?"

"I did, sir, and I thanks you."

"No, I thank you. Have you seen any men loitering here tonight?"

"Nah. Not since the crime, sir. And I bin watchin'! Close."

Since it was all the old man could do, Alasdair nodded sagely.

"I carries a bell now 'cause some young rascals stole my rattle t'other night," he told Alasdair with some grievance. "How else am I gonna alert the populace?"

"Good point," Alasdair said, noticing that the populace hadn't poked one head out any door this time in spite of all the clangs and clattering. "That's the sort of thing that makes me sleep better at night. Carry on."

The Watch put a shaky finger to his forehead in a salute, bowed, and scuttled back to the safety of his box. Which would only be safe if some young bucks didn't come along and tip it over while he was sleeping. They always thought that was particularly hilarious because they were usually too drunk to see how vicious it was. At least Alasdair hoped so. He'd done violence in his time, too. But always for good reason.

He strode on, not as interested in mayhem as he'd been moments before. The incident had unsettled him, and now he felt strangely empty and cold.

It took another street for him to understand why he felt quite so empty. He'd stopped thinking of her. She'd glowed in his mind like an ember, warming him to the remnants of his soul, dangerously diverting him by utterly occupying his thoughts. That was why he felt so bereft. But that was easily remedied, he thought with a smile. Now he could at least plan on more than he'd imagined.

That would have to be later.

For now, he was anxious to be home. He walked faster, keeping alert. And so he saw a glimpse of a shadow that couldn't be cast from a bough of a tree in the wind or a cat slinking by. It was the size of a boy or a small man, and quickly dipped and disappeared back into the darkness as he looked at it.

Alasdair felt a shiver of expectation, a jolt of exhilaration. So, he was being followed. He doubted there'd be any attack. Whoever it was had surely seen he was fully prepared, and was probably wondering what other preparations he'd taken. And he was almost at his own door. He walked on, signaling his intent to his unseen footman, who, on his orders, had also been keeping silent pace with him in the shadows all the way home from the ball.

His footman opened his door for him when they arrived at his house. "I saw the Watch coming toward you, sir. But he wasn't dangerous, and you said as to how I shouldn't reveal myself unless you were in danger," the big young man said as soon as the door closed behind them. "Did I do right?"

"You did," Alasdair said. "Did you happen to see who *was* shadowing me?"

"Sorry, sir. He was too quick for me, but I think it was a lad. There's one who watches the back entrance most nights. It could have been him. We didn't do anything, because you'd told us to only watch. But if you want . . . ?

"I do not. Continue merely to watch him," Alasdair

said. "How else can we be sure of where he is? Thank you, Paris, that will be all for tonight."

When the footman left, Alasdair went to his study to pour himself a glass of brandy in silent celebration. His body was weary, but his mind was racing. He was exuberant, and very pleased.

Love was now possible, and that was a small miracle, but it could wait. If it was there at all, it would have to wait its turn.

For now, the important thing was that his plan was working, and the game was still on.

16

$\mathcal{A}$lasdair studied the fading bruise under his eye, in the mirror. Unattractive, he decided, but no longer terrifying to small children and sensitive young women. Or so he hoped. At least now he could leave the damned patch off. Both eyes were clear at last and matched in size again. The rest of his face still showed evidence of battering, but looked much better than it had a week before. At least now when people stared at him he'd know they were gawking at him, not his wounds, and maybe that look of pity would vanish from Kate's eyes. A man wanted a woman to look at him many ways, but not in sympathy. At least not this man, and that woman.

He smiled with anticipation. He was going to an art exhibition today. He frowned. He was pleased to be going to an *art exhibition*? He shook his head. But it would be amusing, because he'd be with Kate.

He inspected his jacket, his linen, his trousers, his hair, his fingernails. All immaculate. As he, himself, was not. But if skin could heal without scarring, he reflected, if human tissue could mend itself so nicely, surely then, a man's past could also slowly vanish. . . . No. It could not. But his outlook on life could be mended. His future could be cleaner, purer, better, so he could get on with his life, if he seriously wanted to.

Alasdair seriously wanted to—with Kate.

He hesitated, meeting his own sober gaze in the glass. *Was it really Kate he wanted?* He had to be sure before he committed himself to something so profound as marriage, because that was the only future he could have with her. Was Kate the one woman he wanted for life, for wife, friend, companion, and lover? Was she the one he wanted to give his life and word to, and then never have another? Or could it simply be that he hadn't associated with decent women for so long he'd forgotten how pleasant it could be to deal with a female as an equal?

Could there be other women who . . .

He smiled. Nonsense. It was Kate, he was sure of it. She was unique. She'd none of the practiced lures of the elegant women he'd met, and none of the coarseness he'd found in women who were not ladies. She had more than manners and education, charm and allure. Because, strangely, honest and pure as she was, still she matched him in some weird way. She awakened something long hidden in him. Something he'd once been. Whatever that was, he was the best he could be in her company. He found he liked that man, wanted to know him better, and be him all the time.

All for you, then, is it? he asked himself wryly.

Yes. And no. He wanted only the best for her, too.

How quickly she'd captured him . . .

He turned from the mirror. How quickly he'd have to move now to get on with the future. He hadn't counted on that. He'd been dragging his revenge out for maximum excitement. Now he realized he'd done it partly because he'd no idea of how to live his life without his omnipresent goal. Now he did. And so now he had to finish it, end the past, and start the far more exciting future life with Kate promised him.

Of course, other plans had to change, too. The grand denunciation scene he'd been playing over in his mind since he'd met Kate would have to be rewritten. Yes, the Scalbys had to be disgraced, but now not in public. Certainly not in front of Kate. He'd planned to call on them and let them see their denouement in her eyes as well as his own. Now that idea was impossible. It would hurt Kate. It would make him look bad in her eyes. And she might find out more than he wanted her to know.

She hadn't seen the Scalbys in years, and it was best that she never saw them again. Better that they learned they were through and crept out of town without her ever knowing—or meeting with them. It wouldn't be as dramatic, not half so satisfying for him; it wasn't the delightful scenario that had comforted him through countless nights. But it was one that wouldn't haunt her, so it would have to do. He was surprised to discover that though he disliked giving up the ultimate revenge, he could live with it. Because the Scalbys still couldn't.

Since the thing was nearly done, it was time for it to be entirely done. He'd set events in motion.

But as for today? Today he was going to an art exhibition. It was a fine day. Soon he'd be wandering around a stuffy studio in the center of London, crowded in with a bunch of fatuous people making inane comments about inferior paintings. *Wonderful*, he thought, and strode away so he could call on Kate, and do it.

* * *

"*Gone?*" Alasdair asked. "Where?"

"I thought you knew," Lady Swanson said. "The truth is that I was vexed with you, Sir Alasdair, for sending a hackney carriage for her and not calling in person to take her to the exhibition yourself. But Kate said you might be feeling ill after all your recent trials and so we oughtn't stand on ceremony. The messenger said she was to go in the coach and Sibyl should wait, because Lord Leigh would come for her on his own, and so he did, a half hour later, and now they've gone, too." Her eyes grew wide when she saw his expression. Her voice shook as the idea occurred to her too. "That *wasn't* your messenger? . . . or your coach?"

"Or my message," Alasdair said grimly. He looked around the salon. Chloe, Frances, and Henrietta Swanson were there, standing strangely still. Their faces showed excitement, not concern. That could be because of who they were and not what they'd done. Or it could not. Alasdair grew deathly still, though the blood beat loudly in his ears. He had to think clearly and carefully now. "But a maid was with her?"

"Of course," Lady Swanson said, "We are not lost to the proprieties."

"Neither am I," Alasdair snapped. "You might have done better to trust me on that score, madam. I wouldn't treat her so shabbily. My reputation may be dark, but I've never been said to lack manners." He brushed off stammered apologies. "That doesn't matter now. I'll go to the art gallery. If she's not there, I'll be back immediately. Don't leave this house, *any of you*," he said over his shoulder, because he was already on his way out.

* * *

Alasdair returned within the hour, with a grim-faced Lord Leigh and a very shaken-looking Sibyl.

"She never arrived at the gallery," Alasdair reported to Lady Swanson. "So tell me exactly what this messenger said, what he looked like, and what the carriage looked like."

"He was just a man," Lady Swanson said nervously. "One doesn't notice servants in the usual way of things, and there was nothing to notice about him. He was neither young nor old, fat nor slim. He said he was told to bring Kate to the gallery, on your instructions, for you'd meet her there. I didn't see the carriage."

Alasdair shot a look to the three elder Swanson sisters.

"We weren't here," Chloe protested, shrinking back from the fury blazing in his eyes.

"None of you looked down from your windows?"

"To what purpose?" Frances asked bitterly. "So we could sigh over how pretty she looked? You expect us to flock to the window to wave good-bye every time she steps out, congratulating ourselves on the success of our country cousin?"

"Maybe he thinks we ought to stand there twittering with happiness for her," Chloe muttered from behind her sister. "Maybe even brushing away our tears of joy as she goes out and we stay here watching her go."

The look in Alasdair's eyes was murderous.

"You're mistaking the matter," Henrietta told him with a twisted smile, "We aren't fairy godmothers, we're the wicked stepsisters, remember? Believe it, because we never forget it."

"Henrietta!" her mother gasped.

Her daughter ignored her. She kept her eyes on Alasdair. "But even so," she said, "we aren't responsible for this."

Alasdair looked hard at her. She raised her chin. He turned from her to the butler, standing in the doorway to the salon. "I need to know what color the coach was, trim and wheels. That at least will tell me which coaching company sent it."

"It was a commonplace brown, Sir Alasdair," the butler answered readily. "Undistinguished, as was the trim. At least the trim wasn't distinguishable, but that may have been because it was soiled with dirt and dust of the road. A simple coupe, badly in need of a washing, with two horses, both inferior, one dappled white, the other a rusty bay. The coachman had his head turned the whole while. I believed it to be a private coach and remember remarking that it wasn't the sort one would have expected of you, sir."

Alasdair's healing bruises looked darker against his suddenly ashen face. "And no one thought to insist she stay home instead of answering such a cavalier summons? Or at least thought of sending word to me to ask for an explanation, because the vehicle I sent was unsuitable for a well-brought-up young woman, not to mention the fact that my behavior was wholly inappropriate to a gentleman?"

The silence that greeted this told him what they'd thought.

"Well, then," Alasdair told Leigh harshly, "we have a kidnapping, it appears. You have your sources. I have mine. Let's try to find her before whatever demands are made arrive. They had the element of surprise; let's see if we can too.

"My lady," he told Lady Swanson curtly, "please send for your husband and ask him to meet us here in an hour. This is the best place for us to gather because this is where her abductors will send their conditions. Since Kate wasn't snatched from the street, we must assume this wasn't a random abduction. Since she's not wealthy and no one would expect her uncle to pay a high ransom for a cousin when he has daughters who might have been taken instead, we must also assume you aren't the intended victim of this abduction. I, however, do have a certain reputation. It is not undeserved. I have funds, as well. And anyone watching, as your daughters say they were not, would know Kate and I have been seen together often of late."

He turned to Leigh. "I'll put my staff on notice, too. It's possible that's where the ransom demand will be made. For now let's see what we can discover. I'll meet you back here in an hour's time." He paused on his way to the door. "Tell Bow Street, Lord Talwin, and any others you think might find her. Whether I get back here or not, don't stop looking for her. Be sure, I won't."

The coach rolled on. Kate sat quietly now. She'd stopped pounding on the window when the villainous-looking man shoved her shoulder to make her look at him—and the knife he held so close to her nose that her eyes almost crossed looking at it. He sat back when she fell silent. But he didn't put the knife away.

He'd been in the coach when she'd entered it. She wished she was the sort of female who screeched when she was frightened, but all she'd done was gasp when she'd ducked her head, entered the coach, and seen him sitting there glaring at her. Alice, the Swanson's maid, entering the carriage behind her, had gasped, too, but she'd been drawing in breath for a really good screech, Kate was sure of it.

But Alice hadn't uttered more than a groan as she'd slumped down to the floor of the coach, because she'd been struck down from behind by an unseen hand that then slammed the door shut behind them.

By the time Kate gathered her wits together enough to scream, the man sitting in the coach had half risen from his seat, gesturing with the long and horrifying knife, and growled, "Scream and die. Shut up and we'll see. Now sit down. And shut your trap."

"But Alice . . ." she protested, looking at the maid who lay facedown on the floor between the two seats.

Without taking his eyes from Kate, the man reached a hand down to feel Alice's neck. "She'll do," he snarled. "Wake with a sore noggin, but she'll wake. Which is more'n you'll do if you don't put a sock in your mummer, hear? Shut up!" he translated to Kate's look of bewildered dismay.

She did. The coach started up with a jolt that sat her down fast, which was as well because the muscles in her legs seemed to have turned to water anyway. She looked to the windows, but they were closed tight and covered with shades, so she couldn't see where they were going. That was when she hammered on them— and when the man showed her why she couldn't. She'd sat back again, not daring to breathe, or able to easily, because of her panic and the vile odor rising from the man with the knife. He smelled worse than any garbage she'd ever encountered, because at least garbage was disposed of after a few days, or melted away in the rain, which purified it.

Kate almost wished she couldn't breathe, but did, shallowly. She also wished she was the sort of female who fainted when she was terrified, because she couldn't think of how to escape and she'd rather be oblivious to whatever was going to happen to her next.

She tucked her feet in close to the seat to avoid hurting poor Alice further, and sat huddled in a knot in a hopeless attempt to vanish. She glanced at her captor again, then quickly away. He really was villainous-looking, far removed from all her notions of villains gotten from romantic fiction. He wasn't colorful or dashing, the way she'd thought of pirates—the way Alasdair had looked with his eye patch. Nor was he mysterious and dashing, like a highwayman—as Alasdair seemed when he dressed all in black. This man looked like a villain in the rude, crude, ugly way of reality, like a man who had nothing and so had nothing to lose by trying to get something.

She dared another glance. He was short, heavy, and dressed in ragged clothing that might have been brown when it was made, a dozen years ago. The seams in his somewhat simian face were outlined with grime, so though they made him look ancient, he could have been any age. His crooked features had been broken, but his eyes were small and sharp. If he touched her, she would die. She shuddered, as she realized with sinking heart that she wouldn't. Death before dishonor sounded fine, but death didn't come as easily as dishonor. She wasn't a screecher or a fainter, so that ladylike escape would probably be denied her, too.

But he didn't seemed interested in touching her, and that slowed her pounding heart to a mere gallop. They drove on in silence, but the argument going on in Kate's head was louder than the sounds of the carriage wheels on the cobbles.

She should have known Alasdair wouldn't behave in such scaly fashion, even if he had, she shouldn't have held herself so cheap, nipping into a carriage he'd sent for her like a maid answering a summons from her master. Ladies didn't do that—Alasdair wouldn't have done that either, she realized, feeling stupid and shamed. It was what people might *think* he'd do, but he'd always acted like a gentleman and she was well served for imagining even for a moment that he'd act otherwise. But she'd been so eager to see him she'd let what she'd thought of as his little lapse pass. So it was her fault, as well as a crime, that she was there.

The coach slowed. Kate felt herself turn to ice. It stopped, her captor tensed and crouched, knife high in hand. A door cracked open, a face peered in. Kate's captor relaxed. "The mort on the floor's the maid," he said.

The man at the door nodded, reached in, and hauled Alice out. Kate tried to stand on shaking legs, and sat right back as the door was slammed shut and the coach jolted to a start.

"Not you," the man with the knife said.

The carriage rattled on to its unknown destination again. They rode in silence for what seemed like a long time to Kate, though she realized her sense of time was distorted by her dread. Were they leaving London? But she could still hear the mundane, comforting sounds of the city around her. The cries of the street vendors, the rattle of other carriage wheels, the sounds of horses' hooves striking cobbles as they clattered by.

Their own progress was obviously slowed. Because her captor seemed impatient. At least he put a filthy finger at the edge of the shade on his window from time to time to sneak a look out the window, and frowned. It was a small thing, but it gave Kate unreasonable hope. Wherever they were going, he obviously thought it was taking longer than it should.

As time went on and nothing new and terrible happened, Kate's terror began to subside and she became more clearheaded. She tried to reason out her predicament logically. The coach would stop sooner or later, and though she wished it would be later, she'd better be prepared for what lay ahead. She didn't know if she could escape, but she wouldn't dwell on that. If she could guess why she was there, it would help.

She'd been kidnapped. But she didn't have money, so why should anyone bother? Unless it was a mistake. No. As ugly a customer as her kidnapper was, she didn't think he made that kind of mistake. But a man out for money would certainly take one of the Swanson daughters, and she didn't look anything like them. Even an enemy of theirs wouldn't make that mistake—most especially not an enemy, she decided. And she herself had no enemies she could think of, or any suitors so desperate for her hand—or body—that they'd have to take her in this manner.

The only explanation that made sense was that Alasdair was somehow involved in this mad start. Their charade might have been too convincing. It could be someone who thought there might be gain made out of asking *him* for her ransom. It could even be someone from that dark past he continually hinted about. Someone who wanted revenge on him, and would get it by making him bargain for her safety—or worse.

She'd had been thrust into a coach that was driving her to an unknown destination. The maid the Swansons had provided for her had been struck unconscious, then dragged away, leaving Kate alone and utterly defenseless. She was being held at knifepoint by as evil a man as she'd ever seen. But the fact that *Alasdair* would have to pay for her in any way was what she found really horrifying.

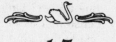

17

All bad things must come to an end, Kate thought as the carriage slowed to a stop again. But this time she worried it might get even worse, because her evil-smelling abductor rose to his bandy legs and gestured to the door with his knife.

"Out," he said.

The door cracked open. Kate swallowed hard, rose, and crept out the door.

The sunlight hurt her eyes, but she was relieved to note it was still daytime. She stood on the top step of the carriage stair and blinked, trying to see where she was through the tears the sudden light brought to her eyes. They were still in the city, but nowhere she'd ever seen.

She'd expected a noisome slum like the one they'd just passed through. She didn't have to see it, its odors had assaulted her nose and there was no escaping the sounds in the streets outside. Although she didn't know that much about London, some things could be deduced by simple reasoning. Good districts didn't have street vendors *selling* rags and bones and bottles. Even closed windows couldn't muffle the earsplitting calls of the criers peddling their wares as they rolled their barrows by, nor shut out the voices of pedestrians as they shouted, quarreled, and whooped at each other. Kate heard them more clearly when they'd paused in traffic, but the accents were so thick she could hardly understand what they'd been saying. What little she did understand made her glad of that. God's name shouldn't be taken in vain, but these people took it and used it any old way, along with ruder things in greetings, jests, and curses.

The noise had faded in the distance, and it had been relatively quiet outside the coach for a while. Kate knew it was too soon a time to have left London far behind, and felt some relief. She realized that was irrational, because terrible things could happen to her anywhere. But somehow the thought of being taken far from her cousins, and especially Alasdair, was even more terrifying.

She'd expected to see tenements or bleak warehouses. That was where a person expected a kidnapper to take them. But they'd arrived at a street of ancient cottages crowded together close to the road, the kind that might be found in any old, depressed part of the countryside.

"Move," her foul captor said, prodding her in the back.

Kate stepped down and walked toward the ramshackle cottage they'd stopped in front of. A door swung open, and, with a sigh that was half a prayer, she stepped inside.

At least the room she'd been locked in met all her expectations, Kate thought drearily as she looked around the tiny attic again. A chair, a cot, and a table were the only furnishings. She supposed she wasn't being deprived on purpose; there wasn't room for a stick more. The ceiling tilted so abruptly a person couldn't pace properly without crouching every seven steps to avoid being slammed in the head. She knew. Her head ached. The one round window was boarded over, a sliver of wood had been broken off to let some air in. Not much did. An eye to the space showed only a glimpse of a neighboring chimney stack and a tiny bit of mangy thatch on that other rooftop.

Kate hadn't seen anyone but her foul-smelling captor, and she hadn't seen him in what seemed like hours. His absence made some of her dread evaporate, because she'd been more afraid of anything he'd do to her than of having been abducted and locked up in a strange room far from friends and family. Much to her relief, though she could occasionally hear snatches of muffled far-off conversation, no one else came near her either.

Now panic gave way to annoyance. She felt more bored than terrified. She briefly marveled at the resilience of the human spirit, then set about trying to think of a way out. Her parents were too far away to help, and though Lord Swanson was clever, he had no experience with such matters. There was one person she automatically thought of as invincible, but in this, he couldn't be. She thought longingly of Alasdair— and almost gave in to despair, wondering if she'd ever see him again, wondering if he'd be devastated at her loss, or merely bemused.

No, she couldn't think that. Certainly he'd be horrified and furious when he heard what had happened. But powerful as he was, he wasn't omniscient, so it was up to her to save herself. She did waste a few min-

utes more imagining his reaction when he heard what
had happened, picturing the look on that dark face,
envisioning how he'd mutter a curse, tighten his lips,
and clench his fists before he leapt into action and
did . . . what? It warmed her to think how worried
he'd be, but she knew that worrying was all he could
do for her. And she certainly could do enough of that
for herself.

So it was up to her. She had to take it step by step.
She'd been stolen, that was the only fact she knew. But
why? What danger was she in? She didn't think her
captor had rapine on his mind. The mere thought of it
horrified her, but he'd looked at her with annoyance,
not lust. She couldn't be mistaken about that. The
thought of rape made her nerves jangle, so she further
reassured herself by doubting he'd been hired to deliver her to someone else for that purpose. None of her
admirers was so overwhelmed with lust as to steal her
away for their dire desires. Of course, one of them had
looked at her with unimaginable depths of desire, but
now they both knew he didn't have to kidnap her to
win a similar response from her. But who else . . . ?

They might have taken her for ransom money, but
she didn't have any, and everyone she met knew that.
She smiled remembering Lord Markham's face when
he'd found out, and didn't doubt he'd told everyone
he knew in revenge. Did they want to extort money
from the Swanson? If so, they could easily have snared
one of her cousins instead. But suppose they'd been
misled. What would they do when they found out she
wasn't worth much?

Enough of imagining terrors, she told herself sharply.
That won't get me anywhere. It might take days to find
out why she'd been taken. She didn't have minutes to
spare. She had to save herself because now even the

mighty Sir Alasdair was helpless. And so she began studying ways out of her predicament again.

The door was bolted. All she got from flinging herself against it was a sore shoulder. The boards in the window had been hammered in securely, and, besides, by the time she'd broken a fingernail and shredded a few others, she realized she couldn't fit out of it even if she could pry it open. Thumping on the floor would only bring up her jailer. But the window drew her. . . .

A little while later her efforts bore fruit.

The door swung open.

Kate blinked. It looked like her captor had taken a bath and shrunk. But another look showed her the small aggrieved boy standing there, hands on spindly hips, was as dirty as the larger version of himself.

"Now, whatcha wanna go and do that for?" he asked angrily. He opened his hand to show her all the bits of paper she'd torn from the little notebook she carried in her reticule, scribbled "HELP" on, and had been squeezing out the window for the past half hour.

"Ain't like no one can read 'em, even if they found 'em, silly bitch," he said. "They come down like snow in August though, so how could I miss 'em?"

Bitter disappointment combined with anger, it made Kate forget how vulnerable she'd felt moments before. Her only hope had been that her kidnappers would have been too busy to notice. But to have been discovered—and then cursed at. By a child?

"I beg your pardon!" Kate asked furiously.

"Well, yeah, right," he said approvingly, "you should. Anyways, I come to tell you to quit it or my da will get mad, and you don't want that, you don't."

The boy's face was almost as filthy as his father's, but his features weren't broken, only small and snubbed, like the rest of him. It was hard to tell if he was seven or twelve. Diminutive as he was, he was as assured as a man and had a rough gravelly little voice. He turned to go.

"Wait!" Kate cried. "I don't know how much you're being paid to keep me here, but I promise you I can get you more."

He looked over his shoulder and grinned. "Aye, more trouble, for certain. Get us scragged, is what *you* can. Won't do you no good. We already got paid, so we gotta deliver or we gets it in the neck one way or t'other."

"My family—my friends—can pay more."

"Yeah, yeah," he said in a bored voice. "That's what my da said you'd say. Listen. It's 'zactly like I said. It's our necks. Broken in a noose or wrung by a hand, don't make no difference, it'd be all the same to us. We don't deliver, we loses our reputation and starves—or worse. And if you does get free, then we gets to take the morning drop at Newgate. Nah. My da said, 'Don't listen to her,' and he's a leery cove. Now stop throwing things out the window, hear?" He began to close the door.

"Wait!" Kate cried again, such panic in her voice that the boy turned round.

"Don't worry. Your gettin' food, ain't about to starve you. Comin' right up, so stubble it, willya?" he said, not unsympathetically.

"But, I need something more," she said, thinking furiously. "I need . . . I must . . . go, you know."

He scowled. "No. What do you need? Ain't likely to get it, but you can ask anyways."

"I have to use the convenience," she announced.

He looked puzzled.

"Ahm . . . I . . ." She sought suitable words, since it was obvious the boy didn't understand the proper ones. Her upbringing presented a problem though, so she tried to explain the need and not exactly what was necessary to meet it. "I had a long ride here, I had a lot to drink this morning, I need to use the convenience, the outbuilding, the . . ."

"Oh," he said, looking nonplused for the first time. "Yeah, right. Shoulda thought. Hang on, gotta member mug downstairs, get it for you."

She looked blank.

"A thunder mug," he said in exasperation.

"Oh. A chamber pot? No!" she said with loathing. "I don't want one. I can't use it, you see," she said, inventing rapidly. "Wouldn't suit at all, not in my . . . present state." She fell silent, hoping the mysteries of female plumbing would embarrass or confuse him.

"Oh!" he said, light obviously dawning. "Flashin' the red flag, are you? Well, yeah. That could be a problem, gotta talk to Da." He turned on his heel, went out, locking the door behind him.

Kate, face aflame, stood waiting.

The door flew open. Father and son appeared in the doorway. Kate cringed at the look on the father's face.

"Use this!" he demanded, thrusting a chipped chamber pot and a filthy rag at her.

Her chin went up. Her nostrils flared. "No, I can't. And I won't. I have needs, but I have standards. You may kidnap me, but you cannot degrade me, or at least I suppose you can, but I won't be party to it. So if I become ill, I suppose it doesn't matter, does it?"

That caused some consternation. His face turned ruddy, even under all the dirt. After a moment's thought he growled at his son. "Take her down to the Jericho, and wait for her. Get her whatever she asks for too. As long as she can't use it to hurt you none."

"Aw, Da. Do I gotta?" the boy whined. " 'Tis a man's work for certain, aint it?"

"*That* it ain't," his father said brutally. "Listen," he told Kate, shaking a filthy finger at her, "he's little, but he's quick, and he knows his knife like you knows your needle. I give him orders. He'll cut you if he got to—and he'll sing out for me, which'll be worse, I promise you. Try any kinda rig, and you'll find out. Now go and take care o' it. Your only gettin' your way 'cause you're a lady, and I don't know much about 'em. But mind your manners, or I'll forget mine."

Kate nodded and, with stiff neck and flaming face, gathered up the hem of her skirt and stepped out the door, with the pair of them at her heels. She took a quick look around the cottage as she marched down the stair and down the short hall to the back. The room on the right was no neater than the one on the left, and had a rusted stove and a table. Blankets on the floor of the room opposite showed it was for sleeping.

"Hold," her original captor said, when they reached the back door. He rummaged in a knapsack until he produced what might once have been a doublet, a dress, or a shirt. He then made a great show of ripping it into long pieces, and handed them to Kate. Her face was so hot it felt swollen, but she accepted the rags, nodded, and allowed herself to be showed out the back door.

The tiny back garden was all weeds, and even they didn't flourish. A path through them led to a sway-backed hut at the foot. Behind it, a high overgrown hedge blocked all view of what lay beyond as well as obscuring the house on the left. The cottage on the other side looked abandoned.

"Well, go in," the boy said when Kate stood still in front of the dilapidated outbuilding. "And 'member, I'm out here."

Kate opened the door to the squalid outhouse, and took an involuntary step back again. It was dark, dank, and incredibly fetid inside. But she held her breath, marched in, and pointedly closed the door behind her.

"*Boy!*" she called imperiously, a few minutes later. "I need some more clean cloths. I *must* have them!"

"Aw, damnation!" the boy said angrily.

"Four," she called again.

"Four?" he asked in disbelief.

"Do you want to see why?" she asked, her voice frigid. Her next words seemed tinged with tears. "*I don't want to show you,*" she said miserably. "But I don't have any choice, do I?"

She couldn't believe the next words he used. When he was done, he grumbled, "Yeah. Anything else, Your Highness?"

"That will do," she replied.

Muttering, he marched back to the house.

She was gone when he got back.

But it took him several minutes to discover that, since she'd managed to wedge the door tight after she'd left.

They caught up with her a half mile down the road. They didn't make a fuss, they didn't raise their voices. Kate felt a prodding at her back, and then the father was at her left side, breathing heavily and glowering at her, and the boy was at her right.

"Silly blowen," the father panted. "Where'd you think you was going? Only got two directions. You wasn't going to scarper cross't no fields, you ain't such a clunch, after all. Still, we run upstairs and looked out a winder, and seen you right off. Now, shoutin' won't do you no good, 'cause the folk hereabout wouldn't care. And if they did, they knows it wouldn't do 'em no good neither. Not many folk live here no more, which is why it's such a good ken fer us. Now, face about and c'mon back."

Kate had only seen two people in her brief race for freedom, both looking old enough to likely expire at merely being shown a knife. She nodded. "You can't blame me, can you?" she asked in a defeated voice.

"Nah," the man said. "Can't. It were the best you could do, though, remember that. You din't need no more towels when you went to the jakes, did ye? I misdoubt you even had your courses."

She ducked her head. It had been a bold ruse, but a terrifically embarrassing one, and now she wondered that she'd even tried it.

He laughed. "Your a canny one, all right, nothin' like a woman's secrets to make a feller look t'other way," he said with admiration. "Sharky here's a regular jemmy fellow, and ought to have twigged to your lay, but he's still a lad. Still, he come for me fast enough when he seen you flown the coop, and he learned from it, so it weren't a waste."

Kate turned and walked down the broken walkways with them. "I can offer you more to let me go," she said.

"Aye, mebbe you can," the older man agreed. "But we got to keep our word or we don't never work no more. And our customer ain't going to cry rope on us, but your fine friends would, and you know it. Leastways, even if you don't, we do."

" 'I don't suppose it would do any good to tell you that though I am not wealthy, I have influential family and friends?"

"No, none," the man agreed amiably enough. "Like I said, it aint the gold, it's the job of work."

"So, you're going to . . ." she swallowed hard and her voice broke, "kill—uhm, *scrag* me?"

The man stopped short and looked at her in astonishment. "Nay, what are you going on about? We ain't in that line. We grabs, we don't put out no lights."

"But why?" Kate asked.

"Not for us to know, or me to say even if I did," the man said primly, as he started walking again, and pulled her along.

"But we ain't got nothin' against you," Sharky put in quickly, looking a bit upset, because Kate's eyes had begun to fill with tears.

She was astonished at her own tears and the boy's reaction to them. She almost never wept, and refused to use them to win an argument, because she had three brothers and felt, as they did, that it was poor sportsmanship. But tears had done what her logic and guile had not. Both father and son were obviously disturbed by them. They were looking grim when they weren't trying to look away. She'd invented one set of female difficulties for a chance at escape, she could certainly invent feminine frailties for the possibility of another.

"It's hard to be stolen away from my friends and family," she said brokenly, swiping at her eyes with one hand, because now that she'd allowed herself to use them the tears were easier to summon. "It's not just because I'm frightened—though I am. But my cousins, the Swansons, are so good to me, Lady Swanson will be devastated by this, and my uncle, unmanned. And my . . . friend, Sir Alasdair, will be distraught."

That was the wrong note. She didn't know why, but father and son exchanged a look, and it was smug and knowing.

"I wonder if I'll ever see my mother and father and my three little brothers again," she went on, letting the tears roll freely down her cheeks. "They sent me to London so I could see the great city, but they're simple country folk. They won't understand. Who could so dislike me as to cause them—and me—such pain?"

"Can't say," the man said abruptly. "C'mon. Tell you what," he added as she bravely gulped back a sob, then let out another, "cuppa tea be just the thing. We'll fix one for you. Aye. You gotta eat, but no one said you gotta do it by your lonesome."

He was as good as his word.

They let her sit at the tilted table while the father brewed tea. The son took a pack they'd stowed under the table and dug out a slightly green haunch of mutton, a hacked-up loaf of bread, and a slab of cheese. Kate wiped her tears and offered to help, but they just looked at her strangely before going on with their chores.

"You could fix your hair," the boy remarked, looking up from where he was placing the cheese on a cracked plate. "You look a regular Blowsabella."

Her hands flew to her hair. *"Blowsabella?"* she asked as she tried to comb her unruly curls into some order with her fingers.

"Aye, it's a word we use for a lass what got hair what looks like a rag doll," the father said, with an actual smile in his voice.

Kate took heart. "Oh. That's why, when you stopped me from running just now, you called me a '*blowen*'?"

Both father and son froze and exchanged a guilty look.

"Nay," the father said curtly, turning his attention back to the pan where he was heating water. "Different word. *That* was because you're the . . . partikilar friend of a swell, a fine gent. See?"

"Oh," Kate said, "but I'm friends with a great many gentlemen."

"Nah," Sharky commented as he sliced a hunk of cheese, "he means 'cause your Sir Alasdair's doxie."

Kate shot to her feet. "I should say not!" she said

angrily. "No such thing! Why, I'm no man's . . . mistress. There, I've said it plainly," she added, her face flaming. "There's nothing I can do about you abducting me, but I don't have to listen to such claptrap. Why," she added, tilting her head to the side, "did those who paid you to do this tell you that? Well, if they did, it's a lie.

"Do you think that matters?' she asked hopefully. "I mean, will it change things? Because if it's some woman who has plans for Sir Alasdair, and believe me, many do," she added, as a sudden vision of the spiteful Lady Eleanora flashed into her mind, as well as a horrifying image of the three spiteful females she was now living with. "Since it's not so, maybe you could tell them that and they'd agree to have you let me go? Because I'm not Sir Alasdair's *particular* friend in that sense at all. I never would or could be," she added with regret, in spite of her efforts to be neutral.

Her two captors didn't miss it.

"Ain't ours to ask," the boy said, but he looked at his father as he did.

"No, it ain't," his father said roughly. "Now, have a cuppa, and some to eat, and you'll feel more the thing."

"But how can I?" she asked, real tears back in her eyes.

"Eatin's got nothing to do with feeling," he said. "Just makes you feel better. Eat," he added, not ungently. "It'll help your mind work so's you can try to outfox us and lope off again."

He flashed a crooked yellowed smile at her, but it was a curiously winning one, and she had to smile back, through her tears.

"All right," she said. "But I must wash my hands."

He laughed. "A good try! But that won't help you do nothin' but get them clean, miss, for we ain't lettin' you get outside again."

"Getting them clean will help," she answered ruefully, holding up both hands to show them how dirty they were from her attempts to break out of the window. She lowered them, looking slightly abashed, when she realized that even so they were cleaner than either of her captors' hands.

The older man saw it, and read her mind. "Aye, but your a real gentry mort, ain't you? We could grow flowers on our mitts and mushrooms on our dimbers and we wouldn't mind. Sharky, get the lass some water."

The boy brought her a bowl of water, a wafer of tan soap, and a square of towel. Kate dipped her hands in the bowl and washed her hands, obviously thinking deeply as she did.

"This just doesn't make sense, you know," she murmured as one hand slowly rubbed the other under the water. "My disappearance won't matter to Sir Alasdair. Well, it will because he *is* a friend. But it won't affect him, or anyone, really, except my parents and brothers. I do have relatives other than the Swansons," she added. "But if anyone's thinking of them, that's folly. Abducting me won't matter much to any of them. They'll feel bad, of course, but I doubt they'll turn the world upside down to ransom me, I don't think. Because though I'd feel sorry for them if anything happened to them, I wouldn't be crushed, and neither would they be for me."

She dipped her face into her cupped hands. "So since none of my rich kinfolk would be *too* devastated," she said when she lifted her face, "who'd profit from this? The Scalbys are my most important relatives in town now, I suppose, at least the most influential. But since I haven't seen them for a long time either, why should they care either?"

She asked, but didn't look at them for an answer because she'd picked up the toweling and was drying her face. So she missed the matching startled looks of regret and fear father and son shot to each other then.

18

"'**E**'s gone to earth, Sir Alasdair," the little man protested. "Lolly's sloped off Gawd knows where. Mind," he added, "don't mean 'e done it or knows 'oo did. Just means 'e knows, like we all do, that you'd blame 'im for leaves falling in autumn. Fact, did 'e know who spirited the gentry mort away, 'e'd be the first to make profit from it from you, wouldn't 'e?"

"So he would," Alasdair said in a flat grim voice that made the little man back farther into the shadows of the alley they were meeting in. "But so he'd want me to think, too. And how did you know what I wanted him for?" he added a shade too gently.

"It's all over," the little man said plaintively. "'Oo don't know? You ain't got no ransom note neither, or we'd know that, too."

Alasdair bit back a curse. So much for preserving Kate's reputation.

The little man anticipated the next question. "'Oo knows who blew the gab?" he asked. "Mebbe a maid at the Swanson ken spilled it to 'nother, mebbe it were a footboy telling a friend, but it's out, and every rogue, bawd, prigger, and peddler in Lunnon's looking sharp, 'cause they thinks there'll be gold in it for 'em if they 'ears ought. So, 'o course, Lolly scarpered— 'e knows how you feel about 'im, don't 'e?"

"I believe you might know his whereabouts," Alasdair said implacably. "But I can't prove it. Could I prove it—or if I do—I tell you now you'd have to leave this country, or this earth, because I'll be *very* vexed with you for not telling me. Lolly has influence here. I have influence everywhere. Remember that, and if you get a sudden insight into the matter, you know how to reach me."

" 'Deed I do," the little man said, ducked a bow, and faded into the shadows.

Alasdair's shoulders slumped. He'd spoken to every snitch and informer, every gossip and news-gatherer he knew in Whitechapel and the Seven Dials, as well as those who floated throughout London, sell-ing secrets and surmises for money or favor. They all claimed ignorance of who'd lured Kate away.

The Runners had been at work, too. The carriage had been found, deserted. They'd found the maid, wandering about with an aching head. She remem-bered getting a glimpse of a man in the carriage with Kate before she'd been struck from behind. But she'd never seen him before and hadn't seen him well. Just a man, she'd said, a dirty, evil-looking man.

Alasdair stood in the shadows and bowed his head. In that moment his face would have been unrecogniz-able to his friends and foes, even to himself. He was shaken to his soul. He could deal with men who com-mitted crimes for profit, for money or personal re-venge, because he himself had gone that route and knew the levers and lures to use to manipulate and catch them in their own schemes. But if no one knew who'd kidnapped Kate, then it could have been a madman bent on rape or murder or both. No one could predict such people, they had no handles. There was no way he could find them or move them if he did, and what would happen to Kate? What had already happened to her?

He groaned low in his throat. He could imagine what might have happened. Too well. He could almost see it in his mind's eye—the man bent over her, after beating or threatening her to hold her still long enough for him to cover her and then, with grunts of triumph, pump his vileness into her while she ran away deep in her mind, where nothing could touch her, ever again . . . *No!*

Alasdair's eyes sprang open and he stared wildly into the dark alley, seeing nothing, his body shaking, cold with sweat. This was different, this was now, this was Kate. He couldn't allow himself to think that. He wouldn't. He'd not got this far from pandering to self-destructive visions. Picturing horrors didn't defeat them. Sickening as they were, they could seduce a man, lulling him into imagining he could rework and change the horrors that befell him, if only in his own mind.

Alasdair knew that route, that ultimate lie. It was really a sickness that made a man relive crimes committed against him. Rather than healing him, reworking the horrors became a way he could punish himself for not having been able to prevent them. That kind of thinking only destroyed his resolve, cheating him of any opportunity of winning. What was done was over, dwelling on it never changed it.

He wouldn't imagine Kate's fate, he'd fight for her instead. He'd search this damned city from sewer to palace, and find her. And if, God forbid, she'd been harmed, he'd cure her. If it took him the rest of their lives, he'd do it. He took a deep breath, straightened, and strode from the alley.

Sir Alasdair St. Erth was not usually seen at London's rat-and-dog fights, where huge amounts of money were wagered each night on which dog would kill the most and how high the stacks of dead rats would grow. Sir Alasdair was seen at them that night though. He dropped in on several of the most popular torchlit, crowded rooms featuring contests between rat and terrier. He didn't mind the stench of tobacco, sweat, and blood as he made his way through the crowded galleries, having a word here with a beggar and there with a bored nobleman. He didn't mind because he didn't notice. He was wholly concentrated on news of Kate.

He left with no news, but let it be known he'd pay for some.

Sir Alasdair was also spied at several exclusive gentlemen's clubs, drifting through the gaming rooms, stopping to talk, pausing to listen. He also visited some of the worst gambling hells, or best ones, depending on how mad a man was for the highest stakes and greatest risks. He wasn't a gambler, but he knew their ways and the games they played. So he waited until the croupiers were raking in their chips, gathering their dice or shuffling their cards before he asked questions. He left each establishment after letting it be known that he'd pay higher winnings for answers, and ask no questions himself.

The bordellos of London seldom saw Sir Alasdair. He usually made his own arrangements for pleasure. But tonight he visited a score of them, from the finest, those that looked like a lady's salon, where only the customers and upstairs maids knew what the merchandise was, to the lowest, where rows of curtained partitions couldn't hide the sounds and smells of the trade. In every one he left his card and his question. Every so often he'd grimace when he pulled out his watch and saw the hours ticking by. Each time he did, he also asked if there were any messages left for him, if any of the lads he'd hired to find him and tell him if there was news had left word. There never was.

Alasdair had spun an invisible web, an unseen network stretched across London that night. Kate's cousin Lord Swanson was making inquiries backstairs at fashionable homes where there were balls and musicales. Leigh was doing the same at the theaters, just as Lord Talwin was at the public masquerades. Other associates and friends of Alasdair's, as well as several of Kate's relatives, were at social affairs. They attended everything from public readings to prayer meetings, searching for clues.

Night was blurring into morning when Alasdair returned to his house. He paused on his doorstep for a moment and closed his eyes, hoping there'd be a message waiting for him there. It was the closest he'd come to praying in decades.

Alasdair hadn't slept all night, but the next morning the only evidence was the shadowing under his eyes and the grim set to his mouth. Otherwise, he looked like himself: spotlessly neat, expertly barbered, cool, aloof, dressed in his usual impeccable clothes. He wore a dark blue jacket and buff pantaloons, with high-polished boots adorned with small gold tassels, every inch the powerful nobleman. Only his friend Leigh could guess his pain, from the bleak and lost look in the back of his eyes.

"Nothing," Alasdair reported, as Leigh entered the study where he was sitting. "She may as well have dropped off the face of the earth."

"And no demands from her abductor?" Leigh asked.

"No," Alasdair said softly. "This is very bad, Leigh, very bad." He gazed out his window. "But perhaps it's not the worst. I've been thinking about it." Alasdair paused and laughed bitterly. "I've been thinking of nothing else since I found out about it. We've heard nothing, but some things begin to fall into place anyway. A madman wouldn't have plotted so well," he said, rising to pace the room.

"Or at least I choose to think so. Because some madmen can lay elaborate plans, and this certainly was one. Still, usually those men leave a trail—in advance of their actions. They don't suddenly take a fancy to a female and then go to such lengths to abduct her with this kind of finesse. Rapists snatch women on the spur of the moment. Elaborate plans are the work of rejected suitors or lovelorn admirers. They write letters, send messages to the object of their affections, pester them in public long before they resort to force. I'd have known if Kate had such an admirer. She'd have said something because the woman is nothing if not candid. Her family would have known, Sibyl, certainly. There was no such fellow.

"So," Alasdair said, locking his hands behind his back, facing Leigh, his face cold and set, "we're dealing with someone who's acting with some other purpose. An enemy, in short. Kate has no such enemies. *I* do. I have legions of such enemies, Leigh. That's Kate's misfortune, but maybe her salvation. Because her abductor must have seen us as we enacted my damned plot. He must have believed us and thought that taking her would hurt me. If that's the case, my knowing is important to him because if I don't know it and see what he's done, it has no meaning. So she may still be unharmed. I know how revenge works. Too well."

"But if that's the case, why hasn't anyone communicated with you?"

"A very good question, because it narrows the field considerably. It's someone who wants me to come to them, Leigh, someone who wants to see me beg and crawl, on their terms."

Leigh grew still. "And will you, if you must??"

Alasdair smiled, it was a true smile, if a weary one. "Would I indeed? I've thought of little else and so I can honestly tell you that if they demanded a finger of me, or a leg, or my liver and lights, they could have them all. They could open my veins and bathe in my blood if they wished. Not only because Kate's innocent in this, and I never intended to involve an innocent in my schemes to this extent—but because . . . I have a care for her."

It was such a cool thing to say after such an immoderate statement that Leigh almost smiled. But he couldn't, because he realized what an enormous declaration about the state of his heart it was for Alasdair to make. "And so who have you narrowed the field down to?" he asked instead.

Alasdair gave him a quizzical look as answer.

Leigh recoiled. "You made sense until now! Damnation, Alasdair, the world doesn't revolve around the Scalbys! Your obsession does, but that can lead you to look in the wrong places. You worked for His Majesty during the war. It could be an enemy you made in his name then. You've twisted noses in England, too. A man can't build your fortune without stepping on toes."

"Toes and noses, Leigh?" Alasdair asked with a small smile, "You're tangling your metaphors."

"Here or abroad, it could be anyone," Leigh went on angrily. "The Scalbys are old now, they're recluses too. Why should you still think of them?"

Alsadair's smile disappeared. "Because I promise you, they still think of me. I made sure of it. Because I have them now, and they know it. I uncovered their vile schemes, and best—or worst—of all, I learned they were enemies of His Majesty, too. Believe me, they think of me every day, every hour, as they wait for me finally to bring them to account. They're old, yes, but so is evil, and it's no milder because of it. They're no less a menace than old serpents hiding under a stone. Turn over that stone, and you *will* be bitten. I've been courting Kate because she's their relative. That must sting. I wanted it to, but I didn't know it would cause Kate harm. I thought even they would draw the line at hurting a relative. I regret that more than you can know."

"But she *is* their relative. So there was no need for them to abduct her. If they summoned her, she'd have gone to them."

Alasdair gave Leigh a patient look. "And I'd have immediately known who'd taken her, wouldn't I? Clearly, they wanted more amusement out of the situation."

"They say that madmen can involve the sane in their mad schemes because they grow so persuasive," Leigh said sadly. "Almost, you persuade me. What are you going to do?" A sudden surmise widened his eyes. "Give up your plans for revenge? That would be very good, Alasdair. It would be the making of you, I think."

"The unmaking, trust me. But I'm a serpent, too. I'll

win her back. It *will* cost me a lot, but I'll bring down their house even if I have to be in it when I do. I'll see her safely out of it first, though, I promise you."

"But what good will that do her?" Leigh asked. "Because I'm convinced she has a care for you, too."

"What good will it do her?" Alasdair shrugged. "If she discovers my whole scheme and finds out just what kind of man I am, it could do her much good, or at least that's what most people would say. They'd probably be right, too. But you underestimate me. I intend to win. It won't be easy. It will probably be very painful. Victory never comes cheap. Maybe Kate will never have to know. I'll go to them and negotiate. That will be the hardest part, believe me, because my self-respect and pitiful attempts at dignity will be demolished. So what? A man can live without dignity and self-respect. Just look at me." He chuckled. "That's just what worries you, isn't it? Stop worrying, I'm not done yet, I've more than a few tricks left to play. While there's breath left in me, they'll have no peace."

"But if you're wrong and they had nothing to do with this?"

Alasdair lifted an eyebrow. "That would be unfortunate, wouldn't it? Then I'd just be pathetic. Well, at least it will brighten their day."

"You'd degrade yourself so for Kate's sake?"

"I can't think of a better reason."

"She means that much to you?" Leigh asked. "Alasdair, that's wonderful."

"Wonderful? Hardly," Alasdair said with a sneer. "But it would be detestable if a man refused to save an innocent young woman if he had it in his power to do so."

"Wonderful that you've found her! You need someone like her."

Alasdair fixed him with a steady look. "Wonderful? When I've lost her?

"Only for now. I'm sure she'll be found, and then you'll see. She's perfect for you. Good, honest, and sincere."

"So she is," Alasdair said. "But a man can't rid himself of evil by associating with purity. That's like pox-ridden men thinking they can cure themselves by having sex with virgins. Nonsense. I'm not one of them, though my disease is as nasty and profound. Saving her won't save me. I'm the one who put her in danger. Whatever my feelings toward her, that was wrong, and must be righted."

"Can I help?" Leigh asked eagerly.

"Can you pray?"

There was one more errand Alasdair had to run before he committed himself to the most desperate one.

He stood in the Swanson salon, the three unmarried Swanson daughters staring back at him. Henrietta spoke first, her voice cold and hard.

"You insult us, sir," she said in response to his terse question.

"That's unfortunate," he said. "But may I have an answer?"

"You think we had something to do with her disappearance," Frances said, and it wasn't a question.

He stood silent, watching them. He'd been evaluating their answers, but watching their smallest movements for a clue as to how honest they were. They were three of the least lovely women he'd ever known. They weren't any easier to talk to than to look at, and even harder to confront. Now, for the first time since he'd met them, they looked vulnerable. He towered over them, they stood close together as though that gave them some comfort, making him realize that they were, after all, only three ill-favored women, and no one had ever given them the benefit of any doubt.

"I have to pursue all lines of inquiry," he said in a gentler voice.

"She came from nowhere with neither title nor fortune, but she became popular and it made us look even less so. We wanted her to go home," Henrietta said with dignity. "But we didn't want her dead."

Alasdair felt ice trickle through his blood. "Who said she was dead?"

"No one," Chloe answered. "But she's been abducted and gone a day. What are we to think?"

He had no answer because he refused to consider the question. "Think what you will. But please, if you know anything at all, tell me now."

It might have been the "please." The three exchanged glances.

"We've been asking, too," Chloe blurted. "We've given good money for answers. Servants know everything, and we've paid for information before. No one knows, Sir Alasdair, no one. She's vanished. We didn't—don't—know her very well. But we certainly wished her no real harm."

"You, however, encouraged her to walk out with some rare examples of British manhood," he said with a bitter smile.

"They were fops and fortune hunters," Frances said, her head high. "Not men who would ever hurt her—until they married her."

"Agreed," he said. He watched them for another moment. "Thank you," he finally said. "If you hear anything, you will let me know?"

"You believe us?" Chloe asked harshly.

"Yes," he answered. "You're far too clever to lie to me."

That made them smile. But they were the sort of smiles that made the sisters look even worse.

There was no more delaying, nothing more to be done except the one thing Alasdair least wanted to do. But he had to do it before he found an excuse not to. As he finally approached the Scalbys' town house that afternoon he found it hard to breathe freely, and his heart knocked against his ribs as though he'd run all the way. He stopped and stared at the prim gray building as though he were looking at a grim fortress guarded by dragons.

He stood rooted to the spot, a tall, powerfully built and handsomely dressed gentleman, standing in the street like a statue of himself. Passersby regarded him curiously. He didn't see them. He'd waited for this moment all these years, had plotted it through most of his adult life, but now that it was here he wanted to leave. Not only because it wouldn't be the triumph he'd sacrificed so much for. But because now that he was on their doorstep dreams fled, and he faced reality. He'd finally have to actually face *them* again.

He felt queasy thinking of the triumph that would light *her* eyes, sicker at the thought of the glee that would be on her husband's sly dark face. The only thing that stopped him from turning away was the thought of Kate and the possible danger she was in. Danger he himself had put her in.

It had been such a simple plan. But he'd been defeated because he hadn't bargained on Kate herself. Now he remembered an incident from when they'd first begun their charade. They'd been dancing, and she'd turned a sparkling gaze on him, and tilted a shoulder to indicate a pair of goggling tulips of the *ton* on the sidelines, watching them. "Am I making you respectable, Sir Alasdair?" she'd whispered. "Or are you making me a scandal?"

"Both, I suspect," he'd said. "Do you mind?"

"I've having too much fun to mind," she'd answered.

"Don't get used to it," he'd told her, "It will stop when they see my heart is pure."

She'd laughed in delight.

But even so, he'd felt a twinge of discomfort. "Does the prospect of scandal bother you?"

"It might," she'd admitted, "if I stayed here. No. Not even then. My friends would know the truth, and that's all I care about."

He'd been pleased by her answer while secretly amazed at her candor, and against all expectation, found himself worrying about her reputation. He should have known then. When had he worried about anything but his own business? Even so, it had been a waste of time. He'd been worrying about her reputation, never realizing he'd have to worry about her very life.

He drew a painful breath as he stared at the house he'd soon have to enter. If he had to sell his soul to protect her, he would. He couldn't begin to understand the force of his feelings, emotions that had been building for weeks, and they came to him in a torrent, blinding him to his own personal danger.

Danger? What danger? he mocked himself. Danger of his life? No. Only that he wouldn't get to throw their defeat in their faces. He'd finish them off anyway . . .

But what if the bargain they made was that he couldn't?

He'd agree, if he had to, he knew, feeling his heart grow heavier. He stared at the door, knowing he'd soon have to walk in and beg from his father's murderers. Because they'd slain his father as surely as if they'd used their own hands instead of forcing him to use his own.

Alasdair tried to assume an expression that might be cold and bland enough to deceive them. He was a master of deception, but it wasn't easy. He hadn't felt pain in so long. Now it threatened to unman him, because now he'd have to beg and bargain with his father's murderers and his own despoilers. Because they'd stripped honor and decency from his life just as surely as they'd destroyed his father.

He had to do it. For Kate and for himself, if he was ever to live easy in his own mind again. *Since when had he worried about living easy in his own mind?* He marveled at the power of his newfound emotions, and in that moment almost hated her for forcing him to this. But he had to save her though it meant he'd lose his heart's desire—both of them. Surely once he'd contracted with them he'd lose Kate, too. Of course they'd tell her all.

He had no choice.

He stood and stared at the gray house like a man preparing to go to his hanging. Just so, he told himself, and so it could be done with style and grace. Condemned men did it every week in London, walking to their deaths with devil-may-care smiles on their faces. If they refused to embarrass themselves before the crowd come to see how gallantly they could die, so could he. He had only to blind that inner eye of his, kill his emotions, freeze his blood and numb his expression so they couldn't guess how much it took for him not to scream. They must never guess how much it cost to swallow injustice, hatred, and pain, and meekly submit to them.

He could. He'd done it before. He could again. He must.

He was so absorbed in his own thoughts that he didn't hear the sound of someone running up to him until the fellow gasped, "Sir Alasdair? Sir? There's a message for you!"

Alasdair spun around and saw his footman, Paris, panting from exertion, holding out a crumpled paper to him. He took the paper and read it rapidly. "Who delivered this?" he asked harshly.

"A lad who turned and ran the second he gave it into Hoskins' hand. I was sent to find you and show it to you as soon as I could. I've been looking for an hour, sir. I was on my way to Lord Leigh's again, when I just happened to see you."

"You've done well. Now go home. I'll be back within the hour."

"Do you have any need of me, sir?" Paris asked hopefully.

Half the household must have read the note, Alasdair realized. They'd scented danger, why else would they send a strapping footman running to him, instead of one of the boys who'd been hired on for just such work?

"Not at the moment," he told his eager footman. "Thank you anyway. Now, go and have everything ready should I need to set out immediately after I get back." *If* I get back, he thought as Paris ducked his head in a bow, before he ran back the way he'd come.

Alasdair read the note again, as relieved as alarmed. It only told him where to go to discover more information. Considering the source, it might be a false claim. But it could come to something. He was momentarily reprieved. He didn't have to plead to the Scalbys yet. They weren't mentioned. And he had a clear course of action to take.

Alasdair turned and strode away, his long legs carrying him away from the tall gray house, his thoughts keeping pace with his wildly racing heart.

And so he never saw the parted curtain in a high window of the town house slowly drop back when he was at last out of sight.

19

The tavern was dark inside, even at midday. The smoke and haze never cleared, which was one of the place's attractions. A man could find never-ending night somewhere outside of death there—but not that far from it either. Alasdair ducked in from the street and strode inside, causing sudden silence as all the denizens of the place eyed him. He scanned every dark corner, looking for the man he sought.

But he wasn't there this time, nor was his giant bodyguard.

Alasdair went to the tap. "Where's Lolly?" he asked the barkeep without preamble.

"Gone," the barkeep said.

"So I've heard, but not from me," Alasdair said in a grim voice, putting the rumpled paper on the scratched and dented counter. "I've a message from him, asking me to meet him here."

The barkeep glanced down at the paper nervously. "Mebbe," he said. "But he ain't here to say no more.

And that's truth!" he protested quickly when he saw the look in his inquisitor's dark and angry eyes. "Look. You could ask Rosie, but I don't know who else could answer you—*would* answer you, now."

"Rosie?" Alasdair asked impatiently.

"My dear sir," a hoarse voice interrupted.

The barkeep, freed from Alasdair's glowering gaze, slipped away.

Alasdair turned to see a mild-looking man of middle years smiling at him. The fellow was bland, dressed in neat ordinary clothing, and had thinning hair and forgettable features. He looked like a second clerk in an inferior countinghouse.

"May I be of some help to you?" the man asked.

"If you can produce Lolly, then yes," Alasdair said. "I've come in answer to his summons."

The man shook his head. "Summons? He summoned you, sir? The very thing that was poor Lolly's downfall," he said sadly. "Presumption. He assumed far too much and presumed even more. How like him to have acted with such effrontery to a gentleman such as yourself."

Alasdair frowned. "You speak in past tense?"

"Oh, indeed I do. It's impossible for you or anyone else to speak to him now. Unless you are of divine origin. Lolly is off somewhere troubling the angels now. Or their counterparts, below."

"And you know this for a certainty?" Alasdair demanded.

The man didn't back away from that murderous glare. "I know this because I witnessed the end of poor Lolly's reign," he said softly. "One might say I precipitated it. But please, never quote me, for I'd deny it—vigorously."

Alasdair studied him. The fellow was too bland, too

cool, too forgettable. He'd met such men before. They were good at what they did, and what they did didn't bear studying too closely. Gang leaders in this district came and went. The only unusual thing about the business was the quality of the man who had obviously replaced Lolly. "Would you know anything about this?" Alasdair asked him, handing over the note.

The man scanned it, then gave it back. "Yes. A little, I think. You are Sir Alasdair?" At Alasdair's terse nod, the man bowed.

"Honored to meet you, sir, if under unfortunate circumstances. It may be I could discover more about this message, given the proper encouragement. Would you care to join me and discuss it?" he added, indicating a table in the rear. "I am Mr. Rose, but my associates call me Rosie.

"Had I known what Lolly was about in this instance, I'd certainly have delayed . . . the matter of his leaving," Rosie said as he settled in his chair at the table. "He was indeed, cut off in the fullness of his sins. But," he added, "that doesn't mean that with time and effort I can't discover all . . . for a fee, of course."

Alasdair looked at him with scorn. Before he could rise from the table again, Rosie added, his mild expression belying the sharp look in his colorless eyes. "I don't speak in vain, sir. I've taken over all of Lolly's obligations, so to speak. I have only to call in certain informants to know more."

"And you'll find out that quickly and easily?" Alasdair asked bitterly.

"No. But I have a good chance to discover all, if only because it's such an unusual crime, sir. You may not believe it, but it's not in our line. It's far too dangerous. Snatching gentry morts isn't our usual business down here. There are too many other ways to make money than meddling in the gentry's affairs. All of you are intimately related to the law in one way or another, if not the throne itself. We may relieve you of your watches, purses, and the odd jewel or two, but not your friends or family. Trouble the rich unduly? I should think not. That way lies Newgate, the topping cheat, or a one-way passage to the Antipodes.

"Everyone knows about your altercation with Lolly the other night, Sir Alasdair. It was one of the things that alerted me to the fact that poor Lolly was reaching too high and too far, and not paying attention to business. Personal feelings don't put bread on the table. Vendettas can be undertaken only with persons of similar rank. It's too costly otherwise, and our business is money, and with the least amount of risk. It's hard enough to fork a purse or fence a handkerchief, and both actions, though trivial, can cost a man his life. Taking a daughter of the gentry is simple suicide.

"Now, if Lolly was accountable for this, Sir Alasdair—and I don't know if he was, no matter what his note says—because he'd want to bedevil you whether he was responsible or not, wouldn't he? It might be that he did it, or it just might be that this was too good an opportunity to vex you for him to pass up. We heard about the matter almost as soon as you did, and everyone claims not to know a thing—although I'm certain I'd find out more if I were given encouragement," he added with a thin smile.

"But if it was Lolly's doing, then it looks like he was acting out of personal spite in this matter as much—or more—as for the gelt," Rosie continued, lapsing into thieves' argot. "Another mistake. Business should be purely business. And so rest easy, my dear sir, because since others involved in our trade also subscribe to that notion, I doubt the young woman has met with any harm—if she was taken at Lolly's command, and is being held awaiting his instructions. Which shall never come now. But I can take over the matter and settle it to your satisfaction, if you like."

Alasdair stared at him, weighing him. "*If* she was taken at Lolly's command," he repeated.

"Yes. And even if not, because I'll make every effort to find her, and that will be considerable. I don't intend to cheat you, sir. You have a certain reputation too, Sir Alasdair," Rosie said. "You're a dangerous man and a wily one. So I assure you that if she's discovered by your efforts before I can find and deliver her to you, I will, of course, issue a refund."

He paused, for the first time searching for words, his gaze wandering the room as he did. Then he leaned forward, fixing Alasdair with a steady look. "I ask only that if I'm wrong, and she *has* come to grief, that I not be held accountable for it, because it would not be a thing of my design or making. My men will not harm a hair on her head, I promise you."

Alasdair nodded. "Then we have an agreement. But you must know that I pay for information as well as for action, and just as handsomely. So since you'll have nothing to lose either way, tell me, do you have any idea of who is responsible?"

"Did I, Sir Alasdair," Rosie said sincerely, "I'd have had your money in my pocket a half hour ago."

Leigh watched Alasdair take another turn around his study, noting his friend's clenched fists, disordered hair, and burning eyes. "Alasdair," he finally said, "we've got everyone we know looking for her, as well as Bow

Street. Now you've got this evil Rosie person, too, and he must have his hordes of villains searching for her. So don't tear yourself apart. It can't do her any good."

"Tell me what can," Alasdair asked bitterly.

"Luck, I suppose. A warning from this Rosie person to the ones who abducted her. And good sense coming to her kidnappers, even if they don't get that word."

"Luck," Alasdair said with a grim smile, "warnings, and good sense. Kate has been stolen away, Leigh. Stolen and likely imprisoned and God knows what else as well. All on a fine summer's day, while she thought she was going to meet *me*! That eats away at me like acid, I can't think straight when I remember that. She got into that coach believing I'd be at the door when it stopped again. I don't want to imagine what she found instead. And I can't stop doing it."

He looked at his friend with rage and pain. "She was abducted by God knows who, and only God knows where she is and what's happened to her. The thing's all over town now, too. Everyone knows, so her reputation will suffer even if she hasn't." His face grew darker and he ran a hand through his hair in frustration. "I'd like to knock their gossiping heads together. It's madness how a woman's honor doesn't depend on her actions, but by what Fate does to her. Madness and cruelty. I never realized it.

"Leigh," he said, his eyes stark, "bedamned to that. The thought of what she might be suffering is near killing me. And it's my damned fault, and I can't do a damned thing about it!"

"Sir Alasdair?" his butler said from the doorway. "Mr. Frederick Loach is here to see you. Will you receive him?"

"Frederick, here?" Alasdair asked, looking up. "In the open? Then he has news. Show him in!"

The Honorable Frederick Loach stepped into Alasdair's study tentatively, letting his walking stick feel the way before him like a blind man worried about obstacles. "Good afternoon, Sir Alasdair," he said nervously. He slid a glance at Leigh but gave Alasdair his full attention. "I came here only because I thought it would be faster than asking you to meet me and . . ."

"Yes, yes," Alasdair said impatiently. "What news?"

Frederick shot another glance at Leigh.

"Lord Leigh has my full confidence, and so should have yours," Alasdair said, "get on with it."

"Miss Corbet was taken by a man in the employ of one Lolly Lou, a low villain from the slums," Frederick reported breathlessly. "I've been told you know this Lolly person and in fact were angry at him. It's thought that revenge for your humiliating him was his motive for stealing Miss Corbet away, since it's been noted you've been paying particular attention to her lately."

Alasdair didn't answer, but the look in his eyes obviously terrified Frederick.

"I don't usually come to people's homes, it's not a good idea for a man in my position," Frederick began to babble. "Secrecy's my hallmark, discretion is my byword, I keep myself least in sight for good reason. Talk about how I earn a few coins here and there isn't good for me, not for my occasional business, nor for my health, if you get my intimation. Because there are people who might be angry with me, but I had to let you know and . . ."

Alasdair lowered his head but raised a hand, like a referee signaling defeat. "Have done, I know. Thank you," he said. "Is there anything more?"

"No," Frederick said sadly.

Alasdair suddenly looked up. "At least have you

heard who this man Lolly employed may be? Or any word of where he is? Where she is?"

"No," Frederick said eagerly, "but I've irons in the fire, I've people listening, and as soon as I know, you shall!"

"Yes, thank you," Alasdair said, the fire in his eyes quenched. He dug in his pocket, withdrew a wallet, and handed Frederick a wad of banknotes so thick that Leigh's eyes widened.

"You have to pay your informants," Alasdair told Frederick. "This should take care of it, and you. I also know it's not good for you to be seen coming from wherever you've been and going straight to my house, so I thank you, and will understand if you must leave at once."

Frederick looked at the stack of bills in awe before taking them and thrusting them into his jacket. He bowed low. "Thank you for understanding my haste to be gone. I'll keep you informed," he added, turned, and hurried away.

"You paid him that much for news you had already guessed?" Leigh asked when he'd gone.

"But he didn't know that. Coming here was a brave act, for him," Alasdair said bleakly. He gazed out the windows that looked out on the street. The afternoon was growing darker than it should have been. "He frittered away his fortune, now he has to sell gossip in order to live. A man can only do what he's capable of, and if he tries to do more, he ought to be rewarded. A storm is coming," he noted absently.

A freshening wind was beginning to paw at the leaves on the trees outside. The sky was filling with fat black clouds, growing so suddenly dark it gave the pavements and buildings an eerie silvery look. Pedestrians were quickening their pace, with a late-afternoon thunderstorm clearly on its way.

"I must be going," Alasdair said dully, "if I want to miss the rain. It looks like it will keep on through the night."

"Where are you going," Leigh asked, though his friend's expression showed him the answer too well.

"To the Scalbys," Alasdair said with a shrug. "It's time. What else can I do? I've only rumors of Lolly being responsible and the Scalbys are the only ones I haven't asked. It's wrong of me not to, no matter my pride. It's the last door, Leigh, I must open it. Maybe that's all they want. Whatever else, I can't just wait. The longer I sit here, wallowing in my pride, the slimmer the chance that she'll come safely home. My pride," he continued, not letting Leigh speak, "should not go before her fall."

"Would you like me to come with you?"

"Thank you. But this, like dying, is a thing I'd rather do alone." He laughed. "Maybe it is better this way. It's time for the damned thing to be done." His eyes kindled. "But, by God, if she *is* harmed, they will die, no less than that, and that I vow!"

"Let me come with you," Leigh said decisively.

"I'll have to wear an oilskin, the storm's coming fast," Alasdair murmured, looking out the window again. "Wish me luck, Leigh. I'll not involve you in this." He strode to the door—and almost collided with Paris, who was rushing in.

"Another note!" Paris cried. "It just came, and this time the lad stayed, you can talk to him, sir."

Alasdair snatched up the note, and his face lit with wild joy.

"It's from her!" he said, as Leigh hurried to read

over his shoulder, "Or at least, so it says. I'll have to
see Sibyl and ask her, or would she have seen Kate's
writing, do you think? And then it will take time, because I'll have to show it to her mother and father and
sisters . . . No, first I'll ask the lad what the lady who
wrote it looked like. That might and answer all."

Leigh began to smile as he read the small even
handwriting.

My Dear Sir Alasdair,

*I have been abducted, but hasten to assure you I've not
come to any harm. Please come to the Excelsior, an inn
to the west, on the high road from London, near to Little Uckbridge, and ask for me. I don't wish to alarm or
involve my cousins, or ask them for the ransom. So if
you'd be kind enough to bring a fair sum with you I'll
see that my father repays you. Please come soon.*

> *I remain, sound in health, mind, and limb,*

> *Kate Corbet*

Leigh frowned to see that the word "*fair*" before the
word "*sum*" had been crossed out, and the word "*gud*"
written in instead, in bold, black, if uneven, lettering.

"A *gud sum*? Do you think she wrote it?" Leigh
asked tersely.

"I think I can't afford not to find out—immediately," Alasdair said. He strode to the door of the study
and shouted orders to his butler, valet and footmen,
calling for his oilskin, his carpetbag, his horse, writing
paper, and for a word with the messenger who'd
brought the note.

As his servants scurried in all directions, Alasdair
went to a safe on the wall, knelt and opened it, took a

sack of coins and a wad of banknotes, slammed the safe shut again, and rose. "A '*gud*' sum," he said with a ferocious smile, waving the banknotes in front of Leigh, "at least to show them." He quickly stowed money in various places on his person, in his waistcoat, jacket and trouser pockets, even stuffing some into his sleeve. "Never a good idea to keep all the money in one place," he told Leigh as he did. "This way even if you are robbed, some may remain. Ah," he said as his valet came in with his carpet bag, "Good. Now bring the set of silver pistols. Yes, and a small sword, the one with the vermeil pommel, and the Venetian dagger, I think."

The valet raced to do his bidding.

"But all that armory?" Leigh asked.

"I don't know where I'm going," Alasdair said as he bent to his bag, tossing out shirts and linen. "I'm not going to a ball," he muttered, "I need to fit this in my saddlebag."

Paris and his valet arrived with the weapons. Alasdair immediately slid the dagger down the side of his boot, and was stowing his other weapons in his jacket when his butler brought in a small, freckled, frightened boy.

Alasdair looked at the boy, who promptly turned so white his freckles stood out like pox. He gave out a small gasp. Alasdair remembered he still held his sword in one hand. He handed it to Leigh, and dropped to one knee so he was on eye level with the boy.

"Here, no need to take fright," he told the boy. "I've only a few easy questions for you. If you answer them right, you get a hot meal, some coins, and a comfortable ride back where you came. Now. Who gave you this note, lad?"

"A pretty lady," the boy said, biting his lip to keep his fear contained.

Alasdair spoke gently but he was large and dark, and his face, whether he knew it or not, was knotted in fierce concentration. "What did she look like, this pretty lady?" Alasdair asked.

"She had skin that was ever so nice, my ma said, and her hair was nice, too," the boy said, shaking slightly.

"Alasdair," Leigh said quietly, "let me. Your idea of gentle is a bit skewed now."

Alasdair stood up.

"First off," Leigh said to the boy, "where do you come from lad, and what's your name?"

The boy brightened. "Edward," he said promptly, "Edward Roger Babbage, sir. I come from the Excelsior, it's on the North Road from London, my folks own it and it's the best inn in all England, sir."

"Excellent," Leigh said, "I must stop there sometime. Now, tell me, how did you come to get this note?"

"Well, see, sir, there was these two who came to the inn with a lady. A man, and a boy, like me, only he was so dirty Ma made him stand under the pump in the back before she'd let him in her kitchen. They came with this pretty lady who spoke so nice, and she asked for some paper and she wrote a note, and she asked Ma if someone could deliver it to Sir Alasdair St. Erth, in London, and get good money for doing it, too. So Ma, she said I could do it, and I could come on the Mail, 'cause I know the coachman, he's my friend because he stops at our place sometimes—if we leave up the flag in the front. So he took me right here, and he's a'waiting outside." He fell still and looked at Leigh hopefully.

"What color was this lady's hair?" Leigh asked.

"Brown," the boy answered promptly.

"What was she wearing?"

"Nice clothes," the boy answered.

Alasdair sighed.

Leigh tried again. "Was there anything in particular you noticed about her?"

"She was pretty," the boy said in a more uncertain voice.

"Did she seemed distressed?" Alasdair's voice grated. He cleared his throat when Leigh gave him a pained look, and seemed surprised at how his voice had broken.

"Don't worry about my friend," Leigh told the boy, who was eyeing Alasdair anxiously. "All he wants to know is if she was upset. He's her friend, you see. Was she weeping? Or looking as though she wanted to?"

"No," the boy said, turning big eyes on Leigh, trying to avoid Alasdair's grim gaze altogether. "I remember, 'cause she was laughing with Sharky—that's the boy's name, and isn't it a funny one? Well, see, her clothes was so pretty but her hair was a terrible mess when she came in, and when Ma and Pa looked at her strange . . ." He paused for breath and plunged on, "Sharky he laughed and said that was 'cause she was a right Blowsabella again, and Ma said he should mind his manners, but the lady laughed and said he was right, and Sharky said Miss Corbet don't mind what he said neither."

Both men let out their own held breath.

"There!" Alasdair said with a sudden grin. "The question we never thought of asking: 'What was her name?' She's there! She's well! I'm going to get her, Leigh." He threw his oilskin cape over his shoulders. "No time to talk to the Swansons. That will be your task. Return the lad home, tell everyone. I've no time to waste at all! I'm going to get her!" he said jubilantly, and, sweeping up his carpetbag, strode out the door.

A few minutes later, as the storm gathered intensity, Leigh watched the bay with its dark rider come galloping from the stables, out by the side alley and into the street. The wind tore at the rider's oilskin cape, making it flap like the wings of a great swooping bird as he bent low for speed and rode off into the striking storm.

Alasdair didn't notice the rain when it came. He was too busy wishing that his horse could fly.

20

Alasdair rode through the storm. It was a late-summer thunderstorm, all rushing clouds, wind and clamor, lightning and driving rain, but in the nature of such storms it was brief. Some half hour or so and its fury would be spent—or would have been if Alasdair had stayed in one place and waited it out. But he couldn't sit still and continued to ride north, and the storm followed him.

The storm clashed all round him as he bent his head low and kept on. He almost preferred it that way. Keeping his horse on the road kept his mind off all the terrible things he could imagine having happened to Kate. Even staying on his horse was a chore, because the animal took exception to every stab of lightning, rearing up when the sizzle of a bolt seemed too near, ears going back at each thunderclap. Sometimes they had to slow to a walk and pick their way, because the rain flooded down in torrents and Alasdair didn't want the beast breaking a leg on the rain-slick road.

But he couldn't stop. He knew where she was now, and he had to be there.

He rode on, the rain beating on his face and sluicing down into his cloak, the wind prying at his collar, making it chafe his skin like sandpaper, the damp finding each finger in his gloves. He rode on, trying not to think about what he'd find when he arrived at the Excelsior, and not succeeding any better than he had done when he hadn't known where she was. The boy said she'd been laughing. He kept telling himself that, hoping it wasn't the laughter of hysteria the lad had heard. He kept telling himself that neat prosaic little note was typical Kate, not a thing she'd have written under duress. Surely, she'd have been able to slide in a warning if it was a trap? If it was, he'd deal with it. At least he knew where to go.

Twilight darkened the sky when the last of the storm rumbled by overhead. Alasdair was wet, weary, and increasingly anxious by the time he finally saw the inn with the sign EXCELSIOR swinging in the diminishing gusts of the departing storm. The boy said it was a good inn. But Alasdair realized it wouldn't matter to those who stopped there, because it was the only structure of any kind to be seen on this lonely stretch of the turnpike that wound through the heath. Highwaymen had ruled there a generation before. Bow Street had thinned their numbers, hardly any plied the trade so close to London anymore. But Alasdair kept a hand on the pistol under his cloak. There were worse things than highwaymen in the world, and some might be ahead. Kate's life might depend on his readiness.

The setting sun glinted at the edges of hurrying clouds, showing the inn to be an old one, timbered in the Tudor style. It was small but neat and tidy, and so Alasdair thought it odd that no ostler or stableboy came running to him as he rode into the yard. Odd and ominous. His hand on his pistol tightened. He sat his horse a moment, looking around. He saw no one and heard nothing but a few tentative birds calling to each other as the clouds blew away—that, and the steady sound of rain dripping from the inn's eaves. He swung down from the saddle and took up his saddlebag with the other hand. Keeping his hand on his pistol under his cloak, he waited.

A short, very dirty man finally came hurrying out of the stable, and touched his cap. "Staying on, sir?" he asked, scrutinizing Alasdair through slitted eyes, from hat to boots. "Or just here for a rest-like?"

"It depends," Alasdair said. "Keep my horse in readiness." He flipped the man a coin and paced toward the inn.

The back of his neck prickled with the awareness of unseen eyes on him and he didn't want to rush in case he alarmed anyone. But he couldn't wait. He pushed the door open, ducked his head, and stepped inside.

The main room of the inn was empty. It was a whitewashed and timbered room with a low ceiling. A quick glance showed a desk by the stair that must lead to the guest quarters upstairs. The door to a room behind the desk was closed. But Alasdair's attention was drawn to a corridor on the right that must have led to the taproom, because he could hear the murmur of voices coming from there. Gripping his pistol firmly, he softly stepped down the little hall, paused, then slowly nudged open the door with the toe of one boot.

He got a quick impression of a large taproom with sloping ceilings, a planked wooden floor, and small, thick, glass windows, a fire mumbling in the hearth opposite him. Alasdair held his breath and withdrew the pistol, using its muzzle to nudge the door open wider. He stared.

Kate was there. He sucked in a breath and held it, suppressing the insane, dangerous desire to run to her. But she was there. She wore a peach-colored gown, a light shawl thrown negligently over her shoulders. She sat at a table with a scrawny young boy and played cards with him. She was smiling. Her smile grew to an expression of wicked delight as she looked at the cards the boy had just dealt her. Then she laughed.

Alasdair felt equal parts profound relief and rising anger. He stood dripping water from every pore, his heart racing, his fear tin to the taste on his tongue, his nerves stretched. He was half-drowned, exhausted and worried and grateful beyond belief, and she was here, snug and content, playing cards, and *laughing*?

She might have felt a draft from the open door, he might have moved, or it just might have been that the force of his presence had somehow communicated itself to her. But she glanced up—and saw him.

She dropped the cards and rose from the chair, her hand to her breast, her eyes wide and bright, filling with tears he could see by the way they gleamed and glistened in the firelight.

He didn't realize he'd stepped forward. He hadn't meant to. But he moved to her. A second later she was plunging across the room, knocking her chair over in her haste. A moment more and she was filling his outstretched arms. He hugged her tightly, his arms going round her until he could feel her heart thudding against his, keeping pace with his own, which was threatening to pound out of his chest.

"Kate," he muttered, "Kate," and buried his face in her curls. They smelled of woodsmoke and peonies.

He inhaled the scent as though it was vital to his continued survival. She was warm and soft and whole, and he'd never known such a feeling of relief.

"Oh, Alasdair!" she murmured. He could feel wetness on her cheeks and his, and knew it wasn't rain because it was warm and welcome on his chilled skin.

He lifted his head and looked down at her. She gave him a tremulous smile. He didn't mean to kiss her. It was a damned stupid thing to do with them maybe in danger, and him not knowing who was watching, or why. But he kissed her anyway because there was absolutely nothing else he could do.

Her mouth was warm and electric with life, and he could feel that tremulous smile on her lips before she opened them to him. And then it was sweet, dazzling beyond anything in his experience, filling him with joy, and relief, and lust. He blinked, shocked at himself. He tore his mouth from hers and stepped back, looking around, remembering what was at stake here and now.

But there was no one but the boy, looking at them with obvious disdain.

"Lor'," the boy said in disgust, "you didn't say you was his fancy piece, Kate. Fact, you said you *wasn't* no blowen."

Kate, flustered, seemed as shocked as Alasdair was at what had happened between them. She touched a hand to her mouth, then dropped it as though her lips were scalding hot. "Well, he's not, and I'm not," she told the boy defensively. "I was just so happy to see him."

"Aye," the boy jeered, "pull t'other one. You was in an inch of makin' faces with him. That's *happy* all right, I s'pose."

Kate frowned. "Making faces?"

"Playin' bread and butter," the boy explained. "fuglin', shaggin', you know, havin' a bit o' . . . ."

"No more of that!" Alasdair said angrily, advancing on the boy as Kate's eyes widened as she figured it out.

The lad stood his ground and put up his chin. "Well, that aint neither here nor there, I s'pose. Jabber don't cut it, does it? Got the grease, Cap'n? That's the point. You post the pony, pay what we needs, you can take her and do whatever you do or don't. You ain't got it, we keeps her, that's the game."

"Are you all right, Kate?" Alasdair asked, keeping her clipped close to his side while he kept his eyes and his pistol on the boy. "Have you been hurt in any way?"

"I'm well, no one hurt me. I was frightened, but I'm fine, I promise."

"This boy abducted you?" Alasdair asked, because he felt the back of his neck prickle again.

"Nah, the lad's good, but he ain't that good," a voice said from an opened door to the side of the hearth that had eased open. "Now, put down that fine pistol, Sir Alasdair, and we'll see how fine Miss Corbet stays. And yourself. I got a barker, too," the voice went on when Alasdair hesitated. "Ain't so fancy, but it spits hot lead, and it's pointed at your head."

Alasdair nodded and slowly lowered the pistol to the floor. The boy darted forward to snatch it up, holding it gingerly and with awe, admiring it. Alasdair turned. The small, dirty man from the stable grinned at him, and motioned him to the table with his pistol.

"Have a seat Sir Alasdair, whilst we has a look in your saddlebag. I 'spect the money's there? I hope so for your sake."

"And if I told you it wasn't?" Alasdair asked, as he took Kate's hand, so they couldn't be separated again. "And added that I've friends coming?"

"I'd believe the bit about your cronies, but not about the gelt," the man said, " 'cause you're too clever to march into a bowmen ken without the ready. Sharky, stop moonin' over the gent's pistol and have an ogle at the bag."

"Where's everyone else?" Alasdair asked.

"Mr. and Mrs. Babbage be in the cellars, having tea with their maid and servin'men, and them few patrons what was unlucky enough to be on the scene. Aw, don't worry, I only give Babbage a dunt in the head to show I meant business. The ostler and stableboy's off to Gawd knows where, for you won't. He's an old friend o' mine, and set up this ken for us before he took his money and loped off. We'll be gone in a lamb-shake, too, if you do the right thing. We ain't in it for nothin' but money, and once we gets that, we're gone."

"Da!" Sharky said excitedly, his hands and face half in the carpetbag he'd just hauled out of the saddlebag. "There's a heap here! What we wanted and then some!"

"Then all's plummy," his father said, starting to back away. "Lemme get a glim. Aye!" he said after a quick look into the bag Sharky held open wide. "That'll do. We'll take it and go, and sorry for your inconvenience, sir. Give you good day, Miss Corbet, it were a treat meetin' you. You're a lady to the bone, that I will say."

"Wait!" Alsdair said. "How do you know I don't have my men waiting outside?"

"They wasn't none there, nor down the road a minute past. I looked. But it makes no never mind 'cause I got 'nother way out. 'Tis a risky business, but it be my livelihood. Now, good day."

"One thing," Alasdair said. "You can take the money and be damned, but one thing I must know. If you don't tell me, I promise you I'll track you to the four corners of the earth to find out. Who sent you to do this piece of business?"

"Close the bag, boy!' the man said, and then shook his head as Sharky pulled the bag together. "Sorry, but that be part of my job. Can't tell nothin' to no one, and that's a fact."

"I think you had better tell me," Alasdair said in a flat, menacing voice.

The man stared. Alasdair no longer held Kate's hand. Instead, he had another pistol—pointed at Sharky, who froze where he was, bent over the carpet-bag. Alasdair nodded. "Yes. Stay where you are, lad, don't even breathe."

Alasdair was a big man who loomed even larger dressed as he was in a great cloak, but he didn't need extra bulk to make their relative positions clearer. He towered over the skinny boy, and the pistol in his big hand didn't waver.

Alasdair glanced at the boy's father, who stood, stricken, in place. "The money caught your eye for a second too long," Alasdair said harshly. "You forget a man may have tricks up his sleeve. Literally."

"Don't hurt him!" Kate gasped. "He's only a boy!"

"To be sure," Alasdair agreed. "But one who helped abduct you."

"Aw, he be but a boy," the man repeated nervously.

"Yes, and so a good bargaining chip, you'll agree?" Alasdair asked. "But I can shoot you, if you prefer." He angled his wrist so the man could get a better look at the pistol, though it remained pointed at the boy. "Or I can get you both, it's an over and under, you see, and does a neat job for one or two. You have only the one shot. Either way you won't be getting this pistol without a fight, and it's one I believe you'll lose."

The room was very still. They all could hear the boy swallow hard, but he didn't stir.

"Now we're at an impasse," Alasdair said conversationally. "Either way there'll be blood shed. Or we can settle this with no fuss. Tell me who sent you and you can walk with the money, if only because you didn't hurt Miss Corbet, and it seems she's taken an unaccountable liking to your boy. Don't tell me, and there'll be death today. My affection for Miss Corbet won't change that. I'm a man who holds grudges. Speaking of which, in case you haven't heard, Lolly has already gone on to his reward. Rosie told me he'd seen to it."

That startled the man. His hand shook.

"But if you say Lolly was responsible for this mess just because he's dead and can't argue the point, I *will* find out," Alasdair cautioned. "And I'll pursue you relentlessly. I've done it before, I can do it again. The stories you've heard about me are all true. So. The real story please. And fast. Was it Lolly? Or perhaps someone more highly placed? The name Scalby is not unknown to me either."

The man backed a step, deathly pale. "Aye, so the lass mentioned. They be her relatives, she said. Listen. We ain't mixed up with the likes of *them*! Nor would we be. They be bad business. It were a simple job o' work for Lolly. He was that angry about your showin' him up at the gin house, see? He sent us to nab the mort, and we was goin' to get half the ready for it. Just to vex you, he said. That be all! We got too much sense to scrag no one. Nor to deal with the likes of the Scalbys! They're way above our touch."

"True," Alasdair said, and the man relaxed. Until Alasdair added, "But I believe there's more. What were you going to do with Miss Corbet?"

The man's eyelashes lowered for a second. He stayed silent.

"Tell him, Da!" Sharky pleaded. "'Cause you'd changed your mind, you said so!"

"So I said," the man muttered, then looked at Alasdair. "You know too much to lie to," he said in a defeated voice, watching Alasdair's hand on the pistol. It never moved. "The truth's that we was to turn her over to Lolly and never look back. But like the lad said, we decided to let her go and make for . . ." He caught himself and said, ". . . another place, by our lonesomes. London's too crowded and too warm for us— 'specially if we took all the loot and not just our share. Which we was goin' to do. See, we keeps our word, but lately Lolly weren't good to work for, he'd a way of makin' sure nobody could prove what he done. All that money woulda greased our way to a new line o' work. Healthier for me and the boy."

He saw Alasdair's expression, his voice grew rough. "We woulda let her go. Can't prove it, o' course. Who else could swear to it? No one, and that's a fact. Who else would know? The boy would lie to His Majesty hisself for me—or for anyone," he added with a gruff laugh, "and don't I know it. He's a natty lad and no mistake. But what I said's the Gawd's honest truth, believe it or don't.

"The lad din't want no harm to come to her, and it weren't no skin off our noses if she went free—after we got the money. So I was goin' to oblige the lad. We was goin' to get word to Lolly she cut and run, and we was goin' to do the same. Who'd know it was a lie but her? And if we asked her to keep it mum, I believe she would of. She's solid as oak. And what would it matter by then? We'd of been gone, good as dead to them in London Town. 'N' if we done that, and stayed, we woulda been," he added with a cough of a laugh.

"So that's truth." The man shrugged. "I din't know what Lolly had planned for her, but I could guess. Can't say one good word about the departed. He was a sad dog even for the likes of us to know, and we wished her well 'cause for all she's a lady she's a rum mort and no mistake."

"Agreed," Alasdair said. He paused, looked at the boy, and then glanced at the man. The boy stayed locked in place, watching him through slitted eyes. The father held his breath. Alasdair saw Kate's expression from the corner of his eye, and could hear her quick and nervous breathing. He gestured with his pistol again.

"So, go," Alasdair told the man. "And fast."

"Thankin' you kindly," the man said. And in a blur of movement, he pocketed his pistol, spun and grabbed Sharky by the shoulder, hauled the carpetbag from the floor, and before Alasdair lowered his pistol, the pair were out the back door and gone.

The room was very still.

Kate's shoulders slumped. "Oh, Lord. It's over? I'm safe? They're gone, and it's all over?"

Alasdair was already at the window. "They had horses tied out back. They're on them and off . . . going through the fields, now into the twilight . . . I can't see so much as a tail in the distance now. They're gone. It's over," he said a second later, from her side. "Poor Kate. I'm sorry." He turned her around and took her in his arms and let her rest against his chest. "I'm so sorry."

"What for?" she murmured, feeling his breath in her curls as his big hand stroked her back.

"They wouldn't have touched you in the first place if it weren't for me," he said bleakly. "They wouldn't have known you existed, or cared. I was the one who endangered you, I contaminated you simply by my presence in your life. I honestly didn't think Lolly would try for revenge, though there were others who might for deeds done long ago. Still, I thought our bargain would be a benign thing. No," he muttered, "that's a damned lie. I didn't care then, I only cared about my own devices. You were the means to the ending I wanted. I'm responsible for your being terrified, being put upon. I put your life, and more, in danger. My God, Kate, you can't know how sorry I am for that. You *are* all right?" he asked suddenly, looking down into her face. "They didn't touch you?"

"I'm fine now," she said. "They didn't touch a hair on my head." She resting against him, reveling in the closeness of his embrace. She felt safe for the first time in days, and in absolutely the right place for the first time in her life.

"I didn't mean for anything like this to happen," Alasdair said. "My God! How could I have guessed it? But the truth is I didn't care—*then*." His arms tightened around her. "By the time I knew how much I cared, it was too late. I didn't want to give up the pleasure I found in your company . . . no. Damn!" he said violently, causing her to pull back and look up at him. "When will I stop lying to you and myself!"

He looked dark as the storm clouds that had just blown over. Kate wasn't afraid of him, only worried for him, because he looked as troubled as angry, and none of his rage was directed at her. "Kate," he said, putting his hands on her shoulders, holding her gently but firmly away from him, "listen."

His voice was gentler, if no less bitter, and he searched her expression for her reactions as he spoke. "I was using you for my own purposes. I wasn't aiming for respectability, I wanted revenge on a pair of people who had ruined my life, and you were the key and the lure and the bait to bring them to their reward. God help me, Kate, but it was your cousins the Scalbys I was after, and nothing else, no matter what lies I told you."

He spoke desperately, his eyes blazing. "They ruined my father and tried to ruin me, they caused his suicide and almost caused my own. I lived only to destroy them, that's all I've wanted these many years. I've finally enough evidence of their wrongdoing to disgrace them publicly, and they know it. They're hiding, waiting for me to strike. Maybe they're waiting for me to bargain with them, they always want something, they probably think I do, too. But all I want is their ruin.

"The waiting is part of my revenge. I wanted them to think I was getting involved with you so I could worry them even more. I didn't know you and told myself no harm would come to you. And yes, since you were their relative, I thought bedamned to you, too, if that turned out not to be so. That's what I thought *then*. I promise that's not what I feel or want, or need now."

"What do you want now?" she asked, and held her breath.

He smiled, a bitter smile with no real humor in it. But he looked in her eyes and what she saw in his took her breath away.

"What do I want?" he said. "You need to ask?"

21

$\mathcal{A}$lasdair continued to hold Kate in his arms, but lightly, so she could move away if she chose. He hoped she wouldn't, it was bliss to hold her safe and close after all his wild imaginings about what harm might have come to her. It was bliss mixed with balked desire simply to hold her close and not be able to do more. They were alone in the taproom of a deserted inn at the edge of a heath in the middle of nowhere. She was pliant, fragrant and docile, yet he merely held her because it wasn't the time to do more. And still, he felt at peace. It couldn't last, he knew that. She'd asked him a question. He thought he'd answered, and now he waited for her response in words or actions.

When she did speak, it was to his cravat, because she kept her head down. "You answer my question with another? No, Alasdair, that won't do. I'm tired of polite games. I've been abducted. I've been terrified. I feared for my life *and* my honor and didn't know which I was more afraid of losing. It turned out that my kidnappers were as kind as they could be to me under the circumstances, but I never really knew what they intended for me. I don't think they knew themselves. I almost escaped once. I didn't break down either . . . well, not often. I think I was very brave." She paused and then said quickly, "I'll be even braver now."

She dared look up, straight into his eyes. "You just admitted you've lied to me all along. You said you used me to get at my relatives. You say you're sorry for it. I asked you what you wanted of me, and you play word games with me! Games, with *me*? After all that?" Her eyes blazed. "Oh, damn and blast—and I don't care what you think of me for saying that, either! How dare you?"

"It was either word games or physical ones, and I wanted to give you the choice," he said gently.

She took in a breath and glanced away.

"You've been through a lot, Kate," he went on. "I didn't want to add my bit to your distress. You kissed me. Don't think I'll ever forget it, don't imagine for a moment I don't want more. But you were wild with relief then. A man's responses under fire are unthinking ones, as are a woman's. They can be forced by events. When you come into my arms for more than shelter, I'll be more than happy to take advantage of you."

She backed a step. He dropped his arms at once, and felt he'd lost much more than one small woman from his grasp.

But she faced him squarely. "What *is* it you want of me now, Alasdair? Do you want anything more of me at all? I suppose the Scalbys know about our arrangement by now. It may be I've answered your purposes, and there's an end to our association. Is it? Please tell me with no roundabout. We should let the poor innkeeper and his wife up from the cellars, but they've been there so long another minute or two won't matter. It will matter to us. Soon as they're here, we'll be back to all the nonsense and manners of polite society again. For once, for now, we can talk honestly.

". . . And,"—she looked down, then up, and blurted—"you also said your revenge on the Scalbys wasn't what you felt or needed or wanted now. So what *do* you want and need and feel? I know flirtation is considered clever, and sincerity isn't fashionable, but I'm so tired of playing games with you. I was tired of it before Sharky and his father nabbed me. I'm doubly so now."

"Triply so, I should think," he said quietly. He stayed still, brooding on some inner argument. Just when she thought she should let it go, shrug, or laugh, suggest they let the innkeeper out of his prison now and worry about it later, Alasdair spoke at last.

"Kate," he said, fixing her with a steady stare, so dark she couldn't read the emotions there, "my mother died when I was thirteen, and my father ran wild with grief. He was a good man, but I never realized how much of that good was her influence, because he was absolutely lost without her. He had few personal friends. Those he had were really her friends, and they dropped away when she was gone. The estate was prosperous, his estate agent honest and diligent, the house ran itself. He had few interests outside of my mother, she made his home and was his life."

Kate saw some hint of emotion besides sorrow passing over his face as he added, "I was their only child and away at school, so he didn't even have a family to occupy his time."

"Surely you don't blame yourself for that?" she asked, startled to realize that fleeting emotion she'd seen had been guilt.

He shrugged. "I was their first and last child, she couldn't have others after I was born, as though I broke the mold and slammed the gate closed after me."

"That's nonsense!" she said with some heat.

"Of course," he said with a sad quirk of a smile, cutting her off. "But we all believe some kind of nonsense or other, don't we? At any rate, there was my father, rudderless, alone, and beside himself with who knows what other nonsensical guilt? He was her husband, after all, he probably had more to believe he should blame himself for.

"Whatever the reasons for his inconsolable grief," Alasdair went on, "he went to London to cure himself. By God, I wish he'd gone to some spa, here or abroad! Sharpers flourish in those places, but they'd only have taken his money, and only to make a profit. Instead, he met the Scalbys in London, and they took his money and his life for the sheer pleasure of it."

His expression was bleak, his voice becoming monotone. "They befriended him and succeeded in diverting him. They were famous for their mindless entertainments, and that was what he was after. He went to their parties, invested in their schemes, sank himself in their debaucheries. But something else was happening, too. Time went by, and as it did, it began to heal him, just as everyone said it would. His numbed senses came alive again, and so did his conscience. He found himself deeply regretting what he'd been doing with his life. I know, because he told me so when I came home from school and met the Scalbys at last.

"You see, I'd passed my vacations with friends for some time. Motherless boys get all sorts of kind invitations, Leigh's house was one of my favorite places for Christmas. But finally, when I was sixteen, Father said I could come home again. I'd written to ask him to please let me see him and our home once more. He wrote back to say yes, come home. I did, and was surprised, because the Scalbys were staying there along with a huge party. I was appalled and fascinated by them and their friends and excesses. That helped wake my father to his responsibilities again."

He smiled at her expression of indignation. "Yes, I blame myself for that, too, and I know it's folly. But if I hadn't come home, my father mightn't have wanted to free himself of the Scalbys just then, and maybe everything would have been different. As it was . . ."

Alasdair turned his head to look out the windows. Kate realized he wasn't seeing anything there, or in the present.

"As it was," he said abruptly, "the Scalbys didn't like being cast off. They called in their debts. Turned out my father had invested unwisely and too well. They owned almost everything he had. They wanted to own it all. So," he said briskly, "they insisted on being paid, or they'd simply take all the rest. My father asked for leniency, they denied it. He couldn't meet them or the world's eyes after his shame, and so he put a bullet through his own eye."

Kate flinched.

"Witnesses said my father killed himself after he'd spoken with them, as they left the house that morning, as they were driving away, in fact. His note to me said merely, 'I'm so sorry. Forgive me. Good-bye.'"

Kate reached to touch him, stopping when she realized it would be intrusive, it was as if he'd forgotten she was there. Nor did she want to recall him to the present. She wanted to hear more, know more, before this rare confiding mood of his had passed.

"I'd been out that morning," Alasdair said. "I came home to find myself an orphan with heavy debts to pay. The estate was entailed, so I kept it. But there was no money to support it. I started trying to recover it that day. I used my friends' advice and connections. I left school and shipped abroad.

"Yes," he added with a wry smile, "my formal education isn't as good as I'd wish, I've tried to correct that, too. I worked very hard after I left school, Kate, with my hands *and* my brain. I was lucky in my past associations, going to school with the richest boys in the land was a great help. I found work as a clerk, then a secretary, then an overseer. I worked on other men's estates and plantations, and in their homes and offices. I went on to be a go-between, a cat's-paw, and finally an agent for friends, enemies, and eventually His Majesty. What money I made I gambled with, but since I hadn't had much luck, I used wit. And since investing isn't all luck, I did well with it. In time I regained everything. Except my father's life, of course. And my honor."

He looked at her, and she realized he saw her again. He paused, started to speak, frowned as if he was about to say something and changed his mind. "I'm a rich man now, Kate," he said more easily. "But the other part of the debt I must repay is much heavier and harder to satisfy. I've been gathering evidence against the Scalbys for years. My father's wasn't the only life they wrecked. They've been cruel, intemperate, and depraved. They suck people in and leave them without their money or reputations. They blackmail, too. The only thing more important to them than their pleasures is their fortune. But their name is the most important thing of all to them. Because whatever they did, they did discreetly, and so whatever their reputation, they still have a place in Society. That's what I want to take from them.

"With all I found, it wasn't enough to ruin them.

Until recently. Now I've proof that they were also trai-
torous. Once the world knows that, they'll be through,
I'll be done with them, and my father avenged. I want
to see their faces when I tell them that, and that's what
I tried to use you for."

"But you only had to explain and ask for my help!"
she cried, "I'd have given it to you, immediately. Of
course I would have! Why, I heard all sorts of stories
about the Scalbys all my life. Why do you think my
parents didn't insist I see them? In fact, they warned
me about them, and said if I saw them, I should keep
my head, and my distance. As if I wouldn't! Some children heard about the bogeymen in their closets. I knew
about their reputation. Society forgives what simple
country folk do not, you see. I suppose I didn't tell you
that because I was ashamed. They *are* family, after all."

He cocked his head to the side. "The scrupulously
honest Miss Corbet keeps secrets?"

"Well, of course," she said, flustered. "Only saints
don't. Everyone has something they don't want to tell,
and if it doesn't affect anyone else directly, why should
they? What a strange world this would be if we said
everything we knew or were thinking! I'd never tell
poor Sibyl she shouldn't wear white because it makes
her look like a ghost, though she asks me about it
whenever she gets dressed. Her mama won't let her
wear anything else, so what good would it do to be
truthful? It would only hurt her. If she had a choice, I'd
be honest. But she doesn't. So I'd have mentioned
something of what I'd heard about the Scalbys to you
before we actually went to visit them. But otherwise,
why should I?"

"Why indeed?" he asked. "Kate," he said suddenly,
urgently, gripping her by her shoulders, "you did tell
me, discreetly, when you kept saying your family was

distant from them and you didn't care to visit them. I didn't want to hear it, or I'd have asked more. I have been persistent in my pursuit of your cousins, and not very scrupulous. Unlike you, it isn't just things I've thought.

"I've done things I'd rather not talk about. I never debauched anyone," he added quickly. "All were willing. I've had affairs, but affairs of the mind or the body, never the heart. I don't know if that makes it worse or not. But I've never been incautious or intemperate. I don't have any diseases, no by-blows, no vengeful cheated lovers in my past. I've been as fair as I could be with whomever I've dealt with, and I'm healthy—in body, at least. Even Leigh has said I'm mad on the subject of my revenge."

"I don't blame you," she exclaimed. "And I forgive you for not telling me all, too, if that's what's bothering you. They did a terrible thing to you and you have every right to seek vengeance. I even understand why you thought you had to use me. I'm only sorry you didn't trust me enough to be honest, but I don't blame you for that either, or for what happened to me. It was this Lolly person who ordered Sharky and his father to snatch me. I heard them talking about it. So don't blame yourself anymore."

"Thank you for forgiving me," he said, watching her closely, "but that's not what's bothering me, Kate. I told you what I was, so you could know me better. No one should make an uninformed decision. You asked me what I want and need and feel. You asked me a question, but before I answer that, I have one question for you."

"Oh?" she asked, her rapid breathing making her breasts rise and fall. Her eyes were bright again, her lips parted, her head tilted toward him as she waited.

"You know what it is," he said roughly.

She stared at him. It certainly sounded like he was going to propose to her. She thought she might die of expectation. If he asked her, she knew what to answer, because she never wanted to leave him again. "Well, in another man I might know, but I can't ever predict you, Alasdair," she said. "And to tell the truth, so much has happened that now I confess I'm muddled and confused. So could you please tell me straight out?"

"It's past time you were as muddled as I am," he said, smiling. He was going to say more, but he saw what leapt to her eyes, and pulled her back into his arms.

This time he took his time, fitting her to his body, settling her in his clasp. She went willingly, and was smiling when his mouth touched hers. He nudged her lips open, sliding his tongue between them. She welcomed him, crowded closer, daring to give him back what he'd given her. He chuckled low in his throat, the sound and vibration making her body thrill. His big hand caressed her cheek, her neck.

His lips left her mouth and placed small nipping kisses on her throat before he sought her lips again in answer to her silent protest at his abandonment of them.

Never, never, never, she thought dazedly, never had she known a man's kisses could turn her inside out like this. She yearned to give him more, be closer still, be part of him. He did his best to accommodate her.

He slid her gown from her shoulder, and when she shivered, closed his hand over her breast, and felt her shiver more. Her breast fit into his hand, the nipple crested. No power on earth could have stopped him from bending his head and tasting the small hot point that had been boring into his palm. It was incredibly sweet, as was the sound of her stifled gasp and tiny moan. Her body tensed, and he knew it wasn't yet ecstasy, so he put his lips on her outflung neck and murmured all the reasons why this was so good, for him, and her, for them.

She clung to him and looked down as his mouth found her breast again. His hair was clean and shining, dark as moonlight on still water, soft and clean against her lips. His scent was faint, but sweet and spicy, dizzying as two glasses of hot Christmas punch. She discovered that her breath in his ear made him shudder, and that made her shake. He radiated heat, he made her head spin and her body tingle. Nothing she'd ever known had ever been this exciting.

"Yes," he murmured as his hand slid to her bottom and pressed her tightly to his yearning body.

She gasped at the unfamiliar feel of his muscular body straining against hers. A woman with three younger brothers had to know what was happening to him. A woman who'd grown up on a farm knew what might happen to her next, too. And a good woman ought to worry. But she couldn't. This man was *Alasdair*, and he wanted her. He was experienced and wise, and surely he'd stop this before the unimaginable happened. That would be too bad, she thought, as his lips met hers again.

She was lost in a world of his making, and he was disappearing into a world where only she existed. They heard their own hearts beating, their own breath catching, the blood thundering in their own ears. But then the real world intruded.

"*Kate!*" Lord Swanson cried.

"*Alasdair!*" Leigh said in exasperation.

Kate sprang away, saw the two men standing in the taproom, saw the direction of their stares, and gasped.

She ducked her addled head and burrowed into Alasdair's arms as he pulled her close again. He turned her so she could pull her gown up over her exposed breasts, as he mildly regarded their dumbfounded gazes. He didn't look embarrassed. He ignored his outraged friend and the shocked Lord Swanson. Instead, he turned his full attention on Kate. The look he gave her was suddenly grave, and full of inquiry.

They stared at each other. She'd doubted, but now she knew exactly what he was asking. Her eyes widened. He gave her a small smile, and nodded. A dozen objections rose to her lips, so many they crowded each other out. She stood silent, trying to choose the right one to say first. *He was only being gentlemanly, he'd been trapped as surely as Lady Eleanora had tried to snare him when they'd met, he could do better. . . .*

And then, in spite of the staggered company watching them, he lowered his head and gave her a long and tender kiss.

Kate was stunned, but after a second, comforted against all reason, and flung her arms around his neck again. When he lifted his head he gazed at her, humor, affection and understanding gleaming in his eyes.

She knew what he'd asked and what she'd answered. The time for talking could come later. Because, Lord! how she wanted this. She closed her dazzled eyes, and nodded.

He grinned.

"Congratulate me, gentlemen," Alasdair said, smiling widely. "I found Kate, as you see. And being lucky beyond my merits, as you can also see, I've found my future wife, too."

22

"**A**re you certain about this?" Lord Swanson asked Kate.

They were sitting at a table in the taproom of the Excelsior, apart from the others in the room. The innkeeper, his wife, son, a few excited travelers who had been guests, and the Excelsior's serving staff, were otherwise occupied, explaining their adventure again to Alasdair, his friend Leigh, some neighbors, and the local magistrate, who'd been rousted from his dinner table to hear the dreadful tale.

This was the first time Lord Swanson had had a chance to speak to Kate alone. She was profoundly embarrassed and looked everywhere but at him. After all, he'd seen her half-naked in the arms of a man, and utterly absorbed in what she was doing with that man. But she discovered that didn't bother her as much as the thought that he'd seen her naked breasts. In fact, she was glad he'd seen her with Alasdair. It made everything simpler.

"I'm certain," she answered. "I'm sorry we were
seen in such a compromising situation, but not because of the reason for it. He'd just asked me to marry
him, you see." That wasn't precisely true, but Kate decided to worry about that later. She'd say anything to
take that troubled look from her cousin's face. His
brow was furrowed, his eyes concerned. "It was an
emotional moment," she added, because that was certainly true.

"Asked you to marry him! Aha!" Lord Swanson
said, sitting back as though that explained everything,
which gave Kate a much better opinion of him and his
marriage. No wonder the Swansons could put up
with their daughters. Kate reasoned a man could put
up with almost everything if he still had that sort of
reaction remembering when he'd proposed to his
own wife.

"He'd just proposed, had he? But had you accepted
him?" he asked shrewdly.

She looked at him with new respect. "Not exactly,"
she answered slowly, "so perhaps this is for the best
then, isn't it?"

"Only if you want him."

She smiled because this time at least she could answer the whole truth. "Oh, I do," she breathed. That
sounded so matrimonial she blushed.

"You don't have to marry him just because we came
upon you at an . . . emotional moment," Lord Swanson
went on doggedly. "You'd been through much. I know
you've said those dastards didn't hurt you, but you
must have been wild with anxiety and overjoyed with
relief when you were freed at last. A person does
strange things at such times. I'm not saying Sir Alasdair took advantage of the situation. But I am saying
that his reputation implies that he might have, and so

neither Leigh nor I would breathe a word of this—or think worse of you—if you were to tell me it was only the excitement of the moment that stirred . . . other excitement. It happens, Kate. I don't want you penalized for it."

"You're kind, cousin," Kate said with heartfelt emotion. "But 'penalized' is the last word I'd use. It's Sir Alasdair who might be that. Because, you see, I've come to care for him very much."

He studied her. "Very well. But if you change your mind, there'll be no harm done, I just want you to know that."

Her gaze flew to his. "Oh, no! There'd be much harm done! At least, to me!"

Then he smiled and looked relieved at last.

It took another hour to get things sorted out, and then the innkeeper wouldn't hear of them not staying to dinner as his guests.

"It'll be raining soon again," he told them after the magistrate had left with a description of the offenders. "Hear that rumbling? Another storm's coming, unless I miss my guess. Fact, my feet tell me it'll be a night of rolling storms. Fine thing to send you out into it without a good dinner after all you've done, Sir Alasdair. Or let you leave so sudden, miss, after the fright you took. Nor have a chance to reward you gentlemen," he told Leigh and Lord Swanson.

"You're ready to reward the immediate world," Alasdair told him with a smile, "but your head must ache, and there's no need."

"Every need!" Mrs. Babbage exclaimed. "My old man here can rest his head, the cooking's half-done. We're a working inn here, sirs, and a fine one, too. We'd like to show you that. And we don't want you bearing away sad memories of the place, miss," she told Kate seriously.

"As if I could!" Kate said, smiling up at Alasdair.

"Yes, then we'll stay," he told the innkeeper, not taking his eyes from Kate, "but only if you bring us your best wines as well as your best food, because we've something extraordinary to celebrate—something much more important than a lucky escape. I'm going to celebrate a luckier capture. I'm to be this lady's prisoner for the rest of my life. So we'll have your finest champagne, if you please."

They had that, and more. They sat and shared toasts with the innkeeper and local gentry who'd come in to hear the exciting story, and then they had a more intimate party, an enormous feast, in the private dining room. Their hosts sent in wave after wave of soups and stews, masses of roasts, shoals of fish, soup dishes filled with custards and jellies, while thunder and lightning harried the night outside their snug parlor.

Lord Swanson had sent word home of Kate's recovery, and now he sat and expanded in the warmth of relief, made merrier by the fine wines and food, and the laughter of his companions. He'd always thought of Sir Alasdair as a formidable fellow, a man of dark depths and wicked ironies, a man to watch carefully. He'd never been easy in his company. But his niece had wrought a miracle. Because though Sir Alasdair was no less masterful tonight, now he was overwhelming in his geniality. He was gracious, warm, full of charming and clever jests. His voice was deep and rich with affability. Even his craggy face looked milder, and it wasn't just a trick of the cheery firelight. It was especially so when he gazed at Kate, which he did constantly.

They all dined so well and drank so many toasts

that when dinner was finally done they sat like a collection of stuffed ducks, unwilling or unable to rise from the table.

"Look at us!" Leigh laughed. "Gentlemen. Kate, I, for one—because I can't be two like you and Alasdair"—he grinned at this sally, because he'd had enough wine to think it was wonderfully droll—"suggest we take the opportunity to test the Babbages' inn further. I don't know about you, but I feel like I've been filleted. Neat as a haddock, not a bone left in my body. It's the food, the wine, and the result of our frenzied ride here, plus the enormous relief of finding everyone whole and well when we got here, and the further pleasure of discovering how well we could celebrate that . . . what was I saying? Ah, yes. What do you think of our staying the night and setting out for London in the morning?"

"You may, certainly," Alasdair said. "I'll do whatever Kate prefers. She might feel the need of a friendly female to confide in after her adventure. What do you say, Kate? Would you be more comfortable going home? Or would you want to stay on here?"

"Thank you," she told him with a warm and only slightly woozy smile. "I'd like to go home, to share the good news with my parents. But that home's too far from here. So I'd just as soon stay on and start back to London in the light."

Her cousin stirred himself enough to summon a worried frown. "You may be engaged to marry, but you aren't wed yet. I don't know about you staying on here without a chaperone."

This made everyone else at the table laugh, though Lord Swanson frowned because he couldn't understand why.

"Cousin," Kate said, taking pity on his confusion,

"I've been abducted. Gone from home in the company of strangers for a full day and everyone must know that by now. I doubt staying on here would make much difference to the gossips, and you, dear sir, are the best chaperone Society could want."

"And she's engaged to marry me," Alasdair said softly, looking at her as though he couldn't quite believe his good fortune, "so I'm afraid her reputation will be in tatters anyway."

"Nonsense!" Lord Swanson exclaimed. "Marriage mends reputations. Well, what do you say, Kate? Mind," he said, frowning again, "we'll get a maid to stay with you, and no hopping out of your chamber on any excuse. And no wandering into any chambers neither," he cautioned Alasdair. They knew how much he'd had to drink when he added, to Kate, "A man's not the father of seven daughters without learning a thing or two. Surest way to snag a husband, but you've done that already, and it would only make me feel guiltier."

"I'll stay," Kate said, "because I feel absolutely boneless, too! I could do with a good night's rest. Though I think I'm still too excited to sleep!"

They decimated a tray of tarts, reduced the fruit and nut bowls to shambles, and finally, as another round of thunder rolled overhead, rose from the table and, after many groans and stretches, began to make their way to the guest bedchambers.

Kate hesitated at the door to the private parlor. "I'd like a word with you," she told Alasdair, her eyes searching his, estimating his mood and sobriety.

But he was clearheaded, because his smile immediately faded. "Of course," he answered, and to a frowning Lord Swanson, added, "Surely you'll permit that, sir? There's not much I can get up to in here now, what with servants coming in to clear every other moment. I promise I'll hand her over to the care of a worthy maid as soon as we have a chance to speak. Come, my lord. I do have a sense of propriety. And we are an engaged couple now. Surely that gives us a chance to speak privately for a few moments?"

Reluctantly, Lord Swanson nodded. And yawned. "Very well. Good night, then. I'll see you all at breakfast—I hope," he added darkly, watching Leigh make his way up the stairs, singing a school song he said he'd got "stuck in his head," and walking like a blind man on ice.

Alasdair smiled. "Don't worry. Leigh's the most amiable drunk I ever met. The only thing alcohol does to him is improve his mood. Don't worry about his safety, or our plans. He can find his way in the dark with a blindfold and his ankles shackled together. He'll be fine in the morning. He rises with the larks with a clear head. I don't know how he does it."

"And you?" Lord Swanson asked.

"Don't worry about me, or Kate," Alasdair said. "I've a hard head. Besides, I don't drink to excess. It's too dangerous a habit for a cautious man. Whatever else I am, my lord, believe that I'm that."

"Cautious indeed!" Kate told Alasdair the moment her cousin had gone. She and Alasdair went to the fireside so they could speak privately as the Excelsior's staff cleared the table. "How cautious can you be?" she whispered, "You got trapped into offering for me."

"What nonsense is this?" he asked, smiling down at her.

"You never actually asked for my hand," she said, her face as filled with worry now as her cousin's had been when he heard she was going to stay in a room alone with Alasdair. "Don't think I don't know that.

Such things are important. One can't *surmise* a proposal, and that's just what I did, because we had to when my cousin walked in, I know. But I am not a Lady Eleanora! We were both carried away, and happened to be caught when we were."

She took a breath. "So," she said a little grimly, "I wanted to tell you now that this doesn't have to go much further." She frowned. "Well, it has to go a little further or my cousin will suspect the truth. So, after we get back to London—give it a week, I think. Then we can announce that we found out we don't suit." She looked everywhere but at him as she hurried on: "That's acceptable, people do that all the time, and their reputations remain intact. But before we do that, I can see that you meet my other cousins, the Scalbys, and do what you have to do. *Then* I can go home and you can . . . What are you doing?" she gasped.

Because the formidable Sir Alasdair had dropped to one knee in front of her. He captured the hand she'd been waving as she'd tried to explain herself. His hand was dry and warm, her cold one trembling in his. He raised it to his lips.

"My dear Miss Corbet," he said, "I know that I am unworthy, but will you do me the exquisite honor of becoming my wife?"

The maidservant who had been clearing the table gasped, and Mrs. Babbage paused with an armful of dirty linen, gaping at them.

But Alasdair went on imperturbably: "I am a man of moderate means and small appeal, but I devoutly hope you'll overlook that. My past doesn't bear speaking of, so I won't. But I'm not yet ancient, and have every hope for my future—but only if you share it with me."

He was smiling, but his expression grew serious as

he looked up into her eyes and added, "I've made many mistakes in my life, Kate. Believe me, this is not one of them. And I vow, here and now, that if there are any in the future, they'll be just that—mistakes. Of time, or fortune, or nature. Because I'll never do anything to hurt, embarrass or dismay you, not of my conscious will. That, I promise. I'll earnestly try to be the best husband you could want. Because I know you deserve even more than that. So. Kate. Will you marry me?"

"Oh, Alasdair," she whispered.

Mrs. Babbage smiled. Then, chivvying at her gaping maid, she hurried her out the door as Alasdair rose to his feet and took Kate in his arms. The door gently closed behind them. Only then did Alasdair lower his head to Kate's. But he paused, his mouth an inch from hers.

"Your answer, please," he said softly. "You'll get no kisses from me, you wicked thing, unless I have your promise. I have a newborn reputation to consider, and it's whole and good and chaste as an egg right now, so I don't want to blemish it by trading kisses with an unprincipled hussy. So, Kate? No moans or sighs, or whatever, now. A simple yes will do." He hesitated, and she saw the gravity in his eyes as he added, "A yes, because I don't think I could survive a no—or at least, would want to—even if it might be the better choice for you."

"Oh, Alasdair," she said, with one of those sighs that he'd said he didn't want. "Alasdair," she added, with tears in her voice, "yes, of course, yes. Indeed, yes. I will, I want to, though I can hardly believe any of this."

She gave herself up to his kiss and soon gave him one of those moans that he'd also specifically said he didn't want. But since it was against his mouth as she squirmed in his arms trying to get even closer to him, and he himself groaned low in his throat at the fiery touch of her tongue on his, he didn't mind at all.

23

The room was dimly lit, even for night. But it was a sultry summer's night, so a fire in the hearth wasn't necessary, and even the glow of a lamp would have made the room feel hotter. Even so, the curtains were drawn tight, closed against any breeze that might possibly be roving anywhere in London that night.

A man sat close to the empty hearth, staring into it, as though he needed it for warmth, and could see pictures in flames that weren't there. The woman seated opposite him stared into the complete darkness at the edges of the room as though she could see moving shadows. Nothing moved except for the faint fluttering of the single candle in the room, set flickering by the slight motion of her hand as she idly plied her fan.

"We received an invitation in the post this morning," she said into the stillness. "Unexpected. But then, perhaps not. The fellow seems willing to go to all lengths. Well, now, despite what I'd thought, it seems our old friend Sir Alasdair St. Erth has actually become

betrothed to our—your—cousin Katherine Corbet. He
rescued her from that abduction, and so many will say
it's because he wished to save her name—as if a man
with a name like his could do that. But whatever they
say, now the thing is official, it was in the papers, and
they're planning a party to celebrate. We've been invited. How amusing."

The gentleman didn't react.

She spoke again. "So, shall we go?" She laughed
when he didn't answer. "Precisely. I think not. But he's
planning to marry her. What do you think of that,
Richard?"

At the sound of his name, the man turned his head a
fraction. He grunted.

"Yes," the woman answered. "Just so. What can one
say? He has evidence, Richard. Evidence that will ruin
us. So why doesn't he simply produce it and have
done? Why should he go to such lengths, eh?"

The man laughed. It was a broken, bitter sound,
with no humor in it.

"Yes, quite," his wife said. "Or perhaps not. Perhaps
he loves her? That would be to our advantage, were it
so. If he does, he could be managed; certainly he
wouldn't want to cast shame on her family. But he has
no shame of his own, and so that's a remote possibility.
Unlikely, as well, as he also has no heart. Still, though
we may pass up this kind invitation, we shall be expected to invite them here. We are known to be social,
you know.

"Damn him to hell," she added conversationally,
though her thin hand clenched to a claw on the handle
of her fan. "He is undoubtedly already headed there.
He wants us to crawl. It's not enough to disgrace us,
which he doubtless will. He wants to see us crawl to

him first. And *then* he will deny us. I imagine he'd find
that amusing. I would, were I he. I expect his plan in-
volves exposing us in front of the family," she went on
moodily. "Then he can cast off the girl, and his revenge
will be complete. But, perhaps not. There may be an
out for us. There might be a way, if he does care for the
girl, there may yet be a way."

The man waved a negligent hand at her, as though
he was brushing away a gnat.

"No, I mean it," she said. "It isn't much of a hope,
but it's all we have left. With all his power, he's only a
man, and we know, God knows we know, he has his
weaknesses. If he didn't, we wouldn't be in this
predicament, would we? So, what's to do? Shall we invite him here? As he expects? As the world expects?
After eluding him so well for so long, shall we at last
be forced to have him here? So we can crawl on our
bellies in our own sanctuary?"

Her husband growled. He turned a livid face to
hers, started to utter something, but sputtered on another snarl and began coughing. His face turned red,
then crimson.

His wife rose from her chair, took a glass from the
table and held it to her husband's lips. He drank so
greedily some of the liquid spilled out of his mouth
and down his chin. He sat back when there was nothing left, gasping, his coughing subsiding.

The woman picked up a bell and rang it. A footman
hurried into the room.

"My husband is having one of his attacks," she told
him in a calm, cold voice, averting her face. "You know
what to do. Get his man and his medicine." When the
footman hurried out, she went to the door, too. She
looked back at her husband, coughing fitfully, but with

less force. "We may not be quite dished. I will consider this carefully. We'll speak of this again, Richard, when you're better," she said, and with a bitter smile, left him alone by the barren fireside.

24

"Mama would like the wedding to be at home," Kate reported, after she skimmed the letter she'd just opened.

Alasdair sat back, listening in silence, his hand loosely circled around the cup of tea she'd poured for him. He watched her closely, taking pleasure watching the way her hands moved when she opened a letter, how her eyes widened when she read something that interested her, and how the sunlight teased gold from her curls.

He smiled at how inane a smitten man could be. The smile grew rueful as he realized there was nothing else he could do but admire her from afar, even if that "afar" was only three feet. He was showing the Swansons how good, how virtuous, how ordinary the wicked St. Erth could be, even when tempted by the tasty tidbit who was his fiancée. He had no choice. They'd been engaged for two weeks, and only now did the Swansons permit him to sit alone with her—at teatime, in the salon, and with the door ajar, he thought with amused resignation.

"And you?" he asked. "What would you like?"

"I'd like it if we'd been married at that inn instead of just compromised there." She colored because of the look that flashed in his eyes.

He noted it. "Does my continuing interest in that 'compromise' distress you?" he asked mildly. "I hope not. I thought you felt the same, and hope it's only your notion of propriety that prevents you from admitting it. Believe me, I'd think it *very* proper if you did."

"It's not that . . . exactly. Well, maybe it is," she admitted. "What I think of what we do—did—isn't something I'm comfortable talking about yet."

"You will be," he promised. "I realize marriage entails decades of dealing with thousands of mundane things that will make up our lives. But I'd be lying if I didn't say that what compromised us is of greatest interest to me right now." He saw her embarrassment and relented. "It's not just the longing for pleasure, Kate. I find myself longing simply to lie with you in my arms, peacefully, talking about how good our life is. It will be. But this isn't getting us anywhere. Warm talk over cold tea isn't much use to a man in a heated condition. No"—he laughed, putting his hand over the cup—"I don't want any more, thank you. What were you saying?"

It took her a minute to remember. She flourished the letter, frowning again. "Plans for our marriage. My cousins say we should wait until next spring, and they're pushing for a fine wedding here, at St. George's. Now here's Mama telling me she's thinking of a wedding in high summer! In our church at home. I don't much care where we're wed, do you? I thought not. But wherever we chose, that's a year away, either way," she said plaintively.

"Even if I didn't mind that, which I do," she added hastily, "what am I supposed to do until then? I don't want to stay here with the Swansons, sweet as they are—and truly, Harriet, Frances, and Chloe are much nicer to me now. But if I go home, you'll have to travel for days to see me, and I won't see you even half as often as I do now—oh, this is impossible. Why should something so simple be getting so baroque!" she asked in frustration. "Why should there be so much time between the decision and the deed? I'm not some giddy young chit, so why don't they trust my judgment? My parents, at least, used to. What's come over them?"

"I believe they may be worried about what people may think came over you—literally," he said wryly. Reaching over the table and taking her hand, he added, "Dear ninny mine, they want the guests at your wedding to see that the wedding isn't strictly necessary. They want it to look like a consummation devoutly to be wished—instead of one that had to be hastily covered up."

She stared at him, perplexed.

He sighed. "We two were away together overnight, at an inn. Even if we hadn't been, there's the matter of who you were away with. Dear Kate," he said gently, to her dawning distress, "they want everyone to see you aren't increasing. The Swansons believe a wedding nine months hence, with you still svelte, should be enough to do the trick. Your parents are more discreet. They don't want the reason for the long engagement to be that obvious. And they might also want to give you enough time to change your mind."

Now she glared. "Never!" she said. "Not my par-

ents at least. They believe what I tell them. Besides,
I've been judge, jury, and referee in our family long
enough for them not only to believe in my good sense,
but to depend on it utterly." She paused, and added in
a smaller voice, "That's just the problem, and why
there may be something in what you say. I doubt they
worry about you—not in the way you mean. I think,
deep down, even old as I am, they aren't ready to let
me go to anyone."

She slipped her hand from his and used her finger
to skim the letter, running it across the crisscrossing
lines. "They say things like . . . ah, here: *'We sent you to
London to have a good time, and hope you don't think we
were trying to be rid of you. We've always mocked parents
desperate to pop their girls off, don't you remember?'* And
here: *'Dearest girl, you know how well we all rub on together here, never think we sent you to visit your cousins because we wanted to marry you off. You're welcome to stay
on here with us as you are, forever.'*

"There," she said with sad satisfaction, looking up
at him again, resting her hand on top of his, as if to
comfort him, " 'Forever,' that's the key word. You see?
It isn't you. You could be an archbishop for all they
care."

He chuckled, but she went on, "It's me, and how
much they need me. But much as I love them, I'd
rather not stay home a year, missing you all the time,
with nothing to do but dream of our marriage. What's
the purpose? So I can assemble some monstrous
trousseau? I can buy linens after I'm married. So I can
arrange for an extra armful of roses at the wedding,
and wait for answers to invitations from relatives in
the Antipodes? Nonsense. All that time at home will
make it harder to leave my family. And they know it.
They want to keep things just as they are. I'm useful to

them. I don't want to sound like an undutiful daughter, but the thing is that now I want to be useful to *you*."

He picked up her hand and brought it to his lips. She was touched, tingling, enchanted, so pleased with him that she forgot what she'd just been complaining about. But it was so comforting to have him sitting there beside her in the afternoon. So domestic, so fulfilling, and Lord, the man looked good in daylight. Night made him seem dramatic, like a great black cat on the stalk. The afternoon sun showed him to be just as virile, equally dangerous but a hundred times more accessible. She yearned to jump from her chair, fling herself into his arms, sit on his lap, and try to discover how long a person could kiss without breathing. Because he'd become as vital to her as breathing.

It wasn't just what he did to her senses. She had enough of them left to realize that marrying a man for one attribute, however agreeable, would be folly. Just as a woman who married for money was a fool because if the fellow lost his fortune, she'd be stuck with the man, physical attraction was very fine but it might also be fleeting. Then, if it ever paled or was somehow lost, she'd be stuck with the man behind the male. But Alasdair was man and male enough for any woman.

He said he longed to lie with her as much as talk with her. She certainly understood that. She was delighted simply to sit and talk with him. She valued his opinion and sought his good opinion of herself. He was reserved, but warm, cool but caring, a mass of contradictions that fascinated her. And she loved to laugh with him. Of course, he lured her senses, too, and though she wasn't sure just what she'd be getting into, she couldn't wait to find out. In all, and in truth, she'd never known she was incomplete until she'd grown to know him. Now she didn't know if she could ever be whole again without him. He lent balance and weight to her life.

So the thought of having to sit so far from his arms and yet so near to him for another hour, much less another year, horrified her. And the suggestion that she might have to sit a hundred miles away from him for that whole year, only dreaming of even this frustrating closeness, devastated her.

She wondered if he felt the same way, and was suddenly afraid to ask. Because maybe he did want her to take that year away from him. Because maybe, in spite of his kiss, and those yearning looks, he wasn't ready for marriage—at least, not to her.

He saw her expression change from frustrated chagrin to something too much like fear. He saw the shadow come into her eyes, her lips parting in a suddenly indrawn breath as she looked at him with worried speculation. And then he saw her small, white teeth begin to worry at her plump lower lip.

A man could only take so much.

He pushed back his chair and surged to his feet. He reached for her, and didn't have to take a step forward because suddenly she was on her feet and in his arms. He held her close and rocked her, one hand clipped round her waist, the other splayed on her back, pressing her near as he whispered, "What? What is it? What's the matter, Kate? Tell me, please."

He felt the breath hitch in her chest, "Oh, Alasdair. Have I presumed? What do I know of such things? Maybe it's only right to wait a year. I don't want to step wrong, I don't know how to go right—Lord, when it comes to you, I don't know a thing! Tell me the right thing to do, please, Alasdair."

He did.

He drew back and cupped her face in both hands.

He searched her eyes and saw no fear of him, but only some deep disquiet that slowly changed to the same helpless, hopeless longing that he felt as he stared at her. Satisfied, he brought his lips to hers.

There was nothing like her kiss. He marveled at it. There was nothing like the sweetness of her mouth, the special essential taste of Kate, the touch of her tongue that sent shivers along his neck, where her hands were now clutching him, locking him right where he wanted to be. He was a man who knew infinite and intricate variations of lovemaking. He knew the ways of the human body at lovemaking better than most physicians did, because he'd been taught much and discovered more in many lands, from expert partners, and yet he'd never felt anything so good as her kiss. It made him want more, but it was so incredibly delicious that even if he were never permitted more, he thought her kiss would be enough.

. . . for a few minutes.

Because, as if of its own accord, now one of his hands sought the roundness of her bottom. She willingly pressed closer. Her hand touched his hair as his mouth sought to taste the corner of her ear. "Kate," he murmured into that ear, delighting at how his breath caused her dainty shudders, "Not a year. Never a year. My God, not a minute more, but certainly not a year."

"Because of . . . this?" she asked, and he could feel her body tense and hear the trace of sorrow in her voice.

"Of course." He laughed and kissed her neck. "And this, and this," he added as he drew a line of kisses down to her shoulder. He was a very tall man, but had no trouble doubling over so he could avail himself of what she offered. He cupped her breast, drawing the neck of her gown down so he could kiss more of her perfumed, rising flesh. "And this . . . But also because I do love you."

He drew back, marginally, and locked both hands behind her back, holding her as though they were connected at the waist. Tilting back a fraction so he could watch her expression, he added softly, "I don't want to sit in stasis for a calendar year, just to placate the gossips. Nor will it matter. Be sure, my reputation will precede me, even if we pass this test, there will be others.

"Kate," he said seriously, "I'll never be able to smile at another female without there being suspicion. I won't be able to come home late to dinner without causing gossip. I promised you before, I'll do it again: I will never betray you. I hope you continue to believe me, but I assure you others will always doubt me. If you can accept that, then, yes, accept me now. A year won't make a difference, except to torment us more. Ten, twenty, won't matter either. I'm flattered and relieved that you want to marry now. Nothing could please me more. Let's do it."

She smiled up at him. He let out a sigh of relief. She closed her eyes. His lips were only centimeters from hers, he lowered his head to remedy that miscalculation.

"Kate!" a shocked voice said.

Alasdair's head went up, and he stepped back. He kept one hand around Kate's waist, but the other fell to his side. Kate turned a flushed, dazed face to her cousin, Lady Swanson. Sibyl and Henrietta were by their mother's side. They all stared. Kate's lips were swollen, her curls mussed, her gown askew. She looked confused, as though she'd just been pulled out of bed during an erotic dream.

"Kate and I have decided that we'd like our wedding to go forth as soon as possible after the banns have been read," Alasdair said. He looked cool and collected—if one ignored the strain in his eyes, and the slightly elevated color on his lean cheeks.

Sibyl was big-eyed; her sister Henrietta stared at the couple enviously.

"So soon?" Lady Swanson said in a faltering voice, gazing from one flushed face to the other.

Alasdair drew himself up. "As there's no reason for a hasty wedding except for our own eagerness to begin a life together, I'd think that those three weeks, plus the two since our adventure, and perhaps three more, should be enough to eventually quell the gossips. And if not, we simply don't give a damn, madam."

"Yes, so I see," Lady Swanson said. "And so, discretion being the better part of valor, I find I must agree. Because speak of discretion! If there's not a problem now, there may be one tomorrow. *At tea!* Sir Alasdair, it is simply not done."

"I agree," he said, wooden-faced. "Nor would I have guessed I'd do it. So, eight weeks of waiting is certainly long enough, you'll agree?"

"Only if the waiting is observed during those weeks, sir," she said sternly.

He winced. "You've my word on it," he said. "Kate?"

"What? Oh, yes," she said, blinking like an owl at sunrise. "Oh my! Eight weeks, yes, please."

Alasdair sat in the bath with a cigarillo clenched between his teeth, and scrubbed at his back with a sponge. "Yes, it's six weeks from now," he muttered through his cigarillo. "The invitation was waiting when you got back to London because we sent them soon as they were ready. We got them out today. The ink must still be wet. You were out of town when it was decided. I sent a letter telling you, but it must have been delivered to Boxwood as you were leaving it. Nothing amiss, was there?"

"No," Leigh said, "Estate matters. But a wedding in six weeks?"

"Eight when we decided. By the time the arrangements were settled enough to issue invitations it was six. Believe me, I keep count. Leigh, I'm as astonished as you are."

His friend leaned back against the porcelain fittings in Alasdair's sumptuous bathing room. "I'm delighted. So I assume there'll soon be another St. Erth arriving on this poor old planet to pester the virtuous and otherwise complicate people's lives?"

Alasdair surged up from the porcelain bath he'd been sitting in. He stood, soapy water sluicing down his body, slopping over the rim of the bath to the mosaic floor tiles. His eyes narrowed, he clutched his sponge till it flowed like a spigot. He was a powerful man and every muscle in his body was corded with tension, most of them on view. He looked dangerous, but his friend only stood and watched him with an expression of inquiry.

"No," Alasdair said through teeth clenched so hard on the cigarillo that they met in the middle. "There is not. By God!" he muttered, obviously checking whatever he was going to say next. He cast the cigarillo into the bathwater and, picking up a bucket of water, poured it over his head to rinse the soap away. "You too?" he asked angrily as he stomped out of the tub and snatched up a towel.

"You could simply say no," Leigh said mildly. "Now your man is going to have to spend the night mopping. There's no sense building yourself such a lavish modern bath if you're going to treat it like a woodland stream. So, it is no? I don't mean to be insulting, but given how lovely she is and how powerfully you react to her, plus how soon you're getting married, I am surprised."

Alasdair ran a hand over his sopping hair. He gave Leigh a level look. "There is no way on earth she could produce another St. Erth right now, trust me on that. I know the proprieties and that she values them, and have *some* semblance of dignity and a scrap of discretion left to me. As well as control. The problem is that it's eroding." He tossed the towel over his hair and rubbed at it. When his head emerged again, his lips were lifted in a curious smile. "Leigh, the thing is, I can't keep my hands off her. *Me!* Isn't that absurd?"

Leigh smiled. "No, that's very good."

"But even at teatime! *Tea time*, in the Swanson parlor! Her aunt walked in along with Sibyl and one of those fierce older sisters. They were shocked. By God, *I* was shocked. We were entangled, but vertical, you can put your eyebrows down now. But that's not like me. I seem to have no control when it comes to Kate, and so I reason we're better off marrying now. Leigh, she's wonderful. I'm lucky beyond my deserts. I'm glad my body made up my mind for me. I don't believe I deserve her, but I can't and won't disgrace her or give her any more cause for concern. Given my past, and the way gossip flies, she'll have enough on her plate just by marrying me. There's nothing for it but wedlock, as soon as may be."

Leigh picked up a shaving brush and admired its silver handle. "Will it be lucky for her, too?" he asked softly.

"I intend to make it so."

"And so you're giving up your vengeful plans for her cousins?" Leigh asked too mildly.

Alasdair swung around and padded out to the door to his dressing room and waiting valet. "No of course not," he said over his shoulder. "The best is yet to come. But don't worry, and don't nag at me. It's almost done. You can wait here, or in the library," he added before Leigh could ask any questions. "I'll only be a moment, then we can be off to dinner. Then, it's the theater, isn't it?" He stopped and turned. "Come to think of it, this may be your final performance at the theater, at least on my behalf. I thank you for all your help, but my mission's accomplished. You don't have to shepherd the littlest Swanson anymore."

"Yes, maybe so," Leigh said. "But if I suddenly cut the child off, it would hurt her feelings, I think. I'll keep accompanying you, if I may, and with Sibyl in tow, at least for a while longer. Given the circumstances, even if she doesn't need me, you may. You need someone who feels free to stop you when you verge on something ill-advised. Kate's obviously too besotted by your famous charm. On the other hand, I am not. If I'd been with you at that fateful tea, you might not be sending out invitations so hurriedly now. For example, I knew you weren't going to hit me when you emerged from the tub. The time to worry about you is when you least think you have to. I'll wait downstairs," he added, as Alasdair laughed.

Alasdair dressed in silence, only replying to his valet in monosyllables, his thoughts far from cravats and waistcoats. Lately he found himself enjoying thoughts of where Kate would be and what they'd soon be doing when were married, especially as he engaged in the most intimate, commonplace activities. He was dressing to go out for the evening. If they were already wed, would she be perched on his bed, casting a critical eye on his toilette? Or would she hint his valet from the room and help him undress instead?

He blinked. Would she want her own bedchamber? He'd have to remember to ask her that, and pretend to be pleased if she did. No, he wanted her with him when he woke in the morning and went to sleep at night. He'd better state his preference, because she was still shy of him. By God, he couldn't wait to see what he could do to end that. He smiled, thinking of all the ways he could.

"Will there be anything else, sir?" his valet asked, because he was done ministering to his master, yet Sir Alasdair stood, not moving from the spot. The valet's keen eye could see nothing amiss. His master's hair was brushed and shining, his jacket fit his broad shoulders without a wrinkle, his black satin evening breeches were flawless, his high neckcloth a work of art, his hose spotless. In all the man was perfection.

"What? Oh. No, you've done well, as always," Alasdair said. "I was just thinking . . . Don't wait up for me."

Alasdair took the long stair downstairs. "No time to dawdle," he called to Leigh as he did, summoning him from the library. His butler helped him on with his evening cape. He took his walking stick, and went to the door his footman, Paris, held open.

Then he paused.

"A moment," he told Leigh. "Was the invitation delivered?" he asked Paris.

"Yes, sir, as you asked."

"And was there an answer?"

"No, sir. But I told their man that he was to give it directly into their hands, and I'd wait for an answer, as you said I should. I waited, and when he returned he said they'd read it, but that neither of the Scalbys had an answer."

"Very good," Alasdair said.

"You said it was almost done," Leigh murmured as they went out the door. "It seems far from it. What will you do if they *do* come to the wedding? Surely you can't mean to accost them there? With all their family around them? And Kate, on her special day?"

Alasdair gave him a tilted smile. "*Surely*? A word I seldom use. I don't know what I'll do if they come. But neither do they, and there's the pleasure in it."

Leigh stopped on the pavement. "A wedding is a holy event," he said sternly.

"And the Scalbys are unholy," Alasdair retorted. "Let be. The plan has a life of its own now. Love is one thing, justice, another. They have nothing to do with one another. If my wedding is accompanied by unholy glee at a final victory, how much sweeter the taste of my wedding feast. What better gift could I be given? For that matter, what better gift for Kate than a husband with a free heart and mind? A clear future, all grudges forgotten, all debts paid—and paid in spades."

"In front of her?"

"Give me more credit than that," Alasdair said. "If it's done in back of her, it's just as good for me."

"But can you give them more credit? Even snakes fight for their lives."

"Their lives, as they knew them, are already over. They know it. Why else are they in hiding? Do you think they'd actually come? The invitation is merely a knife to twist in their wounds. I'll settle it before I face the minister. I have six weeks, after all. Napoleon's defeat at Waterloo took less time, for that matter, so did Creation itself. Forget it. Don't worry. I don't."

Leigh gave him a troubled look as they stepped into Alasdair's carriage. Alasdair told the coachman to drive on, and as they did, he chatted with his friend as though he hadn't a care in his head. He'd told Leigh the truth. Tonight, he didn't worry. He refused to. He didn't forget, though. He never did.

25

Kate's parents didn't dislike him, Alasdair realized, or even distrust him, in spite of his reputation. They just didn't want him.

Marion Corbet was a handsome woman who wore her years well. Though she had blue eyes and was taller than her daughter, it was clear where Kate had got her curly hair and heart-shaped face. John Corbet was a handsome man of fifty-odd. His brown eyes were like his daughter's, except they didn't warm when they looked upon his future son-in-law. Kate had gotten her laughter and easygoing charm from her parents, too, Alasdair realized, to judge from the way they reacted to everyone else, aside from him.

The Corbets hadn't brought their three sons to London to meet their daughter's fiancé, to Alasdair's great relief. Two people ignoring him was enough. He was used to distrust and had expected dislike, but he wasn't used to being so obviously excluded and roundly ignored.

The first night the Corbets arrived in London they were feted at the Swansons' house. There was a merry dinner, a laughter-filled evening, even the grumpy elder Swanson sisters were jovial. There were many tender good nights when the Corbets went back to their hotel. The next night, everyone went to a fine restaurant, where old family tales were retold until the waiters were yawning and leaning against the walls. The third day Alasdair took them in his carriage, with Kate, to drive through the park as Alasdair pointed out the sights to them. That was all he could do, since they addressed all their questions to Kate. Then they all went to the theater, where it was even easier for them to ignore him.

"You were very quiet this evening," Kate told Alasdair that night as they sat on a sofa in the salon. The Swansons were leaving them discreetly alone for a few moments, her parents having gone back to their hotel.

"I didn't grow up in your family," he answered simply.

She flinched. "Right, right," she murmured, lifting one shoulder. "Well, I told you how it was. I just didn't know how it would be. I'm sorry. It's not you." She sighed. "They've already begun involving me. Mother says there's no way *she* can get my brother Simon to go back to school this autumn, since he's taken it into his head to go to the Continent, be a vagabond, and write a journal. *Simon?* Well, you'd have to know him. He was also going to be a balloonist, until he tried his wings by climbing to the top of the barn. He looked down, got dizzy, and fell like a stone. We were lucky all that broke was his wrist."

They shared sympathetic grins, and she went on, "At least I talked him out of running away to join the gypsies. She says I'm the only one he'd listen to. It's true. If he'd told me his plans for becoming an aerialist, I'd have been able to stop it, too. And ditto for my brother Lawrence. He's begun making noises about courting the squire's daughter, and my parents are panicked. He's so rash. He's only sixteen, and you'd have to know the squire's daughter to know what a disaster that would be! And Mama says my brother Robin's sulking because I haven't come home yet, and Father insists no one else can name the new mare but me, since I'm so good at such things. But he reminds me I can't till I see her."

Alasdair took one of her hands in his. "And do you want to? Go home, that is?"

She looked at him helplessly. "I only want to be with you."

They didn't speak again for a while. Then it took all of Alasdair's training and control to finally put her at arm's length, away from him. He steadied his breathing and smoothed back his hair. Looking at her made him reach for her again. Her curls were mussed, her mouth looked as soundly kissed as it had been, her dress was delightfully askew.

"You can't say such things to me," he said in a thickened voice. "You should be able to, but I'm not myself when I'm with you. I hardly know myself when I'm with you," he confessed, looking as exasperated with himself as he was genuinely puzzled by his reactions to her.

She straightened her gown, then fussed with her hair. He smiled to see how she set it to rights by rumpling it more artistically. It was just that kind of absurd thing that made his pulses beat and his heart grow foolishly fond. "You haven't answered my question," he said softly.

"You didn't let me." She ducked her head. "No,

that's a lie. I didn't want to. The truth is that I adore them. But I *cannot* be without you." She looked at him with defiance. "If it tears me in two, that's how it has to be. I don't say it makes me happy, it just about kills me. But I've made my choice, and they can only make me feel guilty and sad. I can't and won't go back on my decision. I've chosen you, because that's the only way it can be for me."

He leapt to his feet. "You can't say things like that to me now," he said in what might have been real indignation. "Not one more word! Not when it's time for me to leave. I hear footmen shuffling at the door. I won't embarrass myself again, I can't, Kate. One more incident, and your family won't trust me to so much as take you for a stroll before the wedding. And who can blame them? But thank you. For your decision, and your trust in me. It isn't misplaced, I promise you."

She got to her feet when he did. He took her hand and kissed it—and then dragged her into his arms.

"Oh, damnation," he groaned against her cheek when he finally was able to find the discipline to say anything. She giggled into his ear. "Now I hear your aunt coughing at the door. Either she's got consumption, or I've done it again."

"Mr. Corbet!" Alasdair said, taking Kate's father's hand before he took a chair next to him in the reception room of the Corbets' hotel. He was pleased to see they sat far away from others who were chatting, loitering, or having tea in the vast room. "So glad you could take the time to see me."

John Corbet eyed Alasdair closely. "You said it was a matter of some importance."

"So it is. Don't get your hopes up," Alasdair said.

"I'm not about to tell you that I'm ending the engagement."

John Corbet's polite smile faded, he looked surprised.

"That's just the point," Alasdair went on doggedly, "and I want to get to that point with no delay. I'm going to marry Kate. She wants that as badly as I do. You and your lovely wife clearly do not."

Alasdair fixed Kate's father with a dark stare. "I can't make you like me," he said flatly. "I can't even make you tolerate me. If you choose not to, that's the way it will be. But I'm here to tell you it will be that way forever, or for so long as I live, and I come from a long-lived family. Baring accident, of course, I intend to be around to be the father of your grandchildren, and great-grandchildren, if I'm lucky. I can live with your dislike. But I don't wish to live with Kate's unhappiness about it. So I came to ask if you'd at least accept that I am here, and will remain so. And to beg you to hide your dislike, at least for her sake."

Kate's father sat still, his eyes on Alasdair. "Well," he finally said, "there's plain speaking."

"Indeed."

"We don't dislike you," the other man said slowly. "It's just that we're not best pleased at losing our little girl."

"She's not a girl, and you won't lose her unless you force her to choose between families. Ours—for when we marry, we will be one—and yours. And I don't ask you to be pleased. Only to accept the facts, and if you can bear to, to occasionally speak to me—at least in front of Kate. I can fully accept your ignoring me when she's not around. It's her happiness I'm here for. I hope that's your goal, too. Whatever you've heard about me, let me assure you her tranquillity is my primary object. I won't mistreat her. I'll always take as much care of her feelings and person as you would. That's exactly why I asked for this meeting, and why I'm here at all."

John Corbet tilted his head, looking Alasdair full in the eye for the first time since they'd met. "Well, you've landed me a facer, haven't you?" he asked roughly. "This is the lofty St. Erth I heard about. The arrogant fellow everyone wrote to me about. And yet unbending enough to ask for a favor? And in the process making me feel smaller?"

Alasdair's expression remained calm, but he winced inwardly. He'd failed. He'd tried to scotch a problem by uncovering it, because he more than anyone knew the dangers of hidden feelings, how they could eat away at a person's soul. The Corbets might only resent him now, but unchecked resentment always grew to be dislike, and worse. But bringing the thing out into the open hadn't ended it, as he'd hoped. He'd have to see if there was anything retrievable. He started to speak, but the older man put up a hand to stop him.

"No, please don't interrupt, Sir Alasdair. You've had your say, now hear mine."

Alasdair sat quiet, bracing himself, reining in his temper.

"You're right," Kate's father said.

Alasdair blinked.

"And if it makes you feel any better, it wasn't you, or your reputation," her father went on. "Your birth is good, your fortune's solid." He cast an eye over how neatly Alasdair was dressed, and added, "You're a good-looking fellow, neither a tulip nor a buck, but seem to be a sound and steady man. I heard about your reputation, and discounted it. My Kate's got a

good head on her shoulders. Which is why we wanted
to keep her, I suppose. That's all it is," he said, shrugging his shoulders and looking glum.

"Her mother and I adore her. Yes, I suppose it is
time she flew on her own. All her friends are married,
what has she got at home but us? That's enough for us,
but for her? I expect we didn't want to see it. Love's a
funny thing. Too much is as bad as too little. It *is* possible to love too well, and that's the plain truth."

"I hope to discover if that's so," Alasdair murmured, his relief easy to see in the way he sat back in
his chair.

"Oh, it is, it is," John Corbet murmured. "Well. I
can't say this was pleasant, but it was for the best. I like
a man who speaks his mind. Now, if you don't mind,
may we just sit a while and talk? I'd like to get to know
more about you, if you'd permit?"

"I'd like that," Alasdair said, and hesitated. "But as
to your good wife?"

"That's just it. She is good. Don't worry, leave her to
me. She'll see the light, but if the messenger is to be
killed for bringing it to her, let it be me. I'm used to it."
He chuckled. "So. Tell me, where do you two intend to
live? In London or on your estate? I hope it's the latter,
because it's closer to us. But you don't look like a
countryman, so I suppose it's to be London."

"My valet mightn't like it, but I was once a countryman and intend to be so again. Only it's not sheep or
pigs I'd like to raise. I've an eye to horses."

"Horses?" the other man asked eagerly. "Well, well.
We do have something in common."

They had the love of Kate, Alasdair thought, but
didn't say it. For the first time, he realized it must be a
hard thing to give up someone you loved, just so she
could be happier. But how could he know that? He'd

never had a choice. The only two he'd ever loved had gone, first one and then the other, without any leave of his. That was what he'd spent his life trying to avenge.

"You don't like Arabian stock?" John Corbet asked in disappointment.

"Oh. No, I always have," Alasdair said, dragging his attention back to what was being said rather than what was going on his head. He buried his thoughts and hid his plans, even from himself, as he'd always done, and went on to pass the morning talking about horses.

Only four more weeks, Kate thought, and shivered, and wrapped her arms around herself, remembering how he'd held her in his arms tonight. She stood at her bedroom window looking out into the dark. She couldn't have seen much even if there was light, except for a narrow alley and the wall of the house next door. But she wasn't looking at anything that was there.

Apart from him for only two hours, and *Lord*, how she yearned for him! Yes, she loved talking to him, and, of course, she relished his wit, and how good it was to hear what he thought about what she did and said. But that was nothing to the way she felt when she looked at him. She got such strange reactions from just watching him do mundane things.

Just a chance glance at his chin tonight showed the first growth of his beard darkening the notch in his otherwise smooth-shaven chin. It sent a surge of warmth to her heart, and regions much lower than that. Even that was nothing to the dizzying feeling of possessive joy she'd felt when she'd looked at his hand on his wineglass. But the bottom dropped out of her stomach when he'd looked back, caught her mooning over him, and caressed her with his dark, equally avid stare.

And when he caressed her! Where he led, she followed. She'd been a prudent girl and was a sensible woman, but when he kissed her and touched her, he made her want to shuck out of her clothes and peel off her skin, anything to get closer to him. She couldn't wait to marry him and join him in bed. She knew it was outrageous. She understood she was in a fever of desire. She didn't care.

Oh, Alasdair! she thought, and hugged herself hard. How can I be so lucky? And so tormented by having to wait four weeks!

Only three weeks, Kate thought, as she paced by her window and saw the first stains of oncoming dawn light the sullen night sky. Three weeks until they were married! And it wouldn't be a moment too soon. Things had gotten so strange and exciting and dangerous tonight, when they'd been alone in the garden after dinner. Such a tiny joke of a London garden, scarcely room for a bird to waltz with his beloved, Alasdair had joked. But it was dark, and the night was so soft, and he'd taken her in his arms, and there was room enough for everything they wanted to do.

His lips at her mouth, her neck, her breasts. Her hands on his chest, feeling the wild beating of his heart and the heat of his skin burning through his thin linen shirt. His hands on her, pushing up her skirt. The way she'd sucked in her breath when his hand caressed her thigh, her inner thigh, herself where only she'd touched herself before while bathing. She'd jerked and started to pull away, and he'd whispered, "No, wait, see, relax, and see, oh, Kate, yes, do you see?"

She hadn't seen anything, but as he'd kept up she'd

felt thrilling new spikes of pleasure, felt a thrumming in her body, a relaxing and yet a tensing of her whole self radiating out from there—there—*there*! She'd been shocked, delighted, weak, and trembling. He'd slowly withdrawn his hand from her flesh, and like a cold breeze blown through a newly opened window, loss had followed the warmth of pleasure. He must have known, he kept his other arm around her.

"There, Kate, it's all right," he'd said. "No one will know but us."

She hadn't been worried about that, she hadn't thought of anyone but him and what else might lie in store. "But what about you?" she asked hopefully, "Shouldn't there be more?"

"Oh yes"—he'd chuckled—"much more. My night will come, and then it will be all our days and nights."

But not soon enough for her, she thought as she paced her bedchamber again, her sheer summer night-gown feeling like grit as it moved over her sensitized skin. She paced until the sun rose enough for her to stop so she could dress and go downstairs and wait for him.

"Two weeks," he breathed into her hair. "We'll be man and wife in two weeks," Alasdair said, loosing his embrace and stepping away. "We can wait until then. So please, go sit over there and smile at me demurely, my dear rogue. It's raining, we can't go out. We're not wed yet, so we have to sit here in this parlor, like lady and gentleman. It's for the best, your brothers are the most vigilant chaperons, that must be why your parents finally brought them here. They wore me out in the park, and at the Tower, and on the Serpentine, I'm too weary for anything more this evening." His smile belied that.

"They're good lads," he added, taking a seat opposite her.

"They're mad about you. Thank you for having Leigh tell Simon about the poetry he studied at Oxford. Now he's on fire to go."

"I'm glad I could set one Corbet on fire without scandalizing everyone," he said, leaning back in his chair.

She giggled at the absurdity of that, and he smiled back at her.

"So, two weeks remain. Is all in readiness now?" he asked.

"My mother and father are ready as they'll ever be, but wistful. They'd have liked the ceremonies at home because London's so thin of company. I reminded them that home would be even thinner of company now, and they conceded that. Don't worry, it's not because they're opposed to you—just the reverse. They want to make the biggest stir. The boys are in ecstasies because you're a 'great gun.' Lady Swanson doesn't think things are in order yet, though. But she'd need two years to get the sort of reception she wants prepared. Lord Swanson is just pleased everything's going forth. Chloe is complaining her gown won't be ready. Frances keeps muttering about unseemly haste. Harriet's in a dither about her new slippers and whether they really match her dress." She frowned. "Sibyl's trying to be brave, but I know she worries she'll never see Leigh again after the wedding. Will she?"

Alasdair shrugged. "I don't know. I don't think his heart's engaged, it's just that his is a soft one. She's too young anyway. Still, who knows what will come in time? But, Kate, are *you* ready?"

"If you don't know, maybe *we* aren't ready!" she yelped.

He laughed. And toyed with his quizzing glass, holding it by its ribbon, letting it swirl in increasingly smaller slow circles before him. "And all the guests have answered?" he asked softly, watching it spin. "Has everyone you've invited accepted, even on such short notice?"

"Almost all! It's amazing. Even on such short notice!"

"Probably the same reason such crowds show up for hangings, to make sure the villain is well and truly turned off," he commented. "So, all's well. I've got very little family, and those that still breathe are coming. But yours . . . Everyone else has replied. But are the Scalbys coming?"

She frowned. "We didn't get *any* answer from them." She gazed at him worriedly. "Should we send round another invitation? Or should we let it be? Alasdair, can you truly bear to see them?

"I truly wish to," he said honestly. Then paused, and added, "Let them see how well I've done. It's the best revenge."

"Well, then, I'd better have Father call on them. It's his duty, and he can find out." She hesitated. "You mean to confront them then? I know you must, but . . ."

"Kate," he said softly, "trust me. I've no desire to ruin our day. I just wanted to know. Forewarned is forearmed. I can't like seeing them on any day, and I don't want them to do anything to ruin that one for me. But I want to be prepared for anything." He caught up his quizzing glass and tucked it away. He looked at his watch. "We have another ten minutes before we're interrupted. Come over here, wench, let's see what trouble we can get into in that time."

She went to him willingly, unwillingly to waste those precious minutes.

* * *

A week, Kate thought as she rode to the dressmakers for the final fitting of the dress she'd wear to her wedding. Just one week left, she realized, as the carriage wheels turned in time with her thoughts: *too long, too long, too long.*

26

The bride wore a gown the color of old pearls and had a soft rosy flush on her cheeks. She carried a bouquet of gardenias and wore a matching crown of them on her curls. The keenest-eyed gossip in church couldn't deny Kate Corbet—now Lady St. Erth, was a slender, graceful sylph of a bride. The gentlemen couldn't deny that she'd curves enough for any man's delight. She made a charming bride, and if gossips were disappointed because they couldn't see if a hasty marriage had been *necessary*, they had nothing to grumble about if they concentrated on the groom.

Damned if the fellow didn't look dangerous, even in church. "Satan at the holy fount," one would-be poet had already titled the poem he envisioned as he watched the groom take his vows, in hopes his romantic epic would rival Byron's wildly successful "Corsair." Not everyone was stimulated to poetry, but more than one guest remarked that St. Erth was the devil of a fellow. There he stood next to his lovely bride, married and appearing to be willing to be so, and yet still he looked untamed.

He stood tall and aloof after the ceremony, his dark gaze slicing through the crowd of well-wishers queuing on the reception line; though he smiled, those smiles could have cut diamonds. True, he didn't look unhappy. And also true that his fierce gaze softened whenever he gazed at his new wife. But where was the joy he should have been showing on this most signal day?

A new groom was expected to look fatuous and permitted to look dazed. Many a fellow looked staggered as he'd stepped down from the altar, as though he'd been hit on the forehead like a bullock at the slaughter. But from the moment St. Erth lifted his fond gaze from his new wife, he seemed, if anything, too aware of his surroundings. He didn't look happy or sad, only distant, distracted, and abstracted. Although he was everything that was proper, he seemed to be waiting for something other than his wedding night.

But who knew what it meant, or what he was thinking? Who could fathom that devil, now or before?

They aren't here, Alasdair thought, fighting to conceal his emotions as he scanned the crowd at the church again. *The damned Scalbys aren't here*. They'd said they would be. Kate's father had gone to their house and presented his card. They'd sent word that though they regretted they couldn't visit with him at that time, they'd certainly be at the church for their cousin's wedding. And they were not.

He'd prepared for them. The moment he heard they'd be there, he could think of little else. He'd been ecstatic. *Finally*, he finally had them where he'd always dreamed, at his mercy in the bosom of their family and in front of all Society. As they'd had him. He was sure they'd accepted the invitation because they were sure he'd spare them now that he was to be related to them. That only showed how little they knew him.

He'd planned to bow and smile, pretend there was nothing between them when they met again, at last, after all these years. He'd sat up the whole night before his wedding, not preoccupied with plans for the night to come with his lovely bride-to-be, but instead thrilling at the thought of the game he'd play with her evil cousins today. At four in the morning, after inventing and discarding so many scenarios, he'd finally come up with the perfect one. He'd smile, accept their congratulations, and when they were about to walk off, whisper sweetly: "Not here, not now, but we have much to talk about. As will all London, and soon." And then turn his head and let them walk away, the way a cat let a mouse it had held in its teeth finally stagger away . . . for a time.

But they weren't there.

Alasdair was relieved, furious, still tensed for confrontation. *Damn them to the hell they were bound for!* He stood on the reception line, nodding to praise and congratulations, his jaw clenched, a muscle in it ticking in time to his rising rage. He didn't think it was possible, but he hated them now more than ever, for ruining his wedding day like this. They'd scored on him once again.

They obviously thought they were still dangerous, at least they were still playing a game. They would pay.

"Alasdair?" Kate asked.

"Yes?" he said at once, turning to her, all his attention now riveted on her because there'd been a troubled note in her voice—he heard it above all the babble.

"Is there anything the matter?"

He gripped her hand more tightly. He hadn't released it since they'd walked back down the aisle. "No."

"Then why do you look so fierce?" she whispered, her eyes searching his.

He laughed. "Do I?"

She nodded. She'd dared mention it to him because there was one of those sudden inexplicable pauses in the wave of guests coming to congratulate them, and she wanted to make use of it. She tried to come up with a jest. Anything to get that terrible look off his face. "You look so grim," she whispered. "And my cousins haven't even congratulated us yet."

He grinned. She relaxed.

"Maybe it's because I like to be on the periphery of the crowd looking in, rather than being the focus of all eyes," he invented quickly. "Everyone watching me so close makes me begin to think I should be doing something worthy of entertaining them. Like juggling, or eating fire."

"Fire eating? That wouldn't be anything new," Leigh laughed as he came up to the newlyweds. "Now, juggling would be capital! Shall I get you some oranges, or would you rather wait for the reception? You *are* going to feed us aren't you?" He clapped Alasdair on the back. "Congratulations, my friend," he said with sincerity. "You're a very lucky man, and the good thing is that you know it. See you don't forget it!"

"As if I could," Alasdair said.

"And, my lady, thank you for taking him," Leigh went on, taking her hand in his and smiling down at her. "Now I can rest easy because I know he's in good hands. You're a charitable lady. I wish you nothing but bright days and beautiful nights, and a score of bright and beautiful children who take after you."

That made everyone within earshot laugh.

"Oh, Kate, I'm so happy for you!" Sibyl said as she hugged her cousin. "And," she whispered into Kate's ear as they embraced, "I'm *so* glad we saved him from the clutches of evil, now aren't you?"

Just thinking of Alasdair's clutches made Kate shiver. "Oh, yes!" she answered Sibyl fervently. "Who says virtue is its own reward? Just look at what I got for it!"

At least she couldn't stop looking.

She gazed at Alasdair throughout the whole long wedding feast. So handsome, so graceful, so big and imposing and yet elegant and charming—when he wished to be. So amusing, and kind, and hers! She could scarcely believe her good luck.

Others couldn't either.

"I never thought you'd actually land him," her cousin Harriet commented when she and her sisters got Kate alone for a minute, when she left Alasdair's side to go to the withdrawing room.

"Thought you were going to have to go home with your tail between your legs, and actually felt sorry for you," Frances said grudgingly.

"*Told* you she'd nab him," Chloe said mournfully.

"How did you do it?" Frances asked Kate. "You can tell us. Not as though it matters anymore, you've got him, you're leaving, we won't see you for a while. He had his pick of the most marriageable and passed them all up. Had his fill of the best demireps, too. What did you do to make him want you?"

"Don't tell us you were compromised at that inn, because we won't believe it, even if you were," Harriet said. "Much that would matter to him. He's slipped out of tighter knots."

They stood around her, enclosing her, glaring at her, and yet she saw a look of entreaty in their eyes and heard a note of what almost sounded like begging in their gruff voices. They really needed to know. It was something Kate had thought a lot about, too.

She cocked her head to the side. "I'm not sure. I know what you mean, though. And I agree, I certainly don't deserve him."

"We didn't say that," Frances protested. "None of us did."

Her sisters nodded.

"I know," Kate said, touched that they'd worry about her feelings. "But I don't know what to answer. I didn't go out of my way to nab him," she told Chloe. She paused. "I think when you empty yourself of expectations and simply go out and meet life, you stand a good chance of finding what you're looking for, even if you don't know that's what you're doing. I tried to do a good thing and met him, almost by mistake."

She saw their looks of puzzlement, and remembered that they couldn't and wouldn't ever know about either Lady Eleanora and how Kate had saved him from her, or the strange bargain she'd made with Alasdair after that. "I mean," she said quickly, "even though he terrified me with his sophistication, I made an effort to make light conversation with him when we first met, because he seemed so terribly bored."

"Well, of course," Chloe said. "He always seemed so, before he met you."

Kate nodded, relieved, and went on to firmer ground, the truth. "Yes. And when we met, there was a connection made. I don't know why. I'll never know, I suppose. But when you meet your match, you feel it long before you know it. It's one thing to feel attraction, this is something very different. It's like a coming home." They were listening quietly, intently. "Yes," she went on, sensing the rightness of what she said as she said it, "there was a sense of knowing, a sharing, a sympathy. That's much more than attraction, though believe me, attraction was not lacking!"

Chloe laughed. "With St. Erth? How could it be lacking?"

Kate smiled. "But we started as friends, and friends we became, and anything can come from that. . . . and did."

The three sisters were silent. Then Chloe spoke up. "Thank you. That makes perfect sense."

"Does it?' Kate laughed. "It still seems a miracle to me!"

The happy couple rode off in a flower-decked carriage, waving farewell to their friends and family. The bride's mama had wept, as had her father, only stopping when they were promised a visit within the month. Her brothers had made merry, pelting the couple with rice and flowers. Few knew where the wedding couple were going on their honeymoon because they'd only made up their minds at the last minute. Not because they were worried about any rambunctious friends planning an embarrassment, hounding the newlyweds on their wedding night with shouts or raucous revelry outside their window. Apart from the fact that the groom's friends were too sophisticated for such vulgar carrying-on, this was Sir Alasdair. No one would dare.

They were going to his town house, and from there, to the Lake Country the following day. He wasn't taking her to his family estate. He might never take her there, he thought, sitting back silently, with her in his arms, enjoying this rare quiet moment of peace after so much hullabaloo. But perhaps, he thought now, as he absently petted her hair, once the matter of the Scalbys

was taken care of, he could one day return to Bright-
stone. Their social death, caused by his retribution,
might vanquish the ghosts that haunted his house,
though he doubted it. He kept it in good heart, but
never visited. He couldn't sell the place because it was
entailed. But he couldn't live in it either.

He'd bought a lovely estate in the Lake District, on
Lake Windermere. He'd modernized the old place and
was proud of it now. It had the lake and a cheerful
brook, and a truly beautiful waterfall. He thought of
Kate standing with him under that waterfall, and
smiled with real anticipation of his honeymoon for the
first time that day.

"What?" she murmured, feeling his smile against
her cheek.

"I was thinking of our honeymoon," he said.

She laughed and shivered, and so he kissed her.
And kissed her. When the carriage pulled up at his
town house, she was eager to go in with him. All her
foolish fears about what they'd do that night had
been burned away by the heat of the lust he'd ignited
in her.

She glanced at the sky as she stepped from the carriage. It was twilight. She paused, frustrated.

He knew her very well. He chuckled, and murmured as he took her hand to help her alight, "So it's
not night. It doesn't matter. We'll pull the curtains and
pretend it is."

She went red as a rosebud. "But the servants," she
murmured.

". . . Have been given the evening off, to celebrate
our marriage. I reckoned that after all our feasting,
we'd be too full to want more than a cold collation for
dinner, and asked them to leave one out for us. I reasoned we could certainly see to the matter of undress-

ing ourselves and getting to bed. Although," he said, as he tucked her hand under his arm and they mounted the steps to his house, "I do earnestly hope you'll allow me to assist you. Dangerous stuff, that removing of gowns. You might get a bit of muslin in your eye."

"You're the one who always has muslin in your eye," she laughed.

"Not anymore, not unless you're wearing it," he said seriously, causing her heart to gallop by what she saw in his eyes.

What he saw in hers made him forget his anger, forget his plans, even forget the triumph he'd missed that day. He saw desire and excitement. And embarrassment in the way she lowered her eyes when she saw his reaction. She was still shy with him. But she was completely his, he knew it. He'd be her first lover, and her only one, he hoped. He aimed to be sure of it.

Alasdair was fluent enough in the ways of love to know that the first time for anyone could be less than satisfactory, was, in fact, likely to be so. But he was wise enough to know that even so, it was perhaps the most important time for a woman, a thing she'd never forget. He had to make it memorable, if not perfect. That night, no matter how vaunting his desire, his lovemaking had to be done with patience, generosity, and absolute love. For her. And for him, too.

That was why he'd wanted to come to her cleansed of the past. He'd thought to celebrate this beginning by making an end to his long nightmare. He couldn't do anything about that now. The Scalbys had ruined his perfect joy in his wedding day, he couldn't let them ruin this night. And since she'd never really know his shame, he was willing, at last, to put down the past, at least for a few more hours.

He told himself no man could have everything. He almost did. He could wait for the rest, he decided, and take—and give—all the joy he could that night. He reached the door, and halted as it swung open.

"Paris," he said in amused exasperation, seeing his youngest footman standing there. "I gave you the evening off. I saw you at the church. You didn't need to wait here for us."

"But I did, sir," Paris said. "There was a message for you."

"There'll be a great many; I was married today," Alasdair said, smiling. "You don't have to hand-deliver every one." He felt Kate stir at his side. He looked down. And bit back a smile.

His bride's hair had been tousled by his fingers, her crown of gardenias was tilted sidewise. Her cheeks were flushed, her eyes shone, her lips were ripe and pink from his kisses, as were her cheeks.

"But you're exhausted!" he told her with mock solicitude. "No need to stand here a moment longer, you've been on your feet all day! Go on upstairs," he told her. "I'll send this overly conscientious fellow off for the night. Then, I'll find a good bottle of wine, and that cold collation I told you about. I'll follow. I won't be a moment. Oh, it's the second door on the right, remember?" he added, just to see her blush grow rosier.

She shot him a reproachful but merry look. And, trying to be casual, lifted her head, nodded, and went to the stair with exaggerated precision. He stood watching her, his eyes growing half-lidded as he saw her swaying bottom. He turned to Paris.

"Thank you, lad, but there was no need to wait. Put the message in that pile on the table. My secretary will see to them. Now, off with you, and have some fun. No need to wait on me tonight. Raise a toast to me with your friends instead, and I'll be satisfied."

Paris shook his head in denial. "Yes, sir, I understand. But the messenger who gave me this said I was to give it into your hand this very night, and no mistake. I knew you'd want to know about it, because I knew him. You've sent me to his master's house before."

Alasdair's smile faded, his eyes gleaming with a dark light. He took the paper from his footman and quickly read it.

We will see you. We realize we must. But it must be tonight. Tomorrow will not do. Tonight. Or never.

Scalby

Alasdair stood stock-still. "Thank you. Go," he finally managed to murmur.

Paris bowed, and left the house. Alasdair stood in the hall until the great clock in the hall chimed the half hour and the outside world entered his consciousness again.

They had to see him *tonight*? *Bastards!* He growled, his hand closing over their message, crushing it. It was his wedding night. Even now, his bride awaited him.

But so did they.

What do they want? Why tonight? Only to vex me? Then damn them to hell, I won't dance to their tune. That was the past, that was what he was about to correct at last. He marched toward the stair and climbed two steps . . . and halted.

But maybe there was a good reason? And how could he enjoy this night with their summons ticking away in the back of his mind? *Damn him, too.* Did his Kate deserve half a lover, half a husband, a man come to her with a divided heart and troubled mind?

No. Of course not, he reasoned with rising excitement that had nothing to do with the hours ahead in his bed.

And since it wasn't yet night, it wasn't, strictly speaking, his wedding night, was it? He'd joked with Kate about that. It was only late afternoon. At most, early evening. He could be there, and gone, and back again, mission completed, returned to her with a full heart and a lightened mind before the moon rose over his rooftop—if he left now.

He stood irresolute. He couldn't leave, without explanation, leaving her alone in a house without servants, on her wedding night . . . evening. *Could he?* He wanted to just go—he could be back before she wondered where he was.

But of course she'd wonder, worry. How long could a bride wait for her husband to come to her? First time, first night, this was too important to get wrong.

Still, if he told her he must leave? Would that be any better? He didn't want to make explanations. She knew his grudge against her cousins. He never wanted her to know more.

He'd planned his revenge for years. It had been his whole life, until Kate. She'd be with him for forever after.

. . . After he'd had his revenge.

She deserved better.

But he could walk fast, he could talk fast. He'd relished revenge long enough, it was time to end the thing, quickly, cleanly, the way you killed a dangerous serpent, by simply snapping its neck. He could face them and tell them, and leave them, triumphantly.

But even that would take time. And his love lay waiting in his bed. His bride expected him upstairs. Kate, his wife, his love, his future, awaited him there.

Alasdair paused on the stair.

Then he turned, stepped down, and strode out the door.

27

The question was, how should she wait for him? Kate stood in the center of Alasdair's bedchamber, seriously considering it. There was that great red-and-gold, lavish, sumptuous, exciting bed of his, just waiting to be used. Just looking at it made her cheeks the color of those outrageous satin bedcovers. But hadn't she been thinking of that bed all these weeks?

So she reasoned that if she, now his wife, waited for him all ablush, dressed to her chin and still in her wedding dress, it would be both foolish, craven, and a very bad start to their life together. What a woman of spirit would do would be to surprise and thrill him by stripping off her clothes and lying back upon that bed like a fine necklace in a velvet-lined box, awaiting him.

She giggled nervously. She wasn't a fine necklace. She was human, had her flaws, and knew them too well. Hadn't she spent last night in the bath, washing and mourning every one of them?

And he'd said he looked forward to helping her off

with her clothing. But it would be such fun to surprise him, so delightful to shock him. After all, once he arrived he'd be the one who'd do everything. She knew what the procedure entailed. But that was like knowing how to drive a coach and four by watching. And she'd never even watched such a thing! She giggled again at the nonsense of that. No, when he came to her she'd follow his lead. So why not have the upper hand just once tonight? she thought with a spurt of hilarity, fueled by the wedding toast she'd drunk.

She quickly stripped off her gown, looked down at herself, gave a little muffled yip of dismay and amusement, flew to his bed, hopped up, and burrowed under all its sumptuous red satin covers.

She waited a second, then in a burst of sheer bravado, raised herself up until only her naked breasts showed. Well, half of them. As much as a man would see if she wore a daring gown. Alasdair had certainly seen more. Well, half a loaf was better than none, she thought, and, flushed and merry, lay back and waited.

And waited.

Where could they have put that cold collation, on the moon? she wondered grumpily, then anxiously. Her body grew as cold as her resolve as she watched the sunset fade outside the windows. *The windows!* She sat up, about to hop from the bed and draw the draperies over them. But she'd set out to be daring, and so she would be. The day was dying anyway. She lay back again and waited.

And waited.

Her jest had grown as cold as she was when the door finally opened. She held her breath. Alasdair stood there at last. She drew in her breath. She'd expected laughter, maybe a leer, certainly interest. He only looked distracted. Until he saw her, and stared.

Alasdair gaped at his bride, all his well-rehearsed words forgotten. He'd run from the house, but had stopped halfway down the street and turned around again. And stood still, then turned back. And turned round again. When he saw passersby looking at him curiously, he realized he was starting to resemble a weather vane. He felt like one, unable to set a true course. There were things he had to do. But he couldn't just leave her without a word. With all he must do, he could never do that.

As he'd climbed the stairs he'd thought of what to say to her, before he left again. But the sight of her made him forget.

She peeped up at him from his bed, smiling mischievously. Her gardenia garland, obviously forgotten, was still perched on her tousled curls, her breasts glowed pink from the reflected shine of the crimson covers they emerged from, she was rosy with delight at her jest, obviously naked beneath those covers, and looked like a slightly tipsy nymph waiting for her satyr.

He smiled, then frowned.

Her smile quavered, disappeared. She tugged the covers up, sat up, and tugged them higher, crossed her arms over her now blameless breasts, and cleared her throat. But she didn't get a chance to speak.

"I have to go out for a little while," he said.

"What?"

"There's an errand, not of my making."

"Leave me now?" she asked incredulously. "Go out?" She gasped. "Has anything happened to my parents? My brothers?"

"No, certainly not. This is something altogether different. I just must go." He lowered his head, avoiding her eyes. "Your cousins, the Scalbys, have summoned me. I have to see them and settle this matter between us for once and for all. I don't want it haunting us the rest of our lives."

"But you can do that tomorrow," she protested. "This is our wedding night."

"It's only late afternoon," he said, glancing at the window, frowning to see that the sky had lost the last blush of sunset and turned the flat gray of first night.

"And it can't wait?"

"No, really it can't. The thing is ripe to be settled. Wouldn't you rather I come to you with a clear head and heart?"

She stared at him. He didn't look himself, she thought, but couldn't tell just why. Then she realized what it was. He looked unsure, and Alasdair St. Erth, unsure, was a very different-looking man. It went beyond a matter of facial features; however upset he was, he was still amazingly attractive. But differently so. He'd worn his certitude like a second skin. Now, without that poise, that cool, amused facade and air of absolute command, he looked like a tragic poet, not a clever man about town. He seemed vulnerable, lost. His features stood out starkly, his eyes dark and blind with despair.

"What is it?" she cried, throwing back the covers, climbing down from his bed and running to him. "Alasdair? What is it?" She stood in front of him, her nudity forgotten by both of them, and peered up into his face as though if she looked hard enough she could see what was troubling him.

He looked at her, really seeing her again. "Oh, God," he groaned, "What in God's name am I doing?"

Her eyes searched his. "What *are* you doing, Alasdair?"

"I'm lying to you," he said softly. "Time, past time I stopped. Before it's too late."

He stepped to the bed, snatched up a cover, and dropped it over her shoulders. She stood still, shocked and confused. With a sound of impatience, he scooped her up and carried her to a chair by the window. He sat her on his lap and tucked the coverlet around her.

"Now, we talk," he said. "We should have before this, but it's not too late. We're married in name only. There's still time for you to get out of this. Kate, I've kept things from you. I told myself it wouldn't matter. It would, it does, and if I'm right, tonight your cousins will see it does even more."

He heaved a great sigh and laid his head on the back of the chair. "Kate," he said, and closed his eyes, pausing before he spoke again. "I told you about my vendetta against the Scalbys. I just didn't tell you all of it. I left out a part, the part that's been eating away at my heart all these years." He looked down at her again, raised a hand, and stroked back a curl from her face, as tenderly and sexlessly as if she were a beloved child he was about to tell a bedtime story to.

"My father got into debt with them, you know that. When I came home from school, they were at our estate with a party of their friends, as I said." His voice was calm, too calm. "Everyone knows that. No one knew the rest. No one but me, the Scalbys, four of their friends, now gone, and now, you. You see, your cousins came to me one night and told me the extent of my father's debt. I was appalled. They said he'd be beggared trying to pay it, and that they doubted he could pay it all, even so. So they offered me the chance to do it, all at once."

Kate frowned. "But you were only . . . sixteen, you said."

"So I was. I had no money, but what I had was more important to them. I was fully grown, fully matured, if not in mind, then certainly in body. They'd noted that, they said, and very much approved of how I'd grown." His voice became wry. "They were younger then, too. She was considered attractive in her fashion, he was . . . active, in his. They informed me of exactly how active they both were, what they and their friends liked to do, and what they wished to do, with me."

Kate swallowed a gasp as he went on. "They proposed sealing the bargain that very night. My father had gone to a friend in the next county to try to raise money. He wouldn't be home 'til morning. They had enough money, they said. But never enough sport. They planned a party, an orgy, to put it plainly, which they did, because they were honest, in their fashion. A party, with me as centerpiece."

"Oh, Alasdair," Kate breathed.

"Oh, indeed. And if I agreed, they'd forget my father's debt, tell him it was charity on their behalf, and bother neither of us again—unless I found their play to my taste. I agreed, of course."

He paused for her protest, and when there was none, nodded, and went on. "I bathed like a bridegroom that night," he said with a small smile. "Then drank as much as I could hold. I wasn't used to spirits, but brandy seemed to smell the strongest, so I grimaced and downed it. I didn't want to join them, you see. I was new to my body, it perplexed and embarrassed me. I didn't want to be naked in front of strange adults. Especially those. I hadn't any sexual experience and recoiled at the thought of having it with them. I suppose I was a backward youth. I had enough lust, of course, most sixteen-year-old fellows do. But I had illusions about love. I was, as I said, mature in body and not mind."

Kate noticed he never mentioned her cousins' given

names, as if by so doing he removed himself from them further. "And he . . ." Alasdair paused. "You see, they told me he'd join in the sport, too."

Kate's breath stopped. "I certainly didn't want that," Alasdair said in cold flat tones. "But if I didn't agree, it was debtors' prison for my father. Who could I tell? What could I do? I seriously contemplated killing them. But what good would that do my father? In the end, I drank the brandy, dressed, and went to the party.

"They were entirely ugly people," he said wearily. "I remember only bits of it, because they had liquors as well as opium to help them and me get on with it. I stripped as they asked, and felt stupid and shamed, my body looked like a plucked chicken to my own eyes, my shoulders too wide, my limbs too bony. They didn't agree."

He paused, gazing past her at something she couldn't see. "I drank and smoked whatever they gave me, though I don't think it was necessary. There's an Eastern philosophy," he said quietly, "a practice that allows men to travel out of their bodies. It takes years of discipline to achieve. It took me only that night. I hardly needed all the drugs. I don't know whose they were, thank God, I remember only hands and mouths and bodies on mine. At some point, I left them, though of course, my body remained.

"I woke," he said dully, "and it was over, they were gone. I grabbed my clothing, dressed, and ran out into the morning. I ran hours before I realized I'd never run far enough from myself to forget. I went home. They'd gone. I went into the house. The neighbors were there, the vicar was there. They told me my father had come home, gone into his study, and killed himself."

Kate sat still, unable to speak until she knew what to say.

"I tried to save him and I killed him," Alasdair said simply, helplessly. "The money didn't matter after all. I've since paid all of it back to them, I refused to honor that part of the bargain, or take one cent from them for what I'd done. It took time, but I did it. Once my father was gone, there was no need for their money. I vowed I'll pay them back in kind, though. I vowed I wouldn't rest until I'd done worse to them. The others there that night are long gone, to their graves or what amounts to it: disgrace and permanent exile. But the Scalbys caused it all, and they remain. But not for much longer.

"Now I'm ready to repay them, that's why I must go to them tonight. I should have told you long ago. In my defense, I didn't want you to ever know and thought you never would. But now it occurs to me that they'll find a way to tell you—scorpions can sting even as they are crushed. I'd much rather you heard this from me."

Now Kate could speak. "*You* killed him?" she cried. "Of course you didn't."

"In a sense, I did," Alasdair said wearily. "The Scalbys were seen leaving his study that morning just before they left. He was found dead after they drove off, slumped over his desk, his pistol still in his hand. The butler discovered him, he'd gone to tell him that his guests were leaving. My father had already left. They must have told him about our bargain. A bargain with the devil always has a trick to it. The money was paid, but I'd incurred a larger debt for him. Poverty he could bear, his son's disgrace, he could not."

"Nonsense!" Kate said angrily. "If he felt anything about what you did, it was guilt, his own. He was probably already sick with worry at what his folly had done to your inheritance. You tried to save him. I don't know if I'd have been that brave in your place, even now. I doubt I would have been at sixteen!"

"Brave?" Alasdair asked with a twisted smile.

"Of course," she said indignantly. "You did whatever you could, bargained with what little you had. But it wasn't little, it was yourself, and *they* should be crushed and damned."

"Kate," he said gently, looking at her with regret, "I remember enough of that night never to be able to forget it. I didn't want to join them, but I remember, indeed, cannot forget, that my flesh, at least, did participate. You'd have thought I'd recoil, shrink—physically as well as mentally. God! If a cold breeze can shrink a man's flesh, you'd think his disgust and despair would do it, too. But I remember, and am damned for it, because I didn't shrink from their demands. I don't know whose hands, body, or lips were served. But I performed, I'm sure of it. There was, in all that shame and anger, still some pleasure for me, all unwillingly. I still despise myself for it. I've tried to cleanse myself in the beds of too many women, but I can't forget. Neither should you."

He gazed at her steadily. "I'm no fit husband for you, Kate. I think I knew it all along. It's only another thing I kept from you and myself. It's as well they summoned me from you tonight—fitting, too. This time they served you well." He spoke more briskly. "A special dispensation for annulment can be arranged if there was no consummation, and you should thank God there wasn't. That much honor I had left. That much I leave to you. Claim whatever you want, I'll agree. You can be free."

"Why should I want to be?" she demanded. "They used you. You were only a boy. A big boy, but not an adult, and drugged and drunk, to boot. As for that, Alasdair, you may know more about flesh than I do, but even I know that we control our bodies only by the most severe discipline of our minds, and they took yours away from you that night."

He shook his head. "Kindly thought, valiantly said, but you owe me nothing, Kate."

"Well, you owe me a wedding night, and a lifetime together," she insisted.

She was both frightened and angry, afraid of losing him, angry that he wouldn't see the truth, and that truth was that she loved him. He'd been brave, but what had happened during his sacrifice was so long ago it was nothing to her, whatever it meant to him. She was so sorry for him she wanted to weep, but knew that would only convince him he was right. This sad, exhausted man wrung her heart and won it even more surely than the cool composed Sir Alasdair St. Erth had done. This man was like that poor abused boy again, she realized, once again sacrificing his body and his heart for someone he loved. That heart was hers, she knew it. Now she had to win it back. Reason wouldn't do it.

Although she'd expected that this night he'd lead and she'd follow him into bliss, now she saw the tables had turned. She'd little experience at lovemaking, except with him. She was still shy, even in front of him. But he needed her, and she realized she had to show him how much she needed him. His grief was beyond words, they'd do her no good.

She put both her arms around his neck. His arms, reflexively, went round her. She didn't give him time to think of what he'd done, she lifted her lips to his. He didn't move. She sighed against his mouth and placed hers over it. He didn't open his lips. She touched the seam of those warm lips with her tongue, and pressed herself against him. He didn't respond. It was like kissing his portrait.

She paused, hurt and confused. Didn't he want her? But then she realized she hadn't shown him anything but willingness. He needed more. He'd always courted her, how did a woman go about seducing him? She couldn't. She could only show him what she needed. He'd always responded to that.

She shrugged the coverlet from her shoulders, so she was entirely bared to him. Then she lay her head against his chest, her hand over his heart. "I love you, Alasdair," she said softly, "And I want to stay married to you, and bedamned to my cousins! Should I spend my life only remembering you with regret because of them? Please, don't let them win again. I want you. I didn't marry you mainly for your flesh. But, oh my, Alasdair! I was *so* looking forward to it!"

Her head moved as his body jerked. And then he was laughing, her head bouncing against his chest. "God, you are amazing." He laughed again.

She sat straight up, nose to nose with him, delighted with herself, grinning at him.

He gazed at her. Her face was flushed, and she looked triumphant, devilish, unutterably seductive, her head thrown back, her small arched breasts bobbing with her laughter, her slender white body rising from crimson satin, offering itself to him. And best of all, and most of all, her eyes filled with humor and love, and perfect fellow feeling. It was, all at once, too much for him.

"Kate," he said, dragging her close, holding her near, "be sure. Are you sure? Decide now. I'm a man. But still too weak to resist. Because it's my heart, my mind, and my flesh that longs for you."

"You're my husband," she said simply. "And I will have you!"

* * *

Her wedding night was everything Kate expected and nothing she was prepared for. Her new husband didn't lead her, and she didn't follow him, they simply tried to devour each other.

When their kisses became too heated, they tried to get closer and stoke up their fires. She was already naked, and they both found his clothing ridiculous, cumbersome, unendurable. He groaned as he dragged his shirt over his head. He shucked off his shoes, pulled off his breeches and hose. She found herself helping him when he got his leg tangled in his small-clothes as he tried to kick them away. Then he carried her to his sumptuous bed, placed her in the middle of it, and with a smile that nearly broke her heart, followed her down to lie with her there.

There was just enough light left in the sky for them to see each other, and it thrilled them.

He'd never seen her entirely naked before, and the loveliness of her body overwhelmed him.

She'd never seen his body, but she knew he'd be powerful and beautiful and she wasn't disappointed. He wore his skin as other men wore their finery, and with good cause. He looked magnificent to her. She couldn't be afraid of the astonishing size and shape of his arousal, because she knew she was the reason for it, and exulted in it.

But they couldn't look at each other for long. They had too many other things to do. They kissed as though the air around them was too thick to breathe, and they could only survive if they took it filtered through each other's lips. He buried his hands in her hair, tasted her, stroked her, and caressed her as she clung to him. She murmured her love, and tried to discover every part of him she'd never been able to touch before.

She'd have been willing to go on like that all night, because she didn't know how much more there could be. He did, and there was only so much he could bear. He paused, finally, his great chest heaving as he gasped for breath. He'd moved her to ready her, preparing her for a long time, or so it seemed to him. But a minute was too long tonight, and he could no longer play. He reared up on his elbows.

"Last chance," he said in a grating whisper. "You can still deny me." But his hand didn't leave her breast, and his body was still a sweet weight on hers as he watched her breathlessly.

She smiled up at him. "No chance," she said, and managed a smile. Which was difficult, because there wasn't blood enough left in her head for her to think, much less speak. It had all retreated to every sensitive part he'd set afire with his breath and lips and tongue, and was pooled there, making her itch and ache and yearn.

He kissed her again and then, with a great sigh, brought his body to hers and made them complete.

She was ready, and yet surprised. She'd expected pain. There was some, of course, he was a very big man, and even with all her expectation, still she was untried. But she was too thrilled, relieved, and amazed to mind. Because there was something else, too. If not rapture, then surely a rapture of the mind, a feeling of wholeness, relief, a sense of utter victory.

He was lost, entirely. So excited and delighted at being irrevocably one with her at last that his troubled mind left his troublesome body as it took them both flying, into ecstasy. He plunged on, reveling in being with her, mind and body, finding this mating so glorious he found oblivion too soon.

She lay back when he collapsed beside her, a little

confused at the storm that had overtaken them, a little sensitive and more sore, and filled with questions about how to make it better next time. But that could wait. She was amazingly happy. She was at last his wife.

He pulled her close as soon as he gathered his wits together, rolled over, and rested on an elbow so he could look down into her face. "Did I hurt you? Did I please you at all? It must been like bedding a thunderstorm for you. Damn, I'm sorry. I never meant to have it this way, I wanted to lure you and lull you, and make slow sweet love to you." He saw her confusion, and added, ruefully, "Yes, I can do it that way. I should and will. We can slow it until it feels like honey dripping down a jar. Kate? Will you say something, please?"

She smiled. "It was fine, I'm very happy."

He groaned. "*Fine*? Lord, that's the last thing a man wants to hear about his lovemaking."

"Glorious?" she ventured.

"What a liar. I'm going to have to make an honest woman out of you. Only not just yet, for your sake and mine. But later, I promise you." His expression became still. "Kate? Thank you."

She smiled and kissed him, a kiss of peace this time, a kiss to nourish, not excite them. They lay there entwined, letting a serene silence settle over them, feeling love and gratitude too immense to put into words, along with an overwhelming sense of rightness. They didn't need to speak. They knew each other's minds. More than their bodies had met tonight. They were one.

"Wife?" he finally said into the utter darkness, when their bodies had cooled and their pulses were steady again.

"Yes," she answered. "It's time. Now. Tonight, as they asked. Only I must go with you."

28

It was late that night when the butler admitted Lord and Lady St. Erth to the Scalbys' house. The pair were dressed soberly but correctly, and were as grave as visitors to a house of death.

"If you will come this way," the butler said. He led them through the dimly lit house and so didn't see the lady slip her hand into her husband's, or his close tightly over it. But then the elegant couple walked so close together no one could have seen that they held hands like children as they went through the silent house to the grand salon.

The salon was huge and furnished richly, but only glances of muted crimson and brown were picked out by the firelight, because the only other illumination was a single candle in a glass on a table. A tall gaunt lady sat in front of that table, her profile and outline all that could be clearly seen. A heavyset man sat in the chair by the hearth, but he didn't turn his head from the play of leaping flames as the butler announced his visitors.

"My, how you've grown," the lady said, as Alasdair and Kate stepped into the room.

Alasdair nodded and answered coldly. "It was inevitable."

"You are now as you were then, though you've matured, but so I'd expected you to. I meant your lady," Lady Scalby corrected him. "Come closer, cousin, and let's have a look at you. They say you've become a beauty."

"They say a great many things, cousin," Kate snapped, staying where she was.

"Oho. Vexed because we missed your wedding?" the lady asked. "Our gift will more than compensate you for that."

"I want no gifts from you," Kate said angrily, but Alasdair's cool voice rose over hers.

"Cut line," he said impatiently. "You asked me to come here. Here I am. You know what night this is, so I assume you've something important to say."

They saw the lady's head dip in a nod. "Yes, to business, then. It's not your wedding I wanted to congratulate you for, though of course you have our felicitations. Cleverly done. Revenge must be extrasweet in this case. No, I wished to salute you for something else. You've done a fine job, Alasdair. You've got us, you know. But of course you do. You've been working at it for years, hiring spies, paying off servants, romancing past lovers, promising anything to anyone who dealt with us and could tell you about it. At first, when we heard of it, we thought you were merely annoying, then amusing. But as the years went on, we realized you were spinning a tight web around us. We took to hiding our activities. It didn't help. You found a great many things that would harm us, but our one misstep will utterly ruin us, and doubtless you intend to use it to do so."

"Never doubt it," Alasdair agreed.

"But why?" she asked, her head moving slightly forward. "Why do you despise us so much, pursue us so relentlessly?"

"You really have to ask?"

"Someone saw us that morning!" she muttered. "Didn't I tell you so?" she asked her husband angrily.

The man by the fire growled what might have been agreement.

Alasdair grew very still.

"So that was it. So, we were craven," she said, turning to Alasdair again. "But surely that needn't account for such vengeance? We didn't want our names in a scandal, can you blame us? Certainly, we *should* have told someone your father was dead. But what difference would that have made? He was past help. We'd our reputations to consider."

Kate felt Alasdair's hand spasm closed over hers, though he moved no other way.

"We went in to say good-bye," the lady was saying, "to tell him his debt was paid, as we promised you. But he was slumped over his desk, awelter with blood. Obviously, he'd put that pistol to his head. It was ghastly . . . well, I'm sure you know. So we ran. That was cowardly, but not criminal."

Kate bit back a gasp of surprise. Alasdair remained still, but his nostrils flared.

"You may say the debt that caused his suicide was our fault," Lady Scalby added harshly when he didn't speak. "But we only introduced him to gaming. As for our other pleasures, he could have said no."

"He was already dead?" Alasdair asked, unable to conceal his shock. "You never told him about our bargain?"

"Of course not. We'd neither the chance, nor the intention," Lady Scalby snapped. "We said we would not. We have our honor," she added, sounding genuinely affronted. "What?" she asked suddenly. "Did you think we murdered him? Is that it? My dear sir, how bizarre. Why should we have?"

Alasdair remained silent. Kate knew that wasn't what he'd thought, and hoped this venomous woman never guessed what his real fears had been, lest she use them to her advantage.

Lady Scalby shrugged thin shoulders. "I imagine his trip to cozen a loan from his old friend was unsuccessful. Pity he was so hasty, because in a few moments he'd have heard his debt was already paid and his rash act unnecessary. He'd just committed it, or so at least, we surmised from the state we found him in, and the smell of gunpowder. The room was still blue with it. If we'd been less discreet, we wouldn't have had to run. But our other friends didn't know of our financial arrangements, we thought it prudent to keep them unaware of it. We'd slipped in to say farewell, tell him he was debt-free, and tear up his vouchers. Instead we found chaos, and ran. So why punish us for what we didn't do?"

"And what you did to Alasdair was nothing?" Kate demanded, so angry she was shaking.

"'What we did to Alasdair'?" Lady Scalby asked slowly. "Oh, child, that was just a bit of advanced education for a young man. I doubt he remembers much of it. Did he tell you about it?" She sighed. "How unexpected. Do you remember it so fondly?" she asked Alasdair.

"Enough," he said absently, obviously still thinking about what she'd just told him.

"Well, that's just what we didn't get," she retorted, swinging her long neck so she could stare at Kate. "Your husband showed great promise. But between one thing and another, he soon left us, if not in body, then in mind and spirit. We were devastated. Especially my poor husband. He never got what he'd anticipated, and had to give up, because your Alasdair was simply passed out, nothing could revive him. Which was a pity, because in those days my dear Richard hadn't yet acquired a taste for such a treat."

"Quiet," Alasdair said, his voice clear and contained again. Kate noticed he stood taller, too. "From your own lips you damn yourself. You and your husband aren't fit company for worms now, much less the society you infected. Why did you ask me here tonight? What was the reason for your untimely summons?"

The lady hesitated. They saw one of her long fingernails scratch at some invisible spot on the shining tabletop. "As you've probably guessed," she murmured, "bringing your bride here quite spiked my guns, as Richard would say. I'd thought she wouldn't know about our little party that night. I'd hoped, rather. Because then we might have made another bargain, you and I. My silence, for yours. I'd thought you'd want to keep your bride ignorant of it. You have either a marriage of the minds, or have taught her to pursue what we tried to teach you."

Alasdair stepped forward. She raised a hand to stop him from speaking. "I neither know nor care," she went on. "But I have nothing to negotiate with now, do I? Still, now that you're here, relieve my curiosity. If it wasn't your father's murder you suspected us of, what on earth caused you to seek our ruin so relentlessly? We kept our bargain."

Kate held her breath, hoping Alasdair wouldn't give her any further ammunition by letting her know it was that bargain itself that haunted him.

"I, too, wanted a trade," Alasdair said. "My father's ruin for yours, lady. You won't hang, you've too many connections and probably more people you can 'negotiate' with. That only buys you so much. You will have to leave England, though. But tell me something, too. Why should you care? For that matter, why did you stay here awaiting my vengeance? You've spent your lives roving in pursuit of pleasure."

"You see, we're old now, Richard and I," the lady said. "I find I wish to die in peace in my own land, and not among strangers. And there is the Name of course. It seems all we have left. So I am reduced to begging, I suppose."

"In vain," Alasdair snapped. "The game's up. I'm done with it, and you. It wouldn't have profited you to murder me either. Even if your minions had been successful, my death would have released the papers I've collected about you."

The lady looked up. "My minions? Many things I've done, sir. But I do not stoop to murder. And," she added with a dry chuckle, "Credit me with knowing that it would have done no good."

Alasdair nodded. It made sense. Lolly had been his enemy, but he'd been seeing this woman and her husband behind every misfortune that befell him. For too long. It was time to end that too. "Even so," he said, "now that's not necessary. I'll send on the information. I suggest you prepare to leave town and the country, if not the entire Continent."

"Nothing I can say will change your mind?" Lady Scalby asked. "If I fall, be sure I will try to drag you down into the mud with me. You, too, have a name to consider, and now a wife and possible children to think of. Do you want the world to know what you did that night?"

"I don't think you'll tell anyone!" Kate said angrily, before Alasdair could answer. "It would only turn opinion against you. Because it was a vile thing to do. He was only a boy. And all he did was to comply. What you did was to instigate, and that's very different."

"And if he found pleasure in that compliance, no matter who instigated it?" the lady asked slyly.

Alasdair paused. "I thought you said there wasn't . . ."

"Indeed," Lady Scalby purred. "I only wanted to make you consider what people would say about what happened."

"Nothing did." Kate cut in. "Don't you see?" she asked Alasdair, urgently tugging on his sleeve. "She's reading your reactions. She's desperate. She saw your distaste at what might have happened. She's inventing now. If she'd known what you thought, she'd never have told you what she did before. She spoke truth then—you'll never hear it from her again."

Alasdair nodded. He touched a hand to her cheek. "Wise wife of mine," he said with a true smile. "Of course. And do you know? I find it doesn't matter anymore. Isn't that astonishing?" he asked with wonder. "But it's so. You showed me there's more than revenge in my life now. I stepped back from vengeance for only a little while, and now I find I can't step back in."

He paused, his eyes searching Kate's. "What do you want me to do?" he asked her.

She was startled, then suffused with joy. He was turning his life's work over to her. She considered it seriously. Then she smiled. She knew the best answer for him, and herself. "Let it go," she told him. "Finally, just let it go. It doesn't matter anymore."

Alasdair nodded. He tore his gaze from her and looked at Lady Scalby. "I have a care for my wife, more than I care about what happens to you, or myself, for that matter. I'm not noble enough to love my enemy and don't believe I'll ever be. But I can sacrifice vengeance for the sake of my love. So yes, I'll let you go. Die here, or live here for all I care. But never think all my work was useless. Without it, without you and what you did, I'd never have met Kate. *That*, my lady, would have been my greatest tragedy. Be damned to you then.

"One thing I don't understand," he added suddenly. "Why does *he* say nothing?" He motioned to the man by the fire. "You asked me here, begged, lied, and demeaned yourself. Why is *he* silent?"

Lady Scalby's laughter rang out. "Did you want to hear him beg? He can't. I will show you what he can do, though, if you wish. Richard!" she said loudly. "Richard!" She huffed with impatience when the man didn't so much as turn his head from the fire. "Food! *Eat*, Richard," she shouted, "*Eat!*"

The man gave a guttural groan, his hands clutched at the arms of his chair. He rose with an inarticulate cry.

Kate took an involuntary step toward Alasdair. He stepped in front of her, his fists balled. The man ignored him, he turned toward his wife, growling.

The lady picked up a bell and shook it. The door to the salon swung open, and a huge man in livery stepped in. "My husband wishes to feed," Lady Scalby told the servant. "Take him and see to it. Then put him to bed. Good night, my dear," she told the man as the servant took his arm and led him from the room.

Alasdair and Kate stepped back to let them by. They stood arrested as Lord Scalby passed, staring at his empurpled face, rolling eyes, the thick lips wet with drool, as he shambled away on the arm of his keeper.

"A little something he picked up on our travels," Lady Scalby said in a brittle voice. "A souvenir of past delights. I told him and told him to stay within our class for his sport, or at least to inspect the treats he bought before he sampled them. But in time, he grew bored with that. Rash fellow. As to that, it started as a rash, can you believe it?" she asked conversationally. "Then a sore, then many sores, then . . . but any medical manual can tell the course of the thing, can't it? One day he lost his balance, then he began to lose little things. He lost his temper frequently, and then he lost his entire mind. Now he remembers nothing but rage and hunger. Syphilis is an interesting disease, is it not?" she asked Alasdair. "You were far, far luckier than you knew that night. I was not. As for me, why, my husband was most generous."

She picked up the candle and held it close to her face.

Alasdair winced. Kate looked away. She'd heard sermons on the rewards for evil living and the miseries of those afflicted with the pox. Nothing prepared her for the ruin she'd glimpsed. It was as if every evil thing Lady Scalby had done had been imprinted on what had been her face. Kate glanced at Alasdair, wondering if this was what he'd looked for in his dreams. Surely it was a more fit punishment than any he could have imagined.

Lady Scalby laughed. "So sorry to disappoint you, but if you sought utterly to destroy us, you are a little too late."

"In this, you win," Alasdair said, bowing. "Congratulations. I couldn't have done more. Indeed, I doubt even I'd have done as much."

"So you really are not going to lay information against us?" Lady Scalby persisted, anxiety finally creeping into her voice.

"No. Not if you never trouble me or mine again. But that could change. I caution you to stop your games now. I'll keep the papers, and use them if I must. I suggest you pray for our continued good fortune and health, too, because should anything happen to me or mine, those papers will be made public instantly. Keep your Name then, and may it bring you joy. I leave you to live, or die, in peace. At least from me. I'm done with you. Good evening, good-bye."

The lady inclined her head in a semblance of a bow. She was close enough to the candlelight for it to show her smile. Kate shivered, because that smile was a reptilian thing to match the bright, flat eyes of its wearer. A turtle's grin, etched in flesh, but not by emotion, made only of lines and creases. Now the lady wasn't capable of more. Kate wondered if she'd ever been.

Alasdair took Kate's hand, and they left her cousin sitting in her chair, staring blindly into the candlelight.

They stepped out of the town house into the night, and it seemed brighter than where they'd just been.

Alasdair shifted his shoulders. He stretched. "Lord! I actually feel lighter now that I've put down that burden. And cleaner, out in the fresh air. I know it's midnight, but I need a walk. And you?"

"Oh, me too," Kate said.

"Go on," he told his coachman. "The night's advanced, but the weather's fine, so we'll walk. But this is London, so follow behind and keep watch."

"If it were just me, I wouldn't care," he told Kate, as he took her hand, "but I take no chances with you."

They strolled home to the sound of the carriage horses' steady clumping along the cobbles just behind them. They held hands, walking in thoughtful and companionable silence.

"I worry," Kate finally said.

"About what?" he said quickly, turning to her. "It's done. She won't trouble us again."

"Oh, I know that," she said softly. "It's not that."

"Then what?" he asked, coming to a halt, holding both her hands and gazing down into her face. "What worries you?"

"Oh, well," she said sadly, looking everywhere but at him. "The thing is, this walk is very pleasant, but it's getting later. I worry about how long it will take us to get back, because there's not much left of our wedding night, and I so was looking forward to it!"

He gave a shout of laughter, swept her up into his arms, and waved to the coachman. When the coach came abreast, Alasdair laughing, carried his laughing bride inside.

"Home!" he called to the coachman, "And hurry! We've a lot of time to make up for," he told Kate as he settled her on his lap, "and only a lifetime left to do it in."

"Not long enough," she whispered, touching a hand to his lips.

"No, not nearly long enough," he agreed, then found a better use for their lips.